Seven Archangels:
Sacred Cups

Seven Archangels:
Sacred Cups

Jane Lebak

Philangelus Press
Boston, MA USA

Other Books By Jane Lebak:

The Wrong Enemy
Seven Archangels: An Arrow In Flight
Seven Archangels: Annihilation
The Boys Upstairs

ISBN: 978-1-942133-04-9
Library of Congress Control Number: 2015931561
Kindle ASIN: B00PB4I7BY

Cover: C.K. Volnek

Dedication

To Kenneth Elwood, who always knew when to push my writing to the next level.

One

Year Zero

After checking over the infant Jesus's new house in Egypt, the Archangel Michael was about to leave when Mary said, "Stop. Who are you?"

Michael's wings flared, and he pivoted.

Mary had been cooking at the fire in the courtyard under a partial roof. Jesus slept in a basket hanging from two hooks.

Uriel looked up from the corner, unruly black hair obscuring wide purple eyes, and seeming just as startled as Michael.

Michael glanced at Uriel, his body language projecting, *She can see me?*

Uriel projected in the negative, then pressed clenched hands up at chest height.

I wish you'd warned me she'd sense my presence, Michael sent to God.

Uriel concentrated, and in the next instant a Guard formed around the house: no demons would be able to enter or listen through it for as long as Uriel kept concentrating.

Mary stood away from the pot. "Who are you?"

With God's permission, Michael made himself visible.

Mary lowered her ladle and positioned herself between the angel and Jesus. "What do you want?"

"I didn't want anything." Michael edged backward. "I was making sure the house was secure."

Mary still brandished that spoon as if it were a weapon. "I'm not going to let you hurt him."

Michael shook his head. "I'm trying to protect him."

Raphael had slipped down off the roof, his six almond-colored wings tucked at his back.

"You're new," Mary said. "I've been feeling that one—" and she pointed toward Uriel's corner, "and that one—" in Raphael's general direction, "but not you."

Noting the other two angels' surprised looks, Michael relaxed a little. He wasn't the only one caught off-guard here. "I don't visit all the time."

Mary frowned. "Why can I see you now?"

"I'm letting you." Michael shifted his weight. "I can leave if you want. I didn't mean for you to be able to sense me at all, so this is more than a little awkward."

Raphael laughed, and Mary turned in his direction. "This is unnerving for me too. I wasn't expecting to keep seeing things like you after the first one." She spoke toward Raphael. "Can you show yourself too, or is that breaking the rules?"

After a moment, Raphael appeared before her, brown-haired and brown-eyed. He opened his hands. "It's a pleasure to greet you."

Mary looked pale, as if she were only now thinking this might not have been the best idea. Still, she turned toward the other corner. "And you—?"

Uriel appeared, bowing with both hands and wings spread.

Mary looked weak, and Michael urged her to sit. He sat before her, and in another moment the other two joined him.

"Where's the other one?" Mary's voice wobbled as she looked from one to the next to the next. "The grey one."

"I'll call him," Raphael said. In the next moment, Gabriel sat on the opposite end of the row so the four archangels sat facing Jesus's mother.

Mary's brow furrowed. "Why can I sense you all?"

Raphael said, "Guesses?"

Then Gabriel started speaking, and Michael sighed with relief. Gabriel was a Cherub, and Cherubim were the teachers. Let Gabriel take over the talking.

And he did. "I would suppose it's your maternal instincts kicking in. Once you spent all that time being close to Jesus in your body, you must have picked up some of his sensitivities. It might be due to his fetal cells having entered your system during the pregnancy. Quite possibly you'll need to have some awareness of us in order to properly mother a child who might be able to detect us too."

She thought about it a moment and to Michael's relief wisely decided not to ask about fetal cells. "And who are you?"

"We're angels," Gabriel said.

"I know that." For the first time she sounded a little irritated, and Raphael chuckled. "Do you have names?"

Raphael bowed his head. "I'm Raphael, a Seraph, Jesus's guardian angel. This is Uriel, a Throne and your guardian angel."

Gabriel said, "I'm Gabriel, a Cherub. I'm not attached to anyone in this household."

Michael said, "I'm Michael, just an Archangel. But they keep me around anyhow."

Raphael and Gabriel both shot him a disbelieving look.

Mary inched backward, the color draining from her cheeks as she faced four multi-winged, many-storied spirits. What did they look like to her, Michael wondered. Creatures of light, human in appearance except for the wings and yet glowing or burning before her. She whispered, "Aren't you all Archangels of the Presence? As in, God's top command?"

Michael looked left at Raphael and right at Uriel and Gabriel. "Don't worry—I feel the same way sometimes. But you have the son of the Most High sleeping behind you, and you aren't afraid of him."

"We're here to serve him." Gabriel shrugged. "You're pretty much incidental."

Mary forced a smile, and Michael relaxed to let Gabriel handle things. Already she seemed more at ease.

"Please don't be afraid," Gabriel said. "We won't harm you, and we'll strive to keep the enemy from harming you as well."

Mary glanced over her shoulder at Jesus. "He'll sleep for a while yet," Raphael said. "I'm watching."

Mary looked at the four of them. "How can I help protect him?"

Raphael smiled. "You're doing just fine now. Your job is to mother him."

"But beyond that." She sat forward. "There's already been one attempt on his life—that's why we're in Egypt. But I can't believe that's going to be the only one. We'll be under attack by he enemies of God as soon as they realize how important he'll be."

Gabriel sat forward. "Do *you* know how important he'll be?"

She looked at him, then down. "No, but I assume he will be, because of the first message."

Gabriel nodded. "We're not sure either, but with Uriel as your guardian and Raphael as his, his mission's going to be big."

Michael said, "But naturally, the enemy is able to figure that out as well, which is why I stop by every day. To check things out."

Mary sat quietly for a while, then started. "Oh, I'm being so inhospitable! Would you like something to eat or drink? Wine?"

The other angels demurred, but Gabriel said, "Actually, if you have a little wine, I wouldn't mind that."

Raphael laughed out loud.

Michael blistered under the look Gabriel shot the Seraph. "A very little," Gabriel said. "Like a mouthful."

"You haven't seen her definition of 'very little.' It would put you in a coma for a week." He turned back to Mary. "He has no tolerance."

Gabriel sighed. "How often do we go solid?"

"Don't listen to him," Mary said to Gabriel. "You're in my household, so you get what you want," and she poured him a cup of wine.

"See," Raphael said when the cup was nearly full. "She doesn't do little servings."

Gabriel took some, and his eyes glistened. "This is wonderful. Angels don't often taste things." He sipped again, then passed the cup to Raphael. "Unfortunately, he's right, and I get sleepy."

Mary brought out bread and cheese.

"We didn't come for food," Michael said.

4

"Nonsense." She winked at Gabriel. "Gabriel said you don't get a chance to taste things often. I'm sorry I haven't got better, but I'll offer you whatever I have."

She passed the dishes to the angels. "Now, I have a favor to ask you."

Raphael said, "The plot thickens."

Uriel's eyes glimmered.

Mary stopped, looking at Uriel. "You didn't speak, but I can feel you talking."

"Angels don't need words," Gabriel said.

Michael opened his hands and inclined his head. *Like this.*

Mary laughed out loud. "That's terrific!" She sat back on her heels. "Is there any way we can redirect the enemy's attacks so they won't target Jesus?"

Gabriel said, "We're here to protect him."

"They've already tried once," she said, "and you said yourself they'll figure it out because of the angels around the household. I assume you don't stop by one house every day for supper?"

"Not for about six hundred years," Gabriel said dryly, and Raphael tensed.

Mary folded her arms. "Then we need to do more to protect him."

"In what way?" Michael said.

"I'm not sure." Mary frowned. "I was hoping you might figure it out."

Raphael looked over at Gabriel, who seemed to be staring a hundred miles away. "Now you've done it." Raphael chuckled. "Give a Cherub a problem to solve, and he won't rest until he solves it."

Michael said, "He could share what he's thinking and let the resident soldier take a crack at it.."

Gabriel wasn't even listening. Raphael said to Mary, "Cherubim are the problem-solvers, and if he engages with a question, he'll either get you an answer or die trying."

"And since angels can't die," Michael said, "he'll get an answer."

Raphael said, "Could be worse. We could have two Cherubim."

Mary said, "What happens if there are two Cherubim?"

"They debate," Michael said.

"And debate," Raphael said.

Uriel nodded, hands opening.

Mary chuckled. "Three Cherubim, five opinions?"

Raphael laughed out loud. "I love that!"

Gabriel spoke as if he'd just awakened. "We can spend our energy deflecting attacks once they've decided on a target, but our energy might be better spent now convincing them to retarget. What if we can persuade them *she* is the reason we're here?"

Michael took a deep breath. "How would we do that?"

"None of them were around when I first told Mary about Jesus," Gabriel said. "They have no information regarding what I said to her about him. Since she's able to sense us, I assume she'll be able to sense them as well."

Michael said, "Have you sensed them?"

"Sometimes." She swallowed hard. "Briefly."

Uriel met Michael's eyes, projecting concern: Asmodeus. Mephistopheles. Belior. Three of Satan's top four demons had been investigating, and it was a certitude they would call in the fourth to confirm their suspicions before bringing in Satan himself.

Michael frowned.

Uriel's eyes lowered, but the Throne's wings half-spread as if for a fight.

Gabriel said, "Uriel's a powerful enough angel that they might think Mary is the point of it all, but only if she can play into their expectations."

"Meaning?" Raphael said.

"She needs to order us around." Gabriel looked right at Mary. "You'll need to act as if you own us and we're your slaves. Would you be averse to that?"

Mary's eyes widened. "Are you kidding me? How could a person give orders to...you?"

"That's not an issue. You'd call for us," Gabriel said. "Then when whichever angel arrives, it's, 'Gabriel, fetch me some water,' or 'Gabriel, bring back the lost sheep.' Whatever you need doing."

Mary shook her head. "I couldn't do that."

Gabriel said, "A charade of that sort would convince them you have a great deal of power. Specifically, some kind of power over us."

"Is there anyone you would take that kind of treatment from?"

All four angels looked at the sleeping baby.

Mary's eyes brightened. "Really?" She sat back. "I'll make sure he isn't rude about it."

Gabriel leaned toward her. "But you had better be. Maybe not rude, but certainly authoritative. No *please*, no *thank you*." He grinned. "Occasionally you'll need to criticize: 'You call that water hot?'"

Raphael chuckled.

Mary knit her fingers. "Could I maybe give you a blanket thank-you once a week?"

"No, and I don't like this plan." Michael bit his lip. "It would only take one time for you to say, 'Is it okay to speak freely?' for Mephistopheles to figure out the entire game. At that point, you'd be in danger."

"Mary knows how to be circumspect." Gabriel looked at her. "But for that reason, no, no expressions of gratitude. As far as you're concerned, we have to look as if we're doing this under duress."

Mary still wavered. "But how would I know if you got angry?"

Gabriel said, "We've existed since the formation of the earth. There isn't any domestic job we'd find either challenging or disgusting."

"At least let me have a code word." Mary nodded. "So after you fill the water jars, I can tell you 'That was satisfactory' and you'll know I mean 'thank you'?"

Gabriel considered. "That would work."

Mary said, "But how will I know if I've overstepped my bounds?"

Gabriel said, "I won't smile when I blow the roof off your house."

Mary startled, but Raphael was laughing, and then Gabriel's deadpan broke. "I trust you wouldn't overstep your bounds, and even were it to happen by accident, we know we're doing it for him."

Mary glanced around. "Would you like some more wine? Fruit? Water?"

"We're fine," Raphael said.

Uriel sat forward. "One more consideration, Gabriel. When our enemies make themselves apparent to her, what then?"

Gabriel said, "Flag her to alert." He looked at Mary. "Uriel will want you to put on an act for them."

Uriel said, "Order us around. Make demands."

She looked uncertain. "Wouldn't that be the best time to keep a low profile?"

"That would be the best time to give them pause, because I assure you, the last thing they'd want is to be in thrall to you, and they won't want to take any chances that you can do to them what you've done to me. Actually, that may be a better way to handle this: I'm the only one in your control." Gabriel gave a small smile. "I may act resentful if they're around, just to convince them it's for real. Don't be afraid. Just keep up the act. They might stick around for a time observing."

Michael said, "It would never occur to them not to order someone around if only they had the power to do so, just the way it would never occur to them to take orders from someone they didn't have to. If you can keep Gabriel in thrall to you, or at least seem to, they'll buy it."

Uriel said, "They'll attack her, though."

Mary turned to Uriel. "But it's for the baby. I don't care what they do to me. That man already said I'm going to have my soul pierced by a sword—if that's what God wants, then what better way for it to happen than mothering my son?"

"They'll still attack him," Raphael said.

8

"But as a hostage." Mary sounded earnest. "It's better than having them attack him directly."

The angels stood, and Mary stood too. "Just call for any of us," Gabriel said. "Michael and I are a word away, and Uriel and Raphael are with you always."

Mary nodded, and the angels vanished. Gabriel and Michael returned to the Ring of Seven before God.

Michael swallowed hard. "Will this work?"

"I have no idea." Gabriel grinned. "But I like how she thinks."

Walking with Jesus through the lamp-lit room, Mary paused, rested her head against the crying bundle of baby. Barely loud enough to hear, she whispered, "Raphael?"

Raphael appeared.

"I'm going to have to ask you to take him." Her eyes were bloodshot. "I can't keep doing this."

Raphael beamed. "Really?"

"You don't mind, do you?"

"No, and you're supposed to be ordering me around." Raphael solidified enough to take Jesus from her arms. "Sleep. You aren't going to get healthy again unless you all get some rest."

Mary seemed reluctant to let him go. "Why is he crying?"

"His throat hurts." Raphael gentled the baby away from her. "I'll see what I can do about it."

Mary said, "You're sure?"

"You're supposed to say, 'That will be satisfactory.'" Raphael began rocking Jesus, such a magnificent armload. "Go to sleep."

With a look back over her shoulder, Mary lay down, then extinguished the lamp.

In the darkness, Raphael held Jesus to his chest and swayed a little, then found that neck-nestle position mothers have used for generations. With Jesus pressed to his chest, he found the proper rhythm of hips and shoulders to keep him moving in a continuous rock.

Gabriel's voice emerged from the corner. "It's the baby slow-dance."

"Did you ever get a chance to do this?"

Gabriel hesitated, looked at Raphael with uncertainty, then projected a positive.

A moment after, Gabriel sent, *I could do it again if you hand him over to me.*

Raphael gave Gabriel a sarcastic smile. *Not on your life.*

Gabriel's momentary disappointment washed over Raphael, but he only held Jesus tighter and continued walking him, his cheek pressed against the fine hair, his eyes closed. Little breaths, that intoxicating baby-scent, miniature limbs curled against his own body.

Do you know how many guardians would love to do this? Raphael sent, his soul overflowing with warmth.

Gabriel had relaxed again. *All of them?*

All of them.

Gabriel sang a lullaby, and Raphael joined him. The second time around, Gabriel took the harmony while Raphael maintained the melody, then repeated one line so they ended up singing as a round. By then their souls were in full bond, trading thoughts and feelings, Gabriel absorbing Raphael's Seraphic fire while imparting on him Cherubic calm. He approached Raphael, and with Raphael's permission he merged into Raphael's form so they were both holding the baby.

He's an incredible little bundle, Gabriel sent. *Thank you.*

Jesus had quieted down while they sang, but now he fussed again.

Gabriel kept his voice low. "He's wet."

Raphael said, "I'd rather not wake up Mary to change him."

"I can change him." And with that Gabriel was solid. He took Jesus from Raphael's arms.

"Are you sure this is a good idea?" Raphael followed Gabriel to the diapers. "Do you know how to do this?"

"Some of us have watched Mary change diapers ten times a day for months," Gabriel said. "You'd know how to do it too if you weren't bedazzled by him."

Raphael chuckled as Gabriel unfastened the baby's clothing. "But maybe—"

He whipped off the wet diaper and grabbed a clean one. "It's a diaper and a baby, and I'm an archangel of the Presence. What could go wrong?"

11

"You realize nine times out of ten, when someone says something like that, a terrible disaster follows."

"Of course." Gabriel handed back a dry-diapered baby. "But I'm ten out of ten."

Raphael looked Jesus in the eyes, and a smile overtook him. In the dark, the baby had opened his eyes fully and watched his guardian angel with a quiet alert stare, as if absorbing every detail of him.

You can see he's intelligent, Gabriel sent.

Raphael bubbled up inside, filled with joy so much that his wings vibrated.

Gabriel drew off the fire, but Raphael burned brighter. He smiled at Jesus, and the baby smiled back.

Raphael took him out into the courtyard and spread his wings.

"About something not being a good idea," Gabriel said, following, "are you sure this is smart?"

That much joy couldn't stay on the ground. Raphael ascended, holding Jesus close to his chest and slicing through the air with his wings.

"You're insane." Gabriel soared beside him. "Your charge has a sore throat, and you're exposing him to the wind."

Raphael rolled so he drifted on his back. "Cold air is good for some kinds of coughs."

Gabriel wore a grin. "And aerobatics—they're good for an upper respiratory infection as well?"

"Not nearly as good as sarcasm."

Gabriel glided a wingspan over Raphael. "Then he's in luck because we're overstocked on both tonight."

Raphael met Gabriel's eyes with a sparkle in his own.

"Aren't you worried you're going to drop him?"

"I'm a Seraph of the presence," Raphael said, "and you're ten out of ten. What could happen?"

Gabriel descended. "The worst that could have happened to me was I could have gotten moistened. Dropping him inhabits an entirely different category of bad."

"I've got him tight."

"I'd prefer if you had him in a sling or a harness."

"You'd prefer I was on the ground."

"That too." Gabriel swung back around so he flew beneath Raphael. "I hope I catch better than you throw."

Huffing in annoyance, Raphael banked and increased altitude. Gabriel sped up to follow him, starlight flashing over his wings.

Raphael looked over his shoulder. "You couldn't catch me at your fastest."

"You've got added drag." Gabriel's eyes glinted. "I'll catch you."

Raphael turned on the speed, leaving Gabriel behind. He tucked the baby closer at his chest, and he adjusted his arms to keep the worst of the wind off him. Six months older and this baby would have been be howling with laughter. Even now, he was reveling in the weightlessness he'd lost after the waters broke and pressure pushed him into an existence of light and temperature.

Gabriel had fallen behind, and Raphael slowed to allow him to almost catch up, but not entirely.

Show-off.

He's loving it. You wouldn't deny Jesus something he loves.

The Cherub-induced thought arose in his head that Jesus wouldn't have loved flying until he'd actually done it, so remaining on the ground wouldn't have fit the full description of denial.

Raphael sent back irritation. He sped up and stripped off his grey-winged pursuer. Up he soared through a clearing in the clouds, the nearly-full moon illuminating his wings. He shifted the baby so he could look into his wide eyes. *God, thank you for him. Thank you, thank you. I never imagined. I had no idea what a guardian felt until now.*

Curling his innermost set of wings around the baby, he arched the other two and went into a spin, supporting Jesus's neck and head against his chest, the other arm beneath his bottom and curled thighs. A flexing of the primary feathers brought him upright so he shot toward the stars, and then he went over backward and dropped, curling his arms and legs up around the baby as if he were doing a cannon-ball into the clouds. Then he flexed his spine and flipped over so he was flying level at speeds that would make a racing horse look chained to a tree.

Against his chest, Jesus gave a belly-laugh, and Raphael laughed out loud too, then spiraled upward. He held the baby out at arm's length and met his eyes again, and this time he was totally lost in the boy's soul, the boy's beauty, and purity and the startling depth of his humanity.

I will do anything for you, Raphael promised.

Drop him? He would never let go. He would never give up. He would never forget this moment, this power, this promise, this love. This soul, entrusted to his care with a bond utterly different than Gabriel's.

The baby studied him, and Raphael felt the answering promise from the boy's soul: he would obey; he would grow in God's love; he would be everything God wanted; and he loved Raphael too.

The Seraph clutched the boy close to his heart and hovered a mile above the earth, his heart rippling with fire and his being vibrating with excitement.

I had no idea, he prayed.

Gabriel caught up, and Raphael tucked his innermost wings around Jesus again.

A momentary unease swept through Gabriel's eyes. Raphael reached through their bond, waiting for the answering fire to spark up inside the Cherub, but Gabriel didn't grasp for it. Raphael kindled him up anyhow from his overflow.

As Gabriel's soul responded, he resonated with confusion as to whether he still belonged with Raphael or whether he ought to distance himself.

Raphael beat his wings to move nearer. "Don't question that! There's room for two. We just need to negotiate things until we adjust."

Gabriel folded his arms and looked aside. "He's your primary concern. I can find other things to do for the next hundred years."

Raphael shook his head "He's my primary concern, but I want you here to balance me out so I can do a better job."

Gabriel nodded. "If only for that, then."

Raphael said, "Just don't keep questioning my judgment."

Gabriel said, "Don't leave me behind again."

Raphael hesitated, then assented.

A moment after, he looked at the baby's slack face, his partially-opened mouth. "He's asleep now. We ought to bring him home."

They flashed to the courtyard, and Raphael walked through the house to bring Jesus back to Mary's bed. He laid down the baby gently, but as he desolidified to let Jesus rest beneath the blankets, the baby made tiny nursing sounds. Mary rolled to her side to latch him on. She murmured, "Was everything okay?"

"No worries." Raphael stroked Jesus's hair. "It was perfectly satisfactory."

Year Three

Gabriel sat alongside the house after the family had breakfast, watching Jesus scratch a finger-sized trench beside the fence with a stick. Raphael had gone to help out a friend guarding a dying man, so for the moment it was just himself and the boy in the sunlight.

Jesus turned to him. "You're Gabriel?"

Gabriel assented.

"What do you do?"

Opting against an exhaustive list, Gabriel said, "I teach."

Jesus tilted his head. "What do you teach?"

He hadn't expected that. "What do you want to learn?"

"Mom teaches me cooking. Dad teaches me the Torah." He jumped up. "Can you teach me numbers?"

Numbers? Really? Gabriel crouched in the dust. "Bring me that stick."

Numbers were life. Numbers were code. You could do anything with numbers, translate anything into numbers. Of course, the Hebrew alphanumeric system wasn't adept enough for the kind of work Gabriel would want, so he skipped the traditional counting systems in both Roman and Hebrew and went straight to ordinal numbers. "This is much more useful," he said, "even though no one else is going to understand you."

Jesus nodded, and Gabriel began writing.

Math. Why hadn't he thought of this sooner? The kid could design bridges and palaces and aqueducts and pyramids. His father was a carpenter, after all. Maybe he'd fulfill God's plans by building something incredible. And for that, you needed a good grounding in mathematics.

Grounding. Gabriel sighed. Writing in the dirt wasn't as useful as it should be, but it was all they had to work with right now.

Jesus caught on, though. He took the stick and made his own characters. He asked questions, and then after hearing the answers asked even more complicated questions. Gabriel gave him just enough information each time to keep him asking more.

He'd just finished writing out a new equation when he felt Raphael approaching at speed. "Watch it!" he shouted, Guarding Raphael off the dirt. "You'll mess things up."

Raphael stopped at the edge of the wall in the shimmering air. "What are you doing? Mess up what?"

Gabriel gestured to the ground. "He's solving for one variable, and he's worked on this for a while."

"Look, Raphael!" Jesus jumped in place. "Seven! The answer is seven!"

Gabriel took down the Guard, and Raphael landed, disturbing the figures in the dirt.

"Tell me you're kidding." Raphael stepped forward gingerly. "Please. This is simply a joke because I was gone longer than you thought I'd be."

Gabriel frowned. Had it been that long? It couldn't have been—unless it wasn't the same day. But no, it didn't feel like that. For one thing, Mary wouldn't have let the child go a full night without sleep.

"You're hopeless," Raphael said.

Hopeless? "He wanted me to tell him about numbers."

"So you taught him algebra?"

"I didn't *start* with algebra." Gabriel put his hands on his hips. "We started by counting, and then he wanted to add, and he realized the limits of a letter-based system for counting, so I showed him base ten counting, and once he got that we kept going."

Jesus was grinning. "It was fun! Can you give me a problem too?"

Gabriel beamed. "He's ready for two variables if you want."

Raphael rubbed his temples. "I think I'd rather go inside and apologize to Mary."

Jesus tugged at Gabriel's wing. "You need to tell me. How do you do two variables?"

Before he could answer, a warning shot through Gabriel, and Mary shouted, "Gabriel!"

Jesus's face went impassive, and Gabriel flashed before Mary. She looked stern, and Uriel's visage had darkened. One of them must have detected a demon.

Mary looked directly at him. "Why were *you* watching Jesus?"

Gabriel said, "Raphael had another assignment."

"Raphael's assignment should be my son." She'd perfected an inflection-free voice that wasn't rude but bordered on condescending. They'd worked on it for an hour one night, trying to achieve the right mix of superiority and standing-on-ceremony. "Is that understood?"

Uriel had a very worried look, so Gabriel smoked his form a bit. "I assumed my presence was sufficient."

"I asked for Raphael. I wanted him with my son, not you." She held up a bag. "Joseph forgot his lunch. Bring it."

Raphael's sword in its scabbard had little flames around the visible blade. Jesus had wandered back into the kitchen. Gabriel tried to look infuriated. "Yes, my lady."

This time he heard it: demonic snickering, and now the irritated look came naturally.

Mary hesitated. "Are you thinking of blowing the roof of my house?"

"I would smile while I did it," Gabriel said by means of reassurance.

"Good," Mary said, a little softer, "because I hope you and I both understand why you're doing this."

Gabriel smiled with an edge sharper than a dagger. "I never forget why I'm doing this."

"That's satisfactory, then. Dismissed."

He vanished to Joseph's carpentry shop.

As he laid the bag on Joseph's work bench, a demon behind him convulsed with laughter. Gabriel took a deep breath and turned to find the Seraph Asmodeus and his bonded Cherub Belior. Together the pair were Satan's top advisors.

"That's completely worth the price of admission." Asmodeus wiped tears from his eyes. "I didn't think I'd live long enough to see anything this funny."

Gabriel frizzled with tension.

Asmodeus said, "Don't worry, we're laughing with you, not at you."

"Actually," Belior said, "if you'll take note, Gabriel isn't laughing, therefore we *are* laughing at him."

Gabriel folded his arms.

"What did you do wrong this time?" Asmodeus said. "First you end up human for a year, and now you're serving humans."

Gabriel bristled.

Asmodeus leaned against the wall. "Why haven't you killed her yet?"

Gabriel answered, honestly, "I don't know how to kill someone God hasn't ordered me to kill."

Belior stepped closer. "I can tell you that. You ask me, and I do it."

"I'm not going to—"

"I won't ask you to curse God," Belior interrupted. "You'll just owe me a favor."

"The price is too high," Gabriel said, "but thanks for thinking of me."

Belior said, "I'm curious, because I have a line of people a mile long who would love to be able to enthrall you. How did she do it?"

Gabriel put two fingers together and touched the back of them to his lips.

"That's powerful," Belior whispered. "You can't even hint?"

Gabriel closed his eyes.

Asmodeus huffed. "It's too bad. Think of the fun we could have had."

Gabriel sighed.

Belior sounded incredulous. "Did she actually demand Raphael be the guardian of her baby? Doesn't that mean she pushed off whichever angel was supposed to guard him?"

"That sounds like a tremendously bad idea, doesn't it?" Gabriel said. Again, totally honest.

"No kidding." Belior's eyes sparked. "Even when the guardian and the charge are a perfect fit, you have trouble keeping a human on a straight path. Mess with the fit and the kid is essentially ours."

Gabriel made his voice low. "I'm under orders to protect him too, so keep that in mind."

"You won't need to protect him because maybe we won't bother attacking him." Asmodeus stretched his wings. "He'll undo himself thanks to her."

The pair looked at one another, and Gabriel shivered as the Seraph and the Cherub (quite probably) reached for one another through their bond. There was a momentary flicker in Belior's eyes, an answering sparkle in Asmodeus', and an instant later both appeared a little stronger, a little more balanced.

Gabriel reached in his heart for Raphael, who sent back reassurance. No demons remained at the house. Also, apparently Uriel had relayed to Raphael that Mary was worried she'd hurt Gabriel's feelings.

Gabriel kept his smile secret.

Belior said, "If you can point us toward the seal she's using, I might consider breaking her hold."

Gabriel's eyes narrowed. "I'm sure you'd hand it right back to me, too."

"Of course I would." Belior's black hair settled over his forehead as he leaned toward Gabriel with a concern that looked genuine. "Just out of respect for our choir, you understand."

Gabriel said, "Respect?"

Asmodeus said, "Are you calling him a liar?"

Here Gabriel couldn't fake it anymore and laughed out loud, bringing steel to Asmodeus' eyes and an added brilliance to Belior's. "You can't fool him," Belior said. "He knows we'd be passing the seal around for the next four thousand years, or at least until Lucifer took our toy away and decided to play with Gabriel himself."

Asmodeus leaned closer. "We're watching her. Eventually she's going to slip, and we'll know how she did it. After that, we own you."

Belior nodded. "Even better, eventually we'll convince her to listen to us, and she'll hand you over without a second's hesitation."

Asmodeus said to Belior, "What you haven't explained yet is how she snared him without losing her soul."

Belior shook his head. "It's an enigma, but she's got some natural power of her own, given the guardian assigned to her." He looked back at Gabriel. "So you can plan on it—eventually you'll be working in thrall to one of our men."

Gabriel swallowed hard. "Charming."

"I was thinking of that magician in China," Belior said to Asmodeus. "The one who sacrifices babies to preserve his youth."

"The witch in Rome who predicts the future would be better," Asmodeus said. "Sometimes she looks too far into the future, and it scares her. But give her Gabriel and she won't have to look any longer. He could tell her what she wants to know, and she won't find out the things she doesn't."

Gabriel thought, *God, allow me at this moment to express my thankfulness that I'm not actually in thrall to any of these humans they're describing.*

The Holy Spirit replied with agreement.

Gabriel turned away. "Thank you for your concern, but I'll be going now."

"Maybe you can help her weed her vegetable garden," Belior called, and Asmodeus laughed aloud.

Gabriel flashed to Heaven, to the Ring of Seven Archangels, and he dropped to his knees.

I really dislike them, he prayed.

It had worked, though—absolutely their deception had worked, and it was evident in Raphael's relief, as well as in Uriel's concern for Mary every time they tempted her, attacked her prayer life, whispered self-doubts into her heart, or tried to sabotage her work. Jesus was growing up shielded from the worst of their weaponry, at least for now. Someday he'd have to cope with their whispering, their lures, the attractions of a world gone dusky, but for now he could have childhood.

As for himself, Gabriel would accept any amount of mockery and harassment. Besides: now it appeared he'd also get to enjoy the occasional hour of algebra.

He learned that so quickly, Gabriel prayed.

God smiled at him.

We'll work on quadratic equations when I get a chance, Gabriel prayed. *And I want to see what he can do with geometry. Joseph is a carpenter, so at some point Jesus will need to learn about lines of force and potential energy, and geometry will be a good complement to the physics he'll need.*

God reminded Gabriel that Joseph himself hadn't learned physics so much as he'd learned about life, about gravity, about stability.

Stability is the bare essential, Gabriel replied, *but geometry is reality.*

God smiled at Gabriel, who returned it with enthusiasm, already planning the next impromptu lesson.

Are we doing all right? Gabriel asked.

God replied, *Perfectly satisfactory,* and Gabriel laughed.

Year Five

Gabriel appeared in response to Mary's summons.

She was tucking a cloth into a basket, and as he appeared, she swept her hair back from her forehead. Gabriel reached out to find Raphael shepherding in a field a mile away with Jesus.

"I'm going to give you an unusual assignment," Mary said, "and if God has any objections, please let me know."

Gabriel inclined his head.

She lifted the basket. "I'd like you to bring this to a man in prison. Last month my cousin's son was apprehended by the Romans for theft, and my cousin is convinced they're not feeding him enough."

God's answer flickered in Gabriel's heart, along with a sense of amusement. "It's allowed, my lady."

A smile ghosted her lips. "That will be satisfactory."

Gabriel took the basket from her. "I'll need his name, of course, and I ought to sneak it in so no one suspects what we've done."

Mary gave him the name. God told him the man was awake, but his guardian would work on correcting that.

While he waited, Gabriel leaned against the wall. "It's generous of you to do this for him."

Mary said, "It's just a loaf of bread and some fruit."

"Even so." Gabriel paused as he realized he'd made a faulty assumption. "Is he unjustly accused?"

Mary bit her lip. "I assume he really committed the crime."

Gabriel started. "And your cousin talked about it with you?"

"Of course she did." Mary shook her head. "No matter the dumb things he's done, he's still her child."

Gabriel didn't reply.

Mary looked abruptly shocked. "Do you think she'd disown him?"

Gabriel nodded. "Perhaps not disown him so much as not disclose his failings to others."

"It'd be hard not to, since he's not around. She can't pretend for a couple of years that he's hiding in a closet." Mary chuckled. "Besides, she still loves him."

Gabriel's eyes widened. "That must make it even worse for her. One assumes she finds his actions embarrassing."

"Probably." Mary shook her head. "You know how the gossip mills work."

Gabriel remained alongside the cooking fire, silent.

Mary picked up her spinning. Over the past few years, she'd grown to treat the angels like frequent guests rather than visiting dignitaries, and he'd gotten used to her working in his presence. He watched the motion of the spindle, taking comfort in the rotation and the twist. "Okay," Mary abruptly said, "this is bothering me. What do you know that I don't?"

Gabriel squinted. "Quite a bit."

"I mean about my cousin. Did God tell you she hates him?"

Gabriel's wings flared. "Absolutely not."

Mary gave the spindle another spin. "So why would you think she'd cut him off?"

Gabriel shrugged. "It just makes sense."

"To whom?"

He opened his hands, and the implication was clear: *To me.*

Mary sounded forceful. "Not to me. It's one action. He's still her son."

Genetics made human relations so much more complicated. The ties of family and heritability and marriage made for more conflict and yet more loyalty than Gabriel had ever understood. "I have no children. I'll take your word on it."

Mary cocked her head, and Gabriel recognized someone about to make a definitive point so she'd win an argument. "If you got into trouble, Raphael wouldn't walk out on you."

Gabriel flinched. "I did get into very serious trouble." He stared at the floor. "To this day, he thinks it's a disgrace."

Mary stopped her spindle and stared at him. "Really?"

Uriel in the corner was staring as well.

Gabriel closed his eyes and wished the prisoner were asleep so he could just bring the bread and end the conversation. Since that hadn't happened, he spoke in a lower voice. "Raphael didn't walk off, but he's also an angel, and we're permanently bonded; under the same stresses, I assume a human would feel free to dissolve the relationship."

Mary sounded heartbroken. "I didn't realize that. He seems so friendly with you."

Gabriel nodded. "He is."

Mary leaned toward him. "But how can something that huge not change the way you interact?"

"Should it?" Gabriel's wings raised. "We ignore what happened in order to continue our friendship."

Mary wound more yarn onto the spindle, but she did it slowly. "What happened?"

Gabriel's shoulders tightened. "It doesn't matter. The important point is how he got punished too because of me, and the blowback on him just worsens my offense. He shared the disgrace at the time, and now he wants it buried." Gabriel tightened his fists. "The fact that he ignores it is a testimony to his charitable nature."

Uriel radiated confusion, and Gabriel perked up. "I'm glad to know it isn't obvious."

Mary returned to spinning, avoiding his eyes. "I'm sorry. I didn't mean to bring it up."

"There's nothing to be sorry for. It's just something that is." He paused. "Your cousin's son is asleep. Will there be anything else?"

Mary shook her head, and Gabriel departed.

Mary turned to Uriel.

"I had no idea," Uriel said. "But he and Raphael are bonded, so if Gabriel said it, you can accept it as true."

"That's sad." Mary twirled her spindle again, turning a sheep's unwanted hair into something useful. "But we're not perfect. Maybe every friendship has something like that inside."

Gabriel balanced on the outer wall of the Roman prison, Mary's empty basket in his hand. The cousin's son had dozed off just long enough for Gabriel to make the delivery, and then the guardian had awakened him to eat before the guards saw. Gabriel had requests from five other guardians to send food for their charges as well, and he debated whether Mary ought to hear about this, because doubtless she would.

Below him were the prison gates. He watched a group of men being released, watched as one was joined by his family, all of whom were thrilled to see him. One young man was escorted by his father, both silent. The rest trudged away without talking, an assortment of firm and discouraged, talkative and brooding, but all of them alone.

Remiel appeared beside him, sunlight in her golden eyes. "Hey, storm-cloud. How's it going?"

He handed her the empty basket. "Would you mind taking this back to Mary for me?"

Remiel said, "Sure. Oh, wait, I forgot—I'm an angel." The basket vanished from her hands even as she snickered. "Do you have any other insurmountable tasks?"

Gabriel shrugged.

"Ooh. This looks serious." She put a hand on his arm and brought one of her gold wings up against his grey ones. "Are you knee-deep in theory, or is something bothering you that I could understand?"

Gabriel bit his lip. "Do you ever find yourself suddenly troubled by something you'd thought settled?"

Remiel huffed. "That's pretty much my life."

Gabriel pulled his wings tighter. "I'm sorry."

"Don't worry. It's not as if I ever forget that I used to have a twin, only he fell." She looked up for the sun. "But if you want to talk about ghosts from the past, I bet I'm the best listener for you."

When Gabriel remained quiet, she said, "You're thinking about when you got thrown out of Heaven for a year?"

Pivoting to stare at her, he took a step back.

She said, "Let's see: you're brooding, you're asking me about old hurts, and you're hanging around outside a prison. I didn't need the entire second choir of angels to help me figure it out."

Gabriel's wings sagged.

Her eyes glinted. "What about it? The fact that it happened at all, or is it something specific?"

He nudged the wall with his foot. "I dragged down Raphael with me."

"He coped with it okay." In the next moment she giggled. "You didn't have to deal with him. At some point he determined the exact minute of the day when God put the hammer down, and for the next several months it was a comedy as we all tried to avoid him at that hour, except that then he'd seek out some unlucky victim in order to announce exactly how many days left until you returned."

Gabriel forced a smile. "I can picture that."

"Ophaniel realized that if he foisted him off on Israfel, she would be just as happy to hear it, only then she got as bad as he was." Remiel tilted her head. "He didn't tell you that?"

Gabriel shook his head.

She said, "He's probably embarrassed."

Gabriel shifted to long-distance vision to track the silent father and son on the road.

"But it's okay," she said.

"I wouldn't use the term *okay*," Gabriel said, "if he's still mortified."

"I wouldn't use the term *mortified* either," Remiel said. "Look, at some point, just tell him you know how he feels about it and that you're sorry, and he'll probably be shocked that you're

even bringing it up, and he'll tell you not to think about it again."
She leaned against Gabriel's shoulder. "You don't need to keep
ruminating over it. It's done, and it's over."

Gabriel said, "I let him down. I can't make that up to him."

Remiel kissed him on the cheek. "I love you, but you're
being dense. Go talk to him. You'll feel better afterward," and
Gabriel flashed away, but not to Raphael.

Two nights later, Gabriel appeared to Mary shortly after
Jesus had gone to bed. Mary wove cloth at her loom while Joseph
sanded wood.

Greetings, Gabriel sent to Mary, and she nodded.

He gestured to his side, where two female angels had
appeared, one golden-haired and the other with black hair, blue
eyes and sky-blue wings. He indicated the golden one. "This is
Remiel. She's a Virtue and one of the Seven archangels who stand
directly before the Most High, like myself." He turned to the
other. "This is Zadkiel, the Chief of the order of Dominions and
Michael's standard-bearer."

Mary acknowledged both of them, not speaking because of
Joseph in the room.

Raphael had come to watch, sparkling with curiosity.

"I trust," Gabriel said to Mary, "that you will find their
combination adequate to baby-sit a sleeping five-year-old boy?"

Beginning to smile, Mary agreed.

"Good," Gabriel said, "because in a moment, Raphael is
going to have to chase me halfway around the world to thrash me
for doing *this*!"

And as he said that, he hurled a snowball at Raphael, then
another, then a third, and then flashed away. Raphael let out a
shout and followed him in a shower of sparks before the
exploding snowballs even had a chance to flurry to the ground.

Mary laughed out loud.

Remiel folded her arms and leaned against the wall. "They
were both so ready for that."

Joseph stared in surprise at the dusting of snow across the floor. Mary left her loom and picked up whatever she could, awestruck as she it melted on her fingertips. "When they get back," she said to Zadkiel, "remind me to ask Gabriel to bring me a box of this."

Raphael appeared at the top of the world only to get pelted with snow. Gabriel was well-armed with snowballs behind the walls of a snow-fort, and Raphael had appeared in the open. Of course—the Cherub had planned it that way.

Gabriel managed to get in five shots before Raphael flashed into the snow fort, only Gabriel disappeared and started hurling more from a second fort that gave him an unimpeded firing line into the back of the first. Gabriel didn't get to use the third one because Raphael knew him too well, and instead of following him into the second, tracked back to the third and commandeered that in advance.

There were shrieks, threats incomprehensible through their laughter, and the invention of the water-balloon when Raphael realized he could form a very thin Guard filled with ice-water. Gabriel fired ice-arrows at Raphael, and Raphael put up a wall of flame to dissolve them in the air. There was hand-to-hand wresting and snow stuffed down shirts, and after an hour, Gabriel's snow-forts were quite well-redistributed along the ground. There was icy debris scattered everywhere and a Seraph-Cherub pair sprawled on the snow gasping for breath.

Raphael rolled onto his side and looked at Gabriel, who lay on his back, arms spread from his side, his wings splayed. Gabriel had made himself slightly more solid to really feel the moment, the cold, the aching where Raphael had struck him in the ribs with an ice-ball. His breath heaved, and slightly solid he put up a little cloud of vapor with every one. A half-smile parted his lips as he lay with his eyes closed. The Cherub was exuding rings of calm, and Raphael absorbed them into his heart as only a Seraph can.

They focused him, centered him both within himself and within God.

Propped on his elbows, Raphael brushed a wing over Gabriel's side and took care of the bruise. Gabriel sent him thanks.

A question and then an answer arose from somewhere between them, and it could have been from either one, but it felt to Raphael as if Gabriel had been the one who asked if this had been fun for him, and he the one who responded that of course it had.

Satisfaction from Gabriel. Pleasure because he'd planned and set up the whole thing himself.

Raphael extended his gratitude. He loved being a guardian, and he would never complain about being with the child, but so much of the assignment was drudgery. The same daily routine, the same people and scenery, the boredom combined with a continuous alert.

Gabriel's eyes opened, and his peaceful aura dissipated. He hadn't realized.

Raphael reflected that he really admired the Angels who did this without the benefit of the thank-yous he got on a regular basis.

Gabriel didn't move from where he lay in the snow, but Raphael could feel him considering: maybe the other archangels could do something, maybe visit every day, maybe give Raphael a breather more often. And then behind it all vibrated Gabriel's impression that the archangels had done as much for him during the year he'd been on Earth.

Oh, no, not the year again. Raphael distanced himself in his mind so Gabriel wasn't sharing all his thoughts any longer.

But Gabriel pressed to get closer into his mind, and Raphael realized Gabriel had set up this outing to say whatever was coming next. Even more, Gabriel was reluctant to say it anyhow.

Don't stop him, said the Sprit in Raphael's heart.

This was so different from the Gabriel of only a while ago, when he would have said whatever it was without concerning himself with how his listeners reacted. Certainly without setting it up, since as far as he'd been concerned truth was truth, and you dealt with it because it was something that was, and what choice did that leave you? Gabriel dealt that way with himself. It was only in the last seven centuries—only since Gabriel had returned from being punished for a year—that he'd acknowledged the legitimacy of the heart-factor in the way you delivered news. He was clumsy, but he was trying to take it into account.

The tension in the Cherub had heightened, and Raphael felt his own soul burning in response.

Gabriel said, "Are some things unforgivable?"

Raphael looked at him curiously. "God forgives anything."

"I meant between friends." Gabriel had a thoughtful frown. "Consider a situation where one lets someone down. Someone important."

Raphael said, "Ask God."

"I'm asking you."

Raphael shifted so he sat cross-legged. "You mean like if I failed Jesus?"

Gabriel focused a long distance away, still frowning, then cocked his head. "Hypothetically speaking."

"It would be a disgrace, I think, not a sin. So technically, it couldn't be forgiven."

Gabriel's eyes widened. "Disgraceful." He drew out the word like Mary spinning the finest of threads.

Raphael raised his eyes to find Gabriel tracing on the ground. Mathematical symbols. Gabriel was running away in his own head.

Gabriel looked only at his calculation. "Nothing could make it right?"

"I wouldn't say that." Raphael shrugged. "You'd probably be able to patch things up, but depending on the amount of damage, you'd always carry some kind of reminder. Remiel certainly does."

"And would I be right to assume," said Gabriel as he diagrammed the problem on the snowtop, "that it would be normal not to fully trust the other person again afterward?"

Raphael nodded. "I think that would be normal after a really big falling-out."

Gabriel frowned again as he started doing whatever it was Cherubim did with numbers. Raphael could feel the equation half-formed in his own head as Gabriel worked it: he was calculating the gravitational influence of two planetary bodies on one another to determine the distance at which the gravitational pull was no longer enough to keep them from drifting apart but not strong enough to draw them together.

What could possibly make Gabriel this tentative? Gabriel was legendary for looking horrible things in the face and saying, "Now we deal with that the way it is."

Who had recently let someone down? Who was not trusting whom?

"Be straightforward with me. What are we talking about specifically?"

Gabriel said, "I'm thinking about that year."

Raphael's heart stopped.

Gabriel used a voice soft as snowfall. "I know how ashamed you feel."

Raphael stared. He couldn't even pray.

That whole year...

His memories of the first hour were blurred: frustration at God, at Gabriel, at himself for how he'd overreacted and in the end been helpless. He was glad he couldn't remember. The worst moment had been watching the two he loved most at odds all at once, knowing his loyalty lay with God but not knowing how to mend the fracture, and next being forbidden even to know what had happened to Gabriel.

But worse than that was the next two weeks consumed by fear that Gabriel had been thrown into Hell, two weeks of wishing he'd seen this coming and headed it off. Suspecting he'd seen hints over centuries but had kept pushing it to the back of his mind as Gabriel turned more toward the minutiae of the law and away from compassion. Then guilt. Shame over his part. He should have done better.

God had pity on him at that point and let him know Gabriel would be returning. But then he endured a year of everyone falling silent whenever he approached, everyone keeping secrets, but him learning to read their eyes and their different caliber silences like a barometer.

And then when Gabriel had returned, he was scarily silent for three months, desperate in prayer, starving to look into God's eyes all the time. Raphael had dealt with that all right.

No, it was the aftermath that was really the worst, when Gabriel came back to himself. First he wrote a letter to the family where he'd stayed, and then he started to process. Cherubim processed endlessly. He spent more years questioning everything in light of what he'd learned, re-defining his entire understanding of God and Creation and his place in it all based on a year where Raphael hadn't been.

In the middle of an assigned task, Raphael would turn to Gabriel to share something exciting, only to find him staring a thousand miles away, always thinking about the same thing.

Every time Gabriel mentioned how strong everyone had been, and how everyone had looked out for him, and how thankful he was for everyone's help, Raphael had heard an accusation: *everyone* meant everyone else.

No other Seraph had so completely failed to help his bonded Cherub, not since the winnowing.

And six hundred years later, here was Gabriel saying he couldn't trust him anymore.

Gabriel continued tracing symbols in the snow. He was doing it left-handed now, having run out of room on his right. "I didn't realize it bothered you that much. I shouldn't have wanted to talk about it."

"None of that should matter." Raphael's hands trembled. "We're together."

Gabriel said, "But it's not good enough if you—"

"No!" Raphael sat up. "You keep doing this! You've got to let off the constant criticism of the way I do things. Let me make my own mistakes for once!"

Of course, when Gabriel was ripped away from him, he'd made his own colossal mistake, and they'd both paid. Flames leaped around Raphael: in the eyes of a Cherub who never forgot anything, he was still paying.

Why was this coming up now? Was Gabriel jealous that Jesus was getting his full attention when Gabriel himself hadn't gotten any in approximately the same position?

Listen to him, urged the Spirit. *I don't want you two at odds.*

He ambushed me!

Gabriel said, "Don't get upset. If you wake him up—"

"Will you listen to yourself?" Raphael got to his feet even as Gabriel sat straighter. "Why should you know how to guard Jesus better than I do? You've always tagged along on my assignments and told me how I'm doing them wrong. *Don't wake up the kid. Don't use a different name. Don't fly with the baby. Don't leave just yet.* When is it time for you to trust my judgment?"

Gabriel inclined his head. Typical Gabriel, backing off to watch the curious phenomenon of a Seraph with emotions. Then a wordless apology.

Raphael unfolded his arms, but his wings were still tight to his back. "It's humiliating enough that you have to be running interference with the enemy. Do you have to come right out and tell me I'm not good enough to do the job God gave me?"

Gabriel raised his hands. "I have absolute faith in you."

"Show it for once!" Raphael kicked a shower of snow into the air. The ice particles glimmered as they settled back onto the surface.

Gabriel bit his lip. "It's a tremendous guardianship, but I can't think of a better angel for it, and God couldn't either, because he gave it to you."

Raphael looked sidelong at him. "I'm going to be right here for him the whole time. I'm not going to let him down."

Gabriel pushed back with his question: if Raphael was done diverting the question, did he still feel the same about the year of Gabriel's punishment?

Fire surged in his heart. "My feelings haven't changed."

The light left Gabriel's eyes. "You still feel ashamed. That it was a disgrace."

"Yes." Sparks showered through the air around Raphael. "Are you happy I said it?"

"Not really, but it's good you were honest." Gabriel looked right through him. "How can I change that?"

"You can't!" Raphael turned so he didn't have to see the thousand-mile stare. "Don't you think if it was possible I would have asked for it by now? You're right—a betrayal of that magnitude can't be undone, and I'm always going to carry that with me, and I can't see anything good that came of one horrible mistake."

"That's a harsh assessment." Gabriel's voice had gone hollow.

"Who better to make it than me?" Raphael folded his arms and squared his shoulders. "I hate that it happened at all, but more than that, I hate that it just keeps coming back as a reminder."

Gabriel had returned to frowning. "Am I to understand you would find it easier if I left?"

He whipped around, stunned. "No!"

How Gabriel could bloodlessly talk about something this wrenching, Raphael would never comprehend.

In the next moment Raphael felt Gabriel balancing out the fire, filling him with those rings of calm until he could think clearly. What would happen if Gabriel decided this would be the last time and simply left, opting not to trust this particular Seraph any longer?

The future spun like a whirlpool, and even though Gabriel steadied him again, he trembled. "Please stay. Just, please, don't keep dragging it up."

Gabriel said, "If that's acceptable to you, then I will, and I won't raise the matter again."

Raphael stared a hole in the snow. Once more came the steel from Gabriel, cool as glass, gentle and focusing. He absorbed it all until that security anchored him and Gabriel felt fully present once more.

"If that's settled," Gabriel said, "there's something else."

Raphael glared at him only to realize "something" was a snowball, followed immediately by a tackle, and in the next moment they were entangled, snow flying, Raphael laughing,

Gabriel's eyes glimmering, the pair together mingling fire and steel in their hearts. Raphael forced the whole conversation aside. It was okay. They were okay.

Half an hour of snow-fighting later, Remiel appeared. "Raphael, I'm sorry, but he woke up, and he's asking for you."

Raphael left. The pair always agreed where his top priority was.

Remiel dropped into the snow beside Gabriel. "Did you have a fun war? I thought I heard you laughing all the way from the Holy Land."

Gabriel nodded.

She leaned closer. "And did you talk with him?"

Gabriel said, "He made it clear how he feels."

She rested her head on Gabriel's shoulder. "I'm glad you straightened it out."

Gabriel tucked in his knees and brought up his wings, staring a thousand miles away. "It's helpful to know where we stand."

Halfway through distributing Mary's bread to the prisoners, Gabriel stopped in place, staring blindly.

He summoned an Angel, handed off the basket, then fled to the rooftop where he stood with his hands on his knees and his head down, chest heaving.

One of the prisoners' guardians appeared by his side, radiating concern.

Gabriel pulled himself up, then held his head aslant. His eyes sparkled.

The guardian rested a hand on his arm.

Gabriel forced a smile, hugged the guardian, then flashed into Heaven.

On the balcony of his library, Gabriel sat on the stone railing, heels knocking the post with a rhythm slower than a man's heartbeat. His fingers traced a stone pomegranate set in the post while he craned his neck to peer at the crowns of his three trees.

Raphael wouldn't want to see him here, doing this. But Raphael wasn't around to watch.

Gabriel's cedars flirted with the wind. Beyond that was a grove of pomegranate trees. In one of the cedars a falcon had built a nest. On the lower levels, smaller birds had nested; the tree harbored a bee hive as well. He would bring Mary some honey. He wouldn't tell Raphael it came from here.

Prisoners.

Bread.

Cedars.

Himself.

He shivered in the breeze.

Just after he'd returned from the year, Gabriel and Raphael had lounged in a field with three musicians. Gabriel sang to accompany, his head on Raphael's shoulder and the Vision live in his heart.

Between songs, Gabriel commented on how good it felt to hear angelic music again, which led to a discussion of the human approximation of music. Gabriel mentioned he'd sung with the shepherds as he worked.

That was when he felt it the first time: a prickle, a peculiar tension, but nothing he could identify quickly. By the time they sang again, the feeling had vanished, but Gabriel listened for it. While the musicians picked their next song, one of them asked whether Gabriel had taught the humans any songs, and as Gabriel told a story about teaching Tobias's grandchildren to sing, the feeling flared.

That came from Raphael, definitely. Gabriel reached for his heart, but Raphael recoiled.

Although familiar, the feeling resisted identification, but while Gabriel continued the conversation, he analyzed it. Wanting to disappear. Discomfort with the subject matter.

Gabriel glanced over his shoulder, and although Raphael looked impassive, the sensation intensified.

I knew I was naked, so I hid myself.

37

Shame?

True, the anecdote was at Gabriel's own expense—but it wasn't that embarrassing, was it? At Tobias's household, that was how friends shared. Or maybe he'd gotten that wrong? It wouldn't be the first time.

Sitting up and away from Raphael, Gabriel wrapped up the tale. One of the musicians shared a similar story about teaching Archangels to sing. Gabriel felt Raphael unkey.

I hid myself.

Gabriel ought to test the theory—maybe by mentioning the punishment again to measure the intensity of the feeling against that of the null state, then using that data positively correlate it with his speaking. He didn't. He couldn't fumble for Raphael's fire right now. He couldn't follow the musician's story. He'd never be able to sing.

He excused himself.

Gabriel reappeared in Tobias's tree from which he'd fallen. On the same branch, he sat with his arms around the trunk, and he tried to pray.

Ashamed. Of him.

Why he hadn't anticipated this, Gabriel didn't understand. Gabriel had never considered Raphael would be anything other than angry, but once he and Raphael had re-bonded and he could feel no anger, that fear dissolved like a nightmare.

But this?

He ought to ask. He needed to ask. In his heart, the Spirit urged him to ask.

But to hear the yes... Why question what Raphael had expressed so eloquently in the tightness around his heart, in his urge to hide?

Query: Could Gabriel live with this?

Assertion: Probably.

Gabriel would constrain himself, not think about the disgrace around Raphael. If other angels mentioned it, he could shut it down if Raphael were around; he could save it for himself and his Father. There had been eternal secrets before. This would be just one more. Over centuries, Raphael would forget. Seraphim could forget when they wanted to.

Gabriel let his hungry eyes soak in the Vision, and he extended his heart to God's love. Here he could be himself. Here there was no shame.

After a time, God gentled him back to awareness.

Raphael had joined him on the branch. Two hours had passed.

"You left abruptly."

Angling away from Raphael, Gabriel stared at his knees. "Were they upset?"

"We figured God called you for an assignment." When Gabriel didn't answer, Raphael said, "Are you okay?"

He had no answer for that. "I'm not injured."

With Gabriel's back to him, Raphael ran his fingers through the grey feathers, interlocking the bases, straightening them and freeing any trapped matter.

Gabriel closed his eyes as Raphael went over the outermost wings. "Making me presentable?"

"You look fine. I wanted to do this when you first returned, but it was so hectic. Wow, you're tense." Raphael brought his hands to Gabriel's shoulders and tried to rub out the knots. "Was it because you were talking about being here?"

Gabriel pulled back his soul from the discomfort prickling over the Seraph.

Raphael said, "Tell them you don't want to talk about it."

"Should I?"

Gabriel's voice sounded so thin.

"Absolutely." Raphael returned his attention to the feathers. "Why do that to yourself?"

Aching in his fingers: Gabriel had clutched the branch hard enough to hurt.

The only sound was the rustle of Raphael's hands through his feathers. Logically, Raphael should blame him for their joint punishment; of course he'd feel the disgrace as keenly as the Gabriel himself. It had been selfish not to consider that.

He'd dragged Raphael down. He'd put him through a year of concern and fear for no reason. No other angel ever had been stripped of the Vision, and as his Seraph, Raphael had to have shared his disgrace. It must have galled him.

It was in both their best interests if Gabriel didn't bring it up again.

Behind him, he felt Raphael gathering himself to speak, and the previbrations of the statement startled him. No, not that. Please.

Gabriel turned quickly. "Thanks. That's better."

Raphael pulled back. "Oh?"

Gabriel raised his wings. "Do you want to do rounds now? It's been a while since I've accompanied you."

The Seraph had brightened, and they'd headed off.

And now, gazing from his pomegranate-decorated balcony at three cedars, Gabriel closed his eyes. Centuries hadn't erased anything. Raphael still felt ashamed.

Gabriel could live with the Seraph's disgust. All it took would be self-control. Bury it alive and eventually it would die underground. Not as effective as burying it dead, but maybe another thousand years could dissolve it.

Gabriel flashed back to Mary's house and bowed before her in case demons watched. "My lady." His voice broke to barely above a whisper. "Barring your objection, I've selected a different angel to transport the loaves in my stead."

Over the next three days, Mary noted that Gabriel didn't leave them at all. "Is the danger high right now?" she asked while Jesus was out with Joseph. "Is that why he's staying?"

"It's normal," Uriel said, and Mary felt the information blossom inside in a way not at all uncomfortable but which had become common with Uriel. She knew all at once that Seraphim and Cherubim, with their unique capacity to bond, had cycles where they moved apart and came together again.

"Is bonding like being married?" Mary asked, and immediately felt it wasn't. The information broke over her like a realization and it kept coming. Bonds were not exclusive like a marriage. Raphael had two other primary bonds; Gabriel had one more primary with Israfel; both had several secondary bonds and hundreds of the low-level tertiaries; there was no physical component.

Jesus sprinted into the house, followed by Raphael and Gabriel. Mary said, "Gabriel, I have an assignment."

He drew up short before her. "Yes, my lady?"

"Snow." She handed him a box. "Please fill this with it for Jesus."

Gabriel opened his hands, and snow filled the container.

Jesus spent the next hour in the sunny courtyard playing with snow, scattering it, and building with it while it turned first into dirty snow, then into slush and then into a puddle. Jesus pointed to it. "Like sin. It looks so new at first, but then you find out it's only water."

Gabriel brought new snow in small doses all afternoon until Raphael decided to keep the air around the snow cold. Then the snow just got dirty but didn't melt. Jesus sculpted it into different shapes, blowing on his hands when the skin began to sting.

Mary brought out a basket of fleece and set up the fleece comb in the sunlight.

Gabriel straightened. "Oh! Could I do that?"

Raphael looked as startled as Mary felt. Inside, she felt Uriel chuckle.

Mary backed away from the fleece comb. "Sure. If you want to."

She couldn't believe how Gabriel smiled as he combed the wool, aligning the fibers and cleaning off the grass and straw bits. Mary got her spindle and began spinning. Jesus used a step-stool to watch Gabriel, and then he put his own hands into the wool to help.

Threading more fleece onto the spindle, Mary said, "Can I ask you a question?"

"Of course you can." Gabriel didn't look up from combing. "But I presume what you intended to ask is whether you can address to me another question other than the one you already did in order to clear the asking of the second question."

Raphael hit him in the wing with a snowball.

Mary shrank on herself. "You can just say no."

"He's trying to say yes," Raphael said. "There isn't a Cherub in creation that doesn't want a question."

Gabriel grinned at Raphael, so he must have been right. Mary smiled. "Oh, okay then. For my *second* question, how did all of you meet?"

Raphael said, "I've always known Gabriel."

Gabriel frowned. "You have not. There was a short time immediately after the angels were created where we hadn't met."

Raphael met Mary's eyes. "So thousands of years, minus a handful of hours, except created time didn't exist yet, so there was no way to measure. But that's more accurate than you needed me to be. Effectively, I've always known Gabriel."

"Those first moments...?" Was it okay to ask this? But if it wasn't, surely they wouldn't answer. "What was it like?"

And there it was again, that information just welling up within her as if it always had been there. This time, though, it came from three directions, and she struggled to keep rooted to here, to now. To a courtyard. To a child. To a spindle.

But oh, to be soft from forging, freshly stamped by the seal of the Creator, new and crisp and everything a wonder and a revelation. Their first awareness had been of a song, a beauty, realization that the song was about the splendor, and then the awareness of warmth and being loved, then loving in return. Then slowly the awareness that oneself was participating in the song, that there was such a thing as oneself and that this one was loved specially. That there were others alongside and they were singing too. Then joy in meeting those others and recognizing them as selves too, wondering if they felt the same and then recognizing in their eyes, their song, the sensations streaming from them that they recognized and felt the love too.

Gabriel murmured, almost to himself, "When all the morning stars sang together."

Mary blinked back tears. "That must have been incredible."

Song after song, but eventually a question of how one had known the song, and after that how one had known the words, how one knew what words were, and what made the music. Gradually attention shifted away from the song and the splendor to those nearby, beings who were beginning to look around just as oneself was. Then questions of how one was producing the song, and how was one perceiving all these things, and then a self-examination and a question of what one was. And with the asking, an answer, a name: *You are My Strength, the Strength of God. You are Gabriel.*

Mary looked at Gabriel, who was concentrating on the fleece comb. Gabriel once said he never forgot anything, and he treasured this memory.

Raphael was sharing a different story, though, about fire and frenzy and joy, not gradual self-discovery so much as hurling all of his heart into the love and into the fire before him, trying to give more and dive back into the oneness of being only to have

God hold him at arm's length and urge him to be himself, to be what he'd been created, *Raphael, God's Healing.*

Gabriel met Raphael's eyes, and Mary realized just how much joy there was in them.

Gabriel's story resumed: the thrill of learning everyone else's name, everyone else's role or purpose, comparing notes on exactly how God's splendor shot through each of them, each one longing to learn about God and who God was and what he wanted from them. Eventually raising one's head and looking further, seeing the throngs of other angels and with a gasp realizing how different each was from the next, how brilliant and splendid, and then resolving to know each one and see God's light the way it prismed a little differently through each of them.

"Then God gave us a command," Raphael said. "Play!"

Mary laughed.

Raphael said, "We shouted for joy, and off we went."

All creation then had consisted of Heaven, and the angels explored it. "Picture an onion," Gabriel said, drawing an image in the air with light. Mary got up so she could touch it, but it felt like nothing. "At the very center imagine the throne of glory, and around that a smaller empty area that served as a spacer. That now is the Ring of Seven, although technically speaking it's a sphere. Around that is a spherical area for the Seraphim. Surrounding that you have another layer, the Cherubim, followed by the Thrones. That's the first tier."

Mary traced her finger around the image. "Can you see one another?"

"There aren't walls or dividers." Gabriel kept adjusting the image in ways imperceptible to Mary but which apparently made all the difference to him. "The layers of the onion serve as a mental guideline for positioning where everything is relative to everything else. Beyond that are three more choirs, or orders, on their own layers: Dominions, Virtues and Powers. The third tier has another three layers: Principalities, Archangels, and Angels. We explored the nine orders first."

"We didn't really explore," Raphael said from behind Jesus. "We played."

"You raced through." Gabriel gave him a narrow look. "I'm surprised you Seraphim learned anything."

In her heard, Mary felt Uriel saying the Thrones had stayed put; there was enough joy just in contemplating the Father.

"We couldn't see him face to Face yet," Gabriel said. "But we could perceive enough to be dazzled. He had to tone it down initially in order for us to individuate."

Once the angels had learned about one another, God opened the inner layers of Heaven and allowed them access to those, each filled with wonders, all kinds of worlds with all manner of terrain. The angels explored, learned, grew to know God and one another and themselves.

"It was a shock to realize not everyone cared about the finer points of detail." Gabriel did look rather shocked. "I'd find something incredible and want to learn everything about it. I'd look up hours later to realize no one else had stuck around to hear what I'd discovered, only some of the others whom it turned out were Cherubim too. Zophiel, Ophaniel, Mistofiel, and I stayed together."

Raphael said, "It's not that we didn't care, but there was so much to experience. It seemed more important to survey the totality and get a sample of everything first."

Gabriel met his eyes with a grin.

Jesus looked up from the fleece comb. "Which way is better?"

"My way," Gabriel said, and Raphael hit him with another snowball.

Mary said softly, "There should be room for both styles."

"God made a multitude of styles." Raphael tousled Jesus's hair. "I think that's the point."

Gabriel winked at Jesus, who giggled. Gabriel corrected Jesus's hands on the fleece, then returned to the story.

There was music. There was adoration. There were debates. There was impromptu worship. There was poetry. Eventually there came stories, first true and then fictional. Then games and contests. Finally a developed liturgy.

"We were still stratified," Gabriel said. "For a long time, Cherubim associated with Cherubim; Thrones with Thrones. God started giving us assignments, and that mixed things up a bit."

"Like what?" Mary said.

Raphael laughed out loud. "You have to tell her yours."

Gabriel rolled his eyes. "I was sent to kill the Leviathan."

Mary's eyes widened. "The Leviathan?"

"The legendary Leviathan, yes. I'd have preferred to study it." Gabriel smirked. "We went on a massive angelic hunt for the thing, only we weren't very organized, and everyone wanted to try it his own way. Most angels who attacked were either driven back or managed to blunt their swords on its scales." Gabriel added, "Lucifer was in charge of the hunt for the Behemoth, or at least he was on that team and took charge. No one took charge of the Leviathan team."

Mary ran her fingers over the yarn on the spindle. "Surely you could have."

Gabriel shrugged. "It never even occurred to me."

Raphael nodded. "You have to realize about Cherubim, they have no social skills."

Gabriel sighed.

"The social cues you'd read as, 'This team needs a leader,' would pass straight over a Cherub's head." Raphael laughed. "Although Gabriel *could* have organized the expedition, Gabriel *didn't*, and with Gabriel around, no one else felt worthy of doing it."

"At any rate," Gabriel continued, "when no one managed to do any damage, Leviathan withdrew to the deepest part of an ocean, and God told me to go kill it. I pulled my head out of a book and figured, no problem, I'm a good little girl, I'll go kill a Leviathan." Gabriel laughed ruefully. "I went out on a boat armed with a net and a fishing pole and still thinking about my book. Shortly it became obvious this wasn't the best plan when Leviathan swallowed the boat and I was inside the Leviathan."

Raphael was laughing with his head thrown back. Gabriel had forgotten the fleece on the table even as Jesus continued combing it. Mary stared open-mouthed. Gabriel said, "That was about the time our intrepid hero realized that every mission ought to have a planning phase."

"I'm on an outcropping on the shore screaming at Gabriel to flash out of there," Raphael said, "and when she didn't flash out, Lucifer held me back because I was going to try to cut the thing open, but he said it was Gabriel's assignment and Gabriel had to do it alone."

"I didn't know you couldn't flash out of a Leviathan." Gabriel was laughing too. "Like I said, really poor planning."

Raphael said, "I can feel through the bond that Gabriel is about to freak out, and I'm trying to calm her—"

"—which didn't help at all." Gabriel huffed. "Imagine smothering a fire with dry grass and lamp oil." Mary choked on a giggle. "He pumped fire into me, and that made it harder and harder to reconnoiter, and I was in the dark amidst all this yuck, and my only weapons were a sword I couldn't swing and a fishing pole I couldn't reach and a net that was entangled in my wings. The only thing I could think was that I'm an eternal creature and *I can't get out of this monster's stomach,* and I'm going to be here forever—"

"—and I felt her open this floodgate inside," Raphael said. "She pulled just about all the energy from me."

Gabriel's shoulders were shaking as he tried not to laugh. "To put it mildly, boom."

Raphael added, "Boom."

"Leviathan bits flew everywhere," Gabriel said, "only I was trapped by the remains of the net and all this offal and yuck and other disgusting things."

Raphael said, "Lucifer still refused to let me go."

"Fortunately," Gabriel added, "that's when I met Michael for the first time. He'd been on shore with his friends, watching in horror and probably wondering what kind of strategy that was. He flashed into the middle of the explosion and grabbed me, then flashed me back to shore."

Mary gasped. "Did he get in trouble for that? I mean, it was your assignment, so—"

"It was pretty much done at that point." Raphael folded his arms. "All except the screaming."

"And so," Gabriel intoned, "an ocean became holy after an angel scrubbed in it for three days."

Mary covered her mouth with both hands, giggling.

"It was in my *hair,* it was in my *wings,* it was soaked into my *clothes...*" Gabriel made a sound of disgust. "But the Leviathan was dead, and the assignment was over. And I never had to do it again."

Uriel shed sparkles. Mary got the impression Uriel had never heard Gabriel tell this story before.

Gabriel looked over at the Throne. "You probably hadn't. It's not exactly my favorite story. Let's tally the failure modes: I didn't plan, I panicked, and then I got covered in ick and had to get rescued by an eighth-order angel."

Raphael shook his head. "You wouldn't trade a minute of it. You learned something."

"Leviathan goo is a great incentive to learn strategy." Gabriel looked at Mary. "If I had to do it again, I would divide everyone into teams. I'd document Leviathan's eating, sleeping and migrating habits. I would have had a large number of Seraphim boil the sea to drive it into shallow waters, then had teams of Angels keep netting around the area to prevent any of Leviathan's food from getting in." He opened his hands. "In retrospect, we had no time limit. If the object was to kill the Leviathan, then death by starvation was just as valid as killing it with a pike." He looked back at Raphael. "If we did have to fight it, I would have made sure we understood all its armor's weak points, potentially what kinds of poisons would have disabled it, and knowing how well it functioned in deep water, I might even have had them carry all the water out of the sea basin in order to beach the thing."

Mary twisted a bit of fleece in her fingers. "You were young."

Gabriel shook his head. "That's no excuse. But after I got calm and clean again, we hung around talking with Michael."

Raphael said, "I remember thinking he had a great sense of humor and was easy to get along with."

Gabriel nodded. "But I didn't think about him again except for a few times our paths crossed. Like I said, we were all so stratified."

Gabriel corrected Jesus's hands again on the fleece so he was putting a more even pressure.

Mary said, "Can I ask you another question?"

Gabriel said, "By which I presume you mean—" and then Raphael pelted him with a third snowball. He regarded the Seraph with an exaggerated patience. "You just don't get tired of doing that, do you?"

"Not until you get tired of the over-specific definitions and the corny wordplay, no." Raphael tossed the next snowball from hand to hand. "I can't see myself getting tired of it."

Mary said, "Then let me just ask it: you were a good little *girl?*"

Gabriel chuckled. "Yes, I was."

Mary's cheeks went hot. "I'm sorry. I assumed—"

"You assumed according to your experience." Gabriel, at least, didn't seem mortified. "But angels aren't in fixed bodies. We change at will."

Mary brightened. "Can you show me what you looked like?"

Gabriel shook his head. "No."

All three angels simultaneously looked up and to one side of the courtyard, and a moment after, Jesus did as well.

"Greetings." The voice came from a visual distortion, as if from heat shimmering near the house, and then it seemed more solid. Without her being able to say when exactly it happened, there stood a figure with his wings tucked, his arms folded, and his eyes glimmering. He wore armor, and he had his chin down so his blond curls dangled over his eyes.

Raphael had drawn his sword, but the newcomer didn't appear to be attacking. "He's putting your son to work." The angel regarded Mary with a steadiness bordering on disgust. "You required Gabriel to handle a task, and he foisted it off on your offspring, then entertained you with stories so you wouldn't notice his trickery." He cocked his head. "Is that the service an individual of your stature deserves?"

"Now that you mention it," Mary said, "it isn't."

Gabriel glared at her. "Do *not* talk to him! That demon is Mephistopheles, one of the Maskim, Satan's high command."

"She can talk to whomever she likes." Mephistopheles bowed. "You're the one shunting off the work she imposed on you, forcing her son to get his hands dirty when you could have done this—" a hand-wave, "—and it would be complete."

The fleece was all combed. Jesus backed away from the table.

"Gabriel resists your authority without appearing to fight." The demon kept his voice neutral, instructive. "That's a common tactic of an angel in thrall: it's called passive-aggressive behavior. He could have combed a hundred fleeces, and instead he diverted you while deceiving your son into doing his work. Is that the action of a trusted servant?"

Mary glanced at Uriel, who regarded Mephistopheles with narrow eyes. Inside she felt repeated urges to caution.

"I'll offer you a trade." Mephistopheles stepped closer. "Hand over your seal on Gabriel, and I'll give you my loyalty."

Mary shivered. "No."

Mephistopheles inclined his head. "If you hand over Gabriel, I'll make him work for you the way he knows he can."

Her mouth went dry. She shook her head.

Mephistopheles came closer still. "He's denying you access to his full power. Can you not know who he is? He's the second most powerful angel in creation, beneath only Lucifer and God Himself in ability."

Mary's heart skipped. She turned to Gabriel, who wouldn't look her in the eyes. Gabriel, who combed fleeces and delivered bread. Gabriel, who threw snowballs and got distracted by math. Her vision blurred.

"They call him the Prince of Heaven, and you have him delivering lunches." Mephistopheles chuckled. "What a waste. Order him to stop the moon in its path or to turn the sun red. Have him topple the Roman Empire. Demand of him the secrets of everything in the universe, because even if he doesn't know how something works, once you ask, he won't stop until he does."

Mary's eyes were riveted to Gabriel, who began vibrating. He wasn't protesting. If anything, he looked uncomfortable, which meant it was probably true. She was playing with power capable of far worse than leveling her house.

Mephistopheles folded his arms and shook his head. "The trouble with retaining a being quite that powerful is that eventually you're going to falter. I guarantee a creature in thrall thinks of nothing more than what he'll do to his keeper once he's slipped the leash. You're safer owning a creature like me and having me control him." He folded his arms and tilted his head. "The last man who kept him didn't seal him when he had the chance, and now he's dead."

Mary looked at Gabriel, horrified. Beside him, Raphael seemed uneasy.

Gabriel's voice was low. "I didn't kill him."

She cringed backward. Gabriel. Killing.

"You were with him the moment he died." Mephistopheles chuckled. "I noted how his guardian didn't think highly of your presence."

Gabriel's eyes darkened. "I had every right."

Mary shifted closer to Uriel, who brushed a wing against her arm.

Mephistopheles parted the hair back from his forehead the better to look Mary in the eyes. "Let me assure you, there is no way to defend yourself. No method of binding one of us is perfect, and they've got you believing all their lies as they act friendly, hoping you'll get careless enough that their comrade can win free. It's not just Gabriel you're fighting. These others want his freedom as badly as he does. A creature of that power with allies that powerful is going to win loose unless you hand him over to someone like myself."

Why weren't they stopping him? Why didn't Uriel make him go away. She looked to Gabriel, desperate for any kind of reassurance. "Would he blow the roof off my house?"

Mephistopheles snickered. "He'll start by flaying your son alive before your face."

Raphael blasted Mephistopheles before he'd even finished the sentence. Gabriel dove over Jesus, shielding him with his wings, and Uriel enclosed Mary, but she pushed forward to get toward her son. Mephistopheles blazed away, and Raphael scorched after him in pursuit.

"Where's Jesus?" she shouted. "Give him to me!"

Gabriel raised his wings, and the boy bolted for his mother.

Mary was chalk-white, and her arms shook, but she pulled him behind her and stood between him and Gabriel.

Gabriel raised his hands. "I would never harm him."

She didn't move.

Uriel stroked her hair, and she flinched away.

Gabriel gathered the combed fleece and set it back in its basket, then looked over his shoulder at Mary and disappeared.

Raphael returned a moment after, flames around his eyes. The first thing he did was hug Jesus. Then he looked around. "Gabriel's gone?"

Mary wanted them all gone – just, away. She never asked for this. She never wanted to see angels or to have demons hanging around or to have a front-row seat to the life of the Messiah. It was always enough to know God was doing these things, but her? She was just a handmaiden, an onlooker, certainly not capable of ordering around angels like a queen and chatting up creatures capable of turning the sun red.

Uriel projected something Mary couldn't interpret, but it left Raphael's eyes sparking. He stepped away, then paused, then looked at Jesus again, and he stopped.

Mary tried to get a grip on her emotions. "Is he still here?"

"Not Mephistopheles, but certainly the others." Raphael looked grim. "I can't feel them, though."

"Why didn't you drive him off sooner?"

Raphael looked away again. "Until he threatened Jesus, I didn't have the authority."

She clenched her fists and looked at her lap, breathing hard. Jesus wrapped his arms around her waist, and she crouched down to hold him. She pressed her face into his hair. "I don't want to see you," she whispered. "Don't go away, but I don't want to know you're around."

Gabriel returned after Mary and Jesus were asleep.

Uriel had gone filmy. "I did my best to convince her you're legitimate."

In the slanting moonlight, Gabriel folded his arms and tilted his head.

"No," Raphael whispered. "The kind of brutality they aimed at her today—do you want that aimed at Jesus instead?"

Gabriel said, "But she's terrified."

"She knew the risks," Raphael said.

"That's easy for you to say," Gabriel said. "You're not the one they scared, and you're not the one that scares her."

"We do scare her," Uriel said. "It wasn't just you. He planted seeds of doubt in her about all of us. Think about how much skill Mephistopheles had to use to scare her like that. Cherubim don't do that, and that means Asmodeus was hidden somewhere, helping him along."

"People aren't designed for this kind of interaction." Raphael's eyes burned. "She's right to be terrified."

Gabriel opened his hands. "So to diminish that—"

"You stay." He grabbed Gabriel's hands and brought up his wingtips to touch Gabriel's. "I want you to stay."

Gabriel drew back. "I want to stay too, but it's not about what we want. It's about what's best for them."

Uriel said, "Then stay because Mephistopheles' appearing means they're escalating, and I'd prefer to have backup."

Mary awoke before dawn and immediately tried to track the locations of the household angels. Raphael: near Jesus. Uriel: close to herself. And then, hesitant, she felt for Gabriel.

Somewhere close, but she couldn't determine exactly where. Not close to Jesus, though. She steadied herself and got up.

She started getting ready for the day, but then she felt Gabriel much closer, as if in the room. Instead of continuing her work, she sat, waiting like a servant.

Gabriel appeared, but on the far side of the room. "Do your work. Treat me as a member of the household, not a guest."

Her voice sounded tight. "Not as the Prince of Heaven?"

"It's a title." Gabriel shook his head. "In a hundred years they're going to call you the Mother of God, so you have the advantage of me in that regard."

Mother of God? Every age really was going to recognize how much God had blessed her? But no, no, Gabriel was distracting her just like the demon had said. "That's not the point, and you know it. I'm only a woman who heard the word of God and kept it. But Mephistopheles claimed you're the most powerful angel in Heaven, and you killed a man."

"I have never killed except on God's orders," Gabriel said, "and I never knowingly did any harm to the man to whom he referred."

That meant he'd killed at all, and that was an uncomfortable thought. Those angels in scripture: the angel of Death had taken the Egyptian firstborn, but it had never seemed like one of these angels could have done something like that.

Gabriel glanced toward the room where Jesus slept. "I'll tell you more later. Raphael doesn't like to hear about my interaction with that man."

After the sun rose and Jesus went out to tend the sheep, Mary took out her spinning. A question came into her mind: was it okay if Gabriel appeared?

In case the demons were nearby, she murmured, "Show yourself."

Gabriel appeared sitting before her. "Could you teach me to spin?"

Of all the things Gabriel might have led off with, that was the last she expected. "You don't know how?"

"I didn't get a chance to learn. I understand the mechanics, but clearly there's more to it than mechanics."

She handed him her spindle. He studied it until he produced an identical one in his other hand. Using her own, she showed him how to wind on the yarn, which he copied exactly, and then she showed him how to twirl and drop the spindle so the fleece twisted into yarn.

Close beside her, Gabriel studied her as she fed in the fleece. He imitated what she was doing, and a moment after, her spindle was still going, and his yarn had snapped and his spindle was on the ground.

"Second try," he said.

Mary gave him pointers, but as it turned out, there were many different mistakes to be made with spinning: overspinning, underspinning, allowing the spindle to backspin, and getting the yarn twisted through the drafting triangle.

"You don't realize what you're doing." Gabriel looked intrigued. "You've extended your senses out into the spindle. Normally you've got your senses firmly seated in the body, but you've made the spindle an extension of your hand, and you're feeling it through the yarn as it moves."

Mary said, "Isn't that just...feeling?"

"It's a body-sense," Gabriel said. "I'm in a subtle body so you can see me, but it's not as finely-tuned as your physical body has to be."

He didn't give up, and he didn't appear as frustrated as Mary would have expected. Every time something went wrong, he would analyze why it had happened and repeat the process to eliminate the problem.

"You wanted to know about the man I worked for," Gabriel said at one point, the spindle out at arm's length and spinning evenly while he fed in the fleece. "I'm Guarding the house so demons can't hear us speaking, so feel free to say whatever you want. Do you remember Tobias, from the Book of Tobit?" When she nodded, he said, "It was him, about forty years later."

The yarn snapped and the spindle fell.

Mary squinted. "That's why Raphael doesn't want to hear about it? Because Tobias was under his protection?"

"I was never a danger to Tobias." Gabriel retrieved the spindle, then wound on the yarn and spun it again. "I told you about my getting disciplined by God for an infraction, and that's what Raphael's disgusted to hear about. I never asked him specifically if it galls him that Tobias helped me when I didn't help him with Tobias. Yet another wrong I can't repay." Gabriel looked momentarily grim. "I ended up working in Tobias's household for six months, but it wasn't a magic situation. I approached him in human form asking to be hired."

Mary said, "What kind of work did you do?"

"Farming. I combed a lot of fleece." He chuckled. "By hand. And he had me teach the children Hebrew."

Mary said, "Did he know how powerful you are?"

Gabriel frowned. "I've wondered that myself. He didn't ask me to make it rain or to help his crops grow, although in the next years I made sure I did. He died five years after my stay, and Mephistopheles is right that I was there, but not to punish him. Asmodeus had a vendetta against him, and I wanted to ensure he stayed protected."

Mary said, "That's kind of you."

Gabriel lowered his eyes. "He thought I was teaching the children, but I learned more from him than he realized."

Mary straightened. "But he was just a man."

"He had a very clear perception of what mattered." Gabriel twirled the spindle again. "If he did know what I was, then he must have thought he was taking me in at great personal risk to his family. But being there transformed me. He's now in Sheol, safe."

The yarn snapped. Gabriel's spindle hit the ground and started rolling away until he called it back to his hand.

"I took two seeds and a cutting from one of his trees." Gabriel looked at the spindle and the newly-spun yarn. "I found a place in Heaven to build a library, and I planted them. It's a reminder."

Mary spoke with her voice just as soft as Gabriel's. "You cared a lot about him."

"He helped me when I needed it." Gabriel looked up. "What Mephistopheles said would be true of a demon in your power. But you don't need to worry. We're here because God sent us."

Year Twelve

After Jesus had gone to bed and while Joseph sat outside whittling, Mary went over the preparations for the festival trip to Jerusalem. They had food, money, blankets, clothing, wine, and water. There were lamps and oil. She recalculated how much they would need for the trip and made sure there would be a little extra. Sometimes they met a less fortunate traveler. Sometimes one of their own companions planned poorly.

Mary double-checked the house, which would be left empty. As she checked the food stores to make sure everything was sealed, she found a wineskin with only a very little wine left, no more than a swallow. She sighed. It wouldn't have killed Joseph to just take that last little bit instead of putting back almost nothing. Who on earth would want no more than a mouthful of wine?

She giggled. Who indeed?

Mary took the wineskin to the table, then found the nicest of their wine cups. She laid out a linen cloth and set the cup in the middle. She lit a lamp on the table near the wine, fighting a grin.

It was all kind of silly, and she wondered what else she could do to make it more over-the-top: incense? Music?

She sat before the table for, praying, *Dear Lord, Lord of the Vine, please bless this cup. Father of Angels, please bless him when he arrives. I think he'll like this.*

Well, either he'd like it or else he'd be insulted that she thought he'd finish her leftovers.

Mary steadied herself. "Gabriel?"

Gabriel appeared immediately.

"Sit."

He took in the scene, and without a word he sat opposite her.

She lifted the nearly-empty wineskin. "I trust you remember the first favor you asked of me."

Gabriel appeared puzzled but then brightened. Good, he'd realized. Mary looked down to hide her smile as she poured the wine into the cup. "Raphael warned you about me, but there's no warning necessary this time."

In darkness lit only by the flame, Gabriel still said nothing.

She raised the cup in her hands and presented it to him. "Take this."

The night felt thicker suddenly, clumsier. As Gabriel reached forward, his eyes glinted. "That will be satisfactory."

In that moment, a third presence made itself felt, a darkness apart from the dark. Even as Gabriel's wings flared, the darker self reached between them, extinguished the lamp and snatched the cup. "I own you now," it said, and it vanished.

"Belior!" Gabriel exclaimed, and abruptly he was gone too.

Mary sat in the dark, her hands hot from where the demon's fingers had brushed her own. "Raphael!" she called. "Uriel!" Her voice shook, and not knowing what else to do, she prayed.

Belior reappeared alongside the Lake of Fire with the cup against his chest, Guarding the wine from sloshing over the sides. Laughing madly, he streaked along the shore, Gabriel at his back. Three, two, one—

Belior zoomed beneath an archway. Gabriel had gotten close enough to nab him, then all at once slammed into a Guard woven by Mephistopheles and Beelzebub. Gabriel pulled backward only to find himself entangled in the Guard's other side.

Asmodeus appeared at Belior's side. "A cup of wine for a seal? How quaint."

"Who cares if it's quaint?" Belior said. "If it enthralled Gabriel, I'd drink my own blood."

Gabriel vibrated, and Asmodeus had enough time to call a warning. Gabriel detonated a concussion blast strong enough to shatter the archway to which the Guard was mounted, but he hadn't broken the guard

"Enchain him," Asmodeus shouted at Beelzebub. "Do it now before you lose him!"

Mephistopheles let go of the Guard long enough to pin Gabriel with his will, then drew on Beelzebub's will to strengthen his hold. Their will solidified as chains encircling his wrists, his waist, his ankles, and spider-webbing him to the spot. Gabriel hung in the air, unable to move as long as the bonded pair focused their entire will trained on keeping him motionless.

Belior frowned into the wine. He couldn't detect any kind of power. No magic, no prayer. There was nothing special about the cup itself. So what had that woman done in order to enthrall Gabriel? And yet clearly it had to be the cup or the wine. A woman alone at night, setting a sacred space, summoning an angel, speaking to him of their past meeting and a favor Gabriel had asked of her, and then presenting him with the cup: what else could it mean other than she had been renewing their covenant?

Asmodeus sparkled at the edge of his awareness. Belior recoiled a little, but he took some of Asmodeus's flames into his heart, and his intellect sparked into a fury. A woman alone at night, a summons, a nominal splash of wine, a reminder, a ceremonial presentation. How else to add that up?

Asmodeus sent, *I suggest we make him drink it.*

We don't know the way she would have done it.

Then we capture her and make her do it in our presence.

Belior studied Gabriel still struggling against chains of willpower. He couldn't match Gabriel's signature to the wine either, but maybe the cup?

Closing his eyes, Belior sent his spirit into the cup to feel the last moments near it, the faintest signature of Gabriel's power—and yet, that signature wasn't the resentment of a free spirit bound up with a living soul. Instead he detected laughter, curiosity, friendship, and a fierce devotion.

Belior kept his face down, but he raised his eyes to get a look at Gabriel.

He felt Asmodeus's curiosity, but that he ignored. He recast everything he knew about the situation and challenged his assumptions in light of what he felt now from the cup and even more what he felt from Gabriel.

Gabriel wasn't radiating nearly enough terror for him to be holding Gabriel's will in his hands. Gabriel was angry, not afraid for himself. Perhaps, though, afraid for someone else.

Belior sent to Mephistopheles and Beelzebub, *I need you to do a little play-acting.*

Their doubled intellect replied, *Why?*

He returned his irritation to the pair, who assented that when he was ready, they would do what he required. He sent a series of instructions, then assumed control over the chains holding Gabriel. As he did so, he made sure they were subtly looser.

Gabriel quieted, and Belior recognized a Cherub biding his time. Good.

Belior shouted, "Now that we have his seal, we can drop that woman into the Lake of Fire. Take her brat too. Go."

Gabriel stiffened as Mephistopheles and Beelzebub both vanished. A moment later they reappeared over the Lake, Mephistopheles holding Jesus and Beelzebub holding Mary. The humans thrashed and screamed.

"No!" Gabriel shouted. "Please! Don't do that!"

"Drop them!" Belior ordered, and both figures plummeted.

With a cry, Gabriel exploded free of Belior's chains.

Belior leaned forward. Yes!

Gabriel caught Jesus in mid-air. The boy met his eyes and grinned.

Even Belior felt the horror ripple off Gabriel as the boy turned into Mephistopheles and the image of Mephistopheles above vanished.

"Hold him again!" Belior hurled aside the cup, even as Asmodeus shouted, "It's the *child?* They were protecting the child?"

Beelzebub, Mephistopheles and Asmodeus attacked while Belior tried to rein in the chains still loose around Gabriel's will. The horror in Gabriel's eyes gave Belior all the confirmation he needed.

"Lucifer!" Belior called. "We need you here!"

Mephistopheles dissociated, adding all his power to Beelzebub. The Seraph tackled Gabriel out of the air and flung them together onto the pebbled shore. Asmodeus grabbed Gabriel by the throat as Beelzebub/Mephistopheles tried to enchain Gabriel again.

Gabriel shone like a star. Belior compulsively shielded his eyes, but Asmodeus drew his sword in preparation. Gabriel blew apart the chains holding him, knocking Mephistopheles into the cliff-face and Beelzebub into the Lake of Fire, and then flashed away.

Asmodeus caught him the instant he flashed, dragging him back into Hell by strength of will, sucking all the power out of Belior in order to keep Gabriel from issuing a warning.

Gabriel was radiating now with a frenzy Belior had never before seen in a Cherub not feeding off a Seraph. This energy was entirely his own, and the awful fact was, despite their strongest efforts, he was winning free.

Mephistopheles struggled to his feet and summoned the armed forces. Instantaneously a legion surrounded Gabriel, but Gabriel had a Guard up so no one else could get close to them. Beelzebub erupted out of the Lake of Fire, his wings engulfed in flame, his head encircled by Seraph fury, but Gabriel's power kept him distant too.

Asmodeus's control slipped, and Belior tried to get a grip of his own on Gabriel, but it wasn't secure. He extended his soul for Beelzebub's power, but theirs was only a weak bond to begin with.

Mephistopheles managed to ensnare Gabriel in a Guard, but it encompassed too much space to be strong. Gabriel expanded his own Guard against it, trying to crack the thing open.

Power swirled into form beside him. Lucifer shouted, "Quit screwing around with him!"

He ensphered Gabriel within a Guard of his own, then slammed it tight so it cracked Gabriel's in pieces. Next he locked Gabriel in place with his will.

Immobilized, Gabriel could only watch wide-eyed as Lucifer inserted his hand through his Guard and discharged an inferno.

Mephistopheles shrieked as his Guard got consumed by flame, and Belior howled as his own chains got shredded away from his heart. Asmodeus fell from the air, his soul raw where Gabriel had been ripped out of his grasp, and Belior dove alongside him, covering him with his wings.

Lucifer's Guard enclosed the flames, a sphere ablaze above the shore of the Lake of Fire like a white dwarf star. All the demons but Lucifer had hands and wings covering their eyes. Half a minute later, the firestorm died, and Lucifer released the field.

Something dropped from it, but it took Belior a moment to realize it was Gabriel.

Belior tried to scream. He tried not to scream. Gabriel was charred to the point where it took imagination to recognize any of his form as part of an angel, and Cherubim are notorious for having little imagination. There was the curve of a wing, a bend that might have been an elbow or a knee. At the last second he must have been able to break the chains enough to draw up his wings and legs, but that hadn't spared him. Where he'd thudded to the ground was a ring of black dust: ashes. He'd been burnt almost to the point of cindering.

Belior extended a hand to finish the job.

"Leave him as he is." Lucifer folded his arms. "It's time to go after the boy."

Still trembling from the ripped chains, Belior fixed his gaze on Lucifer, on his blond hair and green eyes, on his twelve white wings.

Lucifer gestured to Beelzebub. "Secure him if you like."

Beelzebub called a Seraph-Cherub pair from his officers. "Place a Guard around him. Make sure it's unbreakable."

Mephistopheles had made his way to his knees, palms massaging his eyes. Belior helped Asmodeus to a stand. Through their bond he felt how the Seraph ached.

Lucifer looked at Belior and Mephistopheles. "I don't hold you culpable for being fooled by their charade. They made it seem plausible enough. But we've lost a tremendous amount of time, and I need you two working on the child as your top priority from this moment."

Belior and Mephistopheles nodded.

Lucifer put his hands on his hips, wings half-spreading. "I'm going before the throne to demand my rights from God and get us iron-clad permissions as far as testing him. Maybe a communication blackout on the child's guards." He fixed his green eyes on the two Cherubim. "Go after the child. Challenge him. I want to learn what he does if we push."

They left Gabriel on the shore.

Mary sat at the table in tears. Raphael was vibrating enough to shake the walls of the house. Michael and several of his top officers had been coming through the house all night, but they never had any better news to report. They simply couldn't locate Gabriel.

When Mary started shaking, Uriel pressured her to go lie down, even if she wasn't going to be able to sleep. Then Uriel laid a hand over Mary's eyes and forced her to.

The Throne returned to the courtyard where Michael stood looking drawn.

They're around, Michael sent. *I can feel all four Maskim, but they're on the peripheries, and they're totally dissociated.*

Raphael just looked worried.

Michael faced him. *You cannot leave Jesus right now. You and Uriel must—absolutely must—remain with your charges. They're bound to attack either or both of them.*

"I know," Raphael whispered. "But—"

You don't stand any better chance of finding him than Israfel, Michael sent.

Saraquael drew closer to Michael. They'd begun projecting rather than speaking because of the oppressive sense of watching. Saraquael projected his own frustration.

Michael agreed. Then he looked back at Raphael. *You're going to have to leave for Jerusalem with them. Jesus is your first priority. Regardless of anything they might do to Gabriel, his soul could never be in jeopardy. He'd tell you as much.*

Raphael looked aside. The only glimmer he'd gotten from Gabriel had been hours earlier, an indistinct warning, followed a minute later by a flash of pure fear.

Saraquael rested a hand on Raphael's arm. They were doing their best.

Raphael looked at Jesus through the house walls.

"There's no conflict of interest," Michael said. "You stay with him."

Raphael's wings trembled. Michael sent him back inside.

Saraquael indicated that Michael should follow him, and they flashed together to the Ring of Seven.

"The only thing we know for certain," Saraquael said, "is that Belior must have seen Mary give Gabriel the cup of wine and assumed that's how she enthralled him. When he grabbed it, Gabriel followed because that's what you'd expect if it was really his seal." Michael nodded. Saraquael said, "They couldn't have had much time to plan, so Gabriel might have been trapped, but he should have been able to escape."

Michael said, "I assume Belior ran to somewhere in Hell with the cup, since that's the best possible place for an ambush."

Saraquael said, "But unless Gabriel makes contact on his own, I'm not sure how we're going to track him. Zadkiel and I could take in teams to search for him, but Hell has so many nooks where someone could be hidden. Especially in the dark areas or in the ice fields, you could pass within a wingspan of someone and never feel anything."

Michael said, "I'm willing to hear any better ideas."

Saraquael said, "We'll try to capture any officers that might have an inkling of where he is. But beyond that—"

"Beyond that," Michael said, "assign a contingent of angels to the family while they travel. They're our top priority. Gabriel was involved at all only to shield Jesus from their notice. This isn't the first time he's tangled with them over this."

Saraquael shook his head. "You know this is more serious than them throwing insults or trying to get Mary to sign him over."

Michael folded his arms. "It's a danger he was prepared to face. We'll do our part to free him. But the family comes first."

Saraquael sighed. "I'll get a force together to guard them on the route. I want your permission to keep searching Hell myself."

"Denied," Michael said. "I'll appoint Zadkiel and Remiel to coordinate the search. But you're one of my most dependable officers, and I need you with Jesus."

Saraquael's eyes lowered. "I'll do it. But note my protest." And he vanished.

Michael looked toward the throne of the Most High, then dropped to his knees and prayed for the wisdom to guard Jesus the best way possible.

Raphael didn't want to travel to Jerusalem. It was ridiculous, but the house was the last place he'd seen Gabriel, so there he wanted to stay.

Jesus picked up his restlessness, but Raphael assured him they'd remain together. After that, Raphael called for Ophaniel, another Cherub with whom he had a primary bond, and worked hard to keep the worry battened down.

The demons had changed tactics. Without question now Jesus was the focus of their attacks, so the angels dropped the pretense that Mary was the point of it all. Even so, she didn't escape their attention. Uriel dispatched a dozen attacks an hour to the tune of "Gabriel is suffering because of you" and "Your son is going to die because of your mistake."

"It *was* my mistake," Mary whispered to Michael as she trudged toward Jerusalem.

Michael said, "There isn't any guilt on you. You tried to do something nice."

Mary said, "You warned me not to be nice, that it would take only one slip for them to figure things out. You were right."

Michael touched her hand. "But it took twelve years for that one slip."

Mary looked over Raphael walking with Jesus, his eyes a hard shine and an unfamiliar Cherub at his side.

Days passed. Israfel and Raphael both insisted they could feel nothing from Gabriel at all, meaning he must be under a Guard powerful enough to depress a primary bond.

They reached Jerusalem for the festival, Mary subdued and Jesus concerned.

Eight more days. No Gabriel.

Mary traveled with the family caravan back to Nazareth, her mind not on the conversation of the women around her. Jesus traveled with Joseph. It was better that way. She hated seeing the haunted look in Raphael's eyes.

She felt keenly but couldn't express her admiration of him, how he stayed with Jesus even when the boy slept because that was where he belonged despite how Mary knew—and Jesus had confirmed—that Raphael wanted more than anything to be part of the search. But it had been two weeks of relentless spiritual attack. Even the angels looked drawn, and the rare times when she caught sight of Michael, he was stretched thin with strain.

The angels promised Gabriel couldn't be killed, but in some ways might that not be worse, if Gabriel were being tortured? Could demons torture an angel? Uriel wouldn't say.

Mary wondered when the angels would give up hope, when the tension would resolve into grief, and why God wasn't answering their prayers with a very direct answer: find Gabriel *here*. Or, "Gabriel needs you to look harder." Anything other than silence. Uriel said God didn't always answer their prayers the way the angels wanted. Uriel said expecting that would be an attempt to control God.

But surely you could give them a hint, Mary prayed.

Mary prayed a lot while she traveled.

That night she met up with Joseph and set up camp, and when he asked if Jesus was with the other children, a sword went right through her heart.

Zadkiel called Remiel rather than Israfel because Israfel would never hold off long enough to devise a watertight plan. Atop a cliff, she and Remiel lay on their stomachs overlooking the Lake of Fire. On the beach, a Cherub-Seraph pair watched over a knee-high stone cairn with a Guard over it. Curious.

Remiel had all her senses extended toward the structure. "I don't feel him."

"What else could they be Guarding?" Zadkiel whispered. The heat from the lake felt blistering even this far in the air, and she continually resisted the urge to fan her wings. Her feathers spread, and sweat trickled between her shoulders.

Remiel murmured, "It's too small for Gabriel."

"How far does it extend underground?"

Remiel shrugged. "I'm game to attack if you want. Your intuition is better than mine when it comes to searches."

Zadkiel formed her sword. "You take the Seraph. I'll handle the Cherub."

The pair ostensibly on duty paid no attention to their Guard. They had angry flashes in their eyes by turns, backs to one another, and tension rolled off the Cherub even as fury emanated from the Seraph.

Remiel appeared behind the Seraph and in the same second ran her sword through him, but Zadkiel had a momentary struggle with the Cherub. With both unconscious, the Guard came down.

Remiel was flashing the pair out into the Lake of Fire when Zadkiel lifted the paneling over the rocks and got her first look.

She started to scream, but abruptly Remiel had her chained with her will. *"Not a sound!"*

Zadkiel doubled forward, her face in her hands. Beside her, Remiel was saying, "Michael, we've got him. Raphael, we need you here. Now. I don't care. We need... *Then bring him with you!"*

Michael appeared beside Remiel, stepped around Zadkiel, and the shock roll off him as well. Zadkiel tightened up, afraid she was about to start sobbing.

Michael said, "Raphael, *now.*"

It was nighttime in Jerusalem. Jesus had convinced one of the priests to let him have a room. Raphael stood by the window, looking at Jesus. "I can't leave him, Michael. The attacks were vicious today."

From Michael, *I need you here. We have no idea what to do.*

Jesus touched his arm. "Let's go together."

Raphael let Jesus climb up his back, legs wrapped around his waist and arms locked around his shoulders. He put a Guard around himself, and he flashed them both to wherever Michael was.

They landed in Hell, and Jesus flinched as the wall of heat penetrated the Guard.

Michael transferred the Guard around himself, then took Jesus from Raphael. "You'll be all right as long as you're holding one of us."

Raphael didn't have time to protest. Remiel grabbed his hand and dragged him past Zadkiel tearlessly crying on the sand.

She showed him the husk of an angel, and he knew.

Raphael tore the stones from the rock cairn they'd built to make a stronger Guard. Eleven days—burnt to a cinder—left alone—here in Hell—oh, God, why?—I hate them—how could they have done this?

He sent his heart into Gabriel, but he felt nothing.

"He's not suffering," Raphael whispered.

"I didn't think he was," Remiel said.

"We have to get him out of here so we can heal him."

"I didn't want to try moving him." Remiel showed Raphael her ash-covered palms. "He crumbles."

Raphael drew back. No, he couldn't touch him. Not if Gabriel was breaking apart.

Michael came closer with Jesus across his hip and his wings wrapped around the boy. "All our resources are at your disposal. If you want to stay here, I'll call down a legion of Archangels to cordon off the beach."

"There's something about the Lake of Fire that prevents angels from healing well here." Raphael shook his head. "We have to move him."

Raphael wished he had Ophaniel nearby so he could think, or that Gabriel could level the spikes in his thought. Gabriel always came up with something like, "Don't waste time trying to make reality fit what you want. Look at what's really there."

I don't want to look at what's really here. I just want you back. Oh, God, help me to think.

Raphael focused on Remiel. "Can you form a spherical Guard around him and raise the whole thing?"

Remiel did, trying to catch as little of the sand and pebbles as possible. "Now," Raphael said, dropping two sets of his wings and laying them out, "lower him again," and she did. Then Raphael folded his discarded wings over Gabriel, wincing as he crinkled like charcoal after the campfire had burnt out.

Zadkiel had left. Michael had Jesus. Remiel glinted gold, so he turned back to her, the only one capable of doing anything.

She looked blank, but a focused blank, as if she knew he needed her and not her grief. "Where should I take him?"

Jesus said, "Bring him to the room where I'm staying."

A moment later, the angels had flashed there. "Put him in my bed," Jesus added.

"You don't have to." Raphael realized only now how hard he was shaking. He dropped to his knees, putting his hands over his face. He couldn't keep speaking: it wasn't as if Gabriel could feel anything, not in this state. So Jesus might as well sleep in a bed tonight.

There were hands on his shoulders, and he extended his heart to feel Ophaniel beside him, and also Israfel. She was crying angelically, shedding all her emotions without giving them any direction. Ophaniel was trying to keep both of them calm at the same time, but how could he?

Remiel unwound Raphael's wings from Gabriel, and then she shed light on the room so they could examine him.

He was charred. Even though they'd been gentle, the cloth bore a layer of ash in his outline.

Jesus said, "Can you heal him?"

Raphael knelt, running his hands over the air near Gabriel but not touching him. "God, how could you let them do this to him?" he whispered. "This isn't right. It should have been me. He was only trying to protect the family, and that was my job."

Jesus rested a hand on Raphael's shoulder. "It'll be okay. He's with you, and you can help him better than anyone."

"Not this!" Raphael jumped to his feet, standing with Gabriel between his legs. "There's really not a whole heck of a lot I can do about *this* level of damage! They set him on fire! They chained him up and set him on fire, and you think I can just make all that go away? *Gabriel never forgets anything!* How would you like to remember that?"

Jesus backed up a step. "Is he in pain right now?"

"He's unconscious." Remiel sat where they thought Gabriel's head might be. "He can't feel anything at all."

Michael said, "I'm surprised he isn't cindered."

"This damage was calculated." Raphael had flames around his eyes. "At this point, two fireflies lighting up at the same time would push him over the edge. They must have done this over a period of days, getting him right to the edge of cindering without triggering it."

Remiel looked up, her face pale. "We're going to have to finish the job."

"Satan is such a monster," Raphael said. "He knew we'd have to do that. There isn't a hell hot enough for him!"

71

Jesus said, "Raphael, stop!"

Raphael pulled his wings tight around himself. Ophaniel coaxed him to sit, then laid his wings over Raphael's shoulders.

Jesus said, "What is cindering? Why can't you just heal him?"

Beginning to explain, Raphael choked.

Ophaniel rubbed Raphael's arm. "You know that angels can heal from any injury. But it's not instantaneous, and greater damage requires greater time.. A recovery from damage like this might take a couple of months."

"Months?" Jesus's eyes opened wide.

Ophaniel said, "But if an angel gets completely burnt up, that's being cindered. An angelic body will simply regenerate after that. It takes about a day because the whole form is constituting anew, not trying to repair."

Raphael tightened his wings. How could they be talking like this, like an explanation of how many cubits to build some object or what ingredients go into a stew? This was Gabriel. Gabriel, like this.

Michael said, "The problem is, he's on the verge of cindered. We're going to have to burn him the rest of the way to enable him to regenerate."

Jesus had tears in his eyes. "Does it hurt? You said he's unconscious."

Ophaniel kept his arms and wings around Raphael. "If he took a couple of months to heal, he'd feel weak most of that time, and it would be uncomfortable."

Raphael closed his eyes. *And he might spend all that time thinking about what it was like to be set on fire. Repeatedly. Without any help from me.*

Michael said, "Regenerating is uncomfortable too. Mostly it's itchy, but it's a helpless feeling. And there's also the matter that one of us would be forced to burn him."

Raphael shuddered. "I can't do it."

Drawing a breath, Remiel extended her hand.

"Wait." Jesus put his hand on hers. "Is there anything I can do?"

Raphael pushed off Ophaniel's wings and leaned closer to Jesus. Both of them shouldn't be harmed because of this, because of his inability to do his own job. "It's not your hour yet. Don't force yourself. You've never done anything like this before."

Jesus said, "He's not hurting, so there's no need to act immediately. Can't I have a few minutes?"

Jesus reached toward Gabriel, and Raphael grabbed back his hand.

"I need to touch him." Jesus wrapped his hand around Raphael's and squeezed. "I can't just reach through my mind the way you can."

Raphael didn't draw back.

"I'll be gentle," Jesus said, and only then did Raphael release him.

Jesus touched Gabriel so softly that nothing more broke loose. The boy closed his eyes, and Raphael experienced an odd assortment of images, a sense of Gabriel's soul (which made him smile despite the horror) and also a fleeting feeling of how angels were put together, the depth of the damage, the last thing Gabriel remembered (and here Raphael couldn't help but cry out.) Raphael gradually became aware that Ophaniel had a grip on his shoulders, that Israfel watched with her black eyes agleam, and that Michael and Remiel looked worried.

"Oh," Jesus murmured. "Feel this."

Raphael reached into Jesus's mind to sense what Jesus was focusing on.

"This is what's keeping him asleep."

"Don't wake him up," Raphael urged.

"I won't. But that's the mechanism."

Raphael stayed in his mind as he explored other parts of Gabriel's construction.

Jesus shook his head. "I don't know, Raphael. But it feels as if..." He looked up. "The Father gave me authority over you." When Raphael nodded, he continued, "I'm trying to do this the way you would. But maybe I can do it my own way."

Raphael gestured to Gabriel, as if to say *Go ahead.*

73

Jesus braced his hands on the floor and whispered into Gabriel's ear, or where they thought his ear might be. "Gabriel-love, stay asleep, but be whole."

Unable to hope, Raphael remained frozen.

Remiel gasped, and Israfel covered her mouth with her hands.

Some of the black flaked off Gabriel, and beneath it Raphael saw soft grey feathers, unburnt.

Michael whispered, "Oh God, my God..."

Jesus brushed his fingertips over Gabriel's arm, now recognizable as an arm, and the soot came away. There was an angelic body beneath.

Raphael ran his hands over Gabriel, feeling him knit as if he'd never been injured. His soul ignited and he started scouring Gabriel all over to loosen the remains of the ash, unclenching the tight limbs, checking for hidden injuries. There were none.

Jesus sounded cheerful. "Can we awaken him now?"

Raphael assented.

Jesus released that inner mechanism. "Gabriel, be awake."

And with that, Gabriel opened his eyes. He sat up in the center of the angels.

Raphael and Israfel hurled themselves at him, hugging him from both sides at once. Gabriel startled, then, looked around at the others, and saw their relief, felt their awe. He turned to Jesus, who wore a huge grin.

"Are you hurting?" Israfel asked. "Were you in any pain?"

"Only for about three seconds," Gabriel said as the Seraphim released him.

Raphael exclaimed, "They did it all at once?"

Gabriel nodded. "Satan. He surrounded me with a Guard and fired into it. I've got to figure out that technique." He looked from Raphael to Israfel. "Did you burn me out?"

Raphael gestured to Jesus. "He healed you."

Gabriel turned to the boy, eyes wide.

Jesus took Gabriel's hands and kissed his cheek. "Don't be so surprised. You were going to heal anyhow, so it wasn't a miracle. I just upped the timetable."

Gabriel examined himself, and Raphael felt no echo of the damage, no residual signature of Jesus's healing power. Gabriel shifted so he was on his knees. He crossed his arms in front of his chest, and he bowed his head.

Jesus laughed aloud, then put both hands on Gabriel's hair and kissed his forehead. "You're welcome."

Gabriel's eyes clouded. "I made an awful mistake. They figured out the deception, and it's my fault." He lowered his gaze. "I'm sorry. I didn't think before I reacted."

Jesus shook his head. "You did all that work for twelve years, and I appreciate it. Don't you realize what you gave me?" He touched Gabriel's hand. "By protecting me the way you all did, by pretending you had loyalty to my mother but not to me, you gave me a childhood. You gave me time to grow up without being under a cloud of terrorism. That's all I could have asked of you."

Gabriel's downcast eyes focused only on his lap.

Jesus made him look up, then gave him a hug. "I'm so glad we found you, and that you're all right. The rest is incidental."

Late that night, Raphael lay on the floor alongside Jesus's bed, one hand resting on Jesus's hand, his wings up on the low mattress so they draped over Jesus's legs. Gabriel sat against the wall, eyes closed, and Raphael relaxed just being near him after so long.

They were bonded right now about as deeply as they could be, not consciously drawing fire or steel from one another as much as swirled together so they felt like one soul. Gabriel's prayer resonated in Raphael's heart while Raphael augmented it with his native fervor; meanwhile Raphael's thoughts permeated Gabriel even as Gabriel's innate calm focused them and gave them clarity; and yet somehow despite all that, they were still individuals.

Michael sat at the window, looking onto the street. His sword was sheathed, but he remained armored.

Raphael let Michael take the brunt of the watching. With his bonded Cherub on one side and his bonded charge on the other and God sparkling in his soul, he really couldn't imagine being happier.

Gabriel put the image in Raphael's head: they could also be eating ice cream.

Raphael laughed.

Jesus propped himself up on his arms. "Gabriel, I want to ask you a question," he murmured.

Gabriel said, "I think you need to be sleeping."

Jesus said, "Why are there so many of you?"

Gabriel withdraw from Raphael's soul, and Raphael sat away as Gabriel radiated tension.

"When I healed you, it wasn't just you the way I see you here. I also sensed this." He opened his hands the way Gabriel did when they learned math, and he created a picture of Gabriel from long ago, with sharper eyes. "And I picked up this one too, and also this." The second and third figures were Gabriel in a human form and then Gabriel female.

Gabriel had a level tone. "I've been all those."

Jesus frowned. "But Raphael doesn't feel that way to me. Michael doesn't have a lineup like that in his heart."

Michael watched from the window, curious. "I would bet you get two images off me."

"The one you are and the one you are when you're working for the Father?" Jesus shook his head "They're close enough that I'd call them one and the same."

Gabriel said, "There's only one Raphael, and there always ever will be. He's perfect as he is. But do you see this one too?"

Between his hands, Gabriel created a light-sculpture of an Cherub in black armor, his grey wings tucked at his back, helmeted, gauntleted, sworded, and an expression on his face between arrogance and loathing.

Jesus slipped off the side of the bed, and he touched Gabriel's forehead. "That exists only here. And in Satan's desires."

Gabriel wasn't even looking at the figure, as if he couldn't.

Raphael shuddered, nauseated. "Is that—you?"

Gabriel refused to meet Raphael's eyes.

Raphael insisted, "You didn't fall. You would never fall."

Michael said, "Satan showed him that in a dream."

"I thought angels don't dream." Jesus looked over his row of images. "Oh, the second one. He dreamed it." He passed his hand through the space between Gabriel's fingers, and the image broke apart. "You can let go of that one. You won't ever exist as him."

Relief engulfed Raphael, relief from outside himself. Gabriel was taking deep breaths.

Jesus said, "The second one: why were you him, with his sad eyes?"

Gabriel trembled, and Raphael tried to head off the inevitable even as his own heart burned. "But that isn't Gabriel now. Gabriel now isn't sad."

"That's true," Jesus said. "But I have another question if what I'm thinking is right."

Gabriel avoided looking at Raphael. "Then the answer is, God took away the Vision, and I left heaven for a year."

Jesus said, "What did you do?"

Gabriel said, "I survived. I waited a year, and then I came back."

Raphael touched Gabriel's hand because the Cherub felt so cold inside. "You did more than that."

Gabriel physically withdrew from him, not just emotionally, and Raphael flinched.

Jesus said, "I meant what did you do to deserve that?"

Gabriel looked at his lap. "I disobeyed a direct order, but that was just the excuse. Figure number one was stubborn. He needed to be turned into me, which I guess would be figure zero in your lineup."

Raphael tried to kindle his fire within Gabriel, but Gabriel recoiled as if touched by ice, so the Seraph backed off.

Jesus said, "What was it like?"

Gabriel glanced at Raphael, fear flitting over his eyes. "Why do you want to know?"

"I'm afraid I might lose it too." Jesus wrapped his hands in his blanket. "It's too wonderful to be in communion with the Father all the time, and I might get it taken away. I'm only me. And the Father is so big, but I can feel I'm somehow that big too, and it doesn't fit. I'm afraid I might lose that beauty."

Gabriel wouldn't look at Raphael. "You're still in a season of learning, which is as you should be. You've done everything you have to."

Gabriel send through the bond permission to leave if Raphael didn't want to hear this conversation. Raphael tensed but didn't go.

Jesus said, "How did it feel?"

Staring at his lap, Gabriel said, "I wanted to die."

The words sliced through Raphael's heart like a scythe. He'd failed him. He'd failed his Cherub.

Michael said, "Really?"

Eyes hollow, Gabriel made no response.

Michael sounded stunned. "You didn't seem that hard-hit. I wouldn't have let you walk away." Michael crossed the room so he sat right in front of Gabriel. "If I'd realized, I would never have left you alone afterward."

Jesus said, "What had you refused to learn?"

Gabriel stood. "I'm sorry. I can't." And he left.

Flames surged in Raphael's heart. "You left him alone?"

Michael recoiled. "I brought him back with me, but then he left again. He told me it would be better that way. I couldn't tie him up for a year and make him stay, and I thought he knew what was the right thing because he'd always known before. So I let him go. I didn't know him well enough to figure it out."

The unspoken sentence was, of course, *I couldn't ask you.*

Raphael's wings shook. "That's not right! He needed you! I was counting on you to help him, and you walked away?"

Michael looked grief-stricken, for all the good that did six centuries later. "He wasn't crying. I figured no tears, no danger."

"But later, when his strength wore down?"

"He didn't cry for six months! After a couple of weeks, I had to believe he was coping."

"Six months?" Raphael advanced on Michael, who went pale. "You let him suffer for six months?"

Jesus put a hand on Raphael's shoulder, and the Seraph forced himself to rein in the anger.

Jesus said, "Gabriel, come back."

Gabriel returned instantly, but on the opposite side of the room. A moment later, Raphael felt him sending reassurance: he held no anger against him, and he wished Raphael wouldn't either. With a deep breath, Raphael lowered his eyes and let out a long breath. And then in the next moment he wondered whom Gabriel thought he was angry at.

Jesus looked right at Gabriel. "I could order you to answer me."

Gabriel stared through the floor. "I would answer if you did."

Jesus studied him a long moment. Then he said, "Leave if you want."

Gabriel vanished again.

Jesus looked at Raphael. "He didn't go far."

"Only onto the roof," Raphael said. "He also wants to be near us."

Jesus frowned. "That doesn't make sense."

Michael said, "Because we're a community of friends. That's one of the things he learned."

Jesus had been alone in Jerusalem four days when Mary rushed through the Temple and found him sitting among a group of teachers. She stood for a moment trying not to scream in frustration, the blood rushing away from her head until she felt faint. He was here. He was safe. All this demonic activity, and here he was all this time, pestering a group of scholars about the meaning of a passage in Isaiah and how it related to a different passage in Ezekiel.

Joseph strode right into the group and grabbed Jesus by the arm, then announced it was time to be leaving.

Jesus's eyes flew wide as he looked at Joseph's face, then scanned the courtyard for his mother.

For a moment, Mary wanted to be in that group, wanted to tell Joseph not to be harsh even though a moment ago she had wanted to be the one shouting that he'd done something so terribly irresponsible, so inconsiderate, and when he'd realized he'd been left behind, why hadn't he done anything to make himself easier to find?

Joseph escorted Jesus over to Mary. "Why did you do this? We've been terrified looking for you."

Jesus swallowed, and then the tears overflowed. "I'm sorry. I thought— I thought you'd know I'd be in my Father's house!"

Mary grabbed him in a hug and closed her eyes. Jesus wouldn't be this distressed about upsetting them if he were hurt himself. "Are you okay?" she asked. "Have you been eating? Did you have a place to sleep?"

She looked up to see Raphael, who seemed just as disturbed. *Didn't you hear me calling for you?*

He shook his head, projecting a mixture of emotions. Jesus had darted back to the Temple once more before they left, and it had been a demonic attack: he'd gotten distracted by a question, much as Gabriel did when confronted with a tantalizing problem. And Raphael had gotten sucked into it as well, failing to notice the passage of time until the family caravan had departed. At that point it was a question of remaining or trying to find their way by themselves. Raphael could have directed him, but it seemed more prudent to wait. And that night, they'd found Gabriel.

Mary's eyes widened. *You did?*

Uriel started. *Why didn't you send word?*

The angels communicated too rapidly for Mary to follow, and finally Uriel turned toward Mary. *Sometimes God separates us for a short time for a reason.*

Communication blackout, Raphael added. *Satan must have demanded as much if he approached the Lord for special permission to attack.*

Mary swallowed her protest that this explanation wasn't good enough: first God didn't tell them where to find Gabriel, and then God didn't let them tell one another he'd been found, nor where Jesus was.

Jesus wiped the tears from his flushed cheeks. "I'm sorry, Mom. I really didn't mean to worry you. And I was okay the whole time. I kept coming back to the Temple every day, but we must have kept missing each other."

Demonic attack. Demons could rearrange crowds and distractions and maybe it was enough to keep people from finding other people. At least for a while. Mary took a deep breath.

One of the priests touched Joseph on the arm and assured him the boy would be a great rabbi when he grew up. Mary only looked at Jesus and tried to feel thankful that he was with her again, or maybe pride that so many intelligent and holy men recognized his own intelligence and holiness, but instead she felt only the resentment of all the worry.

They started for home immediately, Mary worrying about not having enough supplies but realizing when they stopped for the night that her extra allocation, in case they'd meet someone in need, would see them through.

While Joseph tended the animals, Jesus walked off alone. Mary noticed him an arrow-flight from the camp. Still skittish, Mary called, but he didn't hear, so she followed.

As she drew closer, he asked for Gabriel.

Mary hadn't seen Gabriel yet, so it frightened her to find wariness in his eyes, the way he looked so reserved while talking to Jesus. Before this trip she would have expected to find him wearing an easy smile, maybe head off whatever Jesus was going to say by asking if he wanted a math lesson. Now he looked like nothing more than a soldier reporting to his commanding officer.

How badly had he been hurt? How much did he blame her?

She heard Jesus say, "I overstepped my boundaries with you."

Gabriel opened his hands, and she couldn't read everything Gabriel said. She continued moving closer, not wanting to eavesdrop and knowing they would stop as soon as they saw her if they didn't want her to overhear.

Gabriel looked at her, then back at Jesus.

Jesus said, "I know you're not upset. But even so, I was asking you things I shouldn't."

Again Gabriel opened his hands, and this time he bowed his head as well. Mary caught some of what he projected this time: the answers were his right, and he also had the right to demand them if he wanted.

Jesus said, "But I'm not going to." Then he turned and saw his mother. "I'll come back in a minute. I hurt your feelings before, and I realized when we were traveling, I must have hurt Gabriel's too."

Mary took a step backward, but Gabriel indicated she could stay. He projected a question to Jesus.

"Yes, one more thing." Jesus lowered his gaze. "When I showed you those figures, I realize it made you uncomfortable, but I want you to know..." He tried to meet Gabriel's eyes, but although Gabriel was looking right at him, he didn't seem able to do it. "I want you to know, God loves all four of them. All three figures in my hands. He had a special care for the second one. The one you called the zeroth figure he loves especially. And the final one, the one you showed me, if that was the only one left, he would be heartbroken, but he would love that one too."

Gabriel took a step backward, confusion swirling around him. Mary moved closer as if to steady him.

Jesus looked up. "That was all I wanted to say. I'm sorry I upset you."

Gabriel bowed, and then he kissed Jesus on the forehead.

"Wait," Mary said, "don't go yet."

Smiling, Gabriel turned to her. "I hope you're not going to offer me another cup of wine."

Mary reached her hand toward him, and he brushed his wingtips through her fingers. "I'm sorry I caused so much trouble."

Gabriel shrugged. "I'm not going to blow the roof off your house."

"Smiling or unsmiling?"

"Either way."

"I'm sorry you got hurt because of me."

"Technically speaking," Gabriel said, "I got hurt because of Satan, and because I was protecting Jesus, and because I wasn't clever enough to spot an ambush in advance. I hold you responsible for none of that."

Mary lowered her head. "Thank you."

"Thank you for keeping up the pretense as long as you did."

Mary gave an amused smile. "It's been satisfactory."

"Glad to hear it," Gabriel said, and with that he vanished.

Jesus came toward his mother. "I'm sorry I worried you. I needed to take care of that."

"It's okay," Mary said, seeing Raphael leaning against a tree with a smile on his lips. "I think you just did something very important. Very adult."

Jesus took her hand, and they walked back to the campsite.

Year Eighteen

"*Raphael!*"

Mary's voice in Raphael's mind was so urgent that Jesus dropped his hammer and looked right at him.

Mary, what's happening?

"*It's Joseph. Come now. Right now!*"

Gabriel already vanished, and in an instant he returned. "Joseph is ill. You're needed."

Jesus left the worksite and bolted for home. When he was out of sight of the other workers, though, Raphael said, "Stop. Wait," and grabbed his hand. "Close your eyes. Okay, now open them."

When Jesus looked up again, Raphael had transported them both to an alcove within Nazareth. Jesus got his bearings and pelted for the house.

Just inside, he ran through Gabriel in the doorway and pulled up short beside Mary. She was crouching beside Joseph, collapsed on the floor. "Help him up. Something's wrong and I don't know what."

Raphael laid a hand on Joseph's head and moved with him as Jesus gathered him up, then laid him out on his bed. *What are you getting from him?* Jesus asked Raphael.

Raphael kept his focus on the blood flow through the man's body, the rhythm of his heartbeat, his shallow breaths, the unsteady and tiny blips like lightning flashes in his brain. Gabriel fed him energy, but energy wasn't what Raphael needed. What he needed was permission, and none came. Jesus could give the command and he'd heal Joseph in an instant. For that matter, Jesus could heal Joseph himself, something he was praying for permission to do right now.

Mary looked at Jesus. "Will you do anything for him?"

Will. Not can.

Raphael waited. Jesus brushed the hair from Joseph's forehead and settled him. Joseph never stirred, only kept breathing lightly.

Is that a brain bleed? Gabriel asked.

Raphael acknowledged. *He's not in any pain. But he's not going to recover unless we intervene.*

Gabriel said nothing. He knew the rules as well as Raphael did, but Raphael could feel him praying. He could feel Uriel channeling and delivering Mary's prayer, even if her prayer didn't take the form of words as much as tears.

Jesus too was praying, waiting. And as Mary looked to him, Raphael felt a chalky darkness fall through the house. Asmodeus.

Raphael reached for his sword, but God stilled him. A test, then. It had to be permitted.

Asmodeus' touch permeated the prayer. Wasn't Joseph a good man? A man chosen specially to be Jesus's father? And if Jesus had power, didn't it stand to reason he ought to use it in order to help good men?

Jesus kept praying, but Raphael felt a curious doubling happen to the prayer: there was Jesus's own prayer and then an anharmonic resonance with a prayer that wasn't his own and yet felt as if it could be. What would Mary do without her husband? Who would care for her? If Jesus had a role to fill, who would provide for her in his absence? Life was hard for a widow. She needed Joseph so Jesus could be free to fulfill whatever God wanted.

Raphael bristled, but Jesus's prayers did turn toward that avenue: for Mary's sake, he was asking the Father, please bring healing to Joseph. And for his own – he still needed guidance.

No permission. Only silence.

Asmodeus raised a thought: whatever wasn't forbidden must be permissible. Healing was good. God was good. Healing would be a work of God. It was time to act.

Jesus closed his eyes.

Mary stroked Joseph's hand. "I'm sorry," she whispered, either to Jesus or to Joseph or to both. "I'm sorry."

Jesus leaned forward and breathed over Joseph, but Raphael didn't feel him reaching out the way he'd reached out for Gabriel. Nothing like, *Dad, be whole*. Instead it was more a blessing, a farewell, a wish.

Asmodeus retreated. Raphael sat at the head of the bed with Jesus and remained close until Joseph died. He remained close as Jesus tended the body for burial, and he remained close during the next morning as Jesus shuffled through a fog of grief.

When the sun rose, Mary approached Jesus holding a leather bag. "Take these." Tears glistened in her bloodshot eyes. "They belong to you now."

Jesus accepted the bag, and he headed to the work site.

Dad's tools, he thought to Raphael. They made a familiar sound as they clanked against one another in the bag slung over his shoulder. The bag bore Joseph's sweat, his hand marks, everything he'd worked with on an everyday basis. *He made so many buildings and pieces of furniture and carts. That was his life, and now I have his work left to do.*

At the work site, Jesus reported to the foreman and apologized for leaving but that he'd gotten a message his father was dying. The foreman said he wouldn't be paid for yesterday and sent Jesus out to build a staircase.

He used Joseph's tools. Tools where the flaws were worn down into a part of the instrument, every shortcoming known and every good feature appreciated. In the evening, the foreman paid him for a staircase and sent him home.

Jesus hadn't spoken to Raphael all day, and Raphael had been busy deflecting attacks: guilt that Jesus had let down his mother, plus guilt that he'd stayed his hand and not tried to force a healing or not tried to force God to relent. There was a sense of self-indulgence at his own sadness: why be sad when he'd *chosen* to let Joseph die? And finally discouragement because he wasn't as good a carpenter at age eighteen as Joseph had been at sixty.

Raphael kept sending reassurance: Jesus had done what he was permitted, and that was right.

As the sun dipped over the road, Jesus rounded a bend to find a lone Roman soldier. "You, there!" The soldier pointed at Jesus. "Carry my gear!"

Raphael bristled, but that was the law: a Roman soldier could conscript a man to carry his gear one mile. Jesus, exhausted from the day's work, sighed, but the Roman thrust him his shield and a pack. "Take those."

Jesus shifted Joseph's work bag so he could heft the additional load. The Roman said, "This way."

They headed back up the road the way they'd come, and Jesus sent word to Gabriel to tell Mary he'd be home after dark. The Roman said nothing, but Jesus kept looking at him. Finally Jesus said, "Are you injured?"

The Roman glared at him. "Just carry my gear."

Jesus handed him the waterskin. "Well, regardless, you look thirsty. Here."

The Roman said, "Are you trying to trick me?"

Jesus said, "It's water. You're thirsty. Drink."

The Roman took the waterskin and drank, then tilted it up and gulped down the whole thing. He gasped, wiping water from his cheeks, then handed the skin back to Jesus.

It grew dark. Jesus said, "Are you stationed in Caparnum?"

The soldier grunted an agreement.

"You got separated from your platoon?"

"I was sent to deliver a message."

Jesus smiled. "Some of my best friends are messengers."

The Roman's voice grew tight. "Well, maybe they know the roads around here better than I do. All your towns look the same, so how was I supposed to find the right way to go?"

Jesus said, "Oh, you got lost. That's why you ran out of water."

The Roman said, "How did you know that?"

Jesus raised the empty waterskin. "Your own is empty, and you finished off mine. People aren't overly friendly to Romans, no? You got directed all over the place by the least likely routes. Well, this will get you to Caparnum, and you'll be back with your centurion."

The Roman said, "Are you some kind of rabbi?"

Jesus patted the work bag. "I'm some kind of carpenter."

Nothing more for a while. Jesus looked tired, but not as tired as the soldier. Jesus said, "Your tools weigh a lot more than mine do."

A huff from the soldier. "Because I have to do a lot more than you do."

Jesus said, "Oh, come on. My tools make houses."

The soldier said, "My tools make empires."

Jesus drew a sharp breath, and he looked up for Raphael, who moved around front of the walkers.

My father's tools, Jesus thought to him. *They're carpenter's tools. And this soldier is using his tools to make...well, war and obedience and safety. But what about my real Father's tools?*

In this moment, Jesus reminded him so much of Gabriel enmeshed in a problem, although Jesus could cast the whole question in an emotional and spiritual light that Gabriel at his best never achieved. Jesus kept thinking out loud to him, but the words faded and the thoughts became a series of impulses, so rather than answer, Raphael sent encouragement.

My Father's tools are mercy. And patience. Love. Anger. Redirection. Jesus shook his head. *Water. Manna. Wine. Words. Humans. Touches.*

Jesus picked up speed and tucked his head as he walked, and the Roman unconsciously increased his pace to keep up with him.

What can I make with those tools? Jesus half-thought, half-prayed, and Raphael kept himself out of the prayer because he could feel the Spirit interacting with Jesus: what better guide was there? *You make an empire with swords. You make a house with hammers and an adz and a bow-drill. But what do you make*

89

with mercy, love, the law, and the word? What do you craft with souls?

Raphael limited his work to guiding Jesus's steps, keeping him from stumbling under the weight of the Roman's gear as well as his own and the new gear he was picking up in his mind. What did God use to create history? Time. Justice. Mercy. Good will. But more than that: God used mistakes as well. God used stubbornness. The more Jesus thought, the more Raphael realized God used everything. Everything – maybe God had even used his own abandonment of Gabriel during that wretched punishment.

Jesus's thoughts inverted the problem, a technique for which he could probably thank Gabriel: was there anything God didn't use? Lies? Well, God didn't use lies of His own, but He'd used Joseph's brothers' lies to bring the people down to Egypt. He'd used Pharaoh's hard-heartedness to bring the people out again. He'd used the destruction of the Temple itself to bring about pure monotheism and end idolatry forever.

Is there anything so wretched and brutal that the Father can't use it? Jesus thought to Raphael.

Raphael sent back, *Can you come up with anything?*

Disobedience: used. Adultery: used. No, actually, these things weren't used as much as converted. Weakness. *Despair,* Jesus thought. *I don't think despair is of much use to the Father because despair itself prevents its own usefulness.*

He kept thinking. *Physical pain. But maybe it teaches the one on the receiving end? Or maybe the ones helping?* More walking, more of him reaching into Raphael's power to pull on his reserves, and Raphael gave it all. The Spirit bore a crackling energy now, like a mother offering milk to a hungry baby, and Jesus's spirit was drinking it in.

The Maccabeans certainly died heroically. That mother and all her sons. That was a cruelty God used to inspire others. If evil itself can become a tool in the hands of God, then what remains? Everything is in His workbag.

The Roman said, "Here we are," and Jesus looked up. And gasped. They'd stopped a stone's throw from a crucifixion.

The Roman lifted his gear from Jesus's shoulder, but Jesus had his eyes riveted to the pair of crosses, the men transfixed in agony and needing to trade pain for each breath. "God have mercy," he whispered.

"Maybe your god does," said the Roman, "but you're looking at another one of my tools." He laughed out loud. "Just be glad you didn't have to carry that bit of my gear."

Jesus shivered. The sun lay on the cusp of the horizon, and two men had hours more until they died.

And that? Jesus prayed. *That's a tool too? Men harming men?*

Jesus didn't move as the Roman walked toward his comrades without so much as a word of thanks. *May I do something for them?* he prayed, but it wasn't time, urged the Spirit. Time for compassion, yes, but not time for power.

Jesus sat on the side of the road, his back aching and his legs trembling, and he finished the last of the food in his bag. Raphael wrapped around him, wings over Jesus's shoulders.

What can I build with that? The prayer flowed through Raphael, and he presented it toward God, adding his fervor but nothing else. No answer came back through him. Instead, he could feel the Spirit deep in communion with Jesus's heart, so Raphael just waited on the outside, waited and longed and wondered what the pair were saying to one another.

Jesus whispered, "Raphael, take me home," and he closed his eyes until Raphael prompted him to open them again, and they were in Nazareth.

Through the dark streets, Jesus made his way back to Mary, Raphael again guiding his steps. When he reached their house, Mary hugged him, kissed his cheeks, and tried not to look as drawn as she must feel. Uriel seemed drained.

She had Jesus sit and brought out food for him, then wine, and she sat across the table from him.

Jesus said, "Without Dad to provide for you, I need to stay."

Mary shook her head. "Sweetie, listen."

"I've prayed about this," Jesus said, "and I'm going to stay. Not forever, but for a while. I'll work and save up money, and I'll

91

provide for you so you'll be safe. James and Joses and the rest of them, they'll help, but I'm your son and they're not, so I owe you that much. You've still got the gold they brought when I was born, and I want you to use that too. But when my hour comes, the Father will tell me, and I'll have to leave."

Mary wrapped her hand around his. "Where will you go? Do you know your mission?"

Jesus nodded. "I have my Father's tools now. We're going to build the City of God."

Year Thirty

Midnight. Michael sat atop the house in Nazareth, watching the stars and all too aware of the souls beneath him. Mary lay asleep. Jesus had awakened at midnight, praying.

Michael had Guarded the house, but outside the Guard on the roof he sat, sword in his hands, and he probed through the darkness for their enemies. All four Maskim watched. Satan was suppressing his location, but Michael assumed he was nearby.

Beneath him, Michael felt prayer. Intense prayer. The kind of prayer even Raphael couldn't penetrate because it was God the Son communing with God the Father, and who could plumb that?

I can, replied the Spirit, and Michael grinned.

Point taken. Michael shook his head. *But not us, and I want to make sure he's undisturbed.*

The Spirit swirled through Michael and left him a little giddy, but he settled back down to his job of protecting Mary and Jesus.

Inside the house, he felt Jesus arise, then a tingle as he passed through the Guard to stand in the night.

Michael flashed to Raphael's side.

Jesus watched the stars. He stayed that way for an hour, still deep in communion with the Father and wordless, but Raphael interacting with his spirit.

Grief shot like an arrow through the Guard of the house, and Michael felt it shock Mary out of sleep.

Uriel flared to action inside, soothing and gentle. But the damage was done, and in a few minutes Mary emerged. "You're still here," she whispered, "I had a nightmare that you'd gone."

Jesus turned to her, and he swallowed hard.

Michael glared into the dark. The Maskim could read signs as well as any other angel. They could make predictions. They'd taken a risk about what God was going to do next.

Jesus kissed Mary on the cheek.

She said, "Is it time?"

"It's not my hour yet."

Her voice shook. "But John. What John's been doing out in the Jordan – it's a sign, isn't it?" When Jesus nodded, she ran the back of her wrist over her eyes. "You have to do what your Father asks. But..."

Jesus took her hand. Mary said, "Will I see you again?"

Jesus nodded. "You will. But tomorrow morning, I need to leave."

Mary didn't sleep. Michael felt Uriel guiding her prayers for the rest of the night. When the sun rose, so did she, and she prepared food and other necessities for Jesus. When it was time for Jesus to leave, she had wet eyes and Uriel looked drawn.

Raphael, on the other hand, had flames in his wings and a glow in his eyes, and Gabriel glittered with overflow energy he'd already drawn off the Seraph. In contrast to a silent Mary and Uriel or even a Jesus who prayed as he walked, Raphael chattered in a joyful stream of consciousness, zipping ahead on the road and then back to their group as Jesus headed to the Jordan River. Whatever their adventure was, it began here. Today.

And Michael stayed with them because ministries invited attacks, and the greater the ministry, the more Satan would want to undermine it.

This one's going to be big, Michael prayed.

You know it, replied the Spirit.

Michael had witnessed supernovas that went off with less flare than a Seraph in full joy of living. Thirty years of quiet life, over. Thirty years of protecting against splinters and the common cold, swept aside. Finally Jesus would meet his true purpose.

Building the City of God, Raphael said for the tenth time that morning. *How will he do that? What will our role be?*

Gabriel's response was usually a mischievous, *We haven't figured it out in twelve years, so our odds of success this morning are on the slim side,* but Raphael would just urge him again to guess. And all the time, Jesus kept walking and praying.

The Jordan.

The land grew greener the closer they drew to the river, and with the green came cool, and with the cool came a sense of relief, as if the Earth itself relaxed in a land without thirst. The river itself wasn't much, but it giggled as it moved, and Michael let his spirit resonate with the water's motion.

A voice carried over the water, someone Jesus could hear before he could see, although Michael could detect the man's soul. At his cousin's voice, Jesus smiled compulsively, and his pace picked up.

Fifteen to twenty people stood at the bank, one man in the river preaching. When Jesus neared him, the man stopped.

John shouted, "Behold! The lamb of God!"

Everyone turned. Jesus tensed, but then he walked toward the shore. The angels followed.

Satan appeared before Michael. "Is someone in charge here? I demand to speak to whoever's in charge."

Gabriel and Michael halted. Raphael's sword appeared, but he followed Jesus.

Satan said, "I want my rights."

Gabriel's eyes unfocused, and he spoke in a voice between tenor and soprano. "What do you want of My servant?"

Satan looked disgusted. "Gabriel, tell your puppet master I want full rein to test that servant monkey of his. He's gotten this far on your protection alone, but that's not proof of his worth, only of his hired thugs."

Michael's eyes narrowed.

Still acting as God's voice, Gabriel said, "You may test him."

95

Satan said, "Without any interference from any angels."

Gabriel replied, "There will be no interference from my servants, nor from yours."

Satan said, "I want nothing off limits."

Gabriel's eyes still hadn't focused. "You may not touch his life."

Satan said, "That's not good enough."

"This is not your hour," came the reply. "He will meet you in a fair test. You have forty days beginning now."

Gabriel's eyes snapped to focus, and he blinked as he returned to himself.

"That's sufficient for me." Satan smirked at Michael and waved him off. "You can go now. You're useless enough."

Satan vanished. Michael muttered, "Why do you keep giving him that much freedom?"

God made no reply.

At the water's edge, Raphael's attention was riveted on Jesus, but Michael didn't approach. God had made that much clear: no help. No interference.

"Raphael's not going to like this," Michael said.

Gabriel whispered, "I don't like it either."

At the river, Jesus and John were speaking. Michael said, "Why would Jesus get baptized? Shouldn't he baptize John?"

Gabriel said, "To fulfill the law. Some things are necessary, and some are fitting. Just like his submitting to circumcision, it's God entering a covenant with God. It's unbreakable."

John raised a cup and poured river water over Jesus's head.

As the water cascaded over him, the sky opened. Both angels looked into the Heavens, and Michael gasped as he felt the Spirit descend on Jesus, suffusing him until they saw his whole soul alight with grace. Gabriel stared into the blaze, but Michael looked at the entire scene, witnessed the river not just as water in motion but as grace flooding the world, or rather as the Spirit Himself. Jesus looked into the light, and Gabriel murmured, "He's like a dove," but what Michael saw instead was a river of love engulfing the world.

"You are my beloved Son," he heard the Father saying, "and I am so very pleased with you."

Gabriel dropped to his knees. Michael bowed his head and crossed his arms over his chest.

On the shore, the people were asking themselves if that was thunder. Jesus kissed John on the cheek, then left the water, and he walked back up the path, away from the river.

Raphael flashed to Gabriel. "Why can't I get near him? What happened?"

Michael said, "Satan demanded the right to test him. We can't interfere."

Raphael turned to Gabriel, hurt mixing with outrage. "And you let him do that?"

Gabriel looked surprised. "I didn't let him do anything. He negotiated directly with God."

"You should have asked for mercy. You should have been demanding God let us match whatever tactics Satan was using." Raphael's eyes glinted. "Well? What *are* we allowed to do?"

Michael was about to say they could do nothing, but Gabriel said, "God didn't give Satan free rein. He's got forty days, but he's not allowed to harm Jesus's body. Moreover, although Satan said we're not allowed to interfere," and here Gabriel smirked just a little, "he forgot to stipulate that God couldn't either. I suspect Jesus has far better than us right now."

Forty days. Michael deputized Saraquael to take over his regular tasks and camped out with Raphael in the wilderness. Gabriel never left Raphael's side either, but Michael thought Gabriel seemed worn from the constant steadying he exerted through their bond.

"I can feel him praying," Raphael said. "He doesn't detect us, but I still can't tell if it's because he can't or because he's so deep in prayer. The Spirit is completely suffusing him."

Gabriel said, "Satan can't break through that."

All the same, Michael patrolled, keeping tabs on Satan's movements and noting the subtle changes he made. It had been like this when Satan approached Gabriel all those years ago: a time of intense observation, then subtle pushes with changes to the environment, inconveniences that actually served as pre-tests. Through all this, though, Jesus fasted and prayed and kept his eyes riveted on the Father, and Satan must have been ruing the one demand he'd failed to make.

It was night. In a hollow at the base of a hill, Jesus slept wrapped in his cloak. Raphael had gotten close, but Michael could tell he had no authority right now. Raphael did what he could, making the ground a little softer, keeping the animals and insects at a distance.

As he worked, Raphael whispered, "It's the worst feeling in the world, having someone to protect and not being able to protect him."

Beside Michael, Gabriel shivered.

Raphael halted as if shot with an arrow. For a moment, Michael felt blindsided from two directions – extreme self-consciousness that emerged from both the Seraph and Cherub. "What?" he exclaimed, but both became guarded and neither said a thing.

"Oh," Michael said. "This is like when you couldn't help Gabriel."

Gabriel said, "It's nothing at all like that." He looked up at the moon. "I'm going to patrol and make sure none of the Maskim are hiding out." And he took flight.

Raphael swallowed hard.

Now Michael was the one who felt self-conscious, and he said, "I'm sorry. I didn't mean to upset him."

"It's not as if he wasn't thinking it anyhow." Raphael huffed. "And Satan called *you* useless? I wonder what he'd have said about me."

"You're doing what God wants," Michael said. "That's never useless."

Raphael looked dark. Gabriel returned. "We're right at the end," he said. "Whatever happens has to happen now."

Raphael shook his head. "While he's physically weak and emotionally exhausted and sorting through everything he's learned. His defenses are worn to nothing, and I still can't help."

Gabriel hugged him. Raphael said, "Don't try to reassure me. You're concerned too."

"Satan's...subtle." Gabriel spoke slower. "He's manipulative. But Jesus is smart."

Raphael said, "Would smart alone defeat him?"

Gabriel swallowed hard. "No."

Michael said, "Jesus has grace."

Gabriel said in a low voice, "Yeah. He won't engage the way I did."

Raphael looked up, confused. "What way you did?"

Gabriel folded his arms. "It doesn't matter. What does matter is today — Satan's got the same clock we do, and he's watching it."

When Jesus awoke, he spent the first hour in prayer, then as had become his routine, he alternated walking with prayer and sometimes both. At mid-morning, he reached a dead tree.

Jesus studied the fallen branches. Raphael got a sudden smile as Jesus bent to pick up one of the larger pieces. He took out his knife and began carving.

Gabriel crouched close and studied the little motions of his hands as wood shavings peeled away. Michael by contrast swept his attention over the horizon. Protection meant watching the surroundings, not focusing on the person. He couldn't forget that.

As the wood in Jesus's hands began to transform, the haze in the air smelled of wood smoke and wheat. Why wheat? But the more Michael paid attention, the more he felt a miasma of oppression that meant one thing.

"Alert," Michael whispered.

Gabriel's wings spread. Although he couldn't help, Raphael moved closer to Jesus.

Abruptly Jesus raised his head, and the rocks all around looked like bread.

It would be easy, so easy to speak to them. To say, "Bread," and have the stones themselves give God what He wanted. Hadn't

God made manna in the desert? Wasn't this the desert? What better than to have the Earth itself celebrate its God with Messianic plenty? Bread for all. No more hunger.

Jesus gripped the wood tighter.

Bread, bread for the world. Bread that would feed everyone and give them life, bread straight from the hand of God.

Michael's hand went for his sword. Raphael looked at Gabriel. "Do something!"

Gabriel said, "We don't have permission."

Raphael deepened his voice. "Find something we *do* have permission to do."

"For the past forty days, you don't think I've tried?"

The feeling persisted, the amazing goodness of feeding people. Jesus was hungry, but his was a self-imposed hunger. He could end it at any time by going home, by finding a town and buying bread. But what of the people who couldn't? People starving in lands where nothing grew, places of drought and places wracked by war. Did they deserve their hunger? Did their suffering and death honor God? Did they go into the Pit praising God for emptiness and malnutrition?

Do something.

Do something.

Why would God become a man only to do nothing? To have water poured on his head and pray in a lesser form than he could have just by staying in Heaven with the Godhead?

Wasn't it selfish to do that? Remember Mary's grief after Joseph died while Jesus did nothing. Multiply that a million fold. Think of women just like Mary grieving for their starving husbands, their starving babies.

Gabriel sat beneath the tree, arms wrapped around his knees, wings tucked up. His eyes never left Jesus's face. Raphael grew angrier, but Gabriel wasn't drawing off the fire.

If Jesus didn't intervene, all that suffering was his fault. His. No one else's because no one else's word could turn stone into bread.

Jesus murmured, "Man doesn't live by bread alone, but by every word that comes from the mouth of God."

The push resumed, but Jesus returned to woodworking, and minute later, the heaviness lifted.

Gabriel looked at Raphael. "Satan's in fine form."

Raphael had gone ashen.

Satan stepped into the sunlight, one moment not present at all and the next moment a living shadow formed from the tree's shade, and the moment after that a flaxen-haired, white-winged angel in linen and gold. He folded his arms and regarded Jesus, who Michael realized was able to see him too.

Satan said, "Explain yourself to me."

Jesus said nothing. Satan picked up one of the dead sticks and flipped it in his hand. "You're here, out in the middle of nowhere. You're of the House of David but you were born in a barn and grew up surrounded by sawdust and road dust. You could be working wonders and living legends, but instead you've hidden yourself in privacy for three decades while my men got bored just surveilling you. I can't imagine how bored you've made yourself, and yet here you are, carving spirals into dead wood.

Jesus returned to work with the knife. Satan said, "Are you the Son of God?"

When Jesus said nothing, Satan strode forward. "I asked a question, monkey."

Jesus still didn't reply, as if he hadn't heard him at all, so Satan grabbed him by the wrist and wrenched him through space to the pinnacle of the Temple.

Michael reappeared beside them. Raphael had beaten him there, his wings in flames. "You can't touch his body! You know that! What are you trying to prove?"

Satan stood behind Jesus as a hot wind whipped past him. People milled beneath their feet, oblivious. "If you're the Son of God," he said, "you can throw yourself down and be perfectly safe. You love to quote scripture, so you know He's given His angels charge over you. Surely you realize they're here now, even though they're not going to stop me. Gabriel would dive into fire for you, and Raphael would destroy the Earth before letting you hit the ground. *They'll bear you up on their hands so you don't even kick a stone*. So go ahead. Show everyone the power you command."

Jesus said, "It's also written that you shouldn't tempt the Lord your God."

They were back in the wilderness just like that. Jesus picked up the wood and the knife.

Satan said, "So you do claim to be the Son of God."

As Jesus continued working, Satan said, "I'm going to show you one more thing."

He flared his wings, and in an instant Satan recreated the world in a show of light: monuments and cities, roads, vehicles, machines that built, machines that flew. He cupped his hands and out flared more light in the shapes of musical instruments and jewels and artwork. There was laughter and prosperity, sunrises and fields of crops, seas and skies teeming with life, and flashing through all that were faces of every race and age.

"All this is mine." Satan sounded shocked at his own cleverness, almost delighted. "God gave them a garden and instead I forged them a world. Can you build this, Carpenter? Palaces taller than the clouds? Bridges to span the seas? Ships that dock on the moon?"

Openly surprised, Jesus kept taking it in: the cities, the people, the buildings.

"All this is mine," Satan said, "and can I give it to whomever I want. Don't you want this? I'm not going to let you steal my world from me, but I'm quite willing to share. As soon as you worship me, I'll let you have it."

Jesus shook his head. "The Law says you should worship the Lord your God, and you should serve Him alone."

Satan shrugged. "Naturally that's what the Law says. The Law was written by Him, and I'm smart enough to realize what you said isn't a denial. The Law also says to feed the hungry and to proclaim the works of God everywhere. You've done neither when provided the opportunity. You're the Son of God, and you have an inheritance to collect. That inheritance is in my hands right now, but I'm a proper steward and will present it to you once you worship me."

Jesus said, "It's not just me, and it's not just the law. *You* should serve God alone."

He waved a hand so the images dispersed. "And that's a final refusal. Thank you for your service. You're dismissed."

Satan started to speak, but then he vanished too.

Jesus let out a breath and seemed to deflate, then put his face in his hands. Michael could feel him praying, gratitude for deliverance and strength and the right words to say. Compassion for the people Satan led in circles on a regular basis. And then a question.

The Father answered, and Jesus sagged with relief, smiling.

Raphael wrapped around him. "Can you hear me again? I never left." Jesus nodded. "You did great. You won on all counts."

Gabriel moved before him, holding a bowl with lamb and lentil stew. "I hope you don't mind," he said, "but your mother wanted to feed you."

"Tell her thank you." Jesus took the food and laughed. "It's time to go into the world and build a real city. An everlasting city."

And so it began.

Raphael's joy sparkled through creation like a comet's tail. Remiel followed it until she met up with Jesus walking the road away from the Jordan with Gabriel and Raphael in attendance. Remiel hadn't seen Raphael this delighted in centuries, and given a Seraph's predilection to fully enjoy life, that said a lot. So she stayed. He chattered with a bright enthusiasm that both Jesus and Gabriel must have found infectious, because they were talking right along with him.

Raphael gave her a breakdown on Satan's attempt on Jesus, and she shivered.

They reached the closest town, and at the border, Jesus took a deep breath. He got his bearings, and then headed for the synagogue. And at the entrance, he started to talk to the people in the streets.

Remiel said, "So we're building a city?"

Gabriel said to her, "Cities are made of people."

Remiel grinned. "You said that before."

Gabriel chuckled.

Remiel folded her arms. "What's the strategy? How do you build a city out of people?"

"You'd have to ask Jesus," Gabriel said, "but if you build a city, the first thing you need is a means of support, a natural locus that drives trade to that site and then individuals."

Remiel huffed. "Why are you making it sound so...clinical? And boring. This isn't anthropology."

Gabriel shrugged. "He's using the metaphor of a city, so I'm going to extrapolate his intentions from actual cities. Clearly the grace of God would function as this city's natural locus. What happens next is you create buildings, and then over time the buildings concentrate, and once you've saturated the buildable land, you begin to develop sprawl. We're at the earliest state. He's going to have to find a few individuals who become the foundation of those initial buildings that tap into the natural locus."

Raphael said, "He needs disciples."

Gabriel nodded.

Remiel muttered, "You could have just said that."

Gabriel snickered. "It's more fun to figure it out."

Most people continued their daily lives, but some stopped to listen as Jesus talked to them. It wasn't exactly preaching. Sometimes he'd recite scriptures, but other times he told stories, and through it all, the only constant listeners were the angels. Guardians encouraged their charges to stop, but most only paused and then went on.

When Jesus talked about the City of God, though, one of the passers-by said, "What is the city of God? Jerusalem?"

"No, not Jerusalem." Jesus thought. "What would you compare it to...? The city of God is more like a treasure hidden in a field. If you knew it was there, you'd sell everything you had just in order to buy that field."

Remiel said to Gabriel, "That puts Jesus' value at double yours." When Gabriel started, Remiel added, "Satan only offered you half his kingdom to switch sides. He offered Jesus the whole thing."

Raphael looked over. "What?"

"When Satan was hitting on Gabriel." Remiel put her arms around Gabriel's shoulders. "He kept offering Gabriel co-regency. That's half his kingdom, right?"

Gabriel narrowed his eyes. "No, because if Satan owns you, then you owning half his kingdom is the same as him owning the whole thing. If he got Jesus to worship him, and then gave him everything, he'd still have owned it all. He'd just have had one more puppet string to pull in the process."

Raphael drew up short. "What are you talking about?"

Remiel put her head next to Gabriel's. "You remember. I yanked you in front of God's throne and told you to pray, just pray, even though I couldn't tell you what for. That's when Gabriel was in deep."

Gabriel tightened his wings to his side, and Raphael looked at him with a discomfort that broke over Remiel like goosebumps. "How could you have been in trouble? So Satan offered you the world. You don't want the world."

Gabriel stared at the ground. "I really don't think you want to hear about this."

Remiel shook her head. "He didn't just show up and say, 'Gabriel, old pal, you want half a world?' He orchestrated something vicious."

Raphael's eyes flamed. "You never told me that. I'd have gone after him."

"You don't understand." Gabriel swallowed hard. "I just wasn't prepared. I thought I could handle it, but what he was offering— He just *knew*."

Raphael said, "What did he offer?"

"Everything." Gabriel shivered, and Remiel remembered the terror of watching Gabriel in what looked like an unstoppable freefall. "He offered companionship and music and debates and a library. If he'd been physically seducing me, I'd have been naked and in his arms."

Raphael's eyes widened. "But— Didn't Michael stop him?" He looked at Remiel. "Why didn't you try to stop him? Rather than just sobbing at God's feet and telling me to pray, why weren't you out there with an army?"

"No one came to help." Gabriel sounded desolate. "Satan demanded that concession from God, but I didn't know. One night he hooked me with a poem, and by the end of it I was answering all his questions." Gabriel wrapped his arms around his stomach. "We were debating like two Cherubim, and he said, 'Are we going to argue like this when you're my co-regent?'"

Raphael chuckled. "Only if you want to do it right."

Gabriel froze. "Oh. They told you."

Raphael's eyes popped. "You actually said that?" Gabriel nodded wearily. "No one ever told me anything. It just sounded like something you'd say to me." Raphael sounded pained. "You went through a wringer to stay true, didn't you?"

"You don't understand," Gabriel whispered. "By that point, he had me enjoying it."

A cloud of shame clung to both of them. Remiel's wings flared. "Guys, get a grip. Gabriel didn't go with him. It doesn't matter how close you came. You didn't."

Neither of them would look at one another, and those emotions kept building. Guilt? Shame? "I thought you worked this out," she said. "It's okay. It's over."

Raphael said, "You talked to her about *that*?"

Gabriel bit his lip. "I needed advice."

Raphael bristled, then turned his back and went to Jesus's side.

Remiel put a hand on Gabriel's shoulder. He felt cold like iron in the moonlight. "Please forgive me. I'm sorry. I spoke without thinking because I thought it was funny."

"It's okay." He forced a smile at her. "You're right, except Jesus is worth more than twice what I am. Satan would have overspent for me. Or maybe he just can't pay what Jesus is really worth."

As the sun was setting, Jesus accepted an invitation to stay at someone's house, and the angels trailed him there. His host invited several friends to dinner so they could keep talking, among them a man named Andrew. "I'm only here for tonight," Jesus said. "I need to return to Nazareth tomorrow, to help my family with preparations for a wedding" and Andrew volunteered to go with him. "I've got a brother I want to meet you," Andrew said. "I think you'll like him. His name is Simon."

Chaos in the kitchen.

Mary was baking bread to bring to the wedding, and she'd sent Simon and Andrew to the market for more supplies. Raphael and Uriel guarded from the rooftop while Gabriel and Jesus had talked mathematics for the better part of the morning. Their conversation had continued right through the bread's mixing, kneading, shaping and baking. Remiel remained in a desolid state on the sidelines, but Jesus had looked at her more than once with a smile.

Zadkiel sat cross-legged beside Remiel. She had a flute in her hands, but rather than playing she only ran her hands over the holes.

"There's something about this wedding," Remiel said. "Do you feel it?"

Zadkiel agreed.

Across the room, Gabriel created a design on the table-top, and the light pattern of whatever he was drawing reflected on their faces as he manipulated the light points.

I wish there were anything I enjoyed that much, Zadkiel sent to Remiel.

Remiel laughed. Mary pivoted toward their corner, but Uriel sent reassurance, and she turned back to the bread. Remiel shivered: Mary couldn't feel any difference between the Irin.

Unaware of that simple and yet arrow-sharp exchange, Zadkiel sent, *How much are they going to bake?*

Remiel shook off the feeling. *I guess as much as they can for this wedding tomorrow. They'll pack it up and head out for Cana this afternoon.*

Zadkiel frowned. *How many people attend a wedding?*

I don't know, but it would be embarrassing to run out of something as simple as bread.

Mary looked over Gabriel's shoulder. "I'm uncertain if this is supposed to make sense."

Remiel laughed out loud, and Gabriel shot her a look. "It's just geometry." He stood so Mary could get closer to the lightwork lacing the tabletop. The imagery glistened against the surface, a richer color where it was dusted with flour. Mary knelt beside Jesus before the table, and Gabriel leaned over her, retracing the image with a white light over the blue designs.

"I understand some of it," Mary said, "but then you start talking about four- and five-dimensional objects, and you've lost me."

"It's really not that hard." Gabriel reached over Mary to show her something else.

"Here we go again," Remiel said.

"He has no problem visualizing things that give even other Cherubim a headache," Zadkiel said. "He forgets that angels see things humans can't."

"For example," Remiel said, "other angels."

"That would be one, yes." Zadkiel laughed. "Tesseracts, three- and four-component matrices, sine waves and hyperbolic sine waves together, exponential formulae..."

Gabriel finished his explanation and looked down at Mary expectantly.

Mary inched up and kissed him on the cheek.

Remiel and Zadkiel exploded with laughter as Gabriel's feathers fluffed. He bolted to the far wall, staring at Mary, his cheeks bright pink.

Raphael and Uriel dropped through the roof.

Gabriel and Mary stared at one another, and Mary held her breath as if the world had stood still.

Then Gabriel forced a smile. "You could warn me when you're going to do something like that." His voice was unsteady.

Jesus chuckled. "So you could be in another country by the time she got near?"

Gabriel projected agreement. His wings were trembling.

Mary said, "I'm sorry. You're just... You think a normal person can absorb that?"

Gabriel gestured toward Jesus. "He absorbs it."

"He's a lot smarter than I am. That's my point." Mary stepped away from the table. "I'm sorry. I didn't mean to embarrass you."

Jesus grinned at him. "It's all right. I'm not going to strike you down." He winked. "Don't be afraid. She's just my mother."

"I don't want to think of the penalties for propositioning your mother." Gabriel inched back toward to the table.

"It sounds more like she propositioned you," Raphael said.

Mary said, "Am I that scary?"

Gabriel was looking into Raphael's eyes, and momentarily his whole soul seemed steadier.

Michael appeared in the kitchen, his sword in its scabbard. "Everything all right?"

"Nothing Mary couldn't handle," Remiel said, and Zadkiel smothered a laugh. Gabriel folded his arms and shot a dark look in their direction.

"Gabriel had to fight off a scary force," Zadkiel added.

"*You* may have to fight off a scary force in a minute." Gabriel returned to the table. Raphael's eyes sparkled, and Gabriel continued brightening as he looked at Mary. "You know, I'm flattered, but I couldn't possibly return your attentions. You're so much younger than I am."

Mary ran a hand through her floured hair. "I'll try to nurse my broken heart."

Remiel sent Michael an image of Mary kissing Gabriel, and Michael struggled to contain the laughter. Gabriel rolled his eyes. "Remiel, come here and draw me a tesseract."

"I'll be right there," she said. "As soon as I figure out how to do that."

Jesus said, "We probably need to cut the lesson short anyhow. Let's wrap the bread and get it loaded for the trip."

Mary and Jesus headed to Cana with the disciples. Gabriel left to assist Saraquael with an assignment across the globe. Remiel stayed; on the peripheries, she could detect a curious darkness.

Is something about to happen? she asked Raphael.

Raphael frowned. *You sense it too?*

Remiel folded her arms, sitting intangibly inside the bread and keeping it dust-free as the donkey pulled the cart over the rutted roads.

Raphael sent, *I think our enemies are feeling it as well.*

In lieu of words Remiel drew her sword, laying it across her lap.

Uriel pivoted, concerned.

Remiel kept her senses as broad as possible, scanning. No demons attacked on the road.

Zadkiel patrolled the wedding, armored. Demons were present, as at most human gatherings, but none of the higher ranks, and they limited their activities to specific people.

A haze of worry emanated from the groom's parents, and she drifted toward them where they spoke with the steward. Zadkiel flagged Michael.

Uriel approached, projecting questions.

Zadkiel shook her head. "I'm not sure."

Michael appeared. "Anything wrong?"

They listened in, and it became apparent the steward was reporting an embarrassing problem: someone had miscounted the wine vats. Apparently some were empty or some had been misplaced, or perhaps even stolen. Regardless, after the current supply ran out, they had no more wine.

Mary was looking across the crowd at Uriel. Their eyes met.

Zadkiel said, "Did Mary happen to bring wine with all that bread?"

Uriel chuckled. "She would have if she'd known."

"It's not demons," Michael said. "Not our problem."

Zadkiel said, "Still, I could get some wine from somewhere."

Michael sounded shocked. "Steal it?"

"No, I mean barter without the previous owner exactly knowing about it." Zadkiel winked. "There's plenty of unused wine in this world, and plenty of people who would exchange it for a favor I could easily provide. I'd make sure they were very well-compensated."

Michael shook his head.

In mid-agreement, Uriel paused.

Michael and Zadkiel focused their attention where Uriel had, and they found Mary speaking with Jesus. Zadkiel flashed to them in time to hear Mary say, "They have no more wine."

"What is that to me?" Jesus said.

Mary called over the waiters.

Jesus said to her in a low voice, "It's not my hour yet."

The waitstaff had gathered, and Mary rested a hand on Jesus's arm. "Do whatever he tells you."

They stared at him, more than a little confused. Mary just smiled at Jesus with the same mischievous smile that had kissed Gabriel.

Jesus took a deep breath. To the waiters he said, "Fill six stone vats with water, right to the brim."

Michael radiated surprise. Raphael glowed like the sun.

Zadkiel followed the waiters as they filled the vats. They all emitted a hazy stream of emotions: resentment (the things were heavy); worry (they might not get paid if the wedding was ruined); confusion (what did water have to do with wine?)

As the men filled the stone vats, that sodden sense of the enemy dampened the air around Zadkiel. She turned, sword drawn, to find Asmodeus standing between the waiters and the wedding; a moment later, Belior sat on the well.

"Don't," Belior murmured. "Guests know the difference between water and wine. Who will they blame? The groom? Certainly not. Water down the wine that much and they'll blame the waitstaff for stealing the wine and replacing it with this."

Asmodeus ignited, emitting a sense of danger: if the men returned to the wedding with containers of water, it would go badly for them.

Belior said, "If you're lucky, they'll only withhold your wages. If you're not, the Romans have penalties for theft."

Asmodeus intensified the feeling of danger. The waitstaff regarded one another uneasily.

Zadkiel sent, *Saraquael! Michael!* She flew at Asmodeus with her sword drawn.

Asmodeus raised his sword and braced himself to meet her charge. Zadkiel struck, then flipped so her momentum carried her over his head and she could strike at his back. He snapped up his wings to knock her from the air, but she twisted to avoid the blow. She swung again, but he pivoted and parried.

His eyes glowed with a double-shine: Belior was calculating her movements, giving Asmodeus the advantage of a second set of eyes as well as his power.

Zadkiel called again for Saraquael.

Asmodeus blasted her with his soul-energy. She threw up a Guard in time to deflect it, but the force drove her to the ground. She rolled to regain her footing before he struck again, but he blasted ahead of her, so she yanked backward and found herself staring upward at him.

Remiel streaked directly over Zadkiel's head, tackling Asmodeus off his feet before he could hit a third time. Behind her, Saraquael pulled her upright, then flashed her back to Jesus and his mother. He returned to the fray to help Remiel.

Zadkiel spread her wings and leaped back into the air, her sword glowing. Asmodeus and Belior had called a dozen other demons, but Zadkiel wasn't watching the newcomers. She kept her eyes on the waiters.

Go on, she urged. *Do whatever he tells you. You won't get in trouble. The worst that could happen is they laugh at* him— *and think of the story you'll have! This crazy guy made you fill water vats and pretend it was wine.*

The waiters, unable to see the angelic standoff, resumed carrying the stone vats to the steward.

Zadkiel cheered, then dropped to stand beside Jesus.

He met her eyes. *Do you have any idea what's going to happen?*

She smiled. "I only know they did what you told them."

Jesus smiled.

Zadkiel froze. Satan appeared beside Belior. At a standoff, the angels remained with swords drawn, everyone on highest alert.

The servers returned to Jesus. He said, "Now draw some out and take it to the steward."

They regarded Jesus uneasily.

"Do it," Zadkiel murmured, putting angelic pressure on them. "Do it."

Satan began applying counter-pressure, and she urged them again with her heart.

The server filled a cup and brought it to the steward.

Zadkiel said, "What happens now?"

Jesus folded his arms and tucked down his chin, hiding a smile. *He samples it.*

"And then if an ordinary man or angel had given the orders," Zadkiel said, "he spits it out and gets angry."

Jesus looked coy. *And because I gave the orders...?*

Zadkiel said, "A miracle occurs?"

As she said this, the steward sampled the wine. He paused, took another swallow, and then turned to the groom, surprised. The waiters looked worried, but the steward stopped, as if confused. "Oh, yes," he said, "you can distribute it. This is fine."

Zadkiel shot a smug look to Satan, who hadn't reacted. He'd gone from watching the steward to studying Jesus.

The steward approached the groom, so Zadkiel flashed to his side. The steward said in a soft voice, "Most people serve the better wine first, and then when people have been drinking a while, bring out the lesser wines. But you've saved the best for the end."

The groom looked shocked. "What?"

The steward put a hand on his shoulder. "There's plenty. Don't worry. There's more than plenty."

Back with Mary and Jesus, Zadkiel watched a waiter pouring more wine for both of them, and Mary held it so she could see better. But wine was more than seeing. Wine was in the taste, the smell, the feeling on the tongue and in the throat. It was a physical thing, and she was only in a subtle body.

Zadkiel whispered, "Can I try some?"

Jesus kept his voice low. "Haven't you had wine before?"

"Once." Zadkiel looked up. "The only time I ever took on a human body."

Jesus shrugged. "It probably tastes like that."

"I want the wine you made." Zadkiel stepped closer. "I want to taste wine expressed the way it only can be when my Lord says *wine*." She wrapped her hand around his, and he looked her in the eyes. "If I give you a sense, will you give me a sense? What if I give up my sight?"

Jesus pulled back. "Zadkiel, no."

"How about only when I'm solid?" Zadkiel nodded. "I could retain my angelic sight, but I would be blind when I'm human."

Jesus still looked troubled. "That's not fair unless you would forever be able to recreate the experience."

Zadkiel brightened. "I would do that! I've only ever been solid once before. I can't imagine a future where I'd be missing out on much."

Zadkiel asked permission, and God made her solid. Among the tumult of the wedding she found herself wearing a wedding garment, her long hair loose and her pale wings gone.

She took the cup from Jesus's hands, and he let it go. She ran her fingertips over the smoothness of the pottery, the way it remained warm from his human touch. She swirled the wine in the cup and inhaled the aroma just as the steward had done. The bouquet permeated her, and she thrilled to be here, right here in this moment. She tilted the cup so the sunlight struck the wine's rich red tones.

"Don't be afraid." Jesus put a hand on her shoulder. "Do what you want."

Zadkiel closed her eyes like a bride expecting her first kiss, and she sipped.

Darkness overtook her the moment the wine met her lips. The cool liquid, the alcohol's heat, the bitterness of grapes and its contrast with fermented sugar, the scent of vineyards and the taste of ceramic – they mingled until they'd seared themselves into her heart with a joy that made her smile. Her eyes flared open as she turned to Jesus, but she couldn't see him. She could feel his hand on her, but although she opened her eyes, nothing changed. Not blackness, not swirling grey, simply nothing at all, as if her eyes no longer existed.

Other angels clustered around her with curiosity, concern. But there was that warmth of Jesus at her side, so she glanced toward him again with a pang because she couldn't see him with human eyes any longer. She drank again from the cup and allowed the flavor to wash through her.

Jesus sounded gentle. "You don't have to drink the cup to the bottom."

Zadkiel pivoted toward his voice. "It wouldn't be fair to back out after I've gotten what you promised."

"Is it worth what it costs?" Jesus said.

Zadkiel nodded. "More than that."

Mary stayed on Zadkiel's other side as she finished the cup. Her head reeled, but not enough to worry her. Saraquael joined her, but she didn't speak to him, only lived in the moment. This wedding, this empty cup, this man at her side, this solid body thrilling with joy because of the gift she'd just received.

Saraquael felt worried, so she turned toward him. *It's wonderful!*

His spiritual fingers brushed over her soul. She stepped forward, tilted her head toward where she knew his face would be.

Are you happy? he asked, and she assented. *Then I'm happy for you too.*

Taking her arm, Mary guided Zadkiel through the crowd. The noise lessened, and then she found herself with her hands on the back of a chair.

Mary said, "Do you want to sit?"

"No." Zadkiel smiled. A glorious wedding. Glorious wine. "I want to dance."

The next stop was Capernaum. On the Sabbath, Jesus brought his disciples to the synagogue and read the daily prayers, and then started talking about the scriptures.

Raphael settled in to listen. Flush with power, Jesus right now didn't need a guardian angel the way most people did. With the Spirit directing and guiding Jesus in his ministry, Raphael found his own job changing to more of a supporting role. All the same, he could sense the demonic attention and warned Jesus when they got too interested.

For example, Raphael sent, *that one.*

Jesus looked toward the door just as a man charged in, eyes wild. His soul was wrapped tightly by a demon, and the demon crackled with a dark electricity. "Leave us alone! What have we ever done to you, Jesus of Nazareth?"

Jesus stood, but the man shouted, "I know who you are! You're the holy one of God!"

"Be quiet!" Jesus pointed at the man, and Raphael felt Jesus enwrapping that black spirit with his will. "You! Get out of him!"

Raphael cringed as Jesus ripped the demon right off the man's soul, both the demon and the man screaming as they separated. The man collapsed into a fetal position, hands over his face. The demon snapped out of the world, back into Hell.

Raphael drew closer to Jesus, for all the good that did. Clearly he had the situation under control. But the onlookers had backed away, shocked. *Who was this? How did he do that?*

Jesus crouched on the ground beside the man and helped him to sit up. "It's gone." Then he put an arm over his shoulder, and while seated beside the man, he spoke in a lower voice to the crowd about Isaiah. About deliverance. And the people pushed closer to hear better.

Jesus stayed at Simon's home, but people began flocking to the house. *Rabbi, my daughter is sick. Rabbi, my sister has a demon.* Jesus had healed Simon's mother-in-law, and she was trying to show him gratitude and hospitality by making a meal, but Jesus had no time between visitors to enjoy the food.

You have to eat something, Raphael sent.

Have you been talking to my mother? Jesus replied with a smile.

Raphael grinned at him. *For about thirty years, yes.*

After a few hours, it seemed the whole city had gathered at Simon's front door, so Jesus moved away from the house to give them some space. He healed as many as they could bring to them. "But we need to keep the demons quiet," Jesus told Raphael. "They know who I am, and I'd rather they not try twisting the truth around."

A man came up to Jesus. "I need you to come to my home. My wife is sick. She can't get up. She stays in the dark. She might have a demon."

Someone with him said, "She's been like this for years. There's a curse on her."

The man's guardian took Raphael by the hand, and they flashed together to the wife's side. Her guardian sat with her, radiating hope. "Can he come?"

Raphael couldn't detect anything demonic on the woman. He rested his hand on her head: healthy enough, although a bit weak. Nothing wrong enough to keep her bed-ridden.

Raphael returned to Jesus and sent him the information. Jesus said, "I'll go with you to see her after we send the crowd away."

It took another hour, but Jesus managed to work through the crowd of people. Then the man led Jesus to his home. His wife's darkened room had a dank odor, like yeast and dust untouched by sunlight for years.

"I brought the healer," the man said.

"Tell him to go away. I don't want him."

Jesus settled at the foot of her bed. "There's no demon, and you aren't sick."

She curled around herself. "Make everyone go away. Just make them go."

Jesus said, "Talk to me."

Whenever he'd told the demons to be quiet, they'd quieted right up, but telling a woman to talk didn't have a similar result. She started crying, and her husband held onto her.

"When did this start happening?" Jesus said.

Neither responded.

Jesus said, "Let me touch you."

The man eased his wife's hand from her face, and Jesus clasped it, not recoiling from the tears. He said, "It's been two years."

The man drew a sharp breath.

Jesus said, "You had a baby. But at the end of the labor, the baby died."

The woman kept crying, but now her sharp breaths were audible.

"But it's more than that. They said you were cursed."

The man whispered, "The baby. The baby was...horrible."

Jesus said to the woman, "And they didn't let you see your son."

She sat up. "A boy? The child was a boy?"

Raphael had gone cold, but Jesus only moved closer. "They took the child from you, and they wouldn't let you see him, only told you he was a monster and you must be under a curse, and they wouldn't tell you anything else about him. You never held your firstborn son. And...you haven't had any children since."

The man said, "How can she? She's cursed."

Jesus stroked the tear-stained hand, and the woman leaned closer. "They blamed you. And you accepted that blame, but I'm telling you now, it wasn't your fault."

She whispered, "I'm a sinful woman."

Jesus put a hand on her forehead. "Your sins are forgiven you. The child didn't die because of your sins or because of your husband's sins. There is no curse."

Tears streaked her cheeks. "I want my baby."

Jesus squeezed her hand. "Do you think I can give you back your baby?"

She swallowed hard. "I just want to see him."

The man exclaimed, "He was a monster!"

Jesus turned to the man. "Would you keep a mother from her child? Doesn't God love people despite their sins? And don't men's sins leave them uglier than the worst monster?" He turned to the woman. "Open your arms."

Raphael gasped as Jesus formed an image of light, and the woman reached forward. "It's just a picture," he said, "like a sculpture, not your baby. But it's just how he looked."

She touched him. "Just like this? Exactly?" She rested her hand on the image. "I can feel him! Can I hold him?"

She didn't wait for an answer, just gathered the light-baby into her arms. Her attention was riveted to the tiny boy. "Is this how he looked? This?"

Her husband, ashen, nodded.

"This isn't so bad." She stroked the face with her fingertips. "He's not so bad! You told me he was terrible to look at, that he'd give me nightmares. That I couldn't see him for my own good." She pressed the baby to her chest and looked at him again. "Light the lamps. Let me really see him."

She explored the baby. "He had fingers! He had toes! You said he was a monster. I thought, what if he had claws?"

The baby's face bore the worst of the deformity: he had only one eye, no nose, and a deep cleft through his upper lip. The mother traced his cheeks with her fingers, tears splashing through the light-image onto the arm under the baby's back. "He wasn't so bad," she whispered. "He's perfect. The shape of his head is just like my brother's. And how flat his ears were." She looked up at Jesus. "It wasn't so bad."

Jesus shook his head.

She cuddled the baby up to her chest, just staring at him.

Jesus got to his feet. "Stay with him for a while. When you're ready, tell me."

In the next room Jesus sat at the table, resting his head in his hands.

Raphael said nothing because he could feel Jesus praying. Praying about grief. Praying about a woman with the light flushed from her heart because well-meaning people tried to protect a mother from her own child.

Jesus looked up after a moment. "I want you to remember this."

Raphael said, "I will, but why?"

"Protecting people from themselves. You can't do it." He shook his head. "In the future. Keep that in mind. Imagination is almost always worse than reality. Look at what is rather than what you fear."

Jesus and Raphael prayed together as the night drew on. The lamp burned lower. Eventually the woman emerged from her room. Her hair was ragged and her clothes rumpled, but she was standing and had light in her eyes. "I'll never be ready," she whispered, "but it's time. Thank you. Thank you so much."

She kissed the light baby's forehead, and the baby disappeared. With a choke, she turned down her head and closed her eyes.

Behind her, her husband said, "Please forgive me. I thought I was doing what was best."

Jesus kissed the man on the cheek. "Your sins are forgiven too. Be in peace. Grieve an honest grief."

There were hours more until daylight. Jesus moved toward the door, but the man said, "Please accept my hospitality."

Jesus said, "Thank you, but no."

He went onto the street, Raphael at his side. "Where are we going?"

Jesus said, "Outside the city. Let's find someplace quiet to pray until sunrise, and tomorrow we'll head to other towns. There are more wounds to heal."

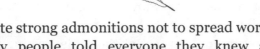

Despite strong admonitions not to spread word of what he'd done, many people told everyone they knew about Jesus's healings, and they came to him in crowds. Some people came, got what they wanted, and left. Others came, left, and came back again. Some began staying all the time, though.

And other people, it galled Gabriel to realize, stayed just to gather information so they could argue.

"It's not supposed to be like that," Gabriel insisted to Raphael as they entered the synagogue. "Yes, Cherubim argue, and skepticism has its place, but some of these people began with the preferred conclusion, and they're gathering only data in support of that conclusion. That's called confirmation bias, and it's not conducive to obtaining accurate results."

Raphael may or may not have been humoring him, but he sent his fire into Gabriel. "You love a good argument."

Gabriel said, "A good argument makes me love the opposing opinion enough to embrace it. Although I may modify it," he corrected himself. "They're not doing that."

People fell into several clearly-defined categories, and Gabriel reviewed those present with Michael: people who wanted something from Jesus. They'd get what they want and leave, no problem. People who didn't care one way or the other: again, not a security issue for Jesus or for his ministry, although obviously it would benefit them to become more interested. "But of the opponents," Gabriel said, "we have some individuals in power who are afraid they're going to lose authority."

Michael ran his fingers over his scabbard. "Like Herod."

"Herod isn't here now. But the Pharisees and the teachers are nervous because he keeps challenging them." Gabriel's eyes lit up. "See, I'd love that, but for some reason they don't. Maybe they don't recognize the ways an honest argument would lead them to a more highly-defined truth, but they're scared. And people afraid of losing power are unpredictable."

Michael said, "I've got forces listening. I'm also monitoring the Romans, but for the moment the Romans don't seem to care."

"The Romans don't worry me as much because their core beliefs aren't being challenged. It's all alien to them." Gabriel shrugged. "Still, I can't help but wonder how Jesus will win them over."

Gabriel followed Jesus to the front where he began teaching. Some of the elders watched with mistrustful eyes, and Gabriel tightened his wings against their stares even though they couldn't see him. The judging looks — too familiar. He'd passed judgment like that in the past. And others had passed judgment on him.

He looked impulsively at Raphael, and Raphael turned to him with a smile. "It's okay."

Gabriel shivered.

Jesus noticed a man whose hand was crumpled, and he walked closer to him.

The nearest Pharisees leaned forward.

Jesus said to the man, "Come here." The man's arm was scarred around the wrist, and his left hand was noticeably smaller than the right. The bony fingers twisted around each other. Raphael probed the man's body and named the problems one after the next: atrophy; neuropathy; the remnants of a crushing injury to the wrist decades old, before the bones had stopped growing.

Jesus turned to the Pharisees. "Is it lawful to do good on the Sabbath or to do evil? Is it lawful to save a life?"

The men didn't answer, but Jesus's face hardened with anger. He turned to the man and said, "Stretch out your hand."

The man seemed surprised, but he opened his hand, and it was whole.

Jesus glared at the Pharisees, but none of them said anything to him. One whispered to another, though, and then both slipped out.

Michael followed, then returned "We may want to get out of here. They're talking about contacting Herod."

"But that was brilliant!" Gabriel exclaimed. "It was beyond brilliant—they can't condemn him because there's nothing illegal about stretching out your hand on the Sabbath. Jesus didn't do anything to indicate he was even performing the healing. In order to claim he healed on the Sabbath, they need to testify to his divine healing power. How can they?"

Michael didn't seem convinced.

Jesus stayed another few hours, then left the town. They stopped at the edge of a Sabbath's journey and waited for sundown, then continued toward the hills. The group at this point was mostly the followers who never left. Andrew. Simeon. Philip. Nathaniel.

At night when the disciples settled down, Jesus went up the mountain to pray, Raphael with him. Gabriel stayed at Jesus's side, enjoying the vibrations of the gentle talk between Father and Son as he went over what was happening and what he planned.

Jesus widened his gaze and looked over the world as the sun rose. *Satan offered me all this,* he sent to Raphael. *But I'm about to engage in a little bit of thievery.*

Raphael chuckled.

Jesus opened his heart, and Raphael stopped laughing to radiate shock. Gabriel reached into Raphael to feel whatever had startled him, and there before him he felt humanity. All of it.

Millions of souls. Billions. Waiting, arrayed through time and space.

Jesus surveyed them all, and he began calling the ones he wanted. Not with his voice, but rather with his heart, as if there were harp strings from each of them back to him and he were the peg holding them into creation. Like a harpist stroking her instrument, Jesus reached into time and strummed through all those souls, finding the ones he wanted especially to serve him and become his apostles. He called them wherever they were hidden, summoning them with the soul's equivalent of music.

Gabriel tucked closer to him, wrapping himself in that harmony of loving God together. Because as Jesus called them, they responded. They neared him even if they didn't know now what it was they longed for. God had time: they didn't need to come now, but they needed to come someday. A young girl raised in a believing family surrounded by holiness all her life. A man deemed ineducable and yet with piercing insight into the human heart. A crippled girl hated by her own family and forced to live in the barn, all the while filled with care for the poor and hungry. A poet who literally stripped naked in the street just to divest himself of the world.

All of these, Jesus prayed. *These are the ones I want.*

The sun nudged above the horizon, and Jesus prayed and summoned and prayed some more. And then, as dawn overspread the world, he descended the mountain into the crowd of people who had followed him this far. He chose twelve.

Simon and Andrew were obvious choices. Another set of brothers, James and John, also joined. There was Philip and Nathaniel. There were two zealots, Judas and Simon.

"This is so exciting," said Nivalis, guardian angel to Judas Iscariot. She and Gabriel sat overhead on a tree branch. "He's always wanted to work for God and change the world, and here he is! I never dared dream he'd come this close to the Messiah!"

They listened to Jesus as intently as the human crowd did, Gabriel hungering to take in these stories and re-create them word-for-word in a document where he could analyze the word choice and the stresses and the vocal tone. He'd heard so many of these stories before, and yet here they came again, and here he listened again, and it was so easy to become the players in these stories. He could be a woman sweeping a house to find a missing coin. He could be a farmer scattering seed (actually, he had been a farmer scattering seed, hadn't he?) and he certainly remembered what it was like to be a shepherd.

Nivalis said, "Wasn't Jesus working as a carpenter? Why doesn't he ever use carpentry in his parables?"

Gabriel chuckled. "I asked him that. He wants people to relate to the situations he's bringing up. Most of them would have no clue what he meant if he said, 'The kingdom of God is like a bradawl.'"

Nivalis said, "The Kingdom of God is like a table built with cedar wood rather than soft pine."

Gabriel laughed. She went on, "To what shall I compare the Kingdom of God? A man uses a level that is flat. If the level is warped, what good then will the shelf be? The resulting furniture is useful for nothing but throwing into the fire."

"There you go," said Gabriel. "He'd make it work, but the people around him would wonder why they'd gotten a carpentry lesson and start asking if he could heal their bunions."

Nivalis said, "They do that anyhow. Judas is just itching for the day they start really building the Kingdom, though. Get these people fired up enough and they could bring down Rome."

Year 31

In the darkness, Mary whispered, "Gabriel? Are you around?"

After so long, she knew how many deep breaths it took until either an angel appeared or else an angel wasn't going to respond. She never asked what caused the slight delay, since they could disappear from one spot and reappear in another without moving through the spaces between, but she imagined it took time to send word and then to take leave of whatever they were doing, and of course if they were on assignment for God, they wouldn't respond at all. As it should be.

This time, on the last breath, Gabriel's presence prickled on the edge of her consciousness. She waited, and he prompted her without appearing: Was she all right?

Mary hesitated. Maybe she shouldn't have asked for Gabriel. Except who else could she ask? Raphael needed to stay with Jesus. Michael was fighting evil. Gabriel had important work to do too, a thing she never doubted, and yet he seemed to have more mobility than the others. But he was so...well, logical about things.

"Oh, you're not all right." He became tangible and seeable, and he reached for her hand. "You're...scared?"

She chuckled weakly. "It's obvious?"

Obvious in the midnight dark. Obvious to an angel's eyes.

Gabriel said, "I'm looking at the chemicals you're putting out in your brain. They look like fear."

"More like worry." She extended a hand, and he took it. "How is Jesus doing?"

He squeezed. "He's the Son of God. He's doing God's work."

"That's not an answer." Her eyes watered, but she didn't sit up and she didn't swipe back the tears. "John— They just beheaded John."

"I know. I was there." Gabriel tilted his head, and his eyes gleamed silver in the dark. "I can't assure you Jesus is perfectly safe and comfortable every hour of every day. But he's eating and sleeping, and he's in good health."

Mary said, "And people want him dead."

Gabriel leaned forward. "If they didn't, he wouldn't be doing his job."

She huffed. "You're not helping."

"Once again, I have no children," Gabriel said, "and my kind don't suffer and die, so it's a struggle to relate to your concerns. I'm trying."

She relaxed back onto her bed. "Thank you."

"But it's not satisfactory." He rested a hand on her shoulder. "Is there any way I can help you, since I can't offer reassurance? I could put you straight to sleep."

She shook her head. "I'll just worry again in the morning."

"Worries are bigger in the dark," Gabriel said. "I remember how that surprised me."

Mary picked up her head. "Tell me a story. Tell me about that time when you became a man."

Gabriel sat back. "That's not a bedtime story."

"Well, then tell me about the winnowing."

Gabriel's eyes widened. "That's even less a bedtime story. You really won't get any sleep."

Gabriel turned his attention to Uriel, and from both sides she felt a back-and-forth too quick to follow. Finally Gabriel said, "If I tell you the story, will you let me spin some of your fleece?"

She frowned in the dark. "Let you?" His discomfort prickled in her mind. "You'd be doing me a favor, and then you'd be doing me another favor in exchange for it?"

Gabriel sounded gentle. "I enjoy spinning, but I can't just sneak into someone's supply closet and use up the fleece supply."

Mary said, "What will I do with it? I mean, I can't sell it."

"Why not?" Gabriel hesitated. "If it comes out sub-par, I'll return it to fleece and you can re-spin it to sell it then."

"That's not what I mean. I mean, yarn made by angels would be priceless."

Gabriel chuckled. "Don't tell them they can't afford it."

A soft noise told Mary the basket and the spindle had appeared in front of Gabriel, and then more sounds got some fleece started on the spindle.

"Okay, so close your eyes, and think about a time when all the morning stars sang together." Gabriel twirled the spindle, paying attention to the fleece as it twisted into yarn. Mary could tell from the sound that he was making it fine, strong.

With her eyes closed, Mary began feeling a sensation she couldn't name. She was, but she wasn't. She felt comfortable, and she'd existed a long time, but a part of her knew she was still young in a way she didn't recognize at the moment. She was Gabriel, a Gabriel back a long time ago.

God called, and Gabriel appeared before Him in a hall with a cavernous ceiling and a throne at the front. She knelt, and the Spirit began speaking inside.

That as the head of her choir, she had an assignment.

That God would engage in a new act of Creation.

That God would take a material form.

That the angels would be expected to worship God in that form.

The story stopped here, and Mary jolted back to herself. Gabriel stopped his spindle, eyes ashine. "You have no idea why that's strange."

Mary rolled to face him. "If God wants to do something, He should do it."

"If God told you He was going to take the form of a sheep, you wouldn't be more than a little disquieted?"

Mary squinted. "You appear disquieted."

Gabriel took a deep breath. "I explained to the Spirit why that wasn't a good idea."

"You didn't!"

A flash of his eyes. Gabriel probably had no idea how fierce he looked when that happened, and Mary shivered. "Absolutely I did! *Let me tell you what it's like,* I said. *You won't know everything. You'll find you have limits. There will be things you have to guess and areas of darkness in your mind. You'll feel clumsy and inadequate at times. Everything is fine the way it is, and I love you the way you are.*"

He spun the spindle again, but it was too fast. That yarn was going to come out thin as a hair and strong as copper wire.

"Let's say God tells you he's going to become a sheep." Gabriel looked ferocious as he worked the spindle. "And your first reaction is, 'But sheep stink. Sheep are stupid. Sheep generate random sheep-pies. Why would you do that?' and He says, 'Because I like sheep.' So your next thought makes it almost palatable: 'It'll be a special kind of sheep? At least able to talk?' No, it's just going to be a sheep. 'But it will at least be a smart sheep?' Not especially." Gabriel shuddered. "Wouldn't you think it was insane? And then God shows you this sheep and says, 'Now worship it.' But it's just a sheep!"

Mary said, "And God didn't change his mind, I take it."

"Close your eyes again," he said.

Gabriel tore out of the Judgment Hall crazed. She flung herself at Raphael, incoherent enough that she needed to explain three times before he even understood what had happened. Yet she had to prepare the rest of the Cherubim for this and help sort out the ones who had problems, when she couldn't even figure it out for herself.

Raphael called for Lucifer, who had just come out of his own interview. Gabriel ranted at him in a rage, and Lucifer held her, soothed her, reassured her that he'd take care of it. He'd talk to God again and it would be fine. *If I can do it, you can do it.* "You're not thinking," Gabriel insisted. "Consider what we're being asked to do. It's not reasonable or sane."

Lucifer said, "It's not God's job to be reasonable or sane, is it? He only has to give the orders, and it's our lot to respond. The whim of God is law to us. God isn't constrained by logic. Work with me. I've got an idea."

"That's the first time," Gabriel said out loud to Mary, "that I ever needed to have faith. Up until then, everything had a reason I could discern. Raphael insisted it didn't diminish us in any way to do this, but it certainly felt like it would."

"I can't imagine you crazed," Mary murmured. "But I still don't see an issue about God in a material form."

"You're a material being." Gabriel sounded a little less strident now. "Worshiping a sheep isn't quite a good parallel for you. Imagine if God asked you to worship him as that loaf of bread, or that cup of wine."

Mary said, "Were animals already around? Did Adam exist yet?"

"Animals, yes. Not yet Adam." A whirl as Gabriel resumed spinning. "I'm not sure it would have made a difference. The intelligence you possess is a mock-up of what we have. It would have been easier to bear if God had suggested he would take the form of a tree or a mountain or an ocean."

Mary hunched down in her bed..

"You asked," Gabriel said. "I don't still feel that way or I wouldn't be here turning fleece into yarn." He offered a smile. "Do you have any other questions that I can answer so you can perceive it as an insult?"

Mary chuckled. "You have a way with words. But the winnowing itself--what happened?"

Gabriel pointed at her, and she laughed as she closed her eyes again.

Mary felt herself again looking through a younger Gabriel's eyes, although she could tell time had passed. From God, a summons to all the angels to gather, and once again they took their places in spheres around the heavenly throne. God asked them to sing, and they did. As the song flowed through Mary, her eyes teared up again. This was the last time, their last song with all the angels together. They didn't realize it.

And then God's aspect revealed itself anew, as three persons in one: the Creator and the Word and the Sanctifier. Mary wondered a moment, but then Gabriel re-cast it as a Word and the Voice that spoke the Word, and then the Word's meaning, but all the same even though they were all a bit different. And as she relaxed into that definition, the Creator presented the Word in a material form. His Son. God, and to be worshipped.

But material. An animal. A hybrid.

Lucifer burst with light and challenged God, demanded an explanation and charged Him with setting whims out as laws. He said it wasn't rational, wasn't right, wasn't fitting. But God insisted.

Lucifer said, "Would you lose all of us to stay that way? Because we will not serve you like that."

Gabriel reached for Raphael through the bond, and Raphael was shocked, but sent reassurance, and then Raphael knelt and crossed his arms over his chest.

Lucifer struck at him. "Gabriel!" he called. "Follow me!"

Gabriel froze as Lucifer called a long roster of angels — more and more, and some came to him. Gabriel flashed to Raphael, who looked stunned. "No," Raphael whispered to her. "Don't go with him."

Lucifer turned to Gabriel with a glare made of liquid fire. He summoned Gabriel a second time, but she wrapped her fingers in Raphael's wings. "Get over here!" Lucifer shouted. "We need you. We need to stand together. And bring Raphael with you."

Raphael grabbed her hand, but she kept looking at Lucifer.

A green light streaked from the outer spheres of the angelic host—Michael, hurtling out of nowhere right in front of Lucifer. *Who is like God?* he kept asking. *Who is like God? We have to worship—we can't refuse!*

Michael drew his sword. He was shaking, and his blue eyes were terrified. "I'll stop you."

Lucifer struck Michael, breaking his sword.

Gabriel tore free of Raphael and rushed to cover Michael with her wings so Lucifer wouldn't hit him again. He was just an Archangel. But Michael dropped his broken sword and pulled Gabriel's from her scabbard, and he flew straight back at Lucifer.

Raphael cheered. Gabriel came to her senses and transferred all her power into the sword in the second before

Michael struck, and Raphael flooded her with his power to feed into the sword as well.

Michael struck. Lucifer blew back all three.

Mary registered surprise. Lucifer was that strong?

Assent from Gabriel: he's still that strong. Gabriel still wouldn't be able to defeat him.

Gabriel and Raphael armored themselves, and around them other Seraph-Cherub pairs did the same. The Cherubim realized quickly they could leverage their bonds to both power the Seraph and guide the Seraph's movements, making the Seraph a much more effective fighter. But then other angels joined up with Lucifer, insisting what God wanted was a disgrace, disgusting, unfathomable. And with that, war broke out in Heaven.

Now they needed not only to restrain Lucifer, but to prevent the spread of the lie. Because Lucifer was dissociating himself and spreading through the entire angelic realm. To each angel he was presenting a different set of reasons to resist God's order, each time carefully matched to the angel's own vulnerable spots. Or in some cases, misuse of their strengths.

Michael didn't get blown back again. Even without Gabriel's sword, he used his own broken blade to fight. None of Lucifer's most powerful allies had as much as noticed Michael before, but Lucifer realized immediately that he couldn't just swat Michael aside.

In fact, Michael's presence alone served as a summons to the other angels to resist Lucifer. That it wasn't enough just to watch, but they had to take sides.

Gabriel guided Raphael and Israfel as they clashed with the other high-order rebels to keep Michael covered doing his own work because clearly God was working through him.

And slowly Michael went from not being overpowered to actually being able to defend, to then pressing forward, to having a distinct advantage. His sword re-formed. His armor shone. He grew faster and stronger, and he pushed Lucifer toward the foot of the throne with his sword at his neck.

Lucifer looked up at the light of the Godhead and snarled, "You are not my God, and I am not your servant. I reject you. I will never serve you."

Michael grabbed Lucifer by the shoulders, and with his eyes a brilliance like the sun, he twisted reality until Lucifer had been flung out of Heaven and into Hell. A Hell that until that moment hadn't existed at all.

Michael turned to the rest of the angels, and with thunder in his voice, he exclaimed, "Choose!"

The ones who refused to serve tried to run, but Michael's forces rounded them up and expelled them from heaven too.

At Gabriel's side, Raphael dropped to his knees and crossed his wrists over his chest.

It was time. Gabriel knew it was time to make her choice, but when she looked at God as a material being, her stomach twisted, and she couldn't understand.

Finally Gabriel knelt. She clenched her teeth and went through with it.

Mary sat up. "Really?"

Gabriel drew his wings close. "It was enough. Barely. I did it in form. Now there would be no question."

Mary closed her eyes.

"It's a testament to God's mercy how He accepted that." Gabriel shook his head and watched the spindle twirl. "And then I took a census of who remained."

Mary didn't respond.

"I'm not proud of the way I handled things." Gabriel hunched his shoulders. "It was easiest to deal with the carnage as a type of intellectual exercise. It was only later that I really saw the hurting around us. One of Michael's closest friends fell. Two of mine. Seraph-Cherub bonds were broken. Remiel lost her twin brother."

Mary sat back. "It sounds horrible."

"I didn't want to believe it at first. God had told us it would be a test. I never dreamed anyone would fail, or that having failed they wouldn't then try again to do it right. Even less that they'd commit to doing it wrong."

Mary closed her eyes again, but the story didn't continue. No, she knew the rest. Lucifer became Satan. Satan accused the people, tested them, tried them, made demands and eventually got Adam to break God's one law for life in paradise.

Gabriel had a spindle full of yarn. "I told you it wasn't a bedtime story."

"No," she murmured. "But it's you. It's your history. Thank you."

He set the spindle in the basket. "God pulls us through. Even when it's as bad as you think it can get, and it makes no sense, God knows what He's doing. Try not to worry about Jesus."

Mary closed her eyes, and Gabriel played music for her. She couldn't place the sound, but the vibrations moved through her as if she could hear them with her ears rather than her heart, and before long she'd drifted to sleep.

"I actually don't need this right now," Raphael snapped.

Gabriel, with a Cherub's typical blindness to the blatantly obvious, said, "True, we aren't the point of his preaching, but surely you agree we can derive some greater understanding from the universality of the teachings he presents the humans."

Raphael turned his attention away from Gabriel back to the crowd. There had to be five thousand people here, maybe more if you counted the children scrambling around. Definitely one more if you counted the three year old sitting on Jesus's lap while he spoke to the crowd about the Kingdom of God.

Jesus had developed a rhythm to his teaching, and the people had gotten used to it, and the twelve were getting good at enforcing it. Jesus would talk loudly for a while, projecting his voice as far as it would go over the plains. Then he'd rest for a bit, have some water, talk to a few people. Sit with a child on his lap while he whittled some fantastical creature the child had never even conceived of. "Look, it's like a horse, but it has a neck as long as two men standing on one another's shoulders!" And the child would laugh, and Jesus would snicker, and Gabriel would say, "Giraffes aren't actually a close relation of horses."

Behind him now, Gabriel was saying, "The point about bad trees producing bad fruit is accurate enough, but he carries it further to say a bad tree can't produce good fruit. And yet we know God works all things together for the good of His children, so in the end, all fruit will in some way be good fruit. This creates difficulties in the process of discernment."

"You don't say," Raphael murmured, trying to keep at least some personal space around Jesus. More children were coming to him asking for silly animals, and he started work on another creation.

"Moreover," Gabriel went on, "within that bad fruit from the bad tree will be seeds, and the seeds themselves will yield good trees, which will then yield good fruit. This further complicates matters."

Andrew came up to Jesus and murmured, "The people have no bread. You need to send them away so they can find food."

Jesus didn't look up from his carving. "Give them something to eat yourselves."

Simon exclaimed, "There have to be five thousand men here! We don't have anything like what it would take to feed them."

Judas said, "Not to mention, we can't afford that much bread. It would take two hundred denarii at least."

Jesus looked up at Philip, who said, "We have five barley loaves and two fish."

Jesus handed the finished animal to a little boy, who laughed because who had ever heard of a rodent with a long flat bill like a duck's? Then he stood and said, "Get the people to sit in groups of fifty."

Gabriel stopped talking, watching with an alertness that matched Raphael's. *What's he going to do?*

Raphael thrilled as the crowd complied, a sea of people parting into little islands consisting of families, neighbors, friends. It took a long time, but then the twelve came back: now what?

Now what? Raphael put his hand on Jesus's shoulder, and Jesus said, "Bring me what food we have."

Just a little while ago, Gabriel sent, *didn't he refuse to turn stones into bread?*

Raphael moved in close to Jesus, feeling through Jesus's own anticipation, his own questions. Jesus set out baskets, breaking bread into all the baskets, and then he stood with the baskets arrayed before him and began the blessing.

Thomas whispered, "What is he doing?"

Judas whispered back, "Just watch. He had us casting out demons and healing the sick a little while ago—I bet he's going to do something."

Jesus looked to the twelve. "Distribute the bread."

Judas rushed forward to grab a basket, and he beamed. "Bread!"

They disciples rushed out with the baskets, but before Simon left with his, Raphael called, "Hey! You forgot someone."

Simon hesitated, then turned back to Jesus and handed him a loaf of bread. "You should eat too. Keep up your strength." He took a step back, then offered a smile. "Um...thank you. Thank you for feeding everyone."

Jesus met his smile with a grin of his own. "You're welcome. Go ahead and feed everyone — but make sure to keep the leftovers, that way nothing is lost."

Gabriel slipped past Raphael and examined the loaf in Jesus's hands. "This isn't just bread. It's Mary's bread." He looked up with light in his eyes. "Her consistency, her style."

Jesus winked at him. *Heaven won't be heaven without bread in it.*

Gabriel replied, *But you went for the familiar.*

How do you know they're not all tasting their own mother's bread?

Gabriel's wings flared, and he pivoted. "Really?" He turned back. "Oh, wait, you're joking around with me, aren't you? Wouldn't you make perfect bread?"

Jesus replied, *Don't tell anyone, but as a matter of fact, I would.*

Raphael kept scanning the crowd. *What next?*

Jesus replied, *They eat.*

The twelve were handing out bread and fish as fast as they could, people crowding up against them to make sure they got some even though the twelve kept insisting there was more than enough. *You eat too,* Raphael said. *You're exhausted.*

A little kid came up to Jesus with the carved giraffe and pushed it face-first into Jesus's bread. Jesus broke off a bit and pretended to feed the wooden animal, and the kid giggled. He fed it some of his own.

As the day waned, the twelve returned, their baskets still filled. Jesus looked back over the bread, but then picked up his head. Listened.

The people were cheering, watching him. "This is the prophet!" some were calling. Raphael went out to take the temperature of the crowd, then returned, trembling.

Jesus leaned closer to Simon. "I'm going to slip away. You keep the bread. I'll meet back with you in Capernaum."

Simon frowned. "Why?"

"Look at them. They want me to become king. I'm not going to do that."

Judas had been watching the exchange. "But why? You've got five thousand men here, ready to take orders from you! We could set up in Capernaum and drive out the Romans from there, then galvanize the rest of the country!"

Jesus shook his head. "That's not why I came. Disperse the crowd once they've finished eating, but I'm leaving now."

Judas called, "But we may never have a chance like this again!"

Jesus left them behind, walking out into the trees. "Raphael," he whispered, and Raphael wrapped around him and carried him away, up the mountain where he could be alone.

Raphael had to do everything but draw his sword that night to keep what seemed like hundreds of guardian angels from approaching Jesus with questions about everything he'd said that day on the mountain. Exhausted, Jesus needed to rest.

He had just settled to sleep when Gabriel slipped past Raphael, knelt where Jesus lay, and touched him on the shoulder.

Before Raphael could protest, Gabriel had awakened Jesus. He looked at the Cherub sleepily.

"I had a question," Gabriel said.

"It could have waited," Raphael snapped.

Jesus shook his head. "It's all right." He turned back to Gabriel. "And you didn't want to ask in front of a thousand people?"

Gabriel lowered his eyes. He had his hands folded. Raphael smoldered because Gabriel was wearing that perfect "servant" look when he'd just awakened Jesus for his own benefit. The disciples' guardians had all stopped their various activities and turned to watch, something Gabriel certainly knew. How private could this question be if he was willing to ask in front of twelve guardians?

"Earlier today, you told the crowd to love their enemies." Gabriel's wings tightened so he looked compact. "I think it's noble. I understand the concept of killing with kindness, but you're taking it step further into being kind because that's how the Father is."

Raphael said, "You woke him just for that?"

Gabriel pulled back in on himself and averted his gaze. "I'm sorry. Go back to sleep."

Jesus said, "Raphael, Gabriel: when one wins, both lose."

Gabriel stood.

"Stay," Jesus said. "I knew you were going to ask this when I said it. You might as well do it now. I'm awake."

Gabriel sat again. "It won't be long. You asked them to love their enemies, bless those who cursed them, and do good to those who persecuted them." When Jesus acknowledged this, Gabriel said, "Do you mean you want us to pray for Satan?"

Raphael's eyes flared. "Are you insane? You woke him up for that?"

Gabriel lowered his eyes. "I'll leave. I'm sorry."

Jesus smiled at Raphael. "Don't blame him. He's a Cherub with a question, and I'm the one who can answer it."

"What I've said is the logical conclusion to your statement." Gabriel wrung his hands. "If you meant that they should pray for those who persecute them, and for their enemies, then who else but their greatest enemy and their first persecutor?"

Jesus said, "You object to this."

Gabriel nodded. "I don't want him to succeed. Praying for good things to happen to Satan would be insincere on my part because the things he would think are good are things that would injure the human and angelic races."

Jesus said, "But good happening to him doesn't mean he would necessarily consider it good. I can name one very good thing that happened to you that you would have given anything to set aside."

Gabriel stared at the ground. "Point taken. But all the same, doing good to him would by my estimation set back all the good we want for others."

Jesus tilted his head and raised his eyebrows. "Do you think it's possible to benefit everyone?"

Raphael began vibrating. "This is an insane conversation." He turned to Gabriel. "You're asking if you should pray for Satan. That's— It's obnoxious. He wants nothing good for anyone. He denied God. He damned a third of the angels, and he seduced the human race. I don't think God would even honor those prayers. Satan is the enemy."

Gabriel turned back to Jesus. "Agreed. He's the enemy. I can't reconcile that with what you said."

Jesus leaned forward "Do you think the Father ever loved him?"

Gabriel's eyes flared. "Of course he did! I never questioned that."

Jesus said, "Does God change?"

A glacial coldness spread through Gabriel, or maybe it was Raphael feeling his own. ANd then he turned and saw standing under a tree the demon Mephistopheles. Watching. From the feel of him, watching for a while.

Gabriel didn't act as if he detected Raphael's defenses. "God doesn't change. But what they did—"

Jesus nodded. "What they did was wrong. But I'm here for mankind, and what mankind has done was wrong too."

Gabriel settled to the side. "He wants nothing good for them. That alone should make you say no, don't pray for him. Don't bless him or his followers. Don't do good for them."

Raphael kept tracking Mephistopheles, but the dark Cherub only stood beneath a tree, his curls wild but his whole body otherwise under strict control. The disciples' guardians armored themselves, and several drew their swords, but Gabriel and Jesus didn't seem to notice the demon beneath the tree.

Jesus said, "Do you think the Father would take them back?"

Gabriel sighed. "The Cherubim have speculated endlessly."

Jesus touched Gabriel's chest. "But you? What do you think?"

"I've argued both sides."

"You're a Cherub." Jesus smiled. "Of course you've argued both sides."

Raphael couldn't help but laugh, and he noticed how Mephistopheles' eyes glinted too.

Jesus opened his hands. "But what's your opinion? Right now, sitting here in front of me, if I told you there was a demon fallen to his knees before the Throne and begging for mercy, what do you think the Father would say?" Jesus snapped. "Quick."

"Yes," Gabriel blurted, then hesitated. "But for a thousand years I thought no. And—" He tightened his fists. "I don't know.

We can't know unless it happens; that's the real answer. And why pray for something impossible?"

Jesus murmured, "I would think you spent a year praying for the impossible."

"I didn't." Gabriel tightened up on himself. "I spent a few minutes praying for the impossible, and then I buckled down and did a different impossible thing."

Mephistopheles had leaned forward to catch what Gabriel said, only he hadn't seemed to hear it.

"Just so you know..." Raphael murmured.

I do know, Jesus sent.

Gabriel tucked up his knees. "Why did he tempt them in the garden?" He shook his head. "It wasn't in question that they're a lesser race. Confusing them and leading them to sin wasn't any more difficult than it would be to train a dog to sit or get a vine to grow on the sunny side of the fence. Defiling them, what did it accomplish? Did he want to prove a point? Was it spite?"

Jesus said, "Have you considered it was to prevent me from coming into their form as I suggested I would?"

Gabriel looked up. "But—"

"If he prevented that," Jesus said, "the question of whether or not he'd worship a God in a lesser form was immaterial because it wouldn't happen. So he seduced them in the garden to ensure the Father would destroy them. If they never had children, I couldn't become one of them, so he asked them to choose death. Only the Father didn't bring death at once, and I'm here anyhow in an even further reduced form to fulfill and redeem them, and eventually to glorify them."

Gabriel looked up, puzzled. "He thought he could prevent it?"

"It was a way for him to win. He could return without capitulating."

Gabriel seemed even more puzzled. "He wanted to return?"

"He wanted to win." Jesus shook his head. "But when one wins, both lose."

Mephistopheles looked openly shocked.

Gabriel's voice ticked up. "I don't want to pray for him to win."

"Nor should you."

"I want the Father to win." His voice wavered. "Would the Father winning mean both sides lost as well?"

Jesus said, "Here's another question: would his repentance mean nothing had been won so much as set straight?"

Gabriel shook his head. "If we start playing with definitions, you'll never get any sleep, and Raphael will drive his sword through my heart."

A momentary frisson flitted across Mephistopheles' features. "I wouldn't do that," Raphael said, "but I intend to talk to you about what a human body needs."

Gabriel frowned. "There's no other way I'd know about that, is there?"

"You've given enough lectures." Raphael folded his arms. "You're due one."

Jesus ran a hand over one of Gabriel's feathers. "Why don't you think about it, and we can talk more another time?"

Gabriel said, "I wanted to know what I should pray for."

Jesus kissed him on the cheek. "You've got a good heart, Gabri'li."

"You didn't answer my question."

"I didn't intend to answer your question." He lay back down on his blanket. "Good night."

Raphael imposed sleep on Jesus (although it wasn't hard – the man was exhausted.) He kept his eyes on Mephistopheles the whole time, but he sent irritation through the bond to Gabriel.

Gabriel sent back confusion: Jesus didn't mind, so why was Raphael upset?

Raphael's heart burned as he projected back to Gabriel. A guardian was supposed to protect his charge, to make sure no unnecessary problems or pain happened, to keep him shielded and make sure his needs were met. And then to just have Gabriel slip in and wake up Jesus when he knew Jesus needed to sleep, that was arrogant. It was counter to Raphael's duty, and Gabriel assumed it was allowed because they were bonded, or because he was above the regulations everyone else had to follow, or because he was—

Gabriel sent him a prompt: Or because he was jealous?

Raphael's heart vibrated.

Gabriel sent reassurance. He was not jealous. He didn't think a nighttime conversation would hurt Jesus, and in the future he would ask Raphael for permission. Would that suffice?

A moment later, Gabriel added that he was sorry he'd upset Raphael.

Raphael sparkled with irritation. Not sorry that he'd done it?

Gabriel's soul retreated from Raphael's, leaving behind only emptiness.

Beneath the trees, Mephistopheles watched again with folded arms, and this time Gabriel caught sight of the demon. How long had he been there?

Mephistopheles laughed and vanished.

Raphael let out a long breath. The steel in Gabriel's eyes drew Raphael's attention to the other guardians nearby. They'd all turned their focus from watching the demon to watching the pair of them.

Raphael sat beside Jesus to make sure he was fully asleep. It wasn't fair, he sent to Gabriel, that Gabriel thought he could take advantage of Raphael for access to Jesus's store of information. Not if he was doing it for himself to satisfy his curiosity, or because he'd finally found a debate partner who could run him in circles.

A thrill shot through Gabriel at the last.

You see?, Raphael thought. And had Gabriel really intended to present himself before God and ask for good things to be heaped upon Satan? And blessings for the army of fallen angels who wanted nothing more than to spit in God's face again? Or had he only wanted to clarify a point of law before going to start an argument with Ophaniel about the nature of antiprotons?

Gabriel stood. "The first thing. At least, in an extremely modified and limited form. We'll see what happens from there." And with that, he left them.

145

Raphael glanced beneath the trees, but Mephistopheles had not returned, and in the next few minutes the disciples' guardians resumed speaking to one another with an awed hush.

Year Thirty-Two

"Ask him," Gabriel said again.

"You ask. I'm a bit busy right now." Raphael kept scanning the streets as they moved through Jerusalem, his heart prickling with the presence of so many souls in such a close space. Every day it seemed the danger levels grew higher, and therefore the guardianship had become rather intense even for a Seraph who craved excitement.

Despite that, Gabriel spent his days asking questions (and probably spent his nights coming up with new ones) when Raphael sometimes would have rather had another set of eyes watching the people.

"He's about as safe as he gets here." Gabriel glanced around. "The people closest to him are the twelve, and they're not going to hurt him."

Raphael's feathers spread. "I'm doing my job, and I'm not writing off anything as a danger."

Gabriel shrugged. "I just don't understand why he got upset at people for doing exactly what he said to do."

The disciples' guardians were watching the exchange, and Nivalis said, "Gabriel, ask him."

Gabriel pushed a question into Jesus's mind, and Jesus looked up. *Go ahead.*

Gabriel said, "The ten lepers you healed — why did you get upset at nine of them for not coming back to you right away?"

Jesus knit his brows. *Only one of the ten gave thanks to God for his healing.*

"That's not how I'm reading the situation," Gabriel said. "I'm reading it that nine of the ten did exactly what you told them to do, and you were irritated at them for following orders."

Jesus shook his head. *I guess that's one reading of the situation.*

Gabriel said, "What am I missing?"

Before Raphael could say Gabriel was missing one of the most basic points of social interaction, a crowd accosted Jesus with shouts. Gabriel raised his wings as several men thrust a barely-clad woman through him, toward Jesus.

The disciples backed away from the woman like water ringlets retreating from a flung stone. Jesus alone stood with the woman before him.

A Pharisee grasped her by the arm. "This woman was caught in the very act of adultery."

The woman's guardian angel went down on his knees before Jesus, then crossed his arms over his chest and bowed his head.

Another man said, "Moses ordered us to stone women of this kind. What do you think we should do?"

Jesus looked at the woman, who was trying in vain to straighten her clothing.

Gabriel brushed a wingtip by Raphael. "Am I to believe this woman was caught in the act of committing adultery *by herself?*'

Jesus glanced up at Gabriel and sent, *You asked me a question, so now it's my turn. What is the integral of sine x^2 from negative four to zero?*

Gabriel hesitated.

This occurred to me last night, but you weren't around to ask. Jesus bent and set up a grid, then drew a sine curve and started writing out a formula.

Raphael stared at Jesus in confusion, because the Pharisees were asking more questions of Jesus, but Jesus finished writing the formula. He looked up at the Pharisee as if distracted. "It only seems fair that the man who hasn't ever sinned should throw the first stone." Then he looked back at the drawing and sent to Gabriel, *How would you solve this?*

"You wouldn't solve that," Gabriel said, "at least not that way, because it doesn't make sense." He leaned over Jesus, gesturing with his hands and rewriting the formula, "This is really the way I'd set it up because that makes it easier to—"

"You know," Raphael said tentatively, "this might not be the best time."

You're right, Jesus sent, and he rewrote the problem. *But you've limited the range of the integral, and I wanted the range to extend to negative two pi.*

"It ceases making sense once you carry it beyond negative pi," Gabriel said.

Jesus changed the range of the integral anyhow. *Now what?*

"Now it stops making sense," Gabriel said, and he changed the graph of the problem to reflect the different range.

"You both stopped making sense a long time ago," Raphael muttered.

Let me do this, Jesus sent.

Raphael looked up as one of the Pharisees got directly before Jesus, where he was writing, saying, "Should we stone the woman or not?" and Jesus did nothing other than move to the side and keep working. Gabriel had begun talking quickly, his wings raised, his eyes bright. Raphael soon lost track of the mathematics, although he could feel the problem taking shape from both sides, one half of him through his bond to Jesus and the other through his bond to Gabriel. Jesus redrew the problem and they started over again, and Raphael disengaged himself enough to look around and find no one in front of them but the woman.

The disciples' guardian angels had large eyes, and a couple of them were laughing.

Gabriel said, "And that's why the range has to be from pi to negative pi."

I see now, Jesus said. *Hold on a minute.* He stood up and looked at the woman. "Woman, where are they?"

Gabriel looked up, his eyes startled as he focused.

The woman shook her head.

Raphael dropped a set of his wings into a cloak around his shoulders, and he passed it to Jesus, who handed the heavy, warm fabric to the woman. "Has no one condemned you?"

The woman swallowed as she pulled the cloak around her shoulders. "No one, sir."

Jesus said, "Then neither do I condemn you."

The woman regarded him in confusion.

"Go," he said, "and sin no more."

The woman ducked her head as she walked away.

Jesus turned to the woman's guardian. "Escort her to make sure she stays safe," then turned the angel solid and wingless. The angel bowed and hurried after the woman.

He turned to Gabriel. *Why does the thing with the lepers bother you so much?*

Gabriel said, "Because that's what I would do: exactly what you told me to do. I wouldn't want to risk losing the healing if I disobeyed, like Lot's wife turning back to look at Sodom burning. I'd have gone straight to the priests, presented myself the way you said, and then gone to look for you."

Jesus nodded. *And doesn't that sound an awful lot like fear? Using rituals to protect yourself from God?*

Raphael stiffened. Gabriel's gaze dropped. "It's about doing things the right way."

Jesus replied, *It's about having an honest relationship without protecting yourself from the people you love. Over time, how can you relate to someone if it's just a matter of doing only what's required?* And then he added, glancing at Raphael, *Remember, Gabriel, what hurts one hurts two.*

Year Thirty-Three

"You realize they're going to kill us," Thomas muttered as they approached Jerusalem.

Raphael turned to him, projecting reassurance. Thomas had been nervous for days, even in the crowd of travelers heading toward Jerusalem.

Nivalis breathed over Judas, who said, "Well, they can try, but he's the Messiah." He shifted his bag. "They've tried before to stone him, remember? He just slips away."

Thomas only shook his head.

Jesus stopped beneath a tree while most travelers just continued on. "Andrew? Philip? I want you to go ahead into the village. You're going to find a donkey there, tied to a tree. Untie it and bring it to me. When they ask you what you're doing, just say the Lord has need of him."

In the shade, they waited watching the road. Nivalis approached Raphael. "Judas has heard people talking about arresting Jesus."

At Raphael's side, Gabriel said, "Michael's keeping tabs on everything. And so far, the Romans are staying out of it."

A traveler stopped before them on the road, but the humans couldn't see him. He had twelve wings and cold eyes. "Nice day for a pilgrimage," Satan said. "One of you has to send a message for me."

Raphael bristled, but Gabriel closed his eyes, and when he opened them, they were duskier. Speaking in a tenor/soprano mix, he said, "Your message?"

"Gabriel, tell your owner I deserve to test that one again. If that monkey's really their Messiah, he's got to do something about ushering in a Messianic age, and I don't think he qualifies."

Gabriel said, "Note that you've been testing him all along through your human servants."

Satan said, "Direct testing. I want authority over the situation."

Raphael's wings flared, but Gabriel said, "You may have your authority."

Satan said, "Unimpeded by any interference this time. That means no angels and no vast transfusions of grace."

Gabriel said, "Granted."

Raphael's eyes widened. "But—"

Satan said, "And free access to his pet monkeys, too."

"You have freedom to tempt the disciples."

"No!" Raphael's eyes threw sparks. "Why?"

Gabriel concluded, "You have one week."

Satan folded his arms. "I demand a month."

Gabriel said, "One week."

Satan sighed, then snapped his fingers. "Okay, Gabriel, you can put your leash back on. I'm done talking to your owner."

Raphael's wings burned, but Satan didn't so much as look in his direction. Instead he studied Jesus, studied the disciples. "Only a week. That still gives me the Passover. So much fun to be had with their little holiday." He turned to Raphael. "Try not to take it too hard. He's only human."

Gabriel still hadn't returned to himself. Satan said, "By the way, your owner is slipping. He didn't forbid me to hurt the monkey's body or take his life. Maybe he's too worried about his Son to think clearly."

Raphael tensed. "Oh, don't worry," Satan said, shooing him as if he were nothing more than a mosquito. "I have no intention of killing him. But usually I get that tired old stipulation, *Only make sure not to touch his life,* when in reality I had no such designs anyhow because they're so much more fun when they're alive."

Satan vanished, but that slick feeling of evil hung over the gathering.

Gabriel turned to Raphael, his eyes still a dusky mix, and in God's voice, he said, "Joy comes in the morning."

"What's that supposed to mean?" Raphael's voice pitched up. "I need to protect him!"

But Gabriel had come back to himself now, and he gave his head a little shake. Then he looked deflated. "Another trial?"

"Is this what you prayed up for us?" Raphael got right in front of Gabriel and lowered his voice. "Is this the good thing you prayed would happen to our enemy? Like some kind of gift Jesus could pay for?"

Gabriel backed up a step, shocked.

"Is this payback?" Raphael whispered. "Because I didn't work hard enough before?"

Gabriel raised his hands. "I have no idea what you mean."

Thomas said, abruptly, "I don't think we should head into Jerusalem."

Jesus looked at him, and in an instant Raphael recognized the heaviness in his eyes, the exhaustion. Satan had reconnoitered the disciples for three years now. He didn't need an intense research phase. He needed instead just permission, and that he'd already obtained.

Thomas said, "They want to kill you. Isn't it better to stay away?"

Jesus said, "And not fulfill the word of the prophets?"

Peter said, "Do we have to go into Jerusalem to fulfill the word?"

Judas exclaimed, "Of course we do! Jerusalem is the City of God! That's where it all happens, whatever it is."

Jesus winced, but Judas continued, "That's where the Temple is, and the high priest. That's where the Romans have their center. If we take that, then the world has to listen!"

Jesus said, "Judas, no."

"Of course this is what has to happen!" Judas turned to him. "Didn't you say no one knows the day or the hour that the Kingdom will come? So why not here? Why not now? All the

153

players are in place! We just need to put them together the right way, and you can restore the Kingdom of Israel!"

Philip and Andrew approached with the donkey, and Jesus said, "I've made it clear I'm not looking for the rulership of the land."

Judas said, "But you could."

Jesus said, "There's a lot of things I could do. That's not why the Son of Man came to you."

Philip threw his cloak over the back of the donkey, and Jesus mounted it. Then with Andrew holding its lead, they headed toward Jerusalem. Judas started singing, and then Simon and Bartholomew joined in, and soon all of them had begun a loud chorus. As they passed through the village, other people began to follow.

Raphael thrummed with excitement as the people began cutting down palm branches and laying them in the road, and soon a crowd formed. Judas tore off his cloak and laid it on the road before Jesus's donkey, and then Simon did the same. Within minutes, cloaks lined the road.

"Hosanna!" Judas started shouting, and then the people took up the chant. "Blessed is he who comes in the name of the Lord!"

Hundreds of travelers. Hundreds of callers. All they needed were harps and cymbals and trumpets, Raphael realized, but the people were making their own music.

They mounted a ridge, and Jerusalem came into view. A sudden sorrow overtook Jesus's face. "Oh, Jerusalem," he whispered. "Jerusalem, you don't know the things that are going to happen to you, and in you. When it's all over, there won't be two stones left on top of one another."

A Pharisee pushed up close to Jesus. "Rein in your disciples! Are you some kind of king?"

Jesus shook his head. "If I tell them to be quiet, even the stones will start crying out."

When they reached Jerusalem, the procession made straight for the Temple. "He's going to do it!" Judas kept saying to Simon. "He's going to bring in the kingdom!"

At the Temple, Jesus got off the donkey and asked Andrew to return it, then brought the whole entourage in with him. And as soon as he reached the sales booths, he shouted, "Everyone out! This is not a marketplace! This is my Father's house!"

Raphael's wings flared, but Jesus rushed for the nearest table and flipped it. Coins rolled everywhere, and the merchants scattered. He set free a cage full of doves, and he called to the people, "This is a house of prayer, not a den of robbers!"

The crowd responded, rushing to set free the animals and shove the sales tables to the sides. The priests fled the scene, and through it all, Raphael couldn't help but notice how Judas smiled, how his face flushed, and how he watched with a bright anticipation.

And how the next day, when Jesus went back to the Temple to teach, Judas was disappointed. And angry. How he argued that they needed to capitalize on the promise of yesterday's crowd.

How when Jesus told him no, Judas became quiet.

How Nivalis looked worried. Then terrified.

How after a while, Judas slipped away, because he'd had a really good plan. All the main players were in place, he'd said. It was just up to a clever man to put them all together.

As the disciples and Jesus settled down for the Passover meal, Nivalis clutched Raphael's side so hard she hurt him, tears streaming down her face as they prayed together. She kept looking at Judas, but she wouldn't stand near him, and for himself, Judas remained stone-faced. But he was excited.

I tried, Nivalis kept praying. *He's so convinced he's doing the right thing.*

Raphael looked at Jesus. He couldn't protect him. Yet again, he couldn't do a thing, and he couldn't even object because it was God's decision. *But I don't have to like it,* Raphael prayed.

Jesus met his eyes. *I don't like it either.*

Mary was in Jerusalem, but Jesus had asked her to stay with relatives tonight. Tonight was just for him and the twelve. Mary had agreed, but her eyes looked weary. She could hear the gossip. She knew the emotional temperature, and she thought Jesus wanted her away so she'd stay safe.

Raphael went cold. *Can't we turn this down? Pray for mercy? We could build the Kingdom right now if we had permission.*

Michael reported back to Jesus. "I've Guarded the room."

Jesus nodded. *Satan will have his hour, but not now. This hour remains mine.*

Jesus looked at all the disciples, and instead of the sadness Raphael expected to see (sifted like wheat? Satan was going to sift them like wheat? Which ones would blow away like chaff? Half? He'd already gotten Judas) Jesus looked steely. Almost proud, like a father.

They began the meal, but before the supper had ended, Jesus lowered his voice and gave thanks, then broke the bread. He gave it to his disciples, saying, "This is my body, which is given up for you. Do this in remembrance of me."

Raphael could hardly see Jesus at all. Remembrance — was he giving up already? Was it over? Where was their city? Their messianic vision?

Gabriel at his side gasped, and he dropped to his knees. A moment later, Michael did the same.

Raphael couldn't tell at first what had driven the others down. But then he realized that sense of Jesus that always burned inside him — it was more. It was everything, because how could omnipresent be more or less, but it was in Jesus, and it was also in the bread. The bread in his hands, and then the bread in his disciples' hands, and then the bread in his disciples. And then he was in them.

Raphael dropped to his knees as well.

Nivalis covered her face. "Please, no. Skip Judas."

Jesus didn't skip Judas. They all took the bread. The presence of God blazed in all of them.

Jesus took the cup, and he said, "And this cup, this is the new covenant of my blood, which is shed for you." They passed it around, and Jesus said, "I will not drink wine again until the Kingdom of God comes." When the cup returned to him empty, Jesus said, "I know my betrayer is here at the table."

The disciples exploded into questions, but Raphael only sought out Gabriel. *What did he just do? I don't understand.*

He said they had to eat his flesh and drink his blood, Gabriel replied. *He made it happen. That bread looked like bread, but it wasn't. I mean, it was, but it was more. It had the essence of him. Same with the wine. But it looked the same. You needed faith to see it, but it's there. They did what he said.*

Raphael touched Andrew and warmed with the same feeling as if he were touching Jesus.

Sift them like wheat. But Jesus had given them wheat that was himself. Did that mean Satan could sift, but there would be no chaff? And what of Judas?

Peter said, "I won't ever betray you."

Jesus swallowed hard as he went to the corner and picked up a bowl. "Peter, before the morning comes, you'll deny me."

Total silence from all. Even Judas looked horrified.

Peter said, "Lord, I'm not going to leave you. I'll go with you to prison. I'll go with you to death."

Jesus said, "Before morning. Three times. You'll deny you even know me."

He removed his cloak and tied a towel around his waist, and then went to Andrew. "Let me wash your feet."

The disciples remained silent as Jesus bathed Andrew's feet and then dried them. He moved next to Peter, who yanked back. "You can't! You don't even trust me."

Jesus looked up with a faint smile. "If I don't do this, you won't be clean."

Peter said, "Then do my head and my hands."

Jesus chuckled, but Peter relented and let him do as he wanted. "No, if I do this, you'll be clean all over. Trust me."

He went around the room, bathing the feet of all the disciples. When he reached Judas, Nivalis buried her face in

157

Raphael's shoulder, but Jesus didn't do anything different for Judas than he'd done for the others. No admonition, no scolding, no shaming. *We can run*, Raphael kept thinking. *I've taken you out of bad situations before. I can take you now. We'll find a spot and build your city.*

He didn't project it to Jesus. And when Jesus asked the disciples to come with him to pray, he followed in mute desperation.

Uriel appeared and bowed to Michael. Raphael said, "Why are you here?" and he got the sense that Mary had sent her own guardian to be with Jesus. That didn't offer Raphael any comfort. It meant Mary was terrified for her son's safety, and he also knew it wouldn't be as easy this time as it was in the wilderness.

They made their way to a garden where Jesus had prayed before. They prayed together, but the disciples were all tired after the four glasses of wine required by the seder. One at a time they grew too exhausted to continue, and the heavy darkness became heavier with the presence of demons, and although Jesus stayed awake to pray, soon he did so alone.

And Raphael, even though surrounded by other angels, felt devastatingly alone too.

Gabriel sat in one of the lower branches, blocked by the foliage but able to sense where everyone sat, when Jesus moved off a short distance to pray by himself, when the eleven fell asleep. Michael stood watch at the garden gate.

Satan was deploying every weapon in the arsenal: Jesus could walk away from his mission now; Jesus needed to realize how weak humans were if they couldn't even remember their loyalties; Jesus should show them his true power so they never again failed him.

Through the third-party bond, Gabriel could feel Jesus's prayer, and he detected flashes of the understanding Jesus had of what was to come. He wanted to disengage, but whenever he drew away, Raphael would clutch his heart all the tighter: *Don't leave.* So Gabriel didn't leave, but he didn't want to look into the future. At the same time he wanted to know because sometimes when you knew something, you could twist it just enough to make a bad thing good.

Find the seed in the bad fruit. Raise a good tree, with good fruit. God always worked that way. It had to happen again.

Raphael burned into a frenzy, and Gabriel calmed him through the bond.

Jesus's prayer flowed through Raphael, and Gabriel picked up a sense of it: a cup, and could it pass him by?

Raphael flashed beside him. "Can you appear to him?"

Gabriel said, "You should do it."

"But it would mean more from you." Raphael took both Gabriel's hands, and he touched his wingtips to Gabriel's. "Assure him we'll be with him the whole time, no matter what else happens. He knows I'll stay because I have to stay. But when you tell him you'll stay, that means more."

Squeezing Raphael's hands, Gabriel assented. He slipped off the tree branch and knelt in a prayer of his own.

Is this allowed?

God's answer came that he could.

Gabriel moved through the garden, avoided the sleeping apostles, and settled on his knees in front of Jesus. He tucked his wings forward to clear the ground. Jesus looked Gabriel right in the eyes.

The Father said to Gabriel, *You will do what I tell you to do, adding nothing and omitting nothing.*

Gabriel went cold. Asking to appear to Jesus right now hadn't been his best move.

Could he even reach for Jesus's hands? The Spirit approved, so he did. At the contact, he poured his strength into Jesus, and Jesus took a deep breath.

"God's strength," Jesus whispered.

He was not told to answer, so Gabriel said nothing.

Raphael urged him to say more.

The cup, God told Gabriel.

Gabriel opened his hands, and an earthenware goblet formed. Looking into it, he watched it fill with black wine, a mist halfway between existence and void. He stared into the depths of the cup as eternity swirled inside, and he would have been lost if God had not prompted again, *The cup.*

He wanted to object. He wanted to hurl the cup to the side, or to drink it himself, or to snatch it close and cover it with his wings.

Instead, Gabriel extended the cup toward Jesus while Raphael stood mute with horror.

Every angel in the garden watched Jesus take the cup, his hands resting over Gabriel's for one stark heartbeat. Then Gabriel relinquished the cup filled with the nothing that before the Word had spoken once encompassed the whole of creation. Jesus raised the cup to his lips.

The instant they touched, Raphael screamed.

God released Gabriel. It didn't matter any longer what Gabriel said or did: Jesus was cut off from the angelic world.

Raphael doubled over as though gutted, and Uriel curled around him but stared only at Gabriel.

Gabriel covered his face with his hands.

Raphael exploded from Uriel's grasp and got right in front of Jesus as he drained the cup to the bottom. "I'm still here! I didn't leave! We're not gone!"

The empty cup slipped from Jesus's hands, hit the ground and vanished. Jesus slumped against the rock, and in the next moment he was battling tears.

Gabriel reached for Raphael's soul.

"Don't you dare!" Raphael spun to face the Cherub. "You cut him off from us! You betrayed him just like Judas!"

Gabriel still saw that cup in his mind's eye, still felt the chill of clay against his palms.

Michael moved between Gabriel and Raphael. "He did what God ordered him! He didn't manufacture that on his own!"

Raphael radiated incoherent rage, and Gabriel sat in shock. All the angels were staring while Michael struggling to contain Raphael and Uriel wrapped him in purple wings.

Darkness closed around the garden. Demons. The sense of Satan's curious patience. On the peripheries were Asmodeus and Beelzebub laughing at the Seraph's frenzy, and with them Belior and Mephistopheles piecing together the hidden from the visible.

Raphael pushed past Michael, but then Saraquael got between them. Uriel put it in Gabriel's heart: *Go to Mary.*

Gabriel wanted to stay. Leaving would be the abandonment Raphael was accusing him of, the abandonment Jesus already feared.

Jesus can't feel you even if you stay, Uriel pushed. *I want someone with Mary. She ordered me here, but she needs someone with her too.*

Jane Lebak

Gabriel reached into Raphael's soul, but the heat drove even his Cherub heart backward.

Michael glared at Gabriel. *Get out of here!*

Gabriel fled.

He appeared in Mary's room, dark himself in the darkness. She had to be asleep, but immediately he heard rustling, and she was on her feet. "What are you doing here?"

"Uriel sent me."

"Go to Jesus," she urged. "I don't care if they attack me."

"Uriel sent me," Gabriel repeated. "Michael ordered me here. I can't go back."

Mary let out a long breath. "How is he? Is he hurt? Have they arrested him?"

"Not yet." Even in the dark, he couldn't look at her "But it's a matter of time."

Mary said, "What's going to happen?"

"I can't say for certain." But he knew what was in that cup, and for the first moment he wondered if perhaps Jesus hadn't been cut off from his Father at the same time as he was cut off from the angels. And he remembered his own past: the Vision, closed away like a blink.

Raphael, screaming. Michael's anger. Demonic amusement. Jesus fighting tears. And this. It added up to death.

Mary grabbed his hand. "What did you just realize?"

"Pray with me," Gabriel whispered. "Please, even if you don't have the words, please pray with me."

Uriel would have yelled at him for not letting Mary fall asleep, or rather for encouraging her to stay awake. Uriel would have been yet another furious guardian because Gabriel as a non-guardian couldn't understand what human beings needed. But Uriel wasn't there, so Mary prayed with Gabriel until she shook with exhaustion, and then he infused her with strength of the same sort he'd given Jesus. At which point, replenished, she joined him again in prayer as if she'd slept for eight hours.

An hour later, Saraquael appeared. Mary turned toward him even before Gabriel did. "What's happened?"

"He's been arrested." Saraquael sounded subdued. "They've brought him before the priests."

Mary said, "Let's go."

Saraquael shook his head. "That won't be wise. They're going to target his followers."

Mary huffed. "I didn't ask if it was wise."

Gabriel said, "Uriel will hand me my head."

Mary folded her arms. "Uriel would want to be near me if I were imprisoned."

"Uriel can't be killed."

Mary said, "If it's the Father's will that I die near my son, then I want that too."

Gabriel looked aside. "What if he's not allowed to see you? We were all cut off from him. If he can't see any of us, it must be for the reason that God wants him to do it alone."

Mary lowered her voice. "But I can be near him, and that's all I'm asking. Aren't all of you doing the same?"

He couldn't argue with that logic. Gabriel prayed, and a moment after he stood before Mary as solid as she was, wingless and human. "Cover us," he said to Saraquael.

She looked stunned. "I didn't realize you would do that."

"I don't usually." He took her hand. "Let's go."

Gabriel and Mary walked through the darkened streets, Gabriel leading because he was better able to see in the dark. Although he inhabited a solid body for the moment, he didn't go entirely human, preferring instead to keep some awareness of the celestial world. Demons watched from the corners and the rooftops the same way men had watched him in Sodom with Michael, and he fought the urge to hide. If rumors of Jesus's arrest had begun to form, Gabriel heard nothing. A working woman approached, then saw he wasn't alone and backed away.

At the high priest's courtyard, Gabriel scanned the area. John was there, as was Peter. He wondered if he could flag John to have him bring Mary inside, but then an older woman walked through the gate, and Mary simply followed. The guard greeted the woman and didn't ask Mary or Gabriel any questions. They were inside.

Peter's guardian approached Gabriel. "Disguise her accent. It's already gotten Peter in trouble."

Mary nodded.

"Do you want to wait with Peter and John?" Gabriel said.

She shook her head. "I want to get closer. I was thinking of cleaning the hallways."

In one dark corner, Gabriel went insubstantial again, and he followed Mary to a room where the servants were cleaning. She apologized for not having her apron, found a job to do, and began working. Gabriel asked other angels for the building's layout, and then he sent Mary directions toward where the priests were interrogating Jesus.

Uriel appeared in the hallway, eyes alight with purple fire.

Mary looked up at Uriel with a smile that diffused the Throne's outrage. She nodded, smiled, then gave a quick glance at Gabriel that Uriel imitated a moment later. Gabriel tucked his wings to himself and waited for the inevitable, but Uriel only stood back and let out a sigh.

I wish you'd convinced her to stay there, Uriel sent, *but thank you for making sure she was safe coming here.*

Gabriel inclined his head.

Mary said to Uriel, "How much closer can you get me to him?"

Uriel led the way, and Gabriel remained behind.

She wants you to follow, Uriel sent.

Gabriel followed.

As he turned a corner he could feel Raphael on the other side of the wall. Though muted, voices floated in the air: questions, pauses, more questions. Mary stopped in an alcove, but Gabriel stayed back to avoid Raphael's line of sight even though Raphael could probably sense him there.

Mary and Uriel stood in perfect silence, but with little motions of heads and hands and Uriel's feathers, still communicating. Uriel's glow spread to enwrap Mary.

Mary turned to him. "Why didn't Judas testify?"

164

"He didn't?" Gabriel said.

"He's not even present," Mary whispered.

Gabriel looked at Uriel, who shrugged.

Will you be all right alone with her for a moment?

Uriel shot Gabriel a tolerant look.

Gabriel flashed to Judas's guardian angel.

Nivalis looked up, her eyes reddened, her hands knit. "I need help," she whispered. "Please pray with me."

Judas had ensconced himself in an unused part of the courtyard behind the stables, knees tucked up, his head in his hands.

Gabriel settled on one side and Nivalis on his other. Her voice wobbled. "He's upset. This didn't work out the way he wanted."

Gabriel said, "Evil people aren't upset when they bring about evil. Good people are."

Nivalis stroked Judas's hair. "If we pray, he may find the strength to ask for forgiveness. Please, let's try."

Gabriel reached out, and for a moment, he found himself engulfed in fog, in a heavy weight. Confusion: what had he done? Isolation: what would the others say? Did they all want him dead? *I know what it's like not to be able to face your friends again,* Gabriel prayed. *I know how hard it is to apologize for something you didn't think through. God, please give him the strength.*

Judas had never meant harm. Jesus had known what was going on, and the Talmud commanded a man to defend himself if people were coming to kill him. Judas hadn't wanted death for him. If he had, Jesus would have resisted. No, this was worse.

Chills knifed through Gabriel. Demon influence: Judas had invited them in, had felt the need to push God's hand, and Satan's 'best intentions' were penned all over his psyche. So attractive: just go out into the world and make Jesus right all the wrongs, force his hand, make him choose to be *that* kind of messiah instead of *this* kind, make him act to save the others. Make him. Force him. Coerce him. Ultimately, sell him.

Skin for skin: a man will do anything to save his life. And he'd known all along Jesus could save himself. But now this.

The tragedy of good versus good. The little good Judas had wanted versus the ultimate good that God intended.

Please, Gabriel prayed, and then he didn't know what to pray for in this man. The hooks, all the labyrinthine logic, the frustration, the disappointment, the yearning. So much goodness, so much genuine misunderstanding that had never wanted to be corrected.

And overlying that, Satan's nylon strings holding back certain thoughts, connecting others, but no longer pumped full of Satan's energy. Judas was no longer necessary to his plan, and so he'd been discarded like a threadbare ragdoll.

Gabriel tried to cut the threads, but Judas held them close in his heart. *You have to let go of your assumptions,* Gabriel sent. *I can't free you if you're clinging to your own prison!*

Frustrated, Gabriel pulled back from Judas's heart.

Nivalis looked up, her eyes terrified.

"Let's try again." Gabriel could once again feel the chilled cup against his hands. He looked into Nivalis's eyes as if he were still looking into the void.

Uriel called. Gabriel returned.

"She can't stay any longer." Uriel stood behind Mary, wings over her and around her, and she slumped with exhaustion.

Mary looked defiant, but Gabriel could tell she'd already protested to Uriel and lost the fight. He took a solid form and escorted her out of the temple area. No one accosted them on the street with Uriel casting power around them.

Mary lay down on her bed. "I already told Uriel this was futile. I'm not going to sleep."

Gabriel said, "You're going to sleep," and laid his hand over her eyes. She was asleep in moments, but he didn't move from her side. Gabriel turned, but Uriel remained in silence. "Do you want me to stay with her so you can go back to Jesus?"

Uriel said, "You could try again."

"Why don't you figure out if Raphael would let me near." Gabriel fought to keep his voice from breaking. "I'd rather be there than here, but not if it sets him off."

Uriel vanished. Gabriel waited, but the Throne didn't return, so he settled in the corner and prayed until dawn.

Mary asked for Uriel as soon as she awoke. Gabriel, who had received updates all night long via Saraquael and Remiel, sat opposite them and listened as Uriel caught her up on the events. Jesus had been re-tried before the Sanhedrin and was being led before Pilate later this morning.

"Why Pilate?" Mary said, and then she cringed. "Oh. They can't. Why would they want that?"

After a moment, she asked, "Did he get any sleep? Did they at least give him something to eat?"

Just before they left the house, Mary reached for Gabriel. He didn't make himself substantial as her fingers brushed his. "Thank you. I appreciate that you stayed."

They flashed to the Roman palace, where in the courtyard a crowd gathered.

Gabriel exchanged a concerned look with Uriel. Then both changed their focus to the rooftop where Satan sat with Belior.

He's far too smug.

Michael appeared behind them. "What do you think?"

"There are too many possibilities." Gabriel kept scanning. "Where is Asmodeus?"

"He's working the crowd." Michael looked dark. "Belior hasn't left Satan's side since last night."

Uriel sighed. "This is going to end with death."

"That's not what he was planning," Gabriel said. "He gloated that he'd gotten permission to kill him but that he wouldn't, remember? He said God was slipping, if he hadn't given him that restriction the way he always had before."

"But having the ability," Uriel said, "he might have decided to use it."

"Satan knows the power of martyrdom." With a gasp, Gabriel raised his head. "What we're not considering is that the Romans use the Passover to free one prisoner."

Uriel turned. "Go on."

"If Pilate wants, he can free Jesus."

Michael looked puzzled. "But what does that get him?"

Gabriel said, "Satan or Jesus?"

"How does freeing Jesus benefit Satan?"

"He can make it appear that Jesus is a puppet of the Romans." Gabriel shrugged. "Nothing else fits."

Uriel said, "Asmodeus is really working the crowd, though, and I've caught snatches of Beelzebub, too. There have to be at least fifteen dark Seraphim inciting the people."

Gabriel whispered, "If Satan gets the crowd to demand Jesus, does Jesus have to become their king?"

Michael sounded irritated. "Maneuvered into taking the thing he insisted wasn't his role."

Gabriel's eyes shifted to glare sidelong at Satan. "Satan's been planning this for three years. His backup plans have backups at this point. But by doing it this publicly, he's forcing Jesus either to accept the mercy of the Romans and appear a puppet to them, or else take command and forge a kingdom on Earth."

"Or die," Uriel said.

Gabriel said, "But Satan didn't want—"

Uriel's voice flattened. "I don't trust that he didn't change his mind."

Gabriel sighed. "Since there's nothing constructive we can do at this point anyhow, why not hope?"

"Hope for what?" Michael kicked a rock on the ground. "Hope that Jesus gets a chance to piece together the shattered slivers of his ministry? Hope that he can unpervert the mockery of a messianic vision Satan wants to establish?"

Gabriel turned to Michael. "I hate thinking we're useless."

Michael opened his hands. "But right now, it's the truth."

Pilate condemned Jesus to death. They took Jesus away. Judas flung his money back in the high priest's face. Nivalis begged for Gabriel again, and Gabriel prayed with Nivalis until she cried and he shook, but Judas fled to the trees. Nivalis screamed. She pleaded. She sent up a wind that might have blown down the tree. She begged for God to send another man, at least someone to distract him. Judas fixed a knot and hanged himself.

Gabriel held Nivalis for an hour while she cried. He covered her with his wings and kept any other angels at bay, but she couldn't get calm, and eventually Remiel came for her.

"I've dealt with this before," Remiel murmured to Gabriel, leaving Gabriel to wonder what he could have done for a guardian whose charge had just condemned himself to Hell.

Gabriel gazed up at the still body in the still tree in the brilliant darkness of Satan's hour, and he wished he could talk to Raphael about what he'd just witnessed. Instead he reached for God and asked him why. God didn't answer.

Michael? he sent.

Michael sent a very shaken acknowledgment.

Gabriel didn't bother saying he was on his way—he just went.

And arriving, he screamed.

Jesus had been whipped, bloodied, his hands bound before him, a scarlet cloak tossed over his shoulders, and in front of Gabriel's glowing eyes, two Roman soldiers braided thorned branches into a circlet.

Gabriel burst into flames, but Uriel grabbed him. He couldn't project coherently for the moment, and it all rippled out at the same time: *how could they he's hurt why on earth what is the matter with human beings what did he ever do to them this isn't fair can't we stop them?*

Turning to the rooftop, he targeted his glare on Satan, whose own eyes glinted with anticipation.

Gabriel! Michael came right up against him. *Don't engage him!*

I'll give him an hour!

I can't have you doing this! Michael enchained Gabriel with his will and flashed him fifteen miles away to the crest of a hill, a road leading north and south on their either side.

"Listen to me!" Michael's eyes burned blue. "Satan was given this power. I don't know why. Jesus was turned over to his control, and Jesus went along with it."

"But it doesn't have to be—"

"God wants it this way," Michael shouted, "and we can't get closer than we have. We can't stop it. There's nothing we've been able to accomplish so far."

"I can stop Satan from making it worse!"

He grabbed Gabriel by the shoulders. "Listen to yourself! This is Satan's hour! You attack him and he'll cinder you on the spot! I'm telling you, we can't do anything!"

Gabriel threw his sword, then clenched his fists, arched his neck, and erupted with enough power to dwarf a supernova. Michael flung up a Guard around himself as the spiritual shock wave blew over the earth, but still his feathers gusted back in the blast.

Gabriel went down on his knees, and he hit the ground with his fist.

Michael dropped to sitting. He said nothing.

After a moment, Gabriel put his face in his hands. He tried to take a deep breath of the sandy air, but it choked him. He tried again. A third time. Eventually he could sit without shaking.

"You need to be with them," he managed.

"I think I need to be with you." Michael spoke softly. "They'll call if I'm needed."

A long silence passed. Gabriel shook his head, trying to obliterate the visions in his memory.

Michael touched his hand.

"Raphael won't leave him." Gabriel's voice was raspy. "This has to be killing him."

Gabriel left the rest of it unsaid: that he wanted to be there too. Even if he couldn't do anything for Jesus, he still could be there with his Seraph.

Michael squeezed his hand. "On some level he has to know this isn't your fault."

"Yeah," Gabriel whispered. "Wouldn't that be nice?"

"It didn't help that you wouldn't even apologize, though." When Gabriel's head snapped up, Michael added, "It looked as if you didn't care."

Gabriel swallowed.

"You had that studious expression." Michael sighed. "It took even me a while to realize you were struggling. But Raphael needed something from you right then, and you gave him nothing." Michael sat back. "I heard about Nivalis."

Gabriel shook his head.

Michael shifted so he and Gabriel were face to face, and Michael took his hands, then brought forward his wings so they touched the tips of Gabriel's wings, and he closed his eyes. Together they prayed, sitting on the road, letting the sun shine through them, and Gabriel tried not to consider everything he had seen.

But he and Michael were together, and for a moment Gabriel relaxed in the strength of his presence. As a unit they reached for the Spirit, and the Spirit swept through them and strengthened them.

What's going to happen? Gabriel prayed.

Michael withdrew, but Gabriel pressed for an answer.

A moment after, the Spirit answered.

Gabriel yanked back his hands from Michael's as if from a hot pan.

Michael whispered, "What?"

Gabriel stared into eternity, denial and fear and fury combined in one silvered expression.

Michael whispered, "Is it death?"

Gabriel couldn't respond. For Michael, silence would be response enough.

They returned to the Roman palace, and Gabriel was stunned to find Uriel with arms and wings around Raphael. He hadn't felt the Seraph's distress, or maybe he couldn't over his own.

Gabriel moved closer and put his hand on Raphael. "We're with you." Raphael didn't acknowledge, but at least he didn't throw Gabriel off. It was a start.

Uriel sent information to Michael and Gabriel: Pilate had washed his hands of the situation. Jesus was to be given a crossbeam to carry to the Skull Place, and he was to be crucified.

Mary sat on a bench, bloodless. Gabriel knelt before her and rested his hand on hers.

"How will he die?" she whispered. "What happens?"

Gabriel's eyes unfocused. *Crucifixion falls into the category of suspension torture, so he'll be stretched. He'll have to inch up for breath. The nails through his wrists and feet will cause him to lose blood, even more than he's already lost by being flogged, but not so much that he loses consciousness. He'll be aware of everything for hours while he asphyxiates because of the weight on his intercostal muscles, unable to draw a full breath, but still able to get shallow respirations so that he doesn't die immediately. The whip lashes on his back will sting, and they'll pull open when he moves on the wooden beam. The nails through his wrists will crush the sensorimotor median nerve, and it will feel like fire. The one through his feet will hit the plantar nerves and do the same. When he's close enough to death, the Romans will smash the bones in his shins so he can't inch up for breath, or when he simply hasn't the strength, then all his weight will bear on his wrists until the mass of his own body crushes the last bit of air out of his lungs, and then he asphyxiates.*

Mary leaned forward. "Tell me."

Gabriel shook himself free of the images. "He'll lose a lot of blood. Blood carries the good parts of the air to the body where it needs it. When he can't get enough air any longer, he'll die."

Mary's eyes teared. "Is it painful?"

Gabriel looked aside. "In the last minute, when there's not enough oxygen, it's actually a euphoric state, as if you're drifting."

Mary accepted this and did not ask about the hours leading to those last moments. "And what about Sheol? What is it like?"

"It's a natural happiness." This much at least was the complete truth. "Imagine awakening in the middle of the night and knowing everyone you love is in the house with you. It's just warm enough, and your blankets are up around your shoulders, and you have a soft pillow. Outside you can hear crickets, but you know you're secure, and you drift back to sleep."

Mary tried to smile. "So, it's not all bad."

"It's never all bad." Gabriel shook his head. "Even when that's how it seems."

Raphael had come up behind Gabriel. Mary looked up at the Seraph, and Gabriel stood.

He didn't meet Raphael's eyes. "I'm going to stay."

"I want to talk to her."

Gabriel gestured toward Mary with a sweep of his hand, then approached Uriel.

Uriel hadn't left Heaven often before becoming Mary's guardian, and this was a tremendous crowd, all of them angry and hungry. Looking unsteady, Uriel reached out a hand. Taking it, Gabriel sent the Throne reassurance, brushing wings against wings.

"I heard about Judas." Uriel's head was bowed. "There was nothing else you could have done."

Gabriel sighed. "I'm tired of hearing that."

"You're going to hear it again before this is over."

"And everyone believes it but me. And him."

173

Uriel said, "You understand Raphael better than anyone else. Quick to detonate, quick to apologize. Nivalis's bond to Judas was broken and she blames herself, so she cries. Raphael's bond to Jesus was broken, and he's blaming you. The only other choice would mean being angry at Jesus for submitting."

Gabriel said, "Then he and Nivalis are a lot alike right now."

Uriel nodded.

Gabriel looked over his shoulder at Raphael. "Sometimes I thank God I'm never going to be a guardian."

"And sometimes," Uriel said, "there's no way I can imagine myself as anything else ever again."

Raphael flashed back to Jesus's side. Gabriel transported with him to the interior courtyard where Jesus had been stripped again and given the crossbeam to carry.

I'll carry it for him, Gabriel prayed.

No.

Please let me give him my strength, then.

No.

Please let him know we're still with him.

No.

Can't I do anything for him? Gabriel prayed.

No answer.

Gabriel went down on his knees.

Raphael looked over his shoulder. *I tried that already.*

But you'd be even more angry at me if I didn't try. He wrapped his arms around his stomach. *Raphael, please believe me. I didn't have a choice in the garden.*

Raphael answered with a frustrated fury.

Don't be angry at me when the one you're mad at is God.

And don't you tell me what I should feel.

Gabriel moved closer to Jesus, his eyes unfocused but the scene etching itself into his mind. The Romans pushed Jesus forward even though he was already walking. Gabriel estimated the weight of the wood from the beam's size and density (about a hundred pounds) and then estimated the distance to the place where Jesus would be crucified (a third of a mile), factored in the heat, dehydration, the way Jesus had already been lashed, his fatigue, the strength Gabriel had been able to give him last night, his sleep-debt, and he concluded Jesus would not make it up the hill.

Please, he prayed, *even though I can't help him, please send someone. Please let someone help him.*

Raphael and Gabriel followed, Gabriel taking to the air when the closeness of the crowd grew too much.

The crowd jeered, hooted, laughed.

Raphael looked up at Gabriel, a sudden hollowness in his eyes.

Gabriel moved close, still aloft but near enough to touch, then settled behind Raphael, wrapping his arms around his shoulders.

Jesus fell, and before he had a chance to get to his feet, the Romans were shouting and the crowd rang with cat-calls.

Raphael swirled with confusion. *How can they laugh?*

I don't know. Gabriel brought his wings up near Raphael's. *These were the same people last week—*

I hate them. Raphael vibrated wildly, and Gabriel didn't reach into his soul to calm him. *If God let me, I would destroy them more thoroughly than Sodom and not think twice. They didn't deserve him, and he certainly doesn't deserve what they're doing to him.*

As Jesus struggled to his feet, Mary pushed through the crowd to help him.

A Roman soldier raised his hand to strike her.

Gabriel shouted "No!" even as Uriel came between Mary and the Roman, eyes blazing purple, a force so thick in the air that the soldier couldn't have moved his hand even if he'd tried.

Gabriel had his will encircling the Roman. Michael stood over Jesus, his sword ablaze, pinning the other Romans in time.

"Please," Gabriel said to her.

Mary looked Jesus in the eyes, and she whispered, "I'm with you."

Jesus swayed on his feet, and Gabriel reassessed him. Blood loss, heat, dehydration, the weight, and now the hatred of the crowd. Jesus had been able to work miracles through the faith of those around him, but this—he'd never make it up the hill against this.

Gabriel moved closer to Raphael, uncertain what to pray for. Certainly dying in the road was better than making it to the top and dying there. But he couldn't force himself to hope it.

I just want him to be freed from this, he prayed. *Don't let this go on. Do something!*

Mary stood up to the nearest Roman soldier. "Let me carry that beam."

Uriel glowed. The Roman guffawed, but she said, "He can't carry it. I'll do it."

"She's right," one of the soldiers said, grabbing a man from the crowd. "But we need someone strong."

The nearest soldier hefted the beam from Jesus's shoulder, scraped bloody by the weight of the wood.

Raphael instinctively reached out with his soul to heal the abrasion, then choked and pulled back because he couldn't.

Gabriel grabbed Raphael's hand in both his.

Mary kissed Jesus's cheek, but then the soldiers pushed her away.

The man from the crowd complained as the Romans impressed him into service while Jesus stood gasping for breath.

"Take it," Raphael hissed.

Gabriel said, "They'll make him take it. It's Roman law."

One of the Romans drew his sword, and the man shouldered the beam.

Gabriel shuddered. Without the weight of the wood in the calculation, Jesus would make it to the top alive.

He'd seen men crucified before. He was going to see it again.

Michael came to them. "I just wanted you two to know," he whispered, "that Beelzebub and Asmodeus pulled back. Satan is watching, but he's holding his army elsewhere."

Gabriel stared. "What is he trying?"

"I have no idea, but it can't be good." Michael glanced around. "He's got the two Cherubim with him, but no one else, and he's moving constantly."

"When his hour is over," Raphael said, "I'm going to beat the life out of him."

Gabriel muttered, "You're going to have to wait in line."

"You're bonded to me," Raphael said, "so you have to share."

"Save some for me," Michael said.

Uriel drew close. "You can't make up for what Jesus is suffering now. It won't take away the pain."

"Or the humiliation. Or the abandonment. I know that." Raphael glowered. "But I'd like to try."

Jesus stumbled again, and even as Raphael reacted instinctively to shield him, Jesus fell through him.

Gabriel felt the grief like a knife across his chest.

"It's okay," Raphael whispered. "I'm still with you. Stay down a moment."

Simon of Cyrene remained in place, still holding the beam, while the Romans hauled Jesus back to his feet.

"He's not going to make it up the hill," Michael said.

"He's going to make it," Gabriel said flatly.

The Romans let him rest a moment, and some women on the sidelines tried to approach. Jesus told them to weep for themselves, not for him.

Gabriel went cold. He looked up to see Satan sitting on a rooftop, listening to their conversation; he appeared horrified. Worse. He looked scared.

Still sitting on the ground, Raphael sensed Gabriel's surprise and followed his gaze.

Jesus took two more steps and fell again. Raphael huddled over himself.

"He's still got to climb the hill," Michael said.

"He's going to make it," Gabriel said. "Even if they have to drag him, they're going to make sure he gets there."

The Roman centurion spoke to the soldiers, letting Jesus stay sitting while he conferred with them. Gabriel focused his hearing on them, then said, "They don't want to risk Pilate's anger if he dies before they can kill him."

Raphael's head dropped.

Michael touched Gabriel, then flashed him away.

"Ask God for permission to kill him yourself," Michael said.

Gabriel radiated surprise.

Michael nodded. "It's kinder."

"Have you already asked?"

Michael nodded again.

"He's only going to tell me the same thing."

Michael urged, "Ask anyhow."

"It doesn't matter." Gabriel stared at the ground. "I couldn't do it even if God gave me permission."

Michael flashed them back. One of the Romans helped Jesus walk even as Simon of Cyrene continued carrying the cross beam. Taking it slowly, they made it to the top of the hill.

Mary had made it to the hilltop before Jesus had, and she'd positioned herself near to where his cross would be. Two other criminals were already hanging on the two sides, and she was looking at them, her eyes red. When she glanced at Gabriel with a mix of anger and despair, he cringed.

Raphael had gone misty at the edges. He brushed his wings by Gabriel. "I'm not sure I can stay."

"Hold onto me," Gabriel said. "If you want to stay, stay with me."

They laid Jesus out on the cross beam, tied his wrists down, and gave him a leather strap to bite. Raphael turned to Gabriel, his fingers wrapped in the tertiary feathers of his innermost wings. Gabriel wrapped his outer pair of wings around them both, and he drew Raphael's head against his shoulder just as the Romans drove the first nail through Jesus' wrist, between the carpals and the radius.

Mary screamed. Gabriel didn't want to look away, but he watched the face of the Roman driving the nails, his hand accurate with the hammer, his brow furrowed with concentration as he did his job, just his job. Later in the day, when it was time, this man would take a larger hammer and smash the condemned men's shins. Just doing his job.

God, Gabriel prayed. *Dear God, oh God...*

Raphael had his hands so tight in Gabriel's wings that it should have hurt, but Gabriel couldn't feel a thing.

Mary Magdalene rushed up to Mary and drew her away, pulling her into the crowd so she couldn't see what the Romans were doing. Mary was in tears.

The Roman nailed Jesus' other hand, and then he nailed his feet.

Raphael tried to raise his head, but Gabriel gripped him harder. "No, not yet."

Raphael tensed. Gabriel kept him looking away as the Romans hauled the cross beam and the cross upright with wooden forks so he wouldn't see the way Jesus's body jerked on the cross in response to gravity, and then the first few moments as he tried to find a way it didn't hurt so much, but of course there really wasn't one.

Gabriel let Raphael go, and Raphael looked, then backed up a step.

There were no more words. Even half in one another's souls, there was nothing to say.

One of the Romans posted a sign over Jesus head: "Jesus: The King of the Jews."

The crowd mocked the men being tortured to death. The other two men must have been robbers because people threw coins. Travelers on the road—and there were many—looked up in fear, glanced at the soldiers, and hurried past. Some stopped to find out who they were, but some only read the signs and laughed. "Who is this Jesus? The Jews don't have a king. Stupid Romans."

The people who had followed from Jerusalem, though, hooted and demanded a miracle. *Aren't you going to rebuild the temple? Take yourself down if you're so great! Heal yourself! Didn't you call God your father? Where's your Daddy now?*

The sky darkened as if for rain, but no rain fell. There were no clouds. It might have been Raphael darkening the sky; it might have been all the angels together. It might have been the Earth itself grieving.

Uriel stood behind Mary, wings wrapped around her body. She was beyond speech right now, beyond tears, only staring.

Gabriel couldn't tell if she was praying. He tried to pray only to feel an emptiness. Dread. Nausea. Finality.

Drink the cup to the very bottom.

Raphael sat at the base of the cross, as numb as Mary, his fire smothered. Gabriel reached through the bond to kindle him, but Raphael didn't respond. He didn't even acknowledge the Cherub's touch. Gabriel sent him whatever strength he had, but it wasn't much.

Beside him, Satan arrived.

Gabriel spun to face him, but Satan said, "We made a mistake."

Gabriel started shaking—with anger, with fatigue, with something, he had no idea what. "You made a *mistake?*"

"This isn't what we wanted." Satan gestured at the cross. "Whatever happens next, we're not going to like it. None of us."

Gabriel's vision whited out. "It's all about you, isn't it? You caused this travesty, and the only problem is what's going to happen to you?"

Satan frowned at Jesus. "The Father is going to destroy us all—you and me and all these monkeys—because of what's happening today."

Gabriel huffed. "Let Him destroy us all. I can't think of a worse condemnation of creation, that it wasn't sufficient merely to spit in God's face, but that created beings had to take up arms against God Himself and hurt him when he joined us to help."

"Get him down from there!" Satan gripped Gabriel by the shoulders. "Do you want to die? Intervene! Do you want him to suffer?"

Grabbing him by the wrists, Gabriel pushed him off. "Of course I don't want that!"

"Then take him down!"

"You take him down! This was your hour!"

"It wasn't supposed to get this far!" Satan shouted. "He was supposed to plead for his life! He was supposed to show his full power, and failing that, the crowd was supposed to demand his release, making him either a laughingstock or else beholden to the people to become the leader they demanded!"

Gabriel opened his hands. "And now—?"

Satan rolled his eyes. "A man should do anything to save his life! He had every opportunity to cast this cup aside and instead he's drinking it to the bottom."

Gabriel's jaw tightened.

"We've tried taking him down." Satan grew urgent. "We tried averting it when it became obvious what was happening. We tried giving Pilate's wife visions to make her coerce her husband. We've tried talking him into leaving. *We can't do it.*"

Gabriel turned away. "I can't do it either."

Satan formed his sword. "I suggest you give it another go."

A different sword came between Satan and Gabriel, followed by Raphael. In his drawn face, his eyes glowed black. "You leave my Cherub alone."

Satan lowered his weapon. "God's going to destroy all creation because of *your Cherub's* inaction."

Raphael advanced. "Gabriel's not going to violate God's orders and get sent to Hell because of you."

Satan didn't back down. "Isn't it better that one individual sacrifice himself in order to save the rest of us?" He glared at Raphael. "That's your charge getting tortured to death. Why aren't you doing anything to save him?"

Gabriel said, "He wouldn't disobey God to save his Son because he'd only lose Jesus anyhow."

Satan snorted at Gabriel. "How about you bottle up that knowledge and allow him to hear his heart for once?"

Mary turned to the angels. "Enough." She glared at Satan, unflinching. "Stay if you must, but do it in silence."

Satan drew breath as if about to protest, but she fixed him with an even firmer look, and he said nothing.

Mary looked back toward the cross.

Gabriel tucked his wings, bowed his head, and prayed.

Raphael's prayer joined his in his heart, and in that moment they were together. Gabriel gave Raphael whatever strength he could offer, and this time Raphael accepted it.

Satan's voice in Gabriel's mind: *Why is he doing this?*

Gabriel refused to answer.

181

Is it all a put-on?

I'm sure it hurts, Gabriel sent. *He's making all the stress hormones human bodies make, and the pain centers in his brain are firing continuously. You've never been in a body, have you?* When Satan sent a disgusted negative, Gabriel continued, *A body monitors itself all the time for whether it's well. If you touch fire, it tells you so you'll pull back your hand. If it needs food, it tells you so you can feed it. It must be like the pain of Hell you feel. Every second, it's telling him about the nails, about the crown, about the lacerations. Every second it's tempting him more than you ever could to set this cup aside and pour out the contents on the ground.*

Then why doesn't he do it? Satan sent, with the nonverbal echo that he'd set it aside if he could.

You never set aside your own pain, did you? You never tried.

Satan sent an impulse that this wasn't the point.

Gabriel looked at Raphael, shoulder to shoulder with him for the first time in this nightmare. *He's doing what our Father asked.*

Why would He ask that?

Gabriel shook his head.

Figure it out, Satan said. *Maybe there's another way to meet the conditions. It could save us all.*

Gabriel cut the contact and took Raphael's hand. It might be the last time they were ever together.

He wasn't sure Satan was right, but Satan was sure. Although Gabriel didn't mind being destroyed if it was God's will, he had an odd reluctance to being destroyed if it meant Raphael wouldn't exist either. So they stood together, one unit in the face of tragedy, and he kept his hand and his heart in Raphael's, his wings touching Uriel's, and his eyes focused on Jesus.

The Father would demand justice. A destroyed race. A second destroyed race. A destroyed world. A destroyed Son.

At the base of the cross, his sword across his lap, Michael sat back on his heels with his neck craned up. Saraquael and Zadkiel sat immediately behind Michael, their swords sheathed.

Gabriel could feel the air thick with angels, all their attention forced on one dying man. Only three demons were there, Satan and his two top Cherubim, but all watching in the same horror at how humanity had done what even Satan hadn't the gall to do.

Justice.

Gabriel shivered, and Raphael squeezed his hand.

Gabriel sent to him, *Do you forgive me?*

Raphael pulled back his heart, and Gabriel blistered with the residual heat. He lowered his head.

Things happened. They offered Jesus wine on a sponge, but he didn't take it. Gabriel felt tears on his cheeks, but he didn't remember crying. Jesus looked at John and told him to care for his mother, and then asked Mary to take John as her son. Speaking was so hard because he had to use so little air. Jesus was dying. Less than an hour and it would be over.

And then Jesus cried out in a loud voice, "My God, My God—why have you forsaken me?"

Mary let out a choked cry, covering her face in her hands. Raphael turned to Gabriel and sobbed into his wings. Gabriel remembered the cup, the void, the moment it had touched Jesus's lips.

Jesus said, "Father, forgive them, for they know not what they do," and then as Gabriel's head raised and Satan behind him gasped at the same realization, Jesus said, "It is finished. Father, into your hands, I commend my spirit."

He bowed his head, and Gabriel felt the moment of death.

Raphael ignited in his arms and emitted a concussion that shook the Earth. He flashed away. Gabriel took off after him.

He arrived in the Temple sanctuary. Raphael had drawn his sword, and with a shout, he threw himself at the curtain and ripped it lengthwise, then flung his sword at the far wall where it clanged against the stone.

Gabriel tried to pull off the fire through the fury, but Raphael turned on him.

"This was your fault!" He burned like a forest fire. "You were always jealous of the bond I had with him!"

Gabriel raised his hands. "I never wanted this!"

Raphael advanced on him. "You had it in your power to stop it earlier, or at least to tell him we hadn't all forsaken him. But he died alone, and he died believing we'd abandoned him, and it's your fault."

Gabriel took a step backward. "Raphael, please!"

"Get out of my heart." Raphael's eyes were a pair of live coals. "I'm no longer your Seraph."

He took his sword and vanished.

Gabriel went down in front of the torn curtain, and he didn't rise again.

Gabriel lay on his side before the curtain, unmoving as a ragdoll. His wings lay scattered, his arms limp, his legs crossed at the ankle. He stared at nothing. The angle of the sun changed, and dust settled, and he didn't stir. One of the priests walked through him. He lay there.

Satan entered the Temple and sat, also unmoving, looking at Gabriel looking at nothing, both facing the same direction, both in absolute silence. Someone else walked through. Much distress about the torn curtain. No tying or sewing on the Sabbath, so torn it must remain. Servants lit the lamps. The sun went down.

Distant prayers sounded. Gabriel didn't move. Satan dismissed Belior with nothing more than "Leave us alone."

Stars shone. The prayers ended. Satan got up and came around to the front of Gabriel.

Gabriel was staring away with the thousand-mile Cherub stare. Satan lifted him by the shoulders into a sitting position and looked him in the face.

After a moment, Gabriel's eyes focused, and he regarded Satan in confusion.

"Do you still have the Vision?"

Gabriel nodded.

"Is the Second Person back on the throne?"

Gabriel shook his head.

"Damn it!" Satan dropped him, and Gabriel collapsed back to the ground. "Do you realize what that means? Do you have any comprehension?"

Gabriel had unfocused into the stare again as if he hadn't been moved, although his wings lay in different positions.

"Is this what you wanted?" Satan shouted. "Don't you realize what's about to happen?"

Satan kicked one of Gabriel's wings, then vanished.

Gabriel didn't move.

More activity in the sanctuary. More priests discussing how to mend the torn curtain after Passover. Stars shifting.

Uriel appeared in the sanctuary and lifted Gabriel to sitting, then coaxed Gabriel to a stand. Uriel put an arm around him and flashed him away.

Distant prayers. Noise from the streets. The sounds of animals outside the temple. A ruined curtain and silence within.

Gabriel arrived at Mary's darkened residence and crumpled in the corner, knees up, arms folded, head on his wrists. Uriel kissed Mary on the forehead and vanished.

Mary came to Gabriel, bloodshot but tearless, and tried to touch him. Only after her fingers passed through him did he make himself semi-solid enough to reach for her hand.

Through the shadows she looked him in the eyes. "I sent Uriel for you. I didn't know where you'd gone."

Gabriel only regarded her.

"You're so grey. You're misting into nothing." She touched his hair. "Where's Raphael?"

Gabriel projected confusion.

"Where is Jesus now?"

Gabriel again projected confusion: not on the throne of glory. Maybe Sheol. Somehow he knew his body lay in a tomb outside Jerusalem.

Mary said, "Shouldn't you be with Raphael rather than with me?"

Gabriel flinched.

Her face fell. "Why would he be angry at you?"

Gabriel's eyes narrowed, and he looked directly at her with a question.

"Because it's easier to take care of you." She forced a small smile. "You're right in front of me."

Gabriel put his hand on her chest right beneath her throat, and then he touched her forehead.

"I'll be all right," Mary whispered, and the tears came. "I...you get cried out sometimes." She looked aside. "I didn't even get a chance to light a lamp before sundown."

Around the room, lamps flared into light.

Mary started. "Doesn't that violate the Sabbath?"

"I don't care." Gabriel tightened his fist. "Created beings just killed the Son of God."

Mary bit her lip. "When they nailed him...he's God's Son, so maybe he didn't suffer the pain. Maybe not all the pain."

Gabriel averted his eyes. "Would you like to believe that?"

"I would. I'd like to believe he thought Peter and James and Philip were all standing behind where he couldn't see them. Or that they got arrested defending him."

"It would be nice." Gabriel rested his head on his knees. "He didn't deserve that. Every man there today deserved it, but not him."

Mary's voice broke. "Why did it have to happen?"

"I don't know." He hit the floor. "Why can people be so stupid about the obvious and simultaneously creative with their cruelty? Why didn't they just cut his throat? Why make a spectacle of death? Who was the sorry cretin who came up with the crown of thorns? It was probably the only idea the man had in his life. Why did he get it then? Why didn't he come up with a way to make water flow uphill?"

Mary shook her head. "Jesus knew he was making people uncomfortable, and he refused to stop doing his Father's work. I would only hope I could do the same."

Gabriel dropped his head. "God's hand can hurt when it works. But the results are worthwhile. Nobody trusts any longer. Humans don't trust themselves, or each other, and it spreads. At the end, they can't trust God either."

Mary said nothing, and Gabriel struggled to keep the dry embers of his heart from scattering on the wind.

Mary sat back a little. "I'm not going to see you again, am I?"

Gabriel lifted his head, confused.

"You were here for him." She bit her lip. "Without him, there's no more need for you to come around, and I have no more need to see you."

Gabriel said, "Uriel won't leave you until death. And I might not be necessary, but I'll still stop by."

Mary took his hand. "You're very sweet."

"I'm hardly sweet," Gabriel said, "but I do whatever I can in God's service."

Mary smiled. "I appreciate it. But will I be able to see you?"

"I don't know," Gabriel said. "I don't know anything anymore."

Mary hugged Gabriel, who wrapped her in his wings. Her tears soaked into his shoulder.

"Would you do me a favor?" she asked.

"Nearly anything."

"If I give you something, will you bring it to his tomb?"

Gabriel nodded. Mary got up to get a knife, then pulled some of her hair apart from the rest and started cutting through it.

"Let me do you two favors." Gabriel flashed to her side and touched the strands where she wanted them cut, and they severed. He tied them together in a bundle. "Put them in his hand?"

"Anywhere in the tomb," she said. "I didn't want to ask Mary Magdalene, but at least I know you won't think I'm crazy."

Gabriel said, "I may leave him a feather too. We can be crazy together."

Mary nodded even as new tears came. "Well done, Gabriel," she said with a long-ago sternness. "That will be satisfactory."

He bowed to her. "It's been satisfactory for me as well, my lady." And with that he flashed to the tomb.

As soon as he arrived, Raphael's flames engulfed his heart. Gabriel reflexively armored himself.

"How dare you?" Raphael advanced on him. "You have no place here."

"Mary sent me," Gabriel said. "And you need to get yourself under control."

"You have nothing to say to me." Raphael folded his arms and flared his wings. "He's my charge."

"He's my God." Gabriel turned away. "Are we like Michael and Satan fighting over a dead man's body? You'll just have to tolerate my presence for one more minute."

Gabriel knelt before Jesus's body and made himself semi-solid to inhale the myrrh and aloes. He passed his hand through the cloth to lay Mary's lock of hair in Jesus's wounded hand, but he avoided the holes from the nails. Gabriel kissed his face through the burial cloth. *I'm sorry*, he sent to nothing. *I love you. I wish there were something I could have done.*

Raphael's heat suffused the room. Gabriel wanted to say more, but the Seraph flames threatened to breach his heart.

As Gabriel got to his feet, Raphael said, "You owe me an explanation."

Gabriel flashed away.

He flashed through eight locations, including one in Heaven and one in another solar system, before he was sure Raphael couldn't pursue him through them all. He returned to Earth long enough to find an abandoned cabin on the other side of the world. It was still daylight on this mountain. He Guarded the walls, then reGuarded them. No one would find him here.

With the corner to his back, he settled on the floor.

Why? he prayed.

No answer.

Gabriel sent his brain into the problem and turned it over, attacked it from as many directions as he could, questioned his answers and then formed new questions, and every explanation came up wanting.

After all this time, he could recognize a "missing piece" problem, the kind you couldn't solve until you had that final bit of information which made the others sensible but which only baffled you without it.

Regardless, Gabriel turned it inside out, turned it backward, tried to reinterpret all of scripture in light of the past day. Although some of it made more sense, more of it made less.

Cherubim weren't designed to work alone. That was the stinging truth. If he wanted to make any progress, he needed at least one other Cherub to refine his ideas. But that meant bringing down the Guard, and bringing down the Guard meant he might have Raphael all over him again within thirty seconds.

Choice: guaranteed Cherub versus possible Seraph.

Choice: (possibility of answer plus risk) versus (safety plus no answer)

Certitude: No answer without Cherub help

Very high probability: Raphael still furious.

Risk = high.

Very slim possibility: answer with Cherub help.

Benefit = either high or zero.

Gabriel played through the scenario for a minimum-risk maximum-benefit result, changing the variables, choosing the Cherub most likely to give his ideas the proper spin, deriving alternatives in case Raphael did find him, and still no perfect solution.

Certitude: He couldn't hide forever.

Probability (reasonable): Raphael wouldn't remain angry forever.

Question: How long until Raphael calmed himself?

Sub-question: Did Gabriel have a responsibility to calm Raphael?

Question: When would Raphael get distracted and find another target?

Sub-question: Was Gabriel culpable if Raphael did find another target?

Question: Was Raphael right to be angry?

Sunset flared, but this Gabriel ignored. The trouble with making himself unseeable was he couldn't see out either. He couldn't even tell if Raphael was summoning him because he'd set up the Guard specifically to repel the Seraph.

Ultimately all the analysis broke down. Gabriel prayed and felt it was time to emerge, so he took down the Guard.

Instantly Michael was in the cabin. "What are you doing?" Emotions streamed from him with such force that he might as well have been a Seraph, and Gabriel pressed into the corner. "We need you now! Even Raphael couldn't find you."

Gabriel was flat into the wall, projecting: he hadn't realized, he just wanted to think, wanted to be alone, wanted to get away—

"You don't have that option!" Michael's eyes fixed on Gabriel's as if he'd rather be screaming. "We're at war, and I need you where I can find you. You're the smartest angel in creation, but that didn't occur to you?"

Gabriel projected no.

For a moment Michael looked about to continue, but then his wings relaxed. "Saraquael, I've got him," he said into the air, then paused for (presumably) Saraquael's response. He turned back to Gabriel, a hand on his sword. "Well, at least you turned up. We're breaking Jesus out of Sheol."

Gabriel shook his head. "Sheol is impenetrable."

Michael nodded. "That's why we need you. You and the other Cherubim are going to figure it out."

Gabriel dropped back to the floor. "I can't. I can't right now."

Michael crouched beside him. "There's no way we can do it without you." He put a hand on Gabriel's knee. "Is it Raphael? He's livid."

Gabriel tucked his head on his arms.

Michael put his head next to Gabriel's. "I'm sorry. I know you recharge best alone, but I can't give you that option."

Gabriel acknowledged.

"Israfel," Michael said into thin air. "Can you come to me?"

"No!" Gabriel's head jerked up. "Michael, don't."

Israfel arrived, and she met Gabriel's eyes. Her Seraph fire curled from her soul, tantalizing. "You had us worried." She squatted before him. "Are you all right?"

Only for Michael's sake, Gabriel let his soul respond to Israfel's through their primary bond. She gave him her fire, and he took it even though he didn't have anything to return. She sat forward and smiled, and his heart raced, and the abandoned building seemed constricting and ugly. He wanted to be moving about again and answering Michael's questions, and there were other Cherubim to debate with and the walls of Sheol to breach.

"I'm fine. Let's go," he said, feeling his heart boiling over, and Michael brought them to the staging area.

However long the angels had been looking for him, it didn't seem to have slowed them down. Several dozen were organizing plans and determining what or whom to bring along on a strike force. Gabriel found Ophaniel, who outlined several approaches they had decided would not work.

Blistering heat in his heart told him Raphael had arrived. *Where were you?*

Thinking.

You ran away from me.

Absolutely I did. Now let me do my job.

Why don't you measure my shock: the legalist is collaborating for an invasion on the Sabbath?

If it saves Creation, that's saving a life, which you might recall is permitted.

And with that, Gabriel cut off contact.

Ophaniel was looking toward Raphael. "He's furious."

Gabriel ignored the veiled request for information. Ophaniel had his own primary bond to Raphael—let him figure it out for himself.

Michael called the Seven and the heads of the orders before him. "It's pretty straightforward," Michael said. "Jesus is in Sheol, and we want him out. Cherubim, you need to come up with a plan of attack. I want the Principalities and the Archangels arrayed to defend if we manage to crack it open, with the Angels, Dominions and Virtues on alert. Powers are to be arrayed between Sheol and Hell to defend if the demons attempt to interfere." He looked around at them. "Gabriel, you have the entire choir of Cherubim at your disposal. Uriel, we want prayer support from the Thrones."

A heaviness filled the air, and then Satan appeared at Michael's side, wearing armor.

Before Michael could react, Gabriel discharged enough force in Satan's face to strip the corona off a sun, then again before the first shot had time to hit, and a third time, and the fourth time he called his sword to his shaking hands to use as a focus.

Raphael ascended behind Gabriel and targeted a blast of his own. "This is your fault!"

Gabriel took Lucifer off-guard with the first shot, leaving him with both hands over his eyes and his outer wings on fire, but now Satan had a Guard up. He deflected Gabriel's last blows and Raphael's follow-up.

Michael pushed between Gabriel and Satan, his sword in his hands. "Your hour? It's over."

Satan glowed hazily, and a moment later he was on his knees, the fire smoldering out, and then he shone far brighter. Saraquael and Raguel enchained Asmodeus and Beelzebub with their willpower. Belior and Mephistopheles stood back-to-back, maintaining a Guard, but they hadn't drawn their swords. All five wore identical black armor, but the three Seraphim wore capes.

Satan pushed to his feet. The fire in his hair and wings flared out, and he shook his head like a man bothered by nothing more than a cloud of gnats. He opened his hands, scanning the angels before him. "Is anyone in charge here? If I could have someone rational listen to me for a moment—"

"I'm in charge," Michael said. "Leave."

"As much fun as it would be to rout your forces while you're sniveling about your friend, I'm actually here to offer my help." Satan folded his arms and tucked his wings at his back. The singed upper feathers had already turned white again. He hadn't taken down his Guard, though, which gave Gabriel a momentary satisfaction. "It sounds to me as if you're breaking him out of Sheol, and frankly, I think the bunch of you haven't a chance. I don't want him in Sheol either, though, and therefore it's in my best interests to make sure you have at least some chance of succeeding."

Raphael stared daggers at him. "Did you forget who put him there?"

Satan stood much more relaxed than the other four demons. "You can't afford to pass up any resources that might make the impossible possible."

Gabriel said, "Thank you for your input. We'll take that under advisement."

Satan glanced at Gabriel. "That was the most gracious way anyone has ever told me to sod off."

Gabriel inclined his head. "Thank you."

"By the way," Satan said with a smirk, "nice shot."

"This is not a joint assault." Michael hadn't relaxed. "I'm not having you stay so I need to defend against you at the same time as—"

"You won't have to defend against me," Satan said. "And you should free my officers. They're under orders not to attack, even if you try something as boneheaded as that again."

Gabriel raised his eyebrows.

Satan continued, "I'm not stupid. If the Second Person of the Trinity is not returned to the throne, the Father is going to exact revenge on all creation. Being a part of creation ourselves, we see no benefit in being destroyed. Our continued existence is contingent on his emergence. Consequently, I put our resources at your disposal." His eyes glittered, and flames crackled around his wings until Gabriel could feel the heat. "I dislike the prospect immensely myself."

"Then you can relax." Gabriel shifted his weight. "He asked the Father to forgive us all because we were too *boneheaded* to realize what we were doing."

"I've felt the Father's wrath firsthand and know how readily He forgives when it's His dignity on the line. You might remember that yourself." Satan huffed. "My people did nothing in comparison to those monkeys today, and He took everything."

Michael said, "You knew what you were doing."

Satan shook his head "The point remains: just because the Second Person asked doesn't mean the First Person will go along with it."

Israfel pulled Michael aside and whispered, and then Michael called over Saraquael and Zadkiel.

Satan said, "You don't need to consult. If you don't want us here, you need to forcibly eject us from the proceedings. Otherwise, we'll remain."

Michael looked at Gabriel, and Gabriel flashed over to him.

How sincere is he?

How should I know? Gabriel sent. But then he remembered as if in a dream Satan accosting him in the Temple, demanding if he understood what was about to happen, and Satan at the Cross telling him they'd screwed up.

Michael must have caught some of Gabriel's thoughts. *You think he's genuine?*

We should never trust him entirely, Gabriel sent, *but his goals may coincide with ours for the time being.*

Michael rubbed his chin. *What have they got to offer?*

Two of the four smartest Cherubim and three of the four most powerful Seraphim are standing two wingspans away willing to help, Gabriel replied. *I'd say that's something.*

Michael turned to Satan. "You can stay until you annoy me sufficiently that I throw you out."

Satan folded his arms and tilted his head. "Appreciated."

Michael gestured to Saraquael to release the four demons from their restraints. Satan brought down his Guard. "Your Cherubim will take orders from Gabriel. The Seraphim you can keep for now. And if you have any ideas on a starting point, you might as well voice them now, since I know you will anyway."

"Only one." Satan turned to Raphael. "You were with him when he raised the dead. How did he do it?"

Raphael said, "He called them. They came."

Satan folded his arms and shifted his weight only a little, but with such control that the tip of his sword in its scabbard carved an arc in the air. "Then maybe you should get to the walls of Sheol and start calling."

Michael said, "You're here against my wishes. You will not be ordering my officers like that. You want him that badly, you go call him."

Satan smirked. "He's not going to come for me."

"Then I'd strongly suggest you be respectful to the ones he might come for." Michael turned to Raphael. "Do you think it would do any good?"

"None."

Gabriel said, "Let's take a look, though. If there's a solution to be found, we might as well be closer."

All five demons and a select group of archangels flashed to the edge of Sheol, where they hovered in a cluster. Sheol didn't have a gate and didn't rest on the ground. It existed as a territory not encompassed by Heaven or Creation, but immediately adjacent to Hell. Gabriel craned back his head to look up the length of it. It resembled nothing more than a polished cube of black granite, without handholds or decoration.

Had you ever been here before? Israfel sent.

No, never. Gabriel extended a hand to the wall and found it cold beneath his fingertips, but cold in the same way a living thing is warm to the touch. The cold pulsed and met him, and having touched it once, Gabriel knew he would recognize it if ever again he touched a part of it. This was Death.

Michael was scanning the structure. "How large is it?"

Satan said, "Measurements that have no meaning. You could glide all day and not reach the top. When you reach the top, it's the same as here."

Gabriel said, "This could be the top," and changed his axis so he stood on the breathing stone. Now at a right angle to everyone else, he crouched on the plane and pressed both hands into it, then laid down and exposed his wings to it as well.

Ophaniel got down beside him. Awe rolled off him.

"Are you getting anything?" Gabriel whispered.

Ophaniel sent a negative.

Belior and Mephistopheles joined them. Gabriel looked up to find everyone standing on the stone watching the Cherubim investigate. His wings tightened involuntarily as he sat up on his heels.

"We've never managed to talk to the wall," Belior said. "It won't talk back."

"There's no entrance." Mephistopheles had discarded his helmet, revealing a mass of blond curls. "No seams. Even on the corners, you don't realize you're around them until you can't see anyone else you were with a moment ago."

Gabriel reached for Raphael instinctively only to feel the heat again; he disengaged and reached for Israfel. She sparkled in his mind, and he shook off the self-consciousness. "How do souls get inside?"

Belior shrugged as he removed his own helmet. "I've followed them from death, and I get stopped at the wall, but they get drawn in without any struggle."

"So we have a semi-permeable façade," Gabriel said, "which appears to be channeled to prevent entrance by certain types of creatures."

Mephistopheles said, "More than semi-permeable. It's almost an osmotic reaction. Put a human soul alongside it, and in it goes, even if it's not yet dead."

Ignoring Gabriel's horrified expression, Belior said, "Leaving out for the moment the fact that if it were truly osmotic, we'd be drawn inside because the concentration of angels inside is clearly less than the concentration of angels on the—"

"Obviously," Mephistopheles said, speaking rapidly, "and the concentration of human souls isn't equalizing either because at this point in time there clearly are far fewer humans outside Sheol than—"

Satan said, "Belior, Mephistopheles, stop."

Gabriel felt Israfel chuckle in his mind.

You're only amused that I didn't get involved too.

You didn't get a chance. Then after a pause, *I just had exactly the same conversation with Ophaniel.*

Gabriel smiled, and her fire swirled through him again. "Is there any way to follow a soul through?"

Mephistopheles said, "If you'd like to attach yourself to something, I'll be happy to dispatch it so you can test what happens."

Gabriel said, "I was thinking more of being an opportunist."

"You don't need to," Saraquael said. "Guardians frequently try to follow their charges into Sheol, especially if the charge is in a poor state of soul."

Gabriel said, "Are they stopped at the wall or can they penetrate to any depth?"

Raphael scowled. "You could ask me, you know. I just tried to follow him in."

Gabriel steadied himself. "And were you stopped right at the edge of the wall, or could you penetrate?"

"Right at the edge."

"Thank you," Gabriel said. "You could have just told us."

Raphael said, "I didn't stop being his guardian the instant he died, regardless of how convenient that would have been."

Gabriel ignored the glance Ophaniel sent him and instead looked at Belior, who wore a thrilled surprise.

Michael said, "All this trickery is interesting, but have you ever tried battering it?"

Satan said, "I can't blow it open."

Gabriel's eyes brightened as both Israfel and Raphael ignited. "You tried?"

Beelzebub laughed out loud, and Asmodeus said, "I was surprised you didn't feel it in Heaven and come running to find out what we'd done."

Israfel projected to Gabriel that she wished she'd seen it. Gabriel said, "Maybe you could try again?"

Satan met Gabriel's eyes with a sparkle in his own. "Would you care to be that impressed?"

Michael looked uncomfortable. "You'll impress me enough if you get him out. We don't need pyrotechnics in addition."

The Seraphim's disappointment was palpable. It wasn't every day you got to see that much power unleashed in one place.

Push it, Israfel sent.

Gabriel turned to Michael. "What if I help him?"

"Better yet," Belior said, "if we get bonded pairs hitting from opposite sides, we could set up a structural resonance that would perseverate and magnify the strength of the initial blow."

Mephistopheles nodded. "If we fine-tune the harmonic and anharmonic tendencies, it might just increase the entropic energy in the wall enough to—"

"Mephistopheles, Belior, stop." Satan looked at Michael. "I'm willing to try."

Michael sighed. "We'll need six teams."

"If you knew anything about resonance, it's only two," Belior said. "We'll want to time it exactly to coordinate the strike."

"What are we hitting it with?" Gabriel said. "Fire won't have any effect. Light isn't going to do anything other than be pretty."

Satan said, "Blast it with undiluted soul-energy."

Gabriel said, "Have you ever tried plasma, nuclear energy, antimatter...?"

"No," Satan said.

Mephistopheles raised a hand. "I have."

Satan looked at him, eyebrows raised.

"I was curious. I segmented off areas and measured them for smoothness and hardness, as well as chemical composition and—"

"Mephistopheles—"

"I documented its null state," Mephistopheles said quickly, "and comparisons afterward showed no significant alteration in any of the measurements."

"Anything insignificant?" Ophaniel said.

"Nothing I couldn't account for by measurement error."

"Soul energy," Satan said. "It gets the most power from a blast because you're not changing or diluting it."

Gabriel agreed.

"You and Israfel go to the opposite side," Satan said. "I'll strike from here."

"If you don't mind my saying," Belior ventured, "that may not be the best tactic."

"Why Israfel?" Raphael said.

Satan shrugged. "She's stronger than you are."

Gabriel sent Raphael reassurance, but Raphael pushed it aside.

"You won't be able to coordinate it finely enough with Gabriel to set up an anharmonic resonance." Belior rubbed his chin. "Timing is going to be of greater import than force."

"Ophaniel or Raphael can give the signal," Gabriel said.

"Even at that," Belior said, "there's time for communication. It would be better to have you and Raphael on one side and Israfel with Ophaniel on the other because you four are primaries to one another. That eliminates any communication glitches."

"What a convenient plan." Michael looked incredulous. "You just assigned my four strongest officers to scatter and then drain themselves of their power."

Gabriel turned to Michael. "It's unfortunate, but he does make sense."

"Then let Belior and Asmodeus hit one side and Mephistopheles and Beelzebub the other." Michael folded his arms. "I'm not objecting to the theory. I'm objecting to gutting my forces."

Saraquael said, "We could still take them."

"I don't *want* to take them," Michael said. "I would rather they not have the time to consider the opportunity."

Satan looked bored. "If we were going to attack, we would have immediately after he died. Besides, my Cherubim are having too much fun."

Gabriel laughed, and Mephistopheles caught his eye, also grinning.

Ophaniel said, "They're not cross-primaries. Belior and Beelzebub are secondaries, and Asmodeus and Mephistopheles are only tertiaries."

Michael shook his head. "It still sounds far too convenient."

Gabriel said, "It would be a deep discharge. We wouldn't be incapacitated for long."

Satan cleared his throat. "If Gabriel wants to bond with me, I'm willing." He frowned. "Don't misunderstand. I don't want to, but I'd agree to it."

Gabriel grimaced. "I don't see that it would give us that much additional advantage."

Satan gestured toward Belior, who looked simultaneously horrified and jealous. "He thinks bonded pairs are the way to go. My power plus yours would not be insignificant." A moment later he added, "You're also smart enough and would be motivated enough afterward to figure out how to break a permanent bond and free both of us."

"That won't be necessary." Gabriel glanced at Raphael, whose face showed no emotion at all: not the jealousy nor the anger he'd have predicted. "If our efforts are just short, I'll consider it again. But not without a compelling reason."

Satan inclined his head in agreement.

Michael looked at Gabriel. "I'm going to leave the decision to you. If you have any reservations about this, it's a no-go."

Gabriel said, "I don't."

Michael opened his hands. "Then set it up."

Beelzebub muttered to Satan, "I'd rather see you blast it."

"If he hits it afterward, he stands a good chance of disturbing the resonance." Mephistopheles put his hand on Beelzebub's arm. "Resonance is a feedback loop. If you want it to work, you need to get it started and then leave it alone."

Satan smirked. "There will be other chances, no worries."

Gabriel said, "Raphael and I will take the opposite side."

Raphael shook his head. "You were going to be paired with Israfel, remember?"

He averted his eyes. "It will be more even if it's you and me against her and him." Then he looked right at Raphael and met the anger face-forward. "It shouldn't be you and me against each other."

Raphael flashed away. Gabriel followed.

I'm with you, Israfel sent through her bond. Then, *What's going on with him?*

Gabriel sent back a sense of hopeless confusion, and then turned toward Raphael. They had arrived on the opposite side and were completely alone. Gabriel again altered his axis so he was standing on the surface. He reached for Israfel and Raphael, and a moment later he felt the Seraphim in contact with Ophaniel.

He and Ophaniel established what they would do, the distance they needed, and then positioned themselves. Israfel gave an all-clear on her side when the other angels had gotten safely distant.

All in one another's hearts, the four didn't speak as much as share one set of thoughts from four different directions. And the longer they remained merged, the more it arose in their collective awareness just how angry one of them was, how impatient another was becoming in response, and how sad it made the other two. Raphael backed off from the others, and Gabriel stopped the line of thought. Later, later. We can deal with it later. Now we have to coordinate the strike.

He and Raphael merged even as Israfel and Ophaniel merged, and at the same time on opposite sides of an impossibly large cube hanging off the side of Hell, Israfel/Ophaniel and Gabriel/Raphael fired their souls' energy at Sheol.

It wasn't a sustained blast. The idea was to hit it once, hard, with all their energy so the shock wave would travel through the structure. The Cherubim had timed the blast, then pumped all their energy into the Seraphim, who sucked it out like a vacuum as they fired everything from their double-store of power.

Gabriel brought up their wings to shield them from the concussion. He wasn't in a form anymore, just a dissociated soul with no energy to simulate even a subtle body. Unable to sense anything, he waited for any of his power to return, because he'd sent everything into that blast.

God—wow.

Sensation returned with a tingle, and he started pulling himself back together.

At some point he realized Saraquael had collected him and brought him back to the others, thrilled but quiet, supporting him but with his attention riveted elsewhere. As Gabriel forced himself back into a spiritual form, Saraquael said, "Can you see it?"

Gabriel couldn't negate it, either with words or nonverbally. Saraquael helped him get his wings under control, and a moment later Gabriel focused in the general direction Saraquael was pointing.

He reached for Raphael and Israfel, found them equally spent, and could not feel Ophaniel through them.

"This is awesome." Mephistopheles hovered on Gabriel's other side. "Too bad you didn't witness the initial blast. Hell lit up with it, and the entire cube is resonating like a bell. Try to listen before it dissipates."

Gabriel extended his soul. All of Sheol pulsed like a wave, a deep drone as the stress passed back and forth, slightly out of tune, a structure leaning one way and then the next. He patched Raphael and Israfel into what he felt, and they reacted with surprise.

"Lucifer's blast was brighter," Beelzebub said.

"That doesn't surprise me." Gabriel struggled to clear his head. "We needed to hit it just right, not harder."

"You hit it just right," Mephistopheles said, "but it's not going down."

Gabriel could tell that on his own. While impressive, the structural resonance was diminishing without the walls noticeably weakening.

Satan said, "This is ridiculous. Belior, could I in theory boost it by hitting it at the right frequency?"

"Theoretically," Belior said. "I'll help you time it."

At Satan's voice, Gabriel tensed and tried to pull together.

Saraquael projected a feeling of safety: he should relax. Besides, Satan had gone now.

Gabriel reached again for Raphael, who checked him over from a distance. *You're spent.*

Gabriel tried to move away from Saraquael and then decided he'd better wait.

At that moment, a blast ignited an entire side of Sheol, illuminating the husk of Hell's outer limits with an orange-white gash. Gabriel shut his eyes and still could see the light rocketing backward from the impact.

Asmodeus and Beelzebub cheered.

"Oh," Saraquael whispered. "I'd forgotten—"

God, that light... So brilliant, so powerful, and such a loss when it had turned to illuminate only itself. *I wish— I just wish he'd stayed.*

Gabriel listened for the resonance. The sound was even more chaotic than before, but after a moment it became obvious the walls still weren't coming down.

Asmodeus huffed. "What did God brace that thing with?"

A second flash blinded them as Satan hit it again (*How much energy does he have?)* but the resonance didn't increase.

Satan returned, shaking but able to stand on his own. Chalky white, Belior glowed for both of them.

Gabriel said, "That was amazing."

Satan smirked at him,. "It was a bit much for Belior."

"I managed." Belior pulled his wings tight to his shoulders in an attempt to keep the feathers from trembling. He glanced at Asmodeus, and then he stood a little straighter.

Gabriel wished he had a Seraph to draw power from too, but the only Seraphim available were just as wiped out as he was.

Michael said, "When you four are recovered a bit, we need another plan."

Gabriel looked around. "Where's Ophaniel?"

From behind him, Michael said, "I've got him."

Gabriel turned to find Ophaniel in Michael's arms. The Cherub was still limp.

"He'll be all right," Raphael said. "I checked him out. I guess he channeled more into Israfel than you did into me."

Gabriel didn't probe further to find out if that was an insult. Sheol's resonance had dimmed to a buzzing, a bell no longer sounding but not yet still.

Michael said, "I'm up for any other ideas."

Mephistopheles said, "I'll check for damage at the impact points," and he flashed away.

"Only human souls can get in," Belior said. "So if one of you wants to become human, I'll kill you."

"Are you serious?" Israfel said.

"No, I'm not." From the way Belior deadpanned it, Gabriel could tell he genuinely hadn't been. "If one of you became human and I killed you, you'd turn back into an angel and not be very happy."

"Ah. Cherub humor." Israfel folded her arms. "The first oxymoron."

Belior glanced at Gabriel with a grin, and Gabriel felt himself smile back.

Mephistopheles returned. "Unchanged."

Michael folded his arms and his wings, and he bit his lip.

Gabriel straightened suddenly.

Raphael and Israfel looked right at him.

Gabriel turned to Belior. "How do you conjure the spirits of the dead?"

Belior shook his head. "Trade secret."

Mephistopheles' eyes sparkled. "We'll tell you only if you join us."

Satan said, "You want to try conjuring him out of Sheol?"

"I'm wondering if we can use the same mechanism to extract him."

"Conjuring is not extraction," Belior said. "It's sleight of hand."

"Go on," Gabriel said.

Behind him, Ophaniel awoke.

"Explain the process," Satan said. "We want him out of there, no matter what we have to put on the table."

Mephistopheles brightened. "There are three fissures in the wall of Sheol—"

"Two," said Belior.

"—that borders on Hell. They're hairline cracks, but it's enough to grab small strands of a person's soul and amplify whatever they want to say."

"How do you find the soul?" Gabriel couldn't picture this at all. "There have to be half a billion people in Sheol already."

Belior made a light image in his hands, rays streaming from a cube. "Even though the humans are dead, they still carry connections to the people and things they were attached to while alive. If they've got unfinished business, they maintain some awareness of that for a while after their death."

Gabriel remembered Jesus on the hilltop, looking over all humanity, and he nodded.

Belior continued, "So with the more recently dead ones, the ones people would want to summon anyhow, you stand a decent chance of tracing them by finding something they were attached to and following it backward."

Gabriel's forehead furrowed. "You're saying you don't pull the person himself out of Sheol."

Belior shook his head. "The fissure is narrow as a thread. Coaxing even the strand out is tricky. Once we have a grasp on the strand, though, we can send and receive, and we amplify it in order to transmit to the living person whatever information we obtain."

Gabriel folded his arms. "I'm still thinking we can use this somehow. Can I study the fissures?"

Belior flashed himself and Gabriel to a cavern within Hell, shining to illuminate the area. After a moment, the other angels began joining them.

Belior showed Gabriel the one flat wall in the cave, the spot where the expected jagged rocks abruptly transformed into a polished smoothness at a right angle to the rest of the area. "There are two fissures, but this is the one we use. It starts here," and he touched a spot at about the limits of his reach, "and it runs like this," he traced raggedly, "until it tapers off here," at about knee height.

Gabriel touched the wall. "I can't feel it at all."

"That doesn't surprise me." Belior shrugged. "Do you want to feel one of those strands?"

Gabriel nodded.

Belior pressed his hands to the wall. While he worked, Gabriel checked out the other angels. Raphael and Israfel looked stronger now, much the way he felt. Even Ophaniel seemed more stable. Satan didn't appear to have been weakened by firing twice, especially now that his wings had stopped shaking.

"Okay, I've got one wrapped up." Belior gestured for Gabriel to come closer. "Try to feel through the wall for the fissure. It's right here." He pressed Gabriel's hand to the wall.

With his hand sandwiched between the stone of death and an angel without grace, ice shot up his arm.

He closed his eyes. At first he sensed nothing, but then he murmured, "Oh!"

"Send your mind into the fissure," Belior whispered. "Follow the line out from my heart into it."

A filament tender as cornsilk, curled around the edges of the stone and then up beneath his touch.

"There." Belior's voice was barely louder than breathing.

Gabriel shivered.

"Trust me, I'd rather not have you touch it either, but you wanted to learn." His voice was a little louder.

Israfel-in-Gabriel steadied him. The strand felt far more solid than it looked, like a vein filled with blood. *What is it?*

It's an old man I own.

Gabriel jerked back from the wall.

"We had an iron-clad contract. He agreed, and I came out to his farm twice a week for the rest of his life to make it rain." Belior smiled as if looking at his own offspring. "Make it rain and you'll never be out of work. He died, and I made sure it didn't rain for six years until someone remembered Granddad's weird old practices. Now I own a family."

Gabriel flinched. "So when you open the fissure, he reaches for you?"

"The connection is there. There's no volition involved." Belior shrugged. "Feel it again, but open your senses out wider. Thousands of strands are poking through."

Now that he knew what he was feeling for, Gabriel could sense them too, but only by the dozens.

"I've always loved making it rain," Beelzebub said from behind them.

Belior said, "And I've always resented the fact that you came up with Ba'al worship before I did."

"You had to love the ceremonies," Beelzebub said. "*Hieros gamos.* Anthropomorphic religion at its very best."

"You're making me sick," Gabriel snapped, "and if I'm in the corner retching, we're not getting into Sheol."

Beelzebub snickered.

Mephistopheles slipped around Beelzebub, running one wing across him as he passed. "Can you recognize Jesus in the threads?"

Belior projected in the negative.

Gabriel leaned against the wall and folded his arms. "Let me run through the sequence of events again. Someone contacts a witch and asks to contact the dead. The witch contacts you, and you identify the person's strand, then send the information back to the witch."

"Essentially," Mephistopheles said. "The boondoggle is in isolating the thread, since not every soul produces one. There are only about ten thousand penetrating from the fissure, and naturally the odds are against grabbing the one they're requesting. That's why we identify something the person was attached to."

Gabriel frowned as he let off a long breath.

"What was he most attached to?" Satan said.

"People," Michael said. "Humanity."

Satan huffed. "I mean what was he really attached to."

Michael's eyes narrowed. "And I mean people. Humanity."

"What else was he attached to?"

"His mother," Israfel said.

Belior rubbed his chin. "He handed her off to one of those guys. There won't be a strand for her."

Gabriel said, "But Raphael had a bond with him, and as he pointed out before, that bond wasn't destroyed by death."

Everyone fell silent.

Then Mephistopheles whispered, "The connection doesn't have to have originated within Sheol. One originating from the outside is just as valid and might be easier to follow."

Belior brightened. "We never had the person's guardian helping us before."

Gabriel stepped toward Raphael. "So let's try with that."

"Well, there are two other conditions," Belior said. "Without meeting them it doesn't work."

Mephistopheles said, "The request has to be made at night. And it has to be made by a female."

"It's still nighttime in Jerusalem," Beelzebub said, "so you're one down."

"Ask his mother," said Asmodeus.

The angels all choked on either objections or laughter.

"What they're trying to say," Michael said, "is that she won't have anything to do with this."

"It's her son."

"There's no way she would get involved." Michael turned to Israfel. "We're going to have to ask you to do the honors."

Israfel said, "But Belior could touch the strands before."

Belior nodded. "Males can touch them. You can't pull on them unless you're female."

Mephistopheles said, "You can pull them, to be technical, but then they snap back like harp strings and make an interesting vibration. You could play music on them if you wanted."

Belior laughed. "You can't put pressure on them to tighten them, so it'd be a matter of remembering which of ten thousand strands plays a B-flat and which one is the G, and so on."

"What would you play?" Mephistopheles said, and Belior answered automatically, "From Out of the Depths."

Satan said, "Belior—"

"I'm joking!" said the Cherub, turning toward him with glinting eyes even as Asmodeus laughed.

Israfel approached the wall. "Show me how to find the strands."

While Mephistopheles demonstrated, Gabriel turned toward Raphael. *Are you all right with this?*

Just get him out of there.

I'm doing my best.

Keep doing it, then. We haven't made any progress.

Gabriel realized his wings were half-spread as if he were preparing for an attack. *I'm going to need to ride through your mind to follow that connection and guide Israfel to pull it out.*

Raphael shrugged. *You've picked through my mind before. You do what you have to.*

209

Sick at heart, Gabriel turned back to Ophaniel. "Can you find any major flaws in the plan?"

"Do you know what you're going to do once you've established contact?"

"If I knew what I was doing, this wouldn't be experimental." Gabriel rubbed his chin. "He's not without power of his own. Once we draw him up close, he might be able to do something from the other side."

Ophaniel sent, *I don't like this.*

Gabriel shrugged. *We haven't got a better option.*

Israfel said, "Gabriel, we've got a problem. I can't find the strands."

Belior glanced over from where he was talking with Asmodeus. "Seraphim sometimes have trouble listening for them. If you get really quiet, you should be able to find them."

Mephistopheles said, "Beelzebub never found one. Come to think of it, neither did Asmodeus."

Belior bristled. "It's not his fault. It's just a Seraph thing."

"But she's a Seraph."

Michael said, "One of you two should change, then."

"Oh, gee, I never thought of that before in four thousand years." Belior folded his arms and cocked his head. "Don't I feel stupid?"

Mephistopheles said, "It has to have been created female."

Israfel said, "Maybe if we call Zadkiel?"

Gabriel felt Raphael's attention boring into him.

He took a deep breath, tried to quell the momentary fear of being in such a close space with so many male angels and five male demons, and letting out that breath, Gabriel had become female. "I'll do it."

She ignored whether any of the others were staring the way Israfel was. Gabriel had been created female. It was this body's normal form, and because gender was as easily changeable to an angel as a suit of clothes—speaking of clothes, she mentally adjusted her armor—being female was fine; it was just more comfortable to stay the other way. She'd been male ever since Sodom because — well, because, but it would be okay for now.

Gabriel sidled around contact with any of the others as she approached the fissure. "I'll still need you bracing me, Israfel. Once I've got it, you should be able to follow my lead and grab hold as well. I don't know how hard it will be to pull."

Satan moved in close. "Do you realize your power is marginally greater in this form?"

Gabriel took an involuntary step backward and felt herself right up against the wall. "Do you realize how little I care about that?" Evil was in her face and death at her spine. "Israfel, are you ready? Raphael, let me in."

Raphael didn't move closer, but Michael had, and his hand was on his sword. "Don't touch Gabriel. Let Gabriel work alone."

The demons backed off, but not before Gabriel caught Beelzebub's glance at Asmodeus.

Michael brought up his wings, and Gabriel met them, forming something of a tent.

You're still weak, Michael sent.

I'm doing all right, Gabriel replied. *It's not hard to recover from a deep discharge.*

Do you think this has any chance of working?

We have to try.

You don't *have to try.* Michael's eyes glinted. *Moreover, you don't have to try right now. I'll send you out of here in a heartbeat.*

Raphael blazed inside her heart, and she closed her eyes.

Michael urged, *Raphael's furious, but that's no reason to push yourself to the brink. You've done enough.*

"Just this one more thing," Gabriel whispered. "After this, we should take a break and think things over."

Michael stepped back.

Gabriel reached through Raphael to his guardian/protégé bond with Jesus, then followed it backward toward herself, then into the fissure. *We've got it, Israfel.*

Gabriel pressed up against the fissure, following the bond with her mind. It didn't curl like the other strands. This one flowed straight and strong like a laser, moving through the cracks without regard to the vagaries of the stone. Gabriel could follow its path a distance, but after that she had to guess where the crevices of the fissure would twist in order to stay near it. At one point she got stuck in a place where she couldn't follow any deeper.

"I need this open a little bit more," Gabriel said.

Israfel put her hands on the wall and focused her power on the fissure. "Does this help?"

Freed, Gabriel sent her thoughts in deeper. She dissociated her angelic body and extended into the fissure, anchored to Israfel.

"Pull it," Mephistopheles said. "Don't follow it."

It's trapped, Gabriel sent. *I can't pull it if it's anchored.*

Mephistopheles took to the air and put some energy into the fissure overhead. "Is this what you need?"

Gabriel assented. A moment after that, Ophaniel was putting energy into the fissure from the bottom, and the path opened further.

Gabriel worked through the twists, stretching thinner, following the beam from Raphael, wondering how far she'd gotten and how far she had left to travel. The cold stone oppressed her mind, but she continued even as the crag grew narrower.

Abruptly it opened wider again. *Thanks,* Gabriel sent to Israfel.

That's Mephistopheles. He got the tip of his sword into the fissure. I'm going to do the same.

Just don't let go, Gabriel sent. *I want to be able to get back once I grab the thing.*

Count on me. I'll hold on with my life.

Every so often the fissure dead-ended and Gabriel would backtrack to find a better route. It was like a maze, except she wasn't sure there was a way out at the end.

Mephistopheles said to tell you you're doing well, Israfel sent.

Gabriel got a sense of the three of them on the outside prying the fissure open, Mephistopheles and Israfel using their swords, Ophaniel bracing it with his hands, Raphael behind Ophaniel empowering him while providing the link for Gabriel.

Belior was helping too, she realized, and the dark Seraphim were empowering the dark Cherubim.

It really is a team effort, Gabriel prayed. *It's kind of neat. I just wish it hadn't been something like this to bring us together.*

Keep your mind on your work, Raphael sent. *You have to get him out of there.*

Gabriel shivered. *I am working.*

You're praying. Keep moving forward. And then, *Don't even consider coming back without him.*

Gabriel went cold.

Hey, are you okay? sent Israfel.

No.

I'm pulling you out.

Don't. I'm moving forward.

Gabriel, don't be stubborn.

I can do this. It was snug but not horrendous, although it felt more constricted now than a minute ago. Gabriel tried to concentrate on the thread to follow it further, but this passage wedged so tight. She fed her thoughts through a bit at a time until she was all in one place further on. Then time to find the next narrow passage and the next opening in the stone afterward.

Then it occurred to her, she didn't need to navigate blindly. All the other threads were emerging from somewhere, so rather than hunting passages by guesswork, why not follow the threads to wherever they entered the fissure and then find Raphael's bond to Jesus once she'd popped into the open on the other side?

Gabriel found a bunch of threads and followed them through, pulling on them to slide herself along the crevasses. Progress grew much quicker.

Belior says you're a genius.

I know I'm a genius, Gabriel sent, fighting a grin.

A shudder groaned through the fissure.

Gabriel?

What was that?

Israfel sounded scared. *It's slipped. Hurry, please?*

I'm going my fastest.

Then get out of there. It's not stable.

213

Gabriel continued moving forward. The pressure didn't seem as great, but the fissure continued shifting around her as she moved. Threads twisted, bent, corkscrewed around channels and moved with purpose, and Gabriel pulled herself along them, sliding when she could, inching when she had to.

Gabriel, come back. You have to get out now.

She could see the fissure through Israfel's mind, opened like a wound. It glowed and tremored. She could feel Israfel half inside and half outside the better to anchor her, Mephistopheles braced just inside in order to anchor Israfel. Belior had Mephistopheles' sword in his hands to keep the fissure propped, and Ophaniel still secured the lowest segment. But it wasn't holding. They couldn't keep it pried open like that.

Gabriel reached a cluster of thousands of threads. *I'm nearly there!*

Israfel yanked her backward, but Gabriel clung to the sides of the fissure.

I need one minute.

You don't have one minute! Back out of there!

And in her heart, Gabriel felt Raphael pumping her full of angry energy so she could keep moving forward.

Israfel pulled her again. Gabriel pushed Israfel backward, and the fissure shuddered. As she crossed some invisible summit, Sheol began sucking her downhill, dragging Israfel with her.

Gabriel, Michael sent, *out. Now.*

The fissure rumbled, and for the second time in her life, Gabriel disobeyed a direct order.

As the stone around her groaned, she gathered all her energy into a blunt-force concussion blast at Israfel. Gabriel broke free, knocking Israfel out of the fissure and at the same time thrusting herself backward with the recoil. The stone walls crashed together.

Sheol slammed shut with a clamor that dwarfed Israfel's screams. Shock ran up her arms as the stone cracked her sword. She dropped the hilt, hurling herself at the sealed wall. "Gabriel! Gabriel! Gabriel! Get out of there! Gabriel!"

A firm grip on her forearms, and someone hauled her off her feet. She thrashed her wings, but green eyes came into focus inches before her own face. "Israfel, silence!" and she clamped her jaw by reflex in front of the Seraph who used to head her order.

Satan dropped her. She caught herself before stumbling.

Michael pushed between them. "Hands off my officers!"

"Screaming does no good," Satan said. "We need to get back in there."

"You'll keep your hands off my officers!" He turned to Israfel. "Are you all right?"

Her sword had been sheared off mid-blade. It lay beside part of the handle of Mephistopheles' sword and the slivered remnants of yellow-tinged feathers. The soup of emotions from all the angels and demons swirled with horror, confusion, pain, and questions.

Israfel grabbed Michael's shoulders. "I couldn't hang onto her! Sheol started dragging us in, and I tried dragging Gabriel out, and then Gabriel pushed me out of the fissure just before it slammed shut."

Michael sounded level, rock-solid. "Can you get any sense through your bond?"

Israfel shook her head.

Michael pursed his lips. "We need to open it back up and get her out."

Raphael said, "Not yet. Give Gabriel time to find him."

Michael glared at him. "We don't know how time passes in Sheol, and we don't know how long it will take to re-establish contact. We're in the position now of needing to pull out Gabriel and then pull out Jesus."

"All the more reason to wait." Raphael folded his arms. "Once they're together, Gabriel can send him through first."

Ophaniel reached into Israfel's mind, and she sent him a cloud of perplexity. Ophaniel sent back his own bewilderment, then pointed her toward Belior, who was exchanging a knowing look with Asmodeus.

Are you unhurt? Ophaniel sent.

Israfel replied in the affirmative.

Michael shook his head. "I disagree. We need it open now."

Raphael huffed even as Ophaniel returned to the wall.

Satan said, "Belior, you and Mephistopheles get a handhold on it." He stopped. "Mephistopheles?"

Gasping and radiating horror, Belior darted away from the other demons, and then Asmodeus jumped back. Israfel bit back another scream.

Beelzebub crouched on the ground, wings like a tent over Mephistopheles, and he looked up helplessly. The Cherub lay curled like an egg, shaking, completely clenched over himself.

Two of Mephistopheles' inner wings had been sheared off just above the joint.

"Raphael," Michael shouted, "help him!"

Raphael was already crouching before Mephistopheles, tracing his fingers over the injured wings. "Look up at me," he said. "Mephistopheles, look up."

Mephistopheles raised his head, his breathing ragged.

"This doesn't hurt," Raphael said. "Listen to me: *you're not hurting.*"

Mephistopheles let out a long gasp, then tried to clench up tight again.

"Easy." Raphael breathed over the wing edges. Mephistopheles tried to recoil, but Beelzebub held him. An amber glow suffused them all. "Relax."

Satan said, "Report?"

Beelzebub looked pale. "He pivoted when he pulled out of the fissure. When it slammed—"

"Easy," Raphael murmured as Mephistopheles flinched.

Beelzebub yanked the Cherub back and closed his wings. "Don't you dare hurt him!"

"I can leave him in agony to regenerate over a couple of days if he prefers." Sitting back, Raphael opened his hands. "He knows it should hurt, and he's a Cherub so it's hard for him to get past what he thinks he knows, so he keeps preparing for it, but I'm blocking the pain."

Satan said, "Let him work."

"Yes, sir." Beelzebub made assent sound hateful. He opened his wings, and Raphael laid his hands on Mephistopheles. The wings had begun to reform, hazy through the amber light.

"I shouldn't even ask this," Michael said.

Satan said, "What are the odds Gabriel got crushed?"

Israfel's vision went white.

Ophaniel said from behind Israfel, "I can't tell. The fissure's gone."

Belior shoved Ophaniel out of the way. He pressed his cheek to the wall and then spread his wings against it. He shifted position, then moved again, then tried in a different place.

Israfel caught the terror on Belior's face just before he turned toward Satan, but when he met his commander's eyes, he was impassive. "It's sealed. The fissure is gone."

Satan's eyes iced over. "It's just gone?"

Belior nodded. "It's sealed itself."

Israfel said, "How are we going to get Gabriel out?"

Ophaniel said, "You said there's another fissure."

"Yes, but smaller." Belior inched backward as Satan stepped toward him. "This happened once before, when we summoned Samuel to speak to Saul. He didn't want to come, and we had to widen the fissure in order to get a grip. If you remember, sir,

Mephistopheles was hauling him from the main one while I was pushing through this, and we had someone guiding from the third fissure as well. When he went back in, the main one sealed, and we only had the two."

Satan had quite a bit of height on Belior. "Locate the third and use that."

Belior was shoulder-to-shoulder with Israfel at this point, Ophaniel right at his back. "I know its location. The difficulty will be, it's smaller and more twisted. We never used it because it was so complicated to get a line out."

Fear frothed off the Cherub. Israfel spread her wings behind Belior and brushed Ophaniel's wingtips with her own. She said, "Let's see what we can do."

Belior couldn't take his eyes off Satan.

Satan sounded dangerous. "Why hadn't you taken steps to make the other fissure accessible?"

"We never needed it!" Belior said. "If I'd predicted we were going to have to pull the Second Person of the Trinity out through it, I'd have come here every morning for the past five hundred years and widened it just a little bit while having coffee. But given the way the first destabilized, we left well enough alone so as not to jostle the single fissure we had in working order."

Israfel checked on Raphael. "Are they itchy?" he asked Mephistopheles. When Mephistopheles nodded, he grinned. "Believe it or not, that's a good thing. Try not to rub them."

Beelzebub said, "Have you ever done this before?"

"It's my vocation," Raphael said. "I don't need to have done it before in order to know how to do it now."

Through the amber glow, Mephistopheles' wings had returned to their full length, though filmy and still without feathers. His face had relaxed, with color again in his cheeks.

Raphael looked right into Mephistopheles' eyes. "I know he doesn't like to hear screaming," he murmured with a nod toward Satan, "but the next time something like this happens, you have my permission to yell your fool head off, that way we'll know to help."

Ignoring the medical drama, Belior glanced at Asmodeus, then back at Satan. "I can't make promises, but I'll maneuver a line through the third fissure."

Ophaniel said, "I'll help."

Belior flashed both of them to a spot a short distance along the wall, and Ophaniel's interest prickled in Israfel's mind as Belior traced the edges of the smaller fissure.

Raphael pulled back from Mephistopheles, who was sitting up on Beelzebub's lap. "You're going to be downy for a little while. There's nothing I can do about that."

Mephistopheles flexed his wings. "They're fine!" Tiny feathers curled up between the flight feathers, waving in even the gentlest motion. Israfel fought a smile. "They don't even itch any longer."

Beelzebub pushed him off, and Mephistopheles staggered to his feet.

Satan said, "Go help them at the third fissure. Figure out a way to get it open and keep it stable. Gabriel's technique doesn't require a female, so we're sending you next."

Mephistopheles flashed to the other two Cherubim.

"Is that our best bet?" Israfel asked. "I'd rather run a line from me to Gabriel and have Gabriel use our bond as a means of climbing out."

Michael nodded. "Forcing Mephistopheles inside might destabilize the last remaining fissure. It might be dangerous for him."

Satan said, "He'll go in if I order him."

"I'm not sure it's necessary," Michael said. "We might be able to come up with another way." He turned and started to say, "Gabri—" Then he shook his head. "Good one, Michael."

Satan snickered.

Israfel brushed a wing past him. "We'll think of something. Gabriel will be waiting with Jesus on the other side. All we'll have to do is work it open enough that Gabriel has a primary bond to follow, and they'll be back out together in no time."

Michael studied her curiously. "Do you believe that?"

Israfel glanced at Raphael, standing with his wings tight and his arms folded while he glared at the working Cherubim. "I have to believe it. We don't have another option."

Gabriel tumbled in unbroken darkness until she spread her wings and stalled herself. With no sense of equilibrium, she couldn't figure out if she was up or down or sideways, so she shone.

Faces, hands, bodies, right in front of her.

Gabriel swept her wings forward to fire herself backward, even at that moment retreating into a masculine body. Sodom and an alley and grasping—

Gabriel blasted out light like a star, and when he looked again he could see he'd had nothing to fear. He hovered in a cavern miles wide and far longer, the walls and floors and even the ceiling lined with sleepers. No grabby hands and no crowd stinking of sweat and sex. All of Sheol lay spread before him like a geode with human jewels sleeping as they glistened around the inside of the cavern.

It was all right. He was safe, and for once the only thoughts in his head were his own.

He reached for the Vision and found it unseeable. Not taken from him—there was no sense of loss the way there had been during the punishment. Just an absence. Strange. He should have been grief-stricken, but instead, nothing. Just peace.

Sheol. A natural happiness.

Of course. How many times had he explained to angels, to people, that Sheol was pleasant and once each soul had settled down to wait, no one would be unhappy while they waited for the redeemer and judgment?

Gabriel pumped out more light, illuminating Sheol lengthwise and scanning to find the ends of the cavern. Sleeping souls mumbled in protest, and he toned down the brightness, but he had visualized the ends of the structure.

He looked up and around but couldn't locate the fissure he'd used as an entrance. Distressing on an intellectual level, to say the least, but Gabriel found he didn't mind. This place was pleasant, like the memories of drifting back to sleep just before sunrise, stealing an extra few minutes of slumber back when he still lived in Tobias's household.

Tobias was here, somewhere. As were Raguel, Rafaela, Angela, Gabelus...

Gabriel shook his head. The first task had to be finding Jesus among the estimated half-billion sleeping souls. Then, after finding him, he would have to re-locate the fissure and open it from the inside.

Gabriel spread his hands and focused his power until he'd created a sphere the size of a pomegranate. He left it glowing in place as a marker so he would have an idea of where to begin searching for the fissure once he'd found Jesus.

No thread of energy led from Raphael to Jesus any longer. When Sheol had closed, all of Raphael had been shut on the other side. It wasn't going to be as easy as following a thread back to the spool, but it had to be possible. He had eternity, and he was a Cherub. It stood to reason that eventually he'd find his target.

How to find him efficiently, though—that was tougher than simply looking at every face one at a time. Were the sleeping souls organized hierarchically according to time of entry? His glimpse of the length of the cavern hadn't revealed a flood streaming through.

Gabriel fell very still, and he opened his mind to take in as much of Sheol as possible. Centered. Quiet. Drifting, he allowed himself to sense the souls about him, peaceful and dreamless, just warm enough.

As long as I don't fall asleep like them.

He grinned and took a deep breath, then tried again.

There, a new soul. It arrived with a pop like the moment a seedling lifts its head from the soil. Another one, not in the same place. A third pop, distant from the others.

Gabriel tucked his wings and folded his arms, still hovering. So Sheol filled evenly, or randomly, but not in one part at a time. He couldn't begin his search with the newest arrivals.

He reached for God, and his heart's hands closed on nothing. Right.

"So it's just you and me," he murmured to Jesus. "And until I find you, just me."

Although come to think of it...

Where are you? Gabriel prayed.

An answering greeting, but sleepy.

Gabriel tried not to think, *Well, you're no help.* He smiled, though, at the familiar touch and the knowledge that he was so close. He shut his eyes and prayed without words, allowing his heart to touch and be touched, to admire and be received, and then without opening his eyes, he allowed himself to drift toward the tug. His heart wanted to be there with him, and not here alone with all these. Let me come to you, his heart prayed, and Gabriel followed, and there was joy in the following, so he followed the joy past the simple happiness of the sleeping. After the joy came a purpose, and the purpose became a whip driving Gabriel forward until he'd picked up speed and blurred past the faces. *Come to me*, and *Let me come to you* met one another. Gabriel pulled up short and opened his eyes.

He beamed. "Jesus!"

Jesus was sitting awake among the sleepers, and Gabriel dove for him, clutched him in a hug, laughed and buried his face in Jesus' shoulder and wrapped him in his wings. Gabriel kissed his cheeks, then his forehead where the crown had been, then his shoulder where he'd hefted the cross beam, then both his hands and his feet. There were no marks from the brutality.

Jesus touched Gabriel's hair and his wings and said his name, and then he laughed as Gabriel sat back, eyes shining.

"I found you," he whispered. "You're here."

"Tone down your light," Jesus murmured. "You're disturbing the sleepers."

Gabriel complied, offering an apology.

Jesus smiled at him "How did you get here?"

223

So Gabriel told him about the fissure, about Satan joining them at the wall, about Michael and Raphael and Israfel and Belior and Mephistopheles, and then he backed up and apologized for handing him the cup and not stopping the Romans from arresting him, and he apologized for leaving to stay with Mary rather than remaining with Raphael so angry, and he reassured Jesus that his mother was being cared for, and then he apologized for talking too much and for not listening, but Jesus listened brightly and assured him he was doing fine.

Gabriel said, "Now you have to come with me, because I'm going to find a way to take you home."

Jesus shook his head. "I didn't come in here to be rescued."

Gabriel said, "But since I'm here, I can take you back out with me."

Jesus rested a hand on Gabriel's knee. "I'm here to fulfill the will of the Father, and for the glory of God. I'm not going to leave with you."

Gabriel's eyes turned silver. "But— How can it be to the glory of God to leave a part of Himself behind?"

Jesus smiled. "Do you believe me?"

"I do." Gabriel settled back on his heels. "I won't contest your authority, but if we're going to be here forever, I was hoping to learn more about the reason."

Jesus looked pained. "Gabriel, you can't stay."

Gabriel's eyes widened. "My place is with you! And I'm here anyhow, so it's perfect."

Jesus chuckled. "You'll get bored."

"I'm as susceptible to natural happiness as anyone else, and anyhow, I'm a Cherub. You know everything, and I want to learn everything, and we'll have a lot of time on our hands." Gabriel smiled. "Pick a topic and we'll get started."

Jesus shifted some of Gabriel's hair from his eyes. "You have to go home."

Gabriel shook his head, then looked down at his lap. He clasped his hands between his knees.

Jesus drew his face up with a finger beneath his chin. "Gabri'li, you have no idea how much I love you. I would love to keep you here with me, but you have your place in creation and among the other angels. You're needed there. You have to return."

Gabriel met Jesus's eyes, so much like Raphael's, and he showed him the anger, the chaos above, the rage: *I'm not needed. They don't want me to return.* And Jesus tilted his head: *They all don't want you to return, or is Raphael so angry at you that it seems as if no one wants you to return?* Gabriel bit his lip: *Just Raphael.* And Jesus said to him, "Don't turn on each other."

"He believes I let you die. He believes I wanted to cut you off from him." Gabriel swallowed. "There are half a trillion angels. After the first couple of weeks no one will miss me. Please let me stay. You don't even have to talk to me. I just want to be near you."

Jesus hugged Gabriel and kissed his forehead. "I'm going to send you back. Give this to Raphael." He held out a golden orb on his palm, the shape of a Brazil nut. "It's a message for him that I wasn't able to say before it happened."

Gabriel took the orb, and it shimmered before vanishing into his heart.

"Please," Gabriel said. "I'm asking once more. Return with me, or let me stay."

"I'm sorry," Jesus said. "Tell them I have to remain for the glory of God."

Gabriel found himself outside Sheol, surrounded by angels.

A sudden outcry from everyone, the demons shocked, Israfel filling him with fire that surged with relief, Michael right in front of him demanding to know what had happened, and a wingspan away, Raphael with folded arms and a dark regard.

Michael repeated, "What happened? How did you get out?"

Gabriel turned his head aside as if to give himself space among the press, and a few angels stepped backward. "I got in. I managed to find him. But he refused to return with me and sent me away." He pulled his soul back to avoid the flames in Raphael's. "He says it's to God's glory if he remains there."

Satan slammed his fist into the wall. "Damnation! What's that supposed to mean?"

Raphael said, "Let's get back in there and talk to him again."

Michael said, "What's that going to accomplish? We barely got Gabriel inside in the first place, and Jesus already refused. I can't argue about God's glory."

Raphael said, "Maybe if you sent in someone who wanted to succeed, it would work."

A collective sense of shock rippled around them. Gabriel turned to Raphael, his eyes flint-hard, and opening his wings, he bound the Seraph with his will and flashed him away.

They ended up in front of Jesus's tomb, a short distance from five Roman soldiers and their very startled guardians. It was just after sunrise.

"Why are you doing this to me?" Gabriel said. "I've done everything I could!"

"You haven't, and you know it." Raphael's wings flared. "You've been avoiding the hard work the whole time, right from the moment you appeared to him in the garden—"

"God told me exactly what to do and told me not to do anything else!" Gabriel stepped closer. "I won't disobey Divine orders! I learned the hard way that it doesn't do any good."

"How would you know?" Raphael shouted.

The nearby guardians were all on alert now.

"Why are you so angry with me?" Gabriel's wings spread. "You're not even making sense any longer."

"So things have to be sensible in order for you to like them? Maybe I'm just finally seeing what's really going on with you."

Gabriel opened his hand to reveal the golden nugget on his palm. "This is—"

Raphael swatted it away, sending it into the hillside. "What is it, your little excuse?"

"It was a *message*," Gabriel said, "from *him*, and clearly you're not in your right mind. Maybe when you get yourself back under control, you can get it and figure out what he wanted to tell you."

"Don't act like you're the perfect one, so trustworthy that everyone wants you running messages." Raphael had flames in his hair. "You didn't do anything for him! You're an arrogant know-it-all block of ice who only cares about the letter of the law and not for the people who live under that law."

Gabriel's heart pounded. "Don't you think I hate that he's dead? I hate that he wouldn't come with me, and it broke my heart to hand him that cup knowing what was going to happen! But God didn't give me any room to maneuver."

Raphael said, "I would have found a way."

Gabriel said, "Would you have? I got kicked out of Heaven for a year and was lonely, abandoned, exhausted, courted by Satan, and ended up with a concussion and a broken arm, but you didn't come. Did you find a way?"

Raphael folded his arms. "You deserved it."

The world turned into one high whine. Gabriel stared, his eyes blanking, his body going numb. *You deserved it.*

Gabriel flashed away, tearing free from the chains Raphael attempted to cast around him. *God, I don't want to be found. I want to go somewhere no one will ever find me again.*

He ended up in the abandoned cabin, and he Guarded it, Guarded it again, Guarded it a third time. It was no good—they'd found him here once. They would once more. He stood with his wings half-unfurled, his breath punctuated, and he closed his eyes. *I don't want to be found.*

Uriel's presence. Gabriel backed away, but Uriel reached for him, and then they were both in Uriel's bungalow.

I didn't want to be found by <u>anyone</u>, Gabriel sent to God, and God replied that Uriel wouldn't tell anyone. Even now, Uriel was putting up a Guard around the house. He'd be untraceable inside.

Uriel wanted him to take down the Guard on the abandoned house on earth, and Gabriel complied. His hands shook as he projected his thanks.

Uriel took a step forward, then halted and backed off, nodded at Gabriel, and vanished.

Gabriel felt control of the Guard in his power.

He stood alone in the front room, feeling the sunlight, the stillness, the solidity of the small structure. Heaven. Not really

Heaven in his heart, was it? But he didn't want to be found, and here he wouldn't be.

He realized what had just happened: Uriel had been about to kiss or hug him, and God had intervened. Gabriel looked at his shaking hands; if Uriel had done that, he would have fallen apart right there.

Arrogant know-it-all block of ice. You deserved it.

Gabriel sleepwalked into the living room and dropped himself on Uriel's pile of cushions. *I don't care,* he thought. *I don't care any longer. I just don't care.*

The tears had come before he could deny that he even cared any longer. Jesus dead. Raphael—like that. Admitting that. Believing that. He choked for a moment, felt the lie in his own denial that he cared, and then it all overwhelmed him. He lay on his back, wings splayed wherever they'd landed, and he let the tears come. The thud of the hammer. The slam of the wood against the cobblestones when Jesus fell. Mary crying. The cup cold against his hands. Michael glaring. Uriel's level stare. Nivalis sobbing. Raphael pouring fire into his heart. Raphael.

His chest hurt. *You deserved it.*

Yes, he'd deserved it, but...but that wasn't...

He flipped onto his stomach, pulling the closest pillow to his chest, tucking his chin and hiding his face beneath his wings. *God, oh God, please—*

This wasn't right. Jesus in Sheol. So silent, so peaceful. *Don't turn on each other.* Why hadn't he just let Gabriel stay with him? God ought to have at least one angel in service, and Gabriel had been ready to stay forever. No one would have found him there. Raphael would never have said that if Gabriel had stayed inside.

Gabriel spread his wings in the sun, then realized the windows were open. He trembled in fear of eyes, but the light felt good, and he didn't want to shut it away. The Holy Spirit moved inside him: no one would come looking, but He could enlarge the Guard if Gabriel wanted. Gabriel asked for it, and then he dropped himself back onto the cushions.

What was wrong with him? He hadn't cried for six hundred years, and now twice in the same day.

If something this horrible had happened three days ago, he'd have fled to Raphael. He'd have talked to Jesus. And now he couldn't turn to either. It wasn't fair.

Raphael.

Was he mad with grief? But Gabriel couldn't bring himself to believe it was only that, not any more than he could convince himself he didn't really care. After centuries of keeping it harnessed, Raphael was finally fed up with him.

"Do you think I came to give peace all over the earth?" Jesus had said. *"No, I came to bring division. From now on, a household of five will be divided, three against two, and two against three.*

But not our household, Gabriel prayed. *Not like this. Please, not like this.*

Folding his arms beneath himself, Gabriel lay in place for a long time until he couldn't tell if he was in tears now or if that had been a hundred years ago. He prayed until he'd prayed himself out, and then he arose as if he'd been dead and looked around the bungalow. He produced a lyre, but he wasn't one of the angels who could play or sing when sad, so after a while he made it disappear and looked through Uriel's books. There weren't many, and these he'd all read before. He pulled one he remembered liking and thumbed through it looking for a good part.

Silence. Peace. Uriel would tell Michael...he had no idea what Uriel would tell Michael. Maybe just that Gabriel was someplace safe, someplace he'd never find. He'd have to leave Uriel's house eventually, but maybe by then no one would care any longer. Maybe no one would want to search, and he could find someplace to just remain in worship and solitude forever.

He was supposed to be reading. He flipped pages back to the beginning of the good part and tried reading it again, but his mind wouldn't travel into the words to be transported away from the horror. Jesus nailed to that wood, himself unable to do more than hand him that cup, and Raphael's scream as Jesus's lips

229

touched the cup and the moment guardian and charge were sliced away from one another.

He hadn't had any alternative. God had told him not to add to or delete from the message. Raphael said he'd have found a way, but it had been iron-clad. The way it had happened, surely Jesus had felt betrayed as someone he considered a friend handed him the blade that cut off contact from the celestial.

I'm sorry, Gabriel prayed.

He had no need to worry, came the answer. He'd done exactly as God had said.

I should have connived more.

God hadn't left him any room to do that.

I should have done it anyhow.

No, came the sense in his heart, the voice of the Spirit, you shouldn't have. You did what you must, exactly as you should have.

Gabriel tossed the book to the side, then looked over his shoulder and replaced it on the shelf where he'd gotten it. Even if Heaven and Earth fell apart, that was no reason to mistreat a book.

He walked through the sunlight into the kitchen, a composite of future and current. A fire always burned in Uriel's home, even though Uriel had been with Mary for the past fifty years.

What would Mary be doing now? Assuming she wasn't angry at him too for disappearing, she'd probably be spinning, maybe cooking. It might be past sundown in Jerusalem. He didn't care to figure out the exact time.

Gabriel made a spindle from his substance and then some fleece, and he started to spin. The twist, the way the wool became yarn, the methodic winding around his hands and then onto the bottom of the spindle, plying the yarn, letting his mind free while his hands worked. He went completely solid, then human. Humans had the primal urge to make something, and now he could forge something solid from fluff. It was useful; it was productive. At the end he'd have something strong, and right now he needed it.

He spun for hours. The silence inside spread, and he focused on God's face while letting the fleece twirl. As the ragged ends of the wool became yarn, so the ragged edges inside wove back together into one unit.

When he'd made two skeins, Gabriel went to the kitchen and stared again into Uriel's fire.

Gabriel prowled the cabinets and the pantry. He lifted the lid on the nearest container with a ceramic scrape. Flour. Another container: dried mushrooms. Oil. Oats. Wine. Several breeds of rice: arborio; jasmine; basamati. There were onions and garlic, and there were glass jars filled with a liquid tinged orange-gold.

Why did an angel need a fully-stocked kitchen? Oh, right. Mary. Because when Mary came home to Heaven, Uriel wanted her to feel welcome.

Gabriel found a large pot and set it over Uriel's perpetual fire, poured out a little oil, and chopped up an onion. Now he'd cried three times today, but he didn't mind this one. He fried the onions and some garlic, then poured a few handfuls of arborio rice into the pot, hearing it hiss as it simmered. He stirred it constantly so it didn't become brown, and then put in some wine.

Mary never measured, only eyeballed a mixture and knew by feel and taste whether it was right. Gabriel could guess at the proportions, and maybe that would be all right. He kept stirring. Something in the rhythm soothed him. He felt the strain in his shoulders, in his forearms.

Simple things. Wine. Oil. Water. Grain.

Friendship. Fury. Death. Love. Grief.

The kitchen smelled of onions, of heated wine. His hands smelled of garlic, and it was good. While the rice simmered, he threw some mushrooms onto another pan and fried them up.

He sent his mind into the shimmering heat of the fireplace. It wasn't Seraphic fire, but something homey, something friendly rather than consuming. The rice had absorbed the wine. He opened the first of the golden jars and ladled in some of the vegetable broth.

He prayed, *Is now as good a time as any?*

The Holy Spirit acknowledged.

231

If Raphael ever wants to know where I am, you can tell him.

Raphael's presence coalesced behind him before he'd finished the last three words.

He hadn't accounted for this possibility, that maybe Raphael had been waiting for a go-ahead. His hands trembled, but he continued stirring the rice without turning from the fire.

Raphael said, "I owe you an apology."

Gabriel ladled out more broth and let the rice continue absorbing it. Whether it would actually taste like anything he couldn't begin to guess.

Raphael said, "Did you call me here to ignore me?"

"I heard you say you owed me an apology, and I didn't actually hear an apology."

Raphael sighed. "Will you stop standing on ceremony about everything?"

Gabriel's heart tightened. His pulse raced again, and he couldn't breathe. *Deserved it.*

"I'm sorry I said all those things to you," Raphael said.

Gabriel could interpret that as the non-apology it certainly was. What had Michael done, pulled him aside and said "You know you'd better apologize. We can't afford to have you two at one another's throats"?

Gabriel said, "But you're still angry at me."

"Of course I'm angry at you. You let him die alone, and then you left him there in Sheol."

"I tried to bring him back with me."

"I know how you do those things. You went in begrudgingly and then you probably found him and said, 'Do you want to come back? No? Well then send me home because it's probably for the Divine Good.'"

Grabbing the container of rice, Gabriel walked away from Raphael and into the pantry before he started shouting, crying, or hurling energy. *I thought you said now was as good a time as any.*

The Holy Spirit agreed.

In other words, this was going to be a war whenever we did it? Gabriel put the container back on the shelf and returned to the fire.

"So we've established that you're determined to believe the worst about me." The rice had absorbed the liquid again, he poured in more broth. He took a spoonful to taste, but it was piping hot, so first he absorbed the heat into himself.

"Sure, bond with the risotto. Maybe the rice won't mind the constant criticism."

Gabriel clenched his teeth. "Then you taste that. See if they're done."

He tried it. "It's okay. Why are you cooking?"

"It felt like the right thing to do."

"Bread is the time-honored comfort food," Raphael said.

"It's not kosher for Passover."

Raphael sparkled with irritation, *Legalist,* but Gabriel didn't respond.

Gabriel sampled the cooled rice, which was still very al-dente but tasted passable. It wasn't the same kind of rice Angela used to prepare at Tobias's household. Hers was thinner, not as well-suited to what he was subjecting it to, and that definitely changed the consistency. This was a blander grain; the rice he remembered was wild, earthy.

"I begged to stay in Sheol with him." Gabriel stirred some more. "He told me he would love to keep me there. But he wouldn't, and he said it was to God's glory to have him remain. So he sent me back."

Raphael didn't reply, but it felt more like grudgingly allowing a statement to stand than acceptance.

Gabriel stirred more liquid into the rice. Predictable fire contained by the stove, heat in the food contained by the pot. He closed his eyes and let it work before him, trying not to think of the inferno sitting across the room. He reached for God's hand and wondered if Raphael was doing the same but didn't want to reach through their bond to find out.

The kitchen smelled like vegetables. Mary's kitchen always had some kind of scent. Whenever Jesus had caught the smell of baking bread, to him it meant home. He'd once remarked to Raphael that Heaven wouldn't seem like home if no one baked bread there. Maybe that was why Gabriel had wanted to make something. Maybe if Gabriel had carried a loaf of bread into Sheol, Jesus would have followed him out. A lot of nonsense, all these maybes, but it made as much sense as anything happening now.

Gabriel added broth again. "Did your message say the same thing he said to me?"

"Don't you know?"

"No, because it was for you, and if you opened it I wasn't in your head at the time."

Raphael didn't look at him. "And I have no idea what he said to you in Sheol because all contact was blocked at that point."

Yes, blessed peace.

Gabriel said, "Jesus said, 'Don't turn on each other.'"

Raphael's eyes smoldered.

This was maddening. Gabriel looked into the pot and wondered how much longer the risotto had remaining, and then glanced at Raphael again. The Seraph was still here, which was in and of itself a wonder. Had Michael given him an order? It was hard to tell whether Raphael wanted to find middle ground or just wanted to win.

Jesus had said, "When one wins, both lose." And at another point, "What hurts one hurts two." *And what can I say,* Gabriel prayed. *You're right. I mean, he was right.*

The Holy Spirit reassured him.

I can't get used to thinking about him in the past tense. He's supposed to be here.

Raphael continued glaring at him. It was unrelenting.

"What would it take to call a truce?" Gabriel said. "At this point I have no hopes for reaching an understanding. I just want to stop fighting."

Raphael said, "I don't know."

"At a minimum," Gabriel said, "you will not insult me in front of other angels again. Ever. That was completely out of line, especially in front of our enemies, but even if it had only been with the other Seven." He crossed his arms. "If you want to criticize me, I'll hear you out, but do it in private."

Raphael glowered. "You're right. That was out of line."

Gabriel said, "And on your side?"

"I don't want to make up a list. You'll adhere to every iota of it and not one bit more."

Gabriel bristled.

Raphael's eyes softened just a bit. Not soft, but softer. "You always acted like an unassigned co-guardian, so I expected you to do as much for Jesus as I would have, and you then didn't. You let me down, and you let him down. I wouldn't have asked you to get involved if I thought you were going to revert to being a legalist just when we both needed you to be compassionate."

"He wasn't angry at me."

Raphael shook his head. "He wouldn't be."

Gabriel pulled his wings close around himself. "He said—" *Gabri'li, you have no idea how much I love you.* He closed his eyes and ducked his head, tucked the wings tighter. *Arrogant block of ice.* Don't cry again. Just breathe.

Raphael said, "I guess my minimum acceptable standard would be that you can't go running away whenever you don't like what I'm saying."

"Someone had to leave in order to stop things from escalating. You weren't about to."

Raphael slammed his hand into the table. "Why do you always need to win the argument? You didn't leave to stop things from escalating—you fled. You didn't want to be found."

"You're here now," Gabriel said.

"I can't have a discussion with you if you keep running away. So that would be my minimum requirement."

Gabriel shook his head. "It isn't wrong to disengage if the discussion isn't productive."

Raphael said, "Then you're not willing to meet me halfway, and you might as well go hide again."

The risotto still needed one more ladleful of broth. He wanted to pull it off now, throw the whole thing away half-cooked and leave, but he didn't go. Eternity was a long time, and if it was going to be a war whenever they settled things out, they might as well do it now. Raw and in the present, before either of them had a chance to rewrite their lives and edit the other out completely.

Raphael said, "I want to get back to the tomb before morning. Mary Magdalene is going to return to finish with the burial."

Gabriel nodded. "What time is it there now?"

"We've got a couple of hours."

At least he'd said "we." That was something, unless it was habit.

"How is Mary?"

"Stunned, worried. John brought her with him to stay with the twelve. Well, the eleven now." He took a deep breath. "Nivalis is beside herself."

Gabriel nodded.

Raphael said, "Michael pulled everyone back from the wall about five minutes after you left. He said if Satan wanted to keep trying to assault Sheol he was welcome to do it, but Jesus's word was the end of the matter as far as he was concerned. We're still on alert, but we don't have anything to attack or defend."

Gabriel closed his eyes. "Michael must be livid."

"He is, and he isn't." Raphael knit his fingers. "He's furious at Pilate, at the Sanhedrin, at the Roman soldiers, but at the same time, he's taking it on God's word that it was all necessary. Jesus asked the Father to forgive them, so he's trying to ignore it, even if he can't forgive them himself. But he's not happy about it. I think he'd bring down the Roman empire right now, given his choice."

The rice was just the right consistency. Gabriel stirred in the fried mushrooms, then a large portion of parmesan cheese and a chunk of butter. He put the lid on the pot and set it to the side, noting with interest how Uriel had done something to the kitchen that suspended the food in time: it wasn't going to go bad; it wasn't even going to cool down. He put away the ingredients and cleaned the bowl, then turned to Raphael.

Raphael wasn't looking directly at him. "Are you ready to head back now?"

"I suppose so."

They stood outside Jesus's tomb, and Raphael walked through the stone. Gabriel checked out the Roman soldiers, playing a game of pig's knuckles. Their guardians all watched with concern.

Inside the tomb, Raphael sat beside Jesus's shroud, his mouth twisted. Gabriel looked away before he felt the urge to reach into the fire and share the pain.

"This isn't fair," Raphael whispered.

Agreement from Gabriel.

Raphael stroked his hand over the shroud where Jesus's head was, not reaching through, just touching the linen.

Gabriel pulled one of the long feathers from the tip of one wing. Raphael nodded, and Gabriel pulled one of Raphael's as well, then tied them together with a strand of hair, and making himself immaterial, tucked the grey and almond feathers beneath the shroud, just over Jesus' hand.

Raphael's eyes were utterly hollow, and he wasn't even praying. Saying nothing, they just sat for a long time in the tomb's unmoving air.

Nivalis appeared, her eyes dim, her power surging. Raphael opened his arms, and she pushed past Gabriel to cry against him. Gabriel tried to meet Raphael's eyes, but Raphael was looking only at her, so Gabriel exited the tomb.

Outside again in the breeze, he looked at the full moon and then made his way to a cluster of trees out of sight of the Romans and their guardians. He settled himself on his stomach along one of the low branches, feet crossed at the ankles so they braced his semi-solid form against the trunk. He folded his arms and laid his head over his wrists.

Insects hummed and chirped, and rustlings in the grass told Gabriel where animals moved. Two nighttime hunters soared overhead. The Roman guard continued their gambling.

"You're back again," said a voice Gabriel recognized as Mephistopheles.

"Did your team get in, or have you given up?"

"Belior and Asmodeus are still at work because Satan wants them to come up with an alternative, but I can't imagine they'll find a way to remove God from somewhere he wants to stay. So I'm here."

Gabriel chuckled.

"You made me lose a bet." Mephistopheles sounded miffed. "When you carted Raphael off, it was a sure deal that you were going to beat the life out of him. No one could believe it when he returned without you, and without being noticeably thrashed." He paused. "Raphael did me a favor back there, so let me give you some advice."

Gabriel turned to regard Mephistopheles directly.

The other Cherub kicked at a stone, his arms folded and his head bowed. "Seraphim will turn on you. Every Seraph will at some point. We'd all been surprised the honeymoon had lasted for you two as long as it did. But at some point, every Seraph is going to turn, and when he does, he goes for your heart. He'll find the one place you're most vulnerable and hit you right there, usually in public, and he'll do it again after that."

Gabriel squinted.

Mephistopheles cracked a stick with the heel of his boot. "There's nothing you can do to prevent it. The only thing you can do is not share anything with them."

Gabriel said, "Bonding is all about sharing."

"Sharing power, yes. But you don't have to share your thoughts, your desires, the places where you're vulnerable." He chuckled ruefully. "It's a shame you didn't find this out ages ago, but he's only doing what Seraphim do. Now he knows all the ways he can hit you hardest. So if he knows, for example, you pride yourself on being effective, he's going to find the one thing you weren't able to do and completely ignore the fifteen impossible things you did accomplish." Mephistopheles looked at Gabriel with his eyes sparkling, his hair even more unruly than usual. "Look at what happened: you got into Sheol, you did it without getting yourself demolished, and you located Jesus among half a billion souls. Even Satan said he's never seen you so effective, but Raphael looks at you and notes only that you failed to bring him out with you, so he calls you incompetent." He looked back at his hands. "If you had any other vulnerable point, Raphael would have hit that too, given a chance."

You deserved it.

Mephistopheles had a very soft voice. "So I'll just pass this along. You have to come up with the worst thing you could say to him, the one thing it would hurt worst in the world for him to hear. Ideally you want two, but one will suffice. Something that strikes him right in the heart. Then you hold it at the ready like a cocked crossbow in your throat, because at some point he'll do it again, and you'll want to fire back on the spot."

Gabriel's eyes widened.

Mephistopheles swallowed. "He'll escalate then, which is why you want two. But he won't try it a third time because he'll know it's not worth it."

Gabriel felt nauseated. "Doesn't that destroy trust?"

"Being prepared does not destroy trust. Trust has already been destroyed." Mephistopheles shook his head. "After they cut out your heart, it never goes back to the way it was. You'll always know what he's capable of, and a part of you is always going to wonder about everything you share, is this the weapon he'll use against me next time?"

Gabriel rested his forehead on his wrists. *Legalist.* "And this horrible thing to say, what happens if you say it first?"

"It's ineffective." Mephistopheles sounded surprised. "You have to hold it back because counterstrikes are all in the timing." He looked up. "It probably took you three seconds to come up with it, but you'll want to go over it in your head a hundred times until you've got it needle-sharp and it penetrates like an arrow to the heart."

Gabriel shivered.

"It's best not to give him a second chance." His amber eyes looked haunted. "At some point he'll give a sincere apology, and it will melt you. You'll want to believe it because you want everything to go back to normal, but *this* is normal. What came before was just honeymoon, and it ends for everyone."

Gabriel couldn't find the moon through the clouds that had drifted overhead.

"You didn't deserve that." Mephistopheles started stripping the leaves off a branch. "I couldn't believe my eyes when you got into Sheol. None of us has ever come up with even a theory of how to do it, and you popped in half an hour after you decided it was necessary."

Gabriel chuckled. "You never needed to as badly as we did."

"I can tell you never had Lucifer give you an order."

Gabriel felt the world around him, the approaching morning, the night creatures beginning to resettle but the diurnal lives not yet stirring. He felt the cells tearing as Mephistopheles pulled the spine from a leaf. Raphael was probably still with Nivalis, but Gabriel checked the impulse to reach for him.

A moment after, Raphael's voice said, "How are the wings?"

"They're fine."

Gabriel looked up to find Mephistopheles showing Raphael the inner right-hand pair of wings.

"You're downy!" Gabriel couldn't stop himself from grinning.

"Not for long." Mephistopheles huffed. "Anyone comes up to me, and it's this—" He made a twist and a yank with his wrist. "*'Mephistopheles, how cute!'* I had to blast a few of them away, but the ones above me I can't stop."

"That's awful," Raphael said.

"It doesn't hurt. It's just annoying." Mephistopheles turned to Gabriel. "Remember."

He vanished.

Gabriel said, "What favor did you do for him? He was drenched in your energy."

"His wings got caught when the fissure closed. I patched him up." Raphael shook his head. "I couldn't do anything about the down."

"I'm sure he's just glad not to be mangled."

"He never said thank you," Raphael said, "so I wouldn't know."

Gabriel rolled his eyes. "Didn't you realize they're entitled to anything that makes their lives easier?"

"Naturally." Raphael took a deep breath. "Was he bouncing an idea off you on how to get back into Sheol?"

"He was telling me all Seraphim are predators."

Gabriel let that statement sit for a moment.

Raphael sounded uncomfortable. "I wonder if Beelzebub knows he feels that way."

"I got the impression it was mutually understood." Gabriel folded his arms. "How is Nivalis?"

"She's a wreck." Raphael looked down, shaking his head. "She wishes she could have done something more, and all I can tell her is that she did everything she could, and that at some point we're just not allowed to interfere any longer, and she can't blame herself for someone else's choices." He stepped closer to Gabriel. "And really, if I'm telling her that, it's not fair to insist that you should have done something more or that you should have gotten more involved than God allowed you to do, or that you're to blame for God's choices."

Gabriel avoided meeting Raphael's gaze.

"So, with all my heart, I'm sorry I've been so angry at you, and that I insulted you in front of everyone, and the way I went off the handle at you before. You're right that I was directing my anger at you instead of at God, and that wasn't fair."

Gabriel's wings dropped. He tilted his head so it lay against his forearm, and he closed his eyes.

Raphael walked away. "And if you're still going to be like this toward me, then I shouldn't have even bothered, should I?"

Gabriel's jaw locked, and his throat tightened. His fingers gripped the tree branch so hard they hurt, and he fought the urge to run by tucking his face down toward the branch and trying just to breathe without seizing.

A moment later he felt Raphael right in front of him. "Oh, blast, Gabriel, I didn't mean to make you cry."

As Raphael reached toward him, Gabriel threw a Guard around himself. It crackled where Raphael tried to touch. Gabriel wrenched himself up onto his knees, wings spread for balance. His glow reflected in Raphael's eyes.

"What more do you want from me?" Raphael snapped.

"I need five minutes alone," Gabriel said.

"Does that mean 'apology accepted'?"

"It means I can forgive you, and I do forgive you, but I don't know—" Gabriel looked at his hands grasping the branch. "I don't know how I can trust you again."

Gabriel locked down tight, avoiding whatever look was in Raphael's eyes.

Finally Raphael said, "Have your five minutes." His voice was subdued. "Come back afterward if you think you can."

He flashed away.

Gabriel stood on the branch and wrapped his arms around the trunk, pressing his forehead into the bark and feeling the tree greet him in return. The tree told him in tree-language about water and sunlight and springtime. He felt through the rings in a living dendrochronology, picking out the wide rings of the wet years, then the tight ones where water had seemed so scarce.

Four minutes left.

He reached for God. *I don't know if I can.*

Mephistopheles was that persuasive?, asked the Sprit.

He didn't say anything I hadn't been thinking. Gabriel shook his head: deserved it, arrogant, legalistic, ice-hearted.

List your alternatives, said the Spirit.

He could keep himself at arm's length, avoiding any kind of real contact, making sure not to slip when things seemed to be going well. He could fear betrayal forever, always uncertain what would happen if he gave Raphael a weapon to use against his heart or if Raphael would use one of the plentiful weapons already at his disposal.

Meaning to be cautious all the time, the Spirit said, and always on edge.

Gabriel nodded. The other alternative was to return and act as if he trusted Raphael again. Then when the betrayal came, it would be sudden and total, one clean pain and after that he would know exactly what to expect. But it would hurt worse because of all the extra ammunition Raphael had accumulated, and he'd look like a fool for having trusted him again.

Three minutes left.

Which would you prefer? asked God. *Would you rather mistrust him or be betrayed by him?*

I'd rather this hadn't happened, Gabriel said. *I'd rather that Jesus was still alive, that I hadn't been the one to give him the cup, that I'd pulled him out of Sheol, and that Raphael didn't think all those things he said about me were true.*

The Spirit moved in close to him.

He's praying for me?

He's praying for both of you. He's very upset.

He should be upset. Gabriel thought that rather than prayed it, but he knew God would hear anyhow.

Jesus had said, "Don't turn on each other." It was easier to weather a storm together than apart, but this was a self-made storm in too many respects. Too many misunderstandings, too many missed opportunities.

Two minutes.

So the choice: forgive and protect yourself, or forgive and offer a second chance.

I hate this, Gabriel said. *Why did you work so hard to make me compassionate if all it was going to do was rip out my heart? Before that year, I wouldn't have cared if he was angry because I'd have known I was right, and I'd have excused him. Forgiving is a lot harder than excusing.*

But if he acted to protect himself, had he really forgiven him? Or was it only responsible for himself to feel skittish after that kind of attack?

He started walking back toward Jesus's tomb. The small group of Roman soldiers didn't notice him; their guardians did.

One minute.

I think too much, Gabriel sent to God, who offered him a hug.

Gabriel passed through the rock and sat beside Raphael. Raphael hugged him, breathing unsteadily. "I'm sorry," he said even as Gabriel said, "I'm sorry."

Raphael said, "Listen."

"You listen. You've said enough." Gabriel let Raphael wrap his wings around them both, and he fought to relax his heart. "It's been an awful two days. I don't want to go around it anymore. I just want to forget."

Raphael said, "I didn't mean a lot of what I said."

"You don't even remember half of what you said." Gabriel shivered. "And you meant every word of it, otherwise it wouldn't have hurt as much as it did."

Raphael deflated.

"But right now the point should be him, not you, not me." Gabriel shook his head. "We can't turn on each other. There's something more important going on, and it should be about him, and about the twelve, and about Mary, and about whatever happens now that he's dead."

Raphael nodded, but he didn't let go.

Gabriel leaned against him but was unable to relax, and he tried not to let himself feel afraid as he extended his heart into Raphael's. Raphael met him halfway, his fire surging for the moment until Gabriel reached in to calm it, and for that moment they existed in unison.

Gabriel and Raphael stayed in the tomb together, Raphael playing a lyre at times, alternating with Gabriel reading aloud from the scriptures. Other angels paid their respects before heading back to their assignments, many offering their condolences to Raphael. Word had spread about many things, and more than a few of the visitors seemed startled to find Gabriel there.

With about an hour until sunrise, as Gabriel read from Isaiah, Raphael gasped and jerked up his head.

Light exploded through the tomb.

Gabriel was on his feet even as Raphael rushed to Jesus's side, radiating surprise and excitement and disbelief. "He's alive!"

Michael's voice shouted in his mind, *Gabriel! Sheol just detonated!*

Better than that—get over here!

Raphael radiated fire and joy as Jesus struggled with the burial cloth. The Seraph ripped off the upper part of the cloth, then loosened the head wrapping and flung it behind him into the corner.

Jesus sat up, grinning.

Shouting, Raphael tackled him with a hug. Gabriel watched from a distance, arms folded, eyes bright as Raphael laughed and refused to let Jesus go.

Jesus stretched, then looked at Gabriel. "You come here too." Gabriel sat next to him, and Jesus hugged him. "It's so good to see the two of you."

"You did it," Raphael whispered. "You're here."

Gabriel dropped a pair of his wings so they became a cloak of sorts, and Raphael handed it to Jesus before doing the same with a pair of his own wings.

The room grew crowded with angels, and Gabriel went insubstantial, backing away so the others could get close. Remiel sobbed into Jesus's lap. Michael knelt at Jesus' feet apologizing for not stopping the Romans. Raphael didn't move from his side. Jesus rested his hands on Remiel's cheeks and guided her to look up at him, and when their eyes met, she cried all the more, but he smiled at her and ran a hand through her hair.

Raphael flagged Gabriel from across the room. *He's hungry.*

Gabriel opened his hands, and then the container of risotto appeared. The angels passed it to the front.

Jesus said, "This is something you learned in Ecbatana?"

Gabriel shook his head. "It's Roman."

"It's good anyway," Jesus said, and Gabriel smiled. "Thank you."

Uriel appeared and bowed before Jesus.

"Don't tell Mom yet," he said. "I'll come to her myself."

With an inclined head, Uriel departed.

It was angelic chaos for a few minutes, everyone talking at once, Jesus eating for the first time in days, and Gabriel watching. Nivalis appeared and apologized, and Jesus pressed his fingers against her temples and promised her he held her blameless. Gabriel felt her frenzy ease, her self-blame, and momentarily even her loss seemed easier to bear.

A moment after that, the angels all fell silent. They cleared a space at the center of the tomb.

Satan had arrived, his four chiefs around him, all five armed. He stared levelly at Jesus, who looked back at him without flinching.

Gabriel armored himself. Michael and several others had done the same and gotten to their feet. Raphael, he saw, remained in place, watching the enemy without seeming prepared to defend, and he fought an urge to warn him.

Satan hadn't said anything yet. Jesus set the risotto to the side and walked toward him.

246

"Was this one lying," Satan said with a gesture at Gabriel, "when he said you preferred to stay dead?"

"He wasn't lying." Satan stood a few inches taller than Jesus, but Jesus wasn't intimidated by the Seraph's posture or his unflinching gaze. "I had to remain in Sheol to fulfill the scriptures and to redeem mankind, but with that done, the Father freed me to return."

Satan glowered at him.

Gabriel flexed his fingers toward his sword. Mephistopheles pivoted toward him, hand on his own weapon and wings spread, face grim. Across his eyes passed a flicker of warning: *Don't.*

"I don't understand you." Satan sounded furious. "You could have saved yourself. Why didn't you attack them the way they attacked you? You see now this race cares nothing for you, that of all those who sang your praises, only a handful cared enough even to remain and watch, and of those none intervened on your behalf, only stood fretting like a nest of mice. You see now that I was not wrong, that human dignity is an oxymoron."

Jesus said, "That isn't all I see. This wasn't their best hour, but I love them."

Satan folded his arms. "What else do you find in them? They're weak, scared, in love with their own comfort, changeable as the wind, and quick to forget what you've done for them. There is nothing honorable in this race of monkeys."

Jesus said to him, "I will glorify them."

"You didn't *have* to glorify us." Satan's voice sharpened. "We were created in your glory from the start."

Jesus shrugged. "That was my decision."

Satan turned.

Jesus said, "Stay with me."

Satan's eyes glinted white. "Not with you like *this*. Not with your expectations unchanged. Not until you admit the futility of cavorting with animals and worse."

Still facing Gabriel, Mephistopheles shifted his eyes toward Jesus. A shiver passed through wings that were appreciably less downy than a few hours ago.

247

Jesus said, "Love doesn't require exclusivity. If I love them this much, how much more—"

"Then your love is worthless." Satan spat on the ground. "If you bestow it on anything just because you made it, then it's not worth having."

He stalked through the angels, who parted before him. Asmodeus and Belior followed, and then Beelzebub.

Gabriel whispered, "Mistofiel, stay."

The Cherub looked Gabriel in the eyes, then at a departing Beelzebub, then back at Gabriel.

Beelzebub turned. "Come on!" He swept out of the tomb.

Mephistopheles followed him away.

Gabriel sagged against the wall.

Jesus shook his head, then turned back to the other angels. "We've got work to do." He looked at Raphael. "First, I want to say thank you for staying with me the whole time, even though you knew I couldn't feel your presence, and even though you weren't permitted to help."

Raphael went down on his knees. "I was only doing what I was assigned to do."

Jesus touched his hair. "You did it well. Michael," and Michael got on his knees as well, "you kept control of the angelic forces, and you prevented the enemy from doing more harm than they did. Thank you." Michael nonverbalized that he, too, was only doing his job.

Jesus looked out over all of them. "I know it was hard for all of you to watch and not stop him, but this had to be done to redeem mankind. Death's hold is broken. Satan's power is shattered. Adam's sin is undone. Humanity can come home."

The angels cheered.

"Now," Jesus said, "the only thing left to do is spread the word. And there's no one better for it—my messengers."

Laughter, more angels crowding up to Jesus, and he had private words with all of them, a momentary touch, a smile, even just a glance.

Raphael returned to Gabriel. Gabriel shifted sideways.

"We're okay," Raphael whispered.

Gabriel said, "It seems that way."

Raphael beamed, but Gabriel avoided it.

"Michael—" and Michael looked up at Jesus, "—Sheol is in a state of chaos. I need you to take a large contingent of angels—use your judgment as to how large, although I want Saraquael and Gabriel to remain with me—and sort the souls. Keep them corralled, and help the angels who are currently keeping Satan's forces away from them. You'll have to get them ready for judgment."

Michael focused one at a time on Raguel, Remiel, Zadkiel and several other angels, then left the tomb.

"I'm going now to see my mother," Jesus said. "Gabriel and Saraquael, Mary Magdalene is outside. Would you mind staying to make sure she hears the good news?"

Gabriel inclined his head while Saraquael bowed. Jesus departed with Raphael and almost all the other angels.

Gabriel looked up to find only Saraquael remaining, but studying him. He recoiled.

Saraquael gestured toward the rock. "Let's get rid of this thing." And with eyes shining, he shoved the rock aside as if it were made of bread. It rolled with a scraping groan against the front of the tomb.

Gabriel remained invisible, but Saraquael strode out of the open tomb and alighted on the perfectly rounded top of the stone, looking out at what the morning had brought.

The guards collapsed. Mary Magdalene and the other Mary regarded him, open-mouthed, ready to run.

Gabriel said, "Play nice."

Saraquael projected his amusement at Gabriel, but he looked only at the women. "Don't be afraid. I know you've come looking for Jesus, who was crucified, but he isn't here. He's risen, just as he said he would."

The women had backed away. Gabriel dissociated himself and swirled around them, offering strength and reassurance. He wasn't sure if they could detect his presence, but it hardly mattered, considering the gravity of the morning. Yes, he injected into their hearts, they were looking at an angel—-but he was not here to hurt them. He was on Jesus's side, and how could an angel in Jesus's service be a danger to them now?

Saraquael slipped down from the rock and gestured to the tomb. "Come and look at the place where he lay. Then run to tell the disciples that he has risen from the dead and is going ahead of you into Galilee. You will see him there." Saraquael bowed. "And now I have told you everything."

Gabriel chuckled. "Show-off."

Saraquael vanished from their sight. The women peered into the tomb, then sprinted back toward the city.

As Gabriel leaned against the side of the tomb, Saraquael said, "Why did you lie to Raphael?"

Gabriel's eyes flew open. "What?"

"I don't know what you said, but I can read people. I'm a poet, remember?"

Gabriel said, "I didn't lie."

"He was clearly asking if everything was all right between the two of you, and you may not have *lied*, but you left him with the impression that it was."

Gabriel didn't answer.

"He wants to believe it badly enough, and you're usually so understated, that he'll accept anything less than a screaming declaration of discontent as evidence that everything is settled."

Gabriel looked up. "Why is that wrong? He's apologized. I've accepted. What more should I ask for?"

"What more do you want?" When Gabriel made no reply, Saraquael added, "You don't need another misunderstanding on top of the first."

"When did my life become everyone else's concern?" Gabriel said. "And when did you become authorized to fix it?"

"I'm a poet," Saraquael said, "and poets meddle."

"Perhaps that's why so many poets in history have been boiled in oil."

Saraquael laughed out loud. "That's the most gracious way anyone has ever told me to shut up." He jumped back onto the stone. "I've said my peace."

"You mean well," Gabriel said, "but we need to let things settle so we can get back to normal."

The angels remained at the tomb throughout the morning. The Roman guards reported to the high priests that the body was gone, and a number of the priests came to see the tomb for themselves. Gabriel and Saraquael remained unseen while the men examined the tomb and argued among themselves: *surely the grave had been robbed...no, grave-robbers wouldn't steal a body...the disciples must have stolen the body...had he been laid in the wrong tomb?...what about the angel the guards had claimed to see?*

Saraquael said, "It's taking more energy for them to do damage control than to believe what the guards saw and heard."

Gabriel shrugged. "Give them some time. Any Cherub worth the name would ask the same questions when faced with the impossible."

Gabriel and Saraquael sang together when there was no one else around, and then Saraquael played the flute while Gabriel sang to accompany, and afterward Saraquael read poetry while Gabriel listened. Peter and John came, but the angels felt warned not to appear to them, so they watched the men search the tomb, take the burial cloths, and then leave.

"Not enough faith," Saraquael said.

Gabriel said, "Peter is pretty shaken by what he saw, not to mention what he did."

Saraquael squinted.

"It's one thing to think you denied your lord when he's dead." Gabriel looked over his shoulder. "It's quite another to know you denied him and you may have to explain why. It's hard to unsay a denial like that."

"Words last," Saraquael said. "They last a lot longer than the sound they make."

Gabriel pulled his wings tighter around his shoulders.

Saraquael clapped a hand on him. "We're free to go now. Let's see if Michael needs any assistance at Sheol."

.

251

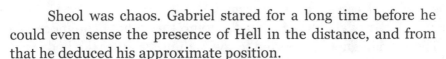

Sheol was chaos. Gabriel stared for a long time before he could even sense the presence of Hell in the distance, and from that he deduced his approximate position.

Raphael appeared at his side. "Incredible, isn't it?"

Gabriel's wings tightened involuntarily, and he sidled toward Saraquael.

Saraquael did a double take. "It's a blizzard of rock bits!"

Indeed, a blizzard of black snow in razor-sharp slivers. Gabriel couldn't see further than a half mile in any direction even with long-distance vision. Intermingled with the shards were larger chunks, ranging in size from fruit to meteoric, and each moving randomly.

Raphael shifted so he had Gabriel cupped in his wings. "You've got to be careful of the larger chunks—angels keep getting hurt when they come together too fast. They've got an attraction for one another."

Gabriel moved away as if trying to get a closer look, then flashed a chunk to himself inside a Guard. It didn't like being contained and kept moving away from him as if by magnetic repulsion. "Why are we here at all?"

Saraquael said, "Gabriel, look away from Sheol. All around."

"Where's away?" He dragged his gaze away from the heart of the tumult and tried to scan long distance.

Saraquael pushed between him and Raphael, pointing. "Follow out that way. See them?"

About to wonder what he could possibly see through the debris, Gabriel hesitated. A glint in the darkness. Another.

"Are those demons?"

Saraquael said, "That looks like an army to me."

Gabriel could see only a couple, but he trusted Saraquael and his Dominion's sense of the hidden.

Raphael said, "Michael thinks it's the whole army."

"But why?"

"Human souls. We need to pull them free and keep them safe until Jesus judges them, but the enemy has to want them too." Raphael put his hands on Gabriel's shoulders. Gabriel tensed as he looked into the bit of darkness Guarded in his hands. "As long as they're trapped in the rock, they stay asleep, so we're getting them out."

Gabriel sent his energy into the Guard, shattering the stone. Three human souls wriggled loose, sleepy and confused.

Saraquael snared them, and a moment afterward there were Angels looking them over to identify them. Within a minute, all three souls had been reunited with their guardians.

Michael appeared, his armor dented and his clothing ripped. "Saraquael, I want you out there with Zadkiel to keep a perimeter against Satan's forces. If they do anything, alert me. In person—we can't communicate through this stuff, so we're reduced to running messages." He turned to Raphael. "You need to get back to helping the wounded."

Raphael took Gabriel by the arm, but Michael put out his hand. "Gabriel's staying with me."

"Oh." Raphael looked suddenly lost, then brushed his wings by Gabriel's. "I'll be back with you as soon as I can."

Gabriel nodded, and Raphael vanished.

"Try not to get separated." Michael wiped the soot from his face but succeeded only in smudging it around.

Gabriel and Michael headed into the debris field. Michael spoke with numerous teams of angels and helped them destroy some of the larger chunks. Angels and Archangels were sifting out the silting bits and reuniting humans with their guardians. Gabriel followed Michael from site to site, assisting when the opportunity presented itself but mostly observing.

After half an hour, Gabriel said to Michael, "What did you want me to do?"

Michael shrugged. "I didn't want you to do anything. I'm keeping Raphael out of your hair."

Gabriel backed up, startled.

"He was all over you, and clearly you weren't comfortable with that, so you're with me." Michael gave instructions to one of the Archangels, then returned his attention to Gabriel. "If you can come up with a better system for harvesting the sleepers out of the stones or for getting the smut out of the atmosphere, I'm all for it. But as far as I'm concerned, keeping the two of you apart is enough."

Gabriel frowned.

Michael returned to work while Gabriel focused on nothing. His senses prickled from the presence of so much death. When he reached out further, to try feeling that dark army just beyond his vision, he felt none of it. Unnerving to say the least. The area swirled with sleep and wakefulness, concern, the joy of reunion and the frenzy of the parted, confusion from the newly-wakened. Another half-hour had elapsed when he said to Michael, "Why?"

Michael turned to him. "Why what?"

"Why did you think you needed to separate us?"

Michael sighed, then waved one of the Archangels away. He moved closer to Gabriel and spoke in a hush. "Look, every time he got near you, you got like this." Michael stood completely stiff, his arms tight to his sides, his wings tense, but his face a startled blank. Shrugging, he returned to his normal posture. "It was obvious to everyone except Raphael that you wanted Raphael gone."

Gabriel bit his lip. "But— I probably should be with him."

Michael waved a hand. "You're free to go."

Five minutes later, Gabriel was still shadowing Michael through the debris field.

"This isn't right," Gabriel said.

"Of course it's not right!" Michael turned to him. "I'm sorry, Gabriel. I owe you a tremendous apology for not stepping in to stop him."

Gabriel shook his head.

Michael grabbed him by the forearms. "I couldn't have stopped him from being angry, but I could have prevented him from harassing you. He was under my command. When you didn't react to all his provocation, I thought you had it under control, but you didn't. You had yourself under control. I needed to step in, and I didn't."

Gabriel reached up for Michael's hands. "You didn't do anything wrong."

"God summoned me in front of the throne," Michael said. "He reprimanded me for allowing one of my officers to be harassed. When I protested that I'd stepped between Satan and Israfel as quickly as I could, He said I hadn't protected *you*." He bowed his head. "I'm asking your forgiveness."

Gabriel hugged him. "You have it. I'm sorry you got into trouble on my account."

"I got into trouble because of what I failed to do." Michael's face darkened. "I'm not going to fail to do it again, which is why you're here." He folded his arms. "What did Raphael say to you after you pulled him away from Sheol?"

Gabriel kept silent.

"Do you realize he was overheard by the guardians of the Romans? Because whatever he said, it sent four of them running for help. I had one in front of me the same instant Saraquael had one in front of him, and in the next minute a third was begging Israfel for help—only none of them would repeat what he said."

Gabriel turned away, bringing up his wings. Michael added, "The fourth ran to Uriel, who found you first."

Gabriel swallowed. "I didn't ask anyone to take sides."

Michael glowered. "I didn't think you did."

A Principality reported to Michael about the status of the perimeter. The damned angels had formed a ring around the field, but they were otherwise silent. Quiet and watching in the void. Their leaders weren't making themselves apparent, but their finger-prints were everywhere. Michael acknowledged and sent the Principality back to Saraquael.

Gabriel said, "Do you have me following you because I'm not trustworthy to finish my assignments?"

Michael stopped in his tracks. "Please tell me you don't believe any of what he said to you. Please."

Gabriel swallowed. "I'm not a very good judge of character."

Michael laughed. "Who is?"

"Well, Raphael." Gabriel watched the debris in full swirl. "I usually follow his lead."

"Am I a good judge of character?" When Gabriel nodded, Michael continued, "Are my other friends all those things he said, the things you won't tell me?"

Arrogant, legalistic, block-of-ice, uncaring. Gabriel began to vibrate with strain. "You may be with me as an act of charity."

"As an act of charity I'll forget you said that." Then Michael stiffened, focused distantly, and turned back to Gabriel. "God says you're going to misinterpret that, so I'll be clear: I love you. I don't spend time with you as an act of philanthropy."

Energy starting rippling from Gabriel, or maybe it was grief. "He wouldn't have accused me of something he hadn't already thought."

Michael softened at the note in his voice. He cocooned them both in his wings, and within that makeshift shelter he shone so he could look Gabriel in the eyes. *Be totally honest. Is the dam about to burst?*

Gabriel looked aside. It had gone down a long time ago.

Michael pressed his forehead to Gabriel's shoulder and Gabriel rested his cheek against Michael's hair. Again from Michael: sorrow. From Gabriel: It was awful, horrible, just too much had happened, but he was stable now. He just needed the ground to stay still under his feet. He needed not to be untrustworthy and all those other things, and maybe then he could forget or at least ignore what had happened.

Ignore it. It had worked for Raphael. It had worked for so long.

Michael pulled back from. "You can stay with me, but you don't have to. You can have a team of your own and keep working. You can leave. It's your choice." Michael smiled. "Should I prove I don't think you're incompetent?" And Gabriel finally smiled.

Michael turned him loose to secure a particularly thick field of debris, assigning him his own team of Archangels. Gabriel sized up the area and immediately dismissed all other angels to work in other areas until he'd secured it. "The sleepers aren't in pain," Gabriel said. "There's no immediacy. The rest of Sheol is not without work to do."

He studied the fragments, fascinated by their attraction to one another. With a little coaxing and the right infusion of energy, a handful of dust-like shards in a Guard could be compressed until they locked together instead of flying apart. He showed the Archangels how to do the same. "This is going to take a long time, but this process might reduce the silt enough to communicate over distances." He pointed to one of the Archangels. "You, get me another Cherub. Anyone."

Gabriel and the other Cherub argued about ways to net the silt. Once they had a method of filtering, he sent the Archangels to promulgate the process while the Cherubim debated ways to control the larger chunks.

"The most obvious is to hold the larger chunks inside a Guard while we detonate them," said the other Cherub, "keeping the Guard permeable to human souls to permit them to escape, then compressing the debris into a sphere to prevent further silting."

Gabriel said, "That has a side benefit that when we find spheres or spheroid objects, we'll recognize them as already harvested and not waste time re-blowing material that's already searched."

The Archangels returned to find the Cherubim arguing about methods of corralling the meteoric boulders. They stepped in between to find out what the two methods were (as it turned out, they'd developed five) and who championed which (neither Cherub could remember) and the Archangels asked permission to begin with the implementation.

Gabriel protested, "We haven't optimized a process."

The Archangel heading the team said, "We don't need an optimal process. We just need a process."

Each Cherub took a small group and instructed them in a different method of grabbing the rock and shattering it safely. As expected, two of the five methods proved impossible to implement; the other three had varying degrees of success depending on the outside factors: the crowding, the silting, the size, the speed, and the number of souls within.

Gabriel had just snagged a medium-sized boulder to experiment with another technique when he felt Raphael excited at his back.

"They found Tobias!"

Heart pounding, Gabriel studied the boulder. "Have you seen him yet?"

"You have to come with me." Raphael zipped around to the front, his eyes afire and his smile broad. "I can stay ten minutes before they need me back with the healing angels. Let's go!"

Gabriel had fallen into the same stiff-limbed stance Michael had made fun of before, and he rolled his shoulders to relax himself. "I'm in the middle of something."

"It can wait." Raphael put his hand on Gabriel's arm, and he went tense again. "I want to see the look on his face when he recognizes you."

Gabriel pulled back more roughly than he'd intended. "I'm streamlining the process so we can work more efficiently. I need to concentrate."

"But—"

"Go without me."

Raphael sounded confused. "I kind of wanted to show you off to him."

Gabriel released the boulder and spun to face him. "Why are we still having this conversation? You're wasting minutes. I told you to go without me."

The confusion yielded to hurt. Raphael's voice dropped. "I don't understand."

"What is there not to understand?" Raphael's sparks made him dizzy, so Gabriel armored his heart against Raphael's fire. "Visit Tobias and have a good time. I'm not going with you."

Inside Gabriel was a flood, and he realized he'd been wrong when he told Michael the dam had already gone down; he'd built a new one in the interim, one that threatened another breach. He couldn't let that happen here, not in front of everyone, not in front of Raphael. So he fled into an analysis of how many seconds of Raphael's ten minutes he'd already spent, how to answer

Raphael's arguments most efficiently, the logistics of how to manage separate visits to Tobias—forever, if necessary.

Raphael lowered his voice. "But he'll want to see you."

"Eternity's a long time," Gabriel looked back into the debris for his boulder. "He'll see me eventually."

Raphael reached for Gabriel's heart, and Gabriel tensed. "Ever since you came back from his household, I've been thinking about how we could see him the first time together. How we'd surprise him."

Gabriel folded his arms. "Far be it from me to criticize your planning abilities, but maybe you should have factored that into the equation before informing me I was a disgrace to you."

Raphael radiated pain. "You're still angry at me?"

Reverted to being a legalist.

Several of his Archangels monitored the exchange from a distance. It couldn't be helped. For that matter, there was a demon army assembled outside the debris field, and they could be monitoring it too. Mephistopheles, laughing because Gabriel hadn't believed him the one time he'd told the truth.

"I'm not angry." Gabriel struggled not to raise his voice. "But I'm also not going to embarrass you in front of him. He's going to want to know why I was in his house for six months, and I'm going to have to tell him."

His eyes huge, Raphael whispered, "I'll explain."

"Did I ask you to explain?" Gabriel stepped forward, his wings spread. "I'm abiding by your wishes. You don't want to hear about that time, but I'm going to talk about it with him. That means we can't visit him together. Am I being clear?"

Gone was Raphael's spark, Raphael's smile.

"Protesting my decision isn't an efficient use of your time." Gabriel gestured with one hand. "Eight minutes and fifteen seconds remain. Go."

Raphael whispered, "You said...before...if I gave you five minutes...you'd trust me again."

Gabriel said, "Perhaps that was an unwarranted optimism," and Raphael gasped.

That pain went right through both of them, and Gabriel wanted to say something, anything that could explain— No. He was only telling the truth, and the truth was the truth: you faced it because you had no choice. There was nothing to say other than what he already had, not without getting into... But he shouldn't need to. His solution made sense. It was just logical to visit Tobias separately so he could explain what happened without disgracing Raphael in the man's eyes. If anything, Gabriel should have made sure to get there first.

Of course, right now Raphael didn't appreciate the logic in visiting separately because with typical lack of foresight he had longstanding plans and couldn't synthesize his conflicting wants.

Raphael finally managed, "Afterward, when I'm not there—" His shoulders hunched. "Afterward, you'll go see him?"

Gabriel perked up. "You do understand."

"I'm afraid I do." And then he was gone.

Too much silt. Gabriel couldn't have called him back.

I'll explain.

It would be disgraceful. Ashamed. Couldn't be forgiven. Just don't keep bringing it up. You deserved it. Reverted to being a legalist. A betrayal of that magnitude can't be undone. I'm always going to carry that with me. Why must you always stand on ceremony about everything?

I'll explain.

I'm no longer your Seraph. I know how you do these things. You'll adhere to every iota of a list and not one bit more. Jealous. You let me down.

"*Tobias, this is Gabriel. Please for the love of God don't ask why he was in your house for six months. It's better if everyone ignores it. I'm horrified that he dragged you into this.*"

"Gabriel?"

I'll explain.

"*Tobias, this is Gabriel. I'm ashamed of him, but he's my bonded Cherub, so I just pretend it never happened, and once you get to know him, you'll see why.*"

"Gabriel!"

I'll explain

Gabriel startled aware. There was an Archangel right in front of him, hands on his shoulders, and seven more clustered around.

Arrogant. Legalist. Deserved it.

"Are you hurt?"

Disgraceful. Shameful. Unforgivable.

"Gabriel?"

"I'm intact." Gabriel realized he'd been off in his own head for several minutes. "I'm sorry. I didn't mean to concern you."

Another Archangel appeared, this one bringing Michael.

"We roused him," said the Archangel directly in front of Gabriel.

Gabriel wrapped his trembling arms around one another. It was so cold. The silt had left him gritty. His eyes stung from the particles.

"What did he say to you?" Michael demanded.

I'll explain.

"He wanted me to visit Tobias with him." Gabriel rubbed at the silt on his arm. "I sent him ahead. That's all."

Michael sized him up. "Leave."

Gabriel's eyes widened. "But I'm okay. I'll get back to work."

Michael shook his head. "You're cooked. Get out of here and recharge."

Gabriel gestured at the debris field with one hand.

"There's a lot left to be done, yes," Michael said, "but if you leave for an hour, you'll come back able to devise a solution that will shave weeks off the work. If you stay like this, you won't do any good, and you won't come up with a breakthrough anyhow. More likely, you'll get hurt. Go. Rest. Pray. Do something else."

Gabriel felt numb. "The demons."

"Satan has every last soldier under his command assembled just outside our communications reach." Michael's voice lowered. "At some point, he's going to launch an assault, and I'm going to need you then. Need you at the top of your game. You're not now. You have to recharge."

Gabriel bit his lip.

Michael said, "Would you disobey a direct order?"

He swallowed hard. "I don't know."

"Let's find out. I'm ordering you to leave."

Gabriel left.

He went home to his library, but he was restless, so he flashed momentarily to Mary's house, then back again to a lakeshore in Heaven, and finally he went before the Throne of Glory, to his spot in the ring of Seven.

He went on his knees and set his sight on God's face, and in the next moment he wanted to hide because God saw him; he was still covered in silt and his heart was leaking confusion. He bowed and stood to leave the ring when the Spirit stopped him.

Gabriel settled back down, but he ran his fingers through his wingtips, getting them deep in the feathers to straighten himself out a bit. He asked permission to leave, and again the Spirit told him to stay.

Self-conscious, Gabriel retreated into himself.

I never minded a little dust, the Spirit replied.

Gabriel shook his head.

It is *more than the dust,* agreed the Spirit, and then Gabriel was clean, his wings and hair lighter. He folded his hands on his thighs. *So let's talk about something other than dust.*

Gabriel closed his eyes. *God—*

Nothing. He couldn't put it into words, the betrayal, the emotions he was struggling so hard to keep under control, the grief and the stunned un-grief, but he was still grieving after all, and the shock of the last three days, and the horrible things he'd seen and the worse things he'd heard, and the realization after all this time that something he'd thought would be enough couldn't be enough after all.

The Spirit prompted him, and Gabriel only prayed, *Help.*

A hug. Gabriel pulled his wings tight and bowed his head, clutching his folded hands to his chest as he let the Spirit enwrap him. He didn't know what else to do, and the Spirit stayed close and urged him just to remain, not to be afraid, to wait and to trust.

What if trust was the thing that was shattered? Gabriel shuddered. What if wasn't enough just to be near someone you loved even though he— even though he had reservations about you? What if you had been wrong all those years when you'd told yourself it was?

Again the warmth from the Spirit, the urging to relax his heart and trust.

Gabriel looked into the eyes of God: All those things Raphael had said—were they accurate? Was that really him? And God replied no; they were all things Gabriel was afraid were true, but they were no more real than that demon image.

Gabriel let out a long breath. Only then could he still himself and allow God's love to flow through him. It was enough that he and God were together, and that was all he needed.

He felt God bringing him back to himself, and as his eyes cleared, the Spirit said, "Go now and visit Tobias."

Gabriel flashed back to Sheol.

Immediately he extended his senses for Raphael, and he sighed when he could feel only traces of the Seraph's fire but no Seraph. Next he took stock of the area. The angels had begun using his compression technique to form platforms for the human souls, even equipping them with their own gravity fields. Hundreds of platters hung in the void, people taking stock of where they were while angels mixed with them. There was a concert taking place on one, and Gabriel chuckled; the music was keeping the people calm.

And oh, in the distance, from here he could feel that demonic presence wrapping around them like a ribbon. Angels harvesting a sea of space for the tiniest of sand grains while all around them swam sharks awaiting a blood frenzy. The people had to be sensing that too, only they didn't understand. Living with evil all their lives, they didn't recognize how wrong it was.

Tobias. He'd been ordered to visit Tobias.

Gabriel followed the traces of Raphael's fire to one of the platforms, and it led to a family he recognized.

The humans in the family were all adults, but some were experimenting with their soul-forms, becoming younger or older. Over time they would learn better control, but for now many remained at the age they had died. Some were surprised at how they had been made whole where at death, or for maybe their whole lives, they had been broken.

Spotting Tobias, Gabriel glided to him, his heart racing. As he landed, Tobias looked up, and Gabriel bowed his head. He took a deep breath to steady himself, then went on his knees. "I want to say thank you, sir."

An old man the way he was when Gabriel lived with him, Tobias took a step forward. "It's you!" He dropped beside him, wonder all over himself.

"Gabriel!" Another human soul rushed him, and Gabriel turned in time to catch Raguel—Tobias' grandson who had brought him to the family and whose room he'd shared. He laughed out loud, and then there was Gabelus, and Angela, and Raguel's mother, and so many others from the family. Everyone was hugging him, and he closed his eyes as he remembered how good it felt to be with them, how it felt to be accepted.

The initial flurry of greetings over, Gabriel stepped back to see them all. Raguel was also an old man; at his side was his wife, and there were his children and grandchildren. Gabriel had followed the family for generations and knew all their names. He could have performed the introductions himself, but suddenly Raguel was telling him about everyone, and telling everyone about him, and he let Raguel do it because that was what had happened the first time, and it had worked so well then.

Gabriel had been half-concerned they'd be stunned into awe on seeing him, but to them, all angels were similar in one respect: too big to comprehend. Their guardians had already assured them not to be afraid, and now they were doing it.

During a pause in the talk, Tobias suddenly said, "Thank you for what?"

Gabriel looked down. "For taking me into your household and demonstrating for me all the things I'd never learned to do. Compassion, acceptance, patience. Community. What it's like to live in a family." Gabriel's cheeks burned. "Did Raphael talk to you?" He knotted his shaking hands. "Did he explain why I was there?"

Tobias said, "I saw Raphael. He didn't mention you."

Good.

For the next two minutes Gabriel explained the past, the choices he'd made, the things he'd refused to learn until God put him into a position where he had to experience them. There was no condemnation in Tobias's eyes, nor in Raguel's, and when they asked questions, it was with no unspoken ridicule: why hadn't he told them? Had they been good enough to him? Tobias thanked him for coming into his household and giving them the privilege of becoming his family, and Gabriel closed his eyes.

One of the household guardians returned to the group looking distressed, and she apologized, but she asked for help. They still hadn't found her charge, Rafaela.

So Gabriel took Rafaela's guardian out a distance from the debris field. It ought to be easy this time: it already had occurred to him that Mephistopheles' and Belior's trick for communicating with a soul should be useful in this mess, and especially with Sheol's walls blown apart, it ought to be that much easier to track a guardian/protégé bond.

"Hold still." Gabriel concentrated to find that thread from the angel to the human. It ought to be there: Raphael had one to Jesus. But after five tries, Gabriel wondered if maybe there wasn't. He asked a nearby angel to find Ophaniel and bring him.

Until he arrived, Gabriel tried a different approach, standing behind Rafaela's guardian attempting to fill her with rings of calm the way he would a Seraph. He couldn't produce those either.

I'm useless here, he prayed.

Rafaela's guardian, a little shaken, said, "We'll find her eventually. There's nowhere else she could be."

Ophaniel arrived. Gabriel said, "I need to find the thread between this angel and her charge."

"But we can't pull it," Ophaniel said.

"She could."

Ophaniel frowned. "Why can't you find it?" He touched Gabriel's shoulder. "You're far too tense. Take an hour and pray over this."

"She needs to find Rafaela, and I already took time to pray." Gabriel swallowed. "Just find her thread for her."

Ophaniel said, "About an hour ago you said something to Raphael that shot right through him. I felt it clear across Sheol."

"I'm not trying to punish him." Gabriel folded his arms. "I gave him an honest assessment of where things stood."

Ophaniel nodded. "I'm not defending his actions—but you understand why it happened."

He looked down. "This isn't the time."

Rafaela's guardian said, "Well, I'm on your side. And it's okay. I'll just keep looking on my own."

Ophaniel extended a wing to the guardian. "Gabriel's going to find her for you."

"Don't make promises for me that I can't deliver."

"You're going to deliver." Ophaniel wrapped Gabriel in his wings while standing behind him. "Relax. You did this before with Satan at your back. Now it's only us."

"Us and a quarter-trillion demons surrounding the field."

"Cozy." Ophaniel took a deep breath. "Be clear and quiet."

Gabriel went still, and immediately words came to the surface of his heart; he went cold and forced them down.

You need to ask God if these accusations are accurate.

He says they're not.

From Ophaniel, a question about why he'd then let the words disturb him; from Gabriel, because Raphael believed them. From Ophaniel: why would Raphael try to make amends if he believed that? And Gabriel's instant reply, from pity.

Ophaniel sent, *He never pitied you.*

Gabriel let his mind open out, searching for the thread. Again words came to the surface, and again he tried to fight them down.

Behind him, Ophaniel flooded him with peace. *If they try, let them come.*

But I can't. You're bonded to him too. What if I damage your relationship with him?

You won't, Ophaniel said. *We have our own bond. You have yours. Let the words rise to the surface.*

And rise they did, but Gabriel closed his eyes and felt through Rafaela's guardian for that bond stronger even than a Cherub/Seraph bond. With Ophaniel at his back and all around him, Gabriel finally detected the thread.

Ophaniel whispered to the guardian, "Can you feel it now?"

The guardian indicated she still couldn't.

Ophaniel squeezed Gabriel. "Have you tried casting rings?"

"It didn't work."

Ophaniel behind him went liquid and exuded rings of calm like steel. Gabriel shivered, but he held the thread, and a moment afterward Rafaela's guardian gasped

She zipped along the thread. Gabriel took off after her, keeping her shielded from flying debris as she crossed the field. By the time he caught up to her, she had in her hand a chunk the size of a grape.

Ophaniel first Guarded and then pulverized it.

The guardian shrieked with joy as Rafaela's soul shook loose, and in the next moment two more burst free. Gabriel snatched them from the void, and momentarily two more ecstatic guardians appeared for their own reunions.

Gabriel exchanged a glance with Ophaniel. "That piece was no more than a pebble."

Ophaniel beamed. "But this is terrific! Now we know how to find the stragglers, when we get down to the final few hundred."

Gabriel had Ophaniel bring his Archangel team back to him. "We've got a new technique," he said, "and for this one, you can thank a couple of demons and the Witch of Endor."

Hours passed. The demons remained assembled without advancing. Michael kept the Powers and the Principalities on military alert while teams of Cherubim worked on the problem of clearing the air. The Sheol material still gave off too much interference for the angels to communicate.

Michael had Saraquael and Zadkiel running messages for him through the mess. "Right now," he sent word to Gabriel, "we need to contain the debris, but not contain it at such a high density that we can't work in it."

Gabriel sent back, "We also want to keep control of this material. If Satan gets ahold of this, he can build an impenetrable containment center."

That drew Michael to him in person. "Are you kidding me?"

When had he last been kidding around? Gabriel formed two hollow half-spheres out of the material, then made a sigil from his soul material. He inserted his sigil and sealed the sphere. "What's in there? Can you feel it? I can't."

Michael shivered. "We haven't been keeping any kind of inventory of all this stuff. That never even occurred to me."

Gabriel cast a Guard in apparently empty space, then drew it tighter until it was the size of an apple seed, and then a tiny bit of Sheol material gleamed. "Given that you can filter out particulate matter at that size, I'd be stunned if Belior isn't already experimenting with miniature eternal death-spheres."

Michael looked up, then sideways at their enemies. "Gabriel, that's... What are we going to do?"

Gabriel looked at the debris field, calculated the density of the pollution both inside and outside, the likely spread of the debris field. As his own dread built, he sent a messenger for Ophaniel. "You've got a new assignment," he said. "I need you to calculate the initial volume of Sheol material in the undetonated cube." He swallowed hard. "And at the same time, I need a second team calculating how much remains."

Ophaniel nodded, frowning. "Who do you think?"

"Physicists," Gabriel said. "Mathematicians. Grab a couple of Seraphim to keep your energy up, but no one who will distract you. And in the meantime—"

"And in the meantime," Michael whispered, "the enemy's moving in."

The first offensive force engaged with the Principalities in a series of guerilla strikes: in and out, in and out, never there long enough to subdue but just long enough to cause problems. By the time the Principalities got out a warning, the demons had managed to break through their guard, and in came the flood.

"The humans!" Michael kept ordering. "Guard the humans! That's what they're after!"

The guardian angels hadn't left their charges, and now they herded them into more defensible locations. Michael deployed his forces into the worst areas, but once the demons had broken through, they scattered everywhere in the Sheol fields. They went for the humans they'd known best during their lifetimes, and some of them dove right into the debris field to find the few remaining trapped souls.

And when they got them, the demons were flashing them out of the field. Probably into Hell itself. Michael grabbed Zadkiel and Saraquael. "I need you to go into Hell," he said. "Find where they're taking those souls, and bring them back out if you can."

They left, summoning the Dominions with them.

The angels needed to get some kind of barricade up again, and it was the Cherubim who began shifting those floating platforms to create makeshift fortresses, spheres with the humans contained inside. When they'd begun doing that, it was the

Virtues headed up by Remiel who streamlined that process to weaponize the blizzarding debris. By clustering the debris around the humans, they could prevent the in-and-out tactics. The angels still hadn't come up with a tactic against the smash-and-grab.

"We need to find Beelzebub!" Michael called.

Gabriel at his side said, "Look for Asmodeus too."

Michael said, "Beelzebub commands the army."

"I'm betting he doesn't any longer. Look." Gabriel directed Michael's sight toward Beelzebub, and at his side Mephistopheles — with no more downy feathers, but instead a smug expression. "That's a promotion. Satan just shook up the ranks."

Michael swallowed hard. "So we've got four Maskim trying very hard to make an impression right now. Where's Satan?"

Although Satan's power surrounded them, they hadn't yet found him. He might well have been dissociated and directing his forces without concentrating his presence in any one place, a tactic that made him simultaneously stronger and weaker. He couldn't focus that way, but on the other hand, within this limited area he could be omnipresent almost the way God was. They couldn't stop that. Michael looked around, livid. "I want him located. I want him forced into one place."

You couldn't battle this way, with demons never in one spot for longer than it took to recognize they were even there. On highest alert you still had only a microsecond during which to act. Michael's forces couldn't leave: they had to stay in this area to protect the humans, and they had nowhere to evacuate them to. And in the meantime, every so often, one of Satan's forces would get lucky and nab a human and carry it elsewhere.

Michael called Israfel and put her in charge.

Next he dissociated so he permeated the whole battle, just as Satan had, and he felt for that dark power spreading like an oil stain through a lake. It was everywhere and nowhere, but now so was Michael, and he spread himself thinner and further. Satan had a battle to coordinate, but Michael had one target, one focus. He tried to push past the panic streaming from the humans, their terror, their grief. The frenzy of guardians whose charges had gotten snatched. The anger of guardians trying to keep their human souls safe. The predator's focus of their enemies. And there, finally, among all that, he felt that slick double-shine over reality that he'd come to recognize as Satan's signature: making darkness brighter but a lie, always a lie.

Michael prayed. Prayed for the same power he'd received back at the Winnowing, for the same authority and for the same reason: because this was God's enemy, and someone had to stop him, but only the power of God could possibly combat this one. *Please,* Michael prayed. *Please.*

God's permission bloomed in his heart, and Michael snapped down like a steel trap.

Satan flared up under him as if he were wrestling an electric eel long enough to wrap around the world. Michael pushed, forced, ordered, and the harder Satan thrashed, the stronger Michael became until his strength was nothing and God's was everything. Michael forced Satan down into the fabric of reality, and as Satan went so did Michael until they were both there, focused, in spiritual forms again in the middle of the battle field.

"Now!" Michael called.

The first to join was Israfel, her eyes a brilliant double-shine with Gabriel's power. Satan met her charge, although he didn't break her blade. She redoubled her attack, but he kept going. A moment after, Raphael had joined, his own eyes alight with power from Ophaniel.

Satan fought off both at the same time. "These are mine! These souls are of Earth, and the Earth is mine! You have no authority here! No right!"

Michael tried to get near, but the undiluted soul-energy of the combat pushed him back. It wasn't enough, though. Even now, with more Seraphim joining the fight, he could tell it wasn't enough.

He flashed to Gabriel, who watched the fight to guide and empower Israfel. "Why are you in Israfel? I need you boosting Raphael."

Gabriel looked at him, suddenly terrified. "I can't!"

"I need you at your strongest. That means you and Raphael. Now. That's an order!"

Ash-white, Gabriel closed his eyes, and the primary pairs swapped: Ophaniel empowering Israfel, Gabriel with Raphael.

Michael grabbed a team of Archangels and went after the the Maskim. Four of them, but effectively two. Locate the two Cherubim and you could disarm the Seraphim, but it never worked in reverse. The Maskim wouldn't bother targeting Gabriel and Ophaniel, since Satan had his own battle well in hand, but take down Belior and Mephistopheles and that left Beelzebub and Asmodeus wide open.

The problem? Seraphim were fast. They had the speed and the reaction time to zip in and out of Sheol taking whatever they wanted and any human soul they had authority over, beginning with the ones they "owned" but extending outward to every human who'd ever sinned.

In other words, all of them.

Michael had Seraphim too, and he deployed them, but even their reaction time was still a reaction, and humans were getting snatched.

He sent for Saraquael and Zadkiel. "Find Mephistopheles," he ordered, and they vanished into the fray. It took them three minutes, three minutes too long, but they found him, and Michael went in for the attack while they searched next for Belior.

Satan, though. Even while working to subdue the others, Satan's protests could be heard through the entire field: that these humans were his, won according to God's own terms. They were sinful, disgusting, filthy, depraved and they had chosen evil over God time and time again.

And he was right. Michael couldn't object, except that they needed protection, and until God stepped in and said not to, that's what he would do.

Satan blew back Israfel and then turned on Raphael, who narrowly resisted the same. Wherever Gabriel was, he must have channeled all his energy into Raphael to keep him steady, but even so, Raphael looked dazed. Michael ordered in more soldiers, but before they could arrive, Satan broke free again, and this time he pulled.

He pulled, and the souls came to him.

Michael shouted, but even as the angels rallied around him, there was no way to stop that inexorable tug of the souls toward the lord of their world. Satan had told Jesus the world was his and he could give it to whomever he wanted, and now he was giving it to himself. They couldn't fight that.

They couldn't fight. But they could try. As the humans responded to the call of Satan's ownership, they did it all at different rates depending on how often they'd served evil during their lifetimes. The angels did their best to stem the tide, but some angels lost hold quicker than others. And in response to Satan's call, they came toward him as if toward a gravity well.

God, what do I do? Michael prayed constantly, and he could tell the other angels were praying as well. *Help us! These are your people! They're sinful, but they're yours, and you died to save them. Please...*

Jesus appeared before Satan. "Hold!"

Satan spun to face him, flames around his wings and eyes. "These are mine! I demanded the right to sift and test them all, and they've failed. Every human soul that's exited this world through death has done so in failure and disgrace."

"Except mine," said Jesus. "And I've destroyed death."

Satan said, "They are mine. They rejected your Father, and they rejected you. What more do you require?"

Jesus said, "Silence."

He turned toward the human souls dotting the field like so many stars. "Be still," he said to the fragments of Sheol, and the storm bits hung in the air. "Gather."

The human souls came close, forming around him in groups the way they had on the plains and in the mountains. Touching Michael on the shoulder, Jesus said, "Go into Hell and retrieve the ones taken there. No one will stop you."

Michael took Saraquael, Remiel and Zadkiel to the gates of Hell, where they did just walk in without any resistance. Unsure how to proceed, Michael shouted, "Come out! Your Lord is calling."

That was, apparently, all it took. The kidnapped souls flooded out. Remiel darted further in with Zadkiel, making sure no one remained trapped, but Saraquael stayed beside Michael, watching the demons who remained frozen at the gates.

The other two returned. "All clear," Remiel said, and they returned to Jesus.

Archangels had begun sweeping up the Sheol material, gathering it away from the human souls, and Michael realized with relief he could see further and feel emotions clearer from all around him. With Raphael at his side, Jesus was moving from group to group of human souls, speaking to them, touching, kissing, embracing, encouraging. Satan still burned like a torch, but he'd simmered down, as if biding his time.

Michael approached Gabriel. "What's he doing?"

Gabriel looked shaken, and only shook his head. At his side, Ophaniel said, "He's telling the good news to the spirits who were in prison."

Michael said, "And...they can come to Heaven with us?"

Ophaniel said, "As best I understand, they have to believe him and want to go with him."

Michael said, "While he's doing that, let's get the enemy secured."

They went through the ranks of fallen angels, pulling out the commanding officers and chaining them. Gabriel worked at Michael's side without speaking, but Michael could feel him strangely non-present, as if insulating himself from the action around him.

As Gabriel secured Mephistopheles, the dark Cherub said, "It's amazing how incompetency rises to positions of power."

Gabriel flinched. Michael said, "Many of us might wonder the same thing. Didn't you just get a promotion?"

Behind Mephistopheles, Beelzebub said, "Don't argue with Gabriel. Remember, he knows it all."

Mephistopheles looked Gabriel right in the eyes. "Not bad for an arrogant block of ice."

Michael snapped, "Quiet."

A smirk distorted Beelzebub's voice. "Do you think I'm going to make him cry?"

Michael commanded every last demon to silence. He turned to Gabriel, eyes ablaze, and he projected fury about Raphael.

Gabriel moved closer. *Michael, no. You don't understand,*

I am not oblivious to the fact that he *robbed me of one of my best officers at a time when I need him at the top of his game.* Michael clenched his fists, then said aloud, "You are under orders to instantly chain, gag, cook, cinder or otherwise punish *anyone* who says anything disrespectful to you."

Gabriel projected, *It's not Raphael's fault.*

Despite his words, Gabriel was projecting a scorching shame, and more. A rawness. Michael wondered for the first time how draining it was for a Cherub to power a Seraph. But Gabriel didn't look drained. Only numb.

Do you need to leave?

No, just don't be angry at him.

The demons quieted down, but several cast unsubtle glares at Gabriel as he worked. Gabriel did his job, but again his attention seemed far away, as if he'd applied a tourniquet to his heart. Cherubim weren't just ammunition for Seraphim to fire, and Michael considered how fragile Gabriel had been before. Maybe he'd ordered Gabriel to open his heart. Michael sent, *I'm sorry I forced you to pair off with Raphael. You weren't ready for that.*

Gabriel made no response whatsoever.

When Jesus finished moving through the crowds of human souls, he released his hold on Satan and on the souls, and he lit up the void himself. He sorted the souls, ranked and ordered them, and at the same time, Satan called all of them toward himself. Not all of them came this time. This time, it was only a portion, but the ones that went toward him flew.

"These should all be mine," Satan shouted. "You changed the rules. The world was given to me, and these things belonged to the world. They could have chosen you, but instead they chose food and sex and pretty baubles. Employers defrauded their workers and workers defrauded their masters, and that makes them mine."

"They chose death. I died for them." Jesus regarded Satan. "That makes them mine. You can have the world. Mine no longer belong to the world."

Jesus pointed to Michael, who moved in fast to secure Satan. "Now," Jesus said, "take your own. The ones who chose you can, indeed, stay with you. But for forty days I bind you and secure you. Your time of testing is over for these."

Michael had Satan chained despite the flames rolling off the Seraph. Jesus said, "Remove him," and Michael brought him into Hell and secured him on the beach at the Lake of Fire. He tied down the Maskim as well.

Satan said, "When forty days are done, beware."

Michael said, "When forty days are done, I'll just trounce you again."

At Hell's gate, Jesus left an Archangel guard to secure it. "Keep the human souls here," Jesus said. "Work with the ones who still need settling. I need to present myself to the Father, and then..." He beamed. "And then I can bring them home."

Gabriel flashed to the upper room where Mary was staying with John. She saw him, then looked up at Raphael when in the next second he arrived. Gabriel looked awful; if anything, Raphael looked worse.

Gabriel staggered to a corner and sat, wings up around himself, his knees tucked. Hesitant, Raphael moved to sit near him.

Mary said, "Is it over?"

Gabriel didn't raise his eyes.

Raphael projected, *For now.*

Mary got a series of images from one or both of them, Satan chained down, her son rebuking all of Hell at the same time, angels engaged in battle, and flames that made her gasp in fear.

Uriel came up behind her. *That's why I asked you to pray. One of the reasons.*

Mary said, "Will you two be all right? Is Michael okay?"

"Michael is fine." Raphael looked at Gabriel. "You need to sleep."

"I'll be all right."

"I really think—"

"I'm fine."

Mary asked for more details, and Raphael reassured her that Jesus was fine (nothing would ever hurt him again) and caught her up on who was where. They prayed together, although she did note that Gabriel didn't move from the corner.

After an hour, an Angel appeared and asked Raphael to come help with some angels who had been injured. Raphael touched a wing to Gabriel, then departed.

Watch, Uriel sent, and when Mary looked at Gabriel, she found him asleep.

I didn't think it would take longer than thirty seconds. Uriel settled on the floor alongside the Cherub, touching his hair.

Mary whispered, "He was too tense with Raphael here?"

Uriel nodded. "That was why I wanted you to pray for them especially. I'm afraid this isn't going to work out well at all."

Gabriel slept for two days. Mary wanted to move him, but she had no idea how, so every so often she would check on him. The way he leaned against the wall, head tucked, chin on his knees, she wished she could settle a blanket around him, but of course he was insubstantial. Raphael stopped by every now and again, but other than commenting early on that he'd known Gabriel was exhausted, he said nothing else.

When Gabriel awoke, he made a noncommittal comment about being out for a while and apologized to Mary if he'd worried her. She told him Raphael wanted to see him, and Gabriel's eyes lowered. He thanked her for giving him the message and left.

Later she learned he hadn't gone to Raphael.

Raphael stopped by the upper room and talked briefly with Mary, kissed her cheek as a message from Jesus, and then prayed with her.

Just before Raphael left, Mary said, "Uriel doesn't want me to ask, but what's happening to Gabriel?"

Raphael tensed. "I'm giving him some space to recharge."

"He looks different." Mary seemed concerned. "He's quiet."

A coldness crept over Raphael's heart. "Looks different?"

"The shape of his face. His eyes." She shrugged. "I know you can look like whatever you want, but I never saw any of you do it."

Raphael called up a light-image of Gabriel, then tried to change it, only he'd never seen Gabriel masculine before the winnowing, so instead he wiped that out and formed Gabriel female from back then.

Beside him, Mary gasped. "Not quite like that, and not female. But kind of like that."

Raphael made the image vanish and flashed to Gabriel.

In the library, Gabriel worked at a tremendous desk, writing furiously with his left hand while tracing words on another page with his right, looking from one to the other without breaking rhythm. He flipped open another book and paged through until he found a line graph. Raphael could feel him working hard at the problem, maybe biology, so he sent an impulse announcing his presence.

Gabriel looked up. Mary had definitely detected a subtle change. It knifed through Raphael, but Gabriel's eyes were wrong, reverting to the way they'd been pre-winnowing. Angels grow to resemble what they love. A long time ago, Gabriel and Raphael hadn't looked alike, and now here was Gabriel drifting back again.

Raphael stood stiffly by the window. "What are you working on?"

Gabriel huffed. "Zophiel wrote a paper about genetics that sounds nice on first reading and is absolute garbage if you bother to scratch the surface, so I'm taking it apart point by point."

That kind of thing would drive any other angel insane; beng a Cherub, Zophiel would love it. No doubt there would be a thesis dropped off on Gabriel's desk in return. These would be distributed among the Cherubim and spark hundreds of debates. At some point Zophiel would swing to Gabriel's side, Gabriel would take Zophiel's original position (though modified) and someday they'd both reach an agreement and move on to the next question.

"Would you like to come with me on rounds?" Raphael struggled to find words. "It's been a while."

"I'm busy." Gabriel went back to the book. "Maybe some other time."

Raphael said, "Could I help with your research?"

Gabriel shook his head.

Raphael hated this. He hated every moment. They'd never been awkward around one another. Tense sometimes, sure; a couple of times hostile. But always they'd had something to say and been comfortable enough to say it. This... He couldn't deal with this. And Gabriel hadn't let go of his little genetics problem the entire time they were talking.

"I'll go then," Raphael said, and Gabriel only looked up at him with blank eyes, sharp eyes. Raphael felt the chill in the air between them where there ought to have been fire and steel. "You're sure? It won't take long."

Gabriel looked back at his book. "Yeah. I'm sure."

I can't ever make it right, can I? But Raphael didn't say it, didn't project it, and didn't try to send the grief through their bond. Instead he flashed to the rooftop of his house.

Raphael's home stood on a hill a couple of miles from Gabriel's library. Gabriel hadn't had the place for a very long time; it was only about a year after he'd returned from Tobias that he'd decided to build it, and he'd asked Raphael to help select a location. Thrilled, Raphael knew the perfect place, and it was here, in sight of his own home. Gabriel had declared it suitable, and he'd begun to make plans.

Gabriel had gone one midnight to Tobias's household and taken two seeds from one tree and then a cutting from it as well. He'd set them in pots where they'd eventually be planted and nurtured them until they were saplings about waist-high. Raphael had asked why he wanted them. Although he'd been evasive, Gabriel had admitted they were to remind him. And Raphael had said, *Why would you want to be reminded of that?* to which Gabriel had replied that he couldn't bear to learn it all again.

Gabriel had inscribed a name over the door, "Three Trees Library," but no one ever called it that. It was always just "Gabriel's library."

It had been so different when Raphael had built his house. He'd done little more than ask the Spirit to make it for him. It had taken him half an hour to find a nice place, and that had been that. Gabriel in contrast had drawn pictures, blueprints, diagrams. He'd made sure there was room to add new wings as the collection required them. He'd changed the slope of the terrain, modified the landscape, and then set out stakes to mark where he wanted the building, the terraces, and the three trees.

Then, with half an hour until the designated time to put the thing together, Gabriel had reversed the design.

Raphael had come up behind him while he was working on the blueprint, and he'd pointed out that as the library grew, the trees would no longer be visible from his house. Without disengaging from the paper, Gabriel had said, "It's better this way." No reason. Raphael knew better than to argue with Gabriel when he felt he had all his proofs in a row, and because Gabriel had been fully engaged in reversing the design, he'd let it stand.

But now, as he sat on the roof of his own house unable to see the trees, Raphael realized Gabriel had kept him from seeing a monument to his failure every time he looked out the window.

Gabriel just back from that year had been so scarily quiet. He'd hung back from group interactions even as he sought them out, analyzing where he fit. No one had treated him differently, but he'd changed the way he treated everyone else: gently, as if fitting them together like piecework. Gabriel had clung to Raphael so hard in those early days, and Raphael had felt Gabriel's rawness because for the first time he was gauging what they thought of him too.

How many times had Gabriel wandered onto the balcony or gazed from the stacks out at those trees, remembering how badly Raphael had let him down? And he'd never given any hint about it.

Raphael focused with long-distance vision through the windows of the library. Gabriel was still at work, books and papers spread over the entirety of the desk.

He lay back on the sun-warmed terra cotta tiles. *I did all I could,* he prayed. And when the Sprit prompted him, he added, *All he's let me do.* The Spirit swirled through him, and Raphael flared up into a simmer. *No, I don't want to let him go.* And then nothing, and he wondered, and he thought.

Gabriel had faced something like this three decades ago, when he'd lured Raphael out with that snowball fight. It must have been difficult to plan it all, just because that kind of thing was alien to a Cherub. Maybe he could make some kind of peace overture, and maybe in that way coax Gabriel to reopen the dialogue. How to do it, though?

It took Raphael two weeks of searching Creation to find the perfect gift for Gabriel, something as engaging to a Cherub as the snowball fight had been to him. In frustration he rejected idea after idea, wondering if maybe the reality was there was nothing Gabriel hadn't studied in total. But when he found it, he knew, and he bubbled with a barely-leashed excitement he kept suppressed in case Gabriel were to sense it.

It had taken Gabriel ten minutes to come up with the idea for a snowball fight and two days to plan it; it had taken Raphael two weeks to find a gift and three minutes to come up with how to present it.

When Raphael brought it to Gabriel, there were other angels gathered with Mary, and a sharp-eyed Gabriel wore the same cautious tension he'd had for a month. Raphael kept the gift cupped in his hand, shielded but emitting little pulses of its power.

The other angels watched. Gabriel prickled with curiosity.

Raphael started to part his hands as Gabriel came forward. But then he took a step backward, and Gabriel followed. Raphael laughed inside, and Gabriel darted for him, trying to see the object.

Raphael launched away, and Gabriel took off in pursuit.

Left behind with Michael, Remiel said, "I think we just witnessed Raphael deciding eternity wasn't long enough to wait for Gabriel to make the first move."

Raphael streaked through Creation, always faster than Gabriel but careful not to strip him off, keeping enough power streaming from the gift to make him curious. He left a trail for Gabriel to follow as he chased him from place to place. At every moment Raphael could feel Gabriel's determination growing, and before it yielded to frustration, he carried the thing to its home.

There Raphael turned to face Gabriel as he arrived, his hands cupped and the gift easily visible. The smaller gift, that was.

And Gabriel got to see it, round and singular and beautiful like a lone question mark in a sea of periods and commas. He probed it without self-consciousness before Raphael's delighted eyes, only Raphael still vibrated with anticipation.

Gabriel looked up, and in the next moment gasped with awe.

Raphael laughed out loud. Gabriel opened his senses to take it all in: a star field, the space dust, and two black holes within a light year of one another. The black holes working against one another had dotted the entire area with singularities, contorting the fabric of space itself and bending light into insane folds. The thing Raphael had held was one of the singularities. The real gift was the location.

Gabriel went loose in it, first surveying, then examining, getting it from every angle. No angel had been here before Raphael; even when he had, he'd kept his signature suppressed to leave no trace. Gabriel was the first, and he played with it, tested it, explored it. He popped in and out of the pair of black holes, pushed through space so thick it would have taken five years to move a wingspan's distance (until Raphael flashed him out). He encircled the singularities, then watched the rippling energy of the black hole pair warp space again to generate a new one.

Raphael burned. He started to reach for Gabriel, but the Spirit cautioned him to wait.

Gabriel immersed himself in the wild geometry of contorted space, ecstatic with the learning. Then, when Raphael felt the Cherub on the verge of reaching for his fire, just when Raphael would have expected to feel that cool grasp in his heart, instead Gabriel clenched his teeth and kindled up on his own.

Raphael protested to the Spirit, who again urged patience.

But I could have fired him up!

He had to learn to do this when you were separated, the Spirit replied. *It takes the edge off. It's not the same.* A moment later, *Wait for him. He's as hungry as you are.*

283

Abruptly Raphael realized what violence this was to Gabriel's nature. This inner fire wasn't something Gabriel wanted to do nor found easy. It must have been awful for him to be fire-free and excluded from his Seraphim for an entire year. Raphael had seen Gabriel get nauseated after a week's immersion in a theoretical problem. Multiply that by fifty. Just something else to regret about that year. Raphael had never wanted to know.

The Spirit was right, though: it wasn't much of a fire, a candle to Raphael's hearth. Enough to help in a pinch, but it couldn't meet the need.

Gabriel extended his senses until he located a cluster of space dust, which he streamed toward the black holes like a river. They watched the particulate matter churn like rapids over rocks around the singularities, picking up speed as it rushed toward the pair of gravity wells.

Isn't it beautiful? Raphael glowed, and the particles picked up a hundred different hues of his light, shimmering as they frothed.

Gabriel started forward, then stopped. He clenched his hands. "I can't." Raphael stared, but Gabriel shuddered. "You're giving me a gift I can't accept."

"Why not?" The heat inside scorched him, and Raphael's entire plan vibrated on the edge of collapse. "You keep not letting me work it out with you. I don't want you to keep punishing me for one mistake for the rest of our lives."

Gabriel's eyes gleamed. Raphael reached out his hands. "I'm sorry. With everything I am, I'm sorry."

Gabriel was locking down, but Raphael felt the Spirit telling him to stay, that whatever they did they needed to settle this now.

Gabriel choked, "Why do you want me around?"

"How can you ask that?" Raphael shook his head. "You're my friend."

Gabriel was shedding the sensation of a fruit with its rind stripped away: exposed, naked. *Friend* wasn't going to do it for him. Raphael said, "You've got an incredible perception of the world, and I love hearing the way you see things."

Gabriel's voice broke. "Know-it-all."

Raphael said, "You keep calm in a crisis."

"Ice-hearted."

Raphael clenched his hands. "You don't mind changing the things you think if you find a better way to do something, and you're always looking for a better way."

Gabriel wouldn't look at him. "Arrogant. Legalistic"

Raphael shook his head. "I hit every one of your best characteristics and twisted them into something awful. I was wrong. But that's not you. That's me."

Gabriel still looked ready to run. It was probably an act of God that he hadn't fled already. "But you also told me... I deserved getting kicked out of Heaven. You said what I did to you can't be forgiven."

Raphael's vision fuzzed. "What?"

Gabriel's voice was thready. "A long time ago, you told me nothing good had come of the year."

Raphael blinked. "I wouldn't have!"

"You did!" Gabriel's head snapped up. "So just like that, you negated everything I learned because of that year, so you must think I'm still that same wretched soul!"

"I never thought that!" Raphael exclaimed.

"And if you're still just as ashamed and disgusted with me as I was at myself—"

"Wait a minute," Raphael said. "Stop! I don't feel anything of the sort!"

"The way you said *You deserved it* means that all of it you were glad for—that you were gloating—that you *laughed* at the way everyone walked away from me, the isolation—"

Raphael was right in front of him, face to face. "I never laughed!"

Gabriel shoved him away. "I can't go on as your bad debt!"

Gabriel covered his face, hemorrhaging grief and shame.

"I don't understand!" Raphael couldn't feel anything over the emotional torrent. "You don't owe me anything! I accepted that God said it was necessary. But I never, not for one second, felt smug. I prayed for you every day. I didn't give up on you."

Gabriel doubled forward. What was going on? What did he mean by a bad debt? When it was Raphael who owed him from the start?

Raphael touched the edge of Gabriel's wings with his own. "Look at me. Please. You don't owe me anything. I don't spend my spare hours compounding the interest on any kind of debt."

Gabriel whispered, "You said I can't make it right."

Raphael shook his head. "You came home, and that made it right."

Gabriel wrapped his arms around his stomach. "That's not what you said! That's not the reality you've lived with every day — every day. You said— We had an agreement." His voice broke. "You said if I wouldn't talk about it, then you would ignore it, and we'd be okay." Gabriel huddled down on himself in space. He wasn't running, but Raphael could feel him pulling clouds of matter toward himself. Like Adam in the garden: I was naked, so I clothed myself. Raphael burned inside, horrified: what had he done? How had he done this to *Gabriel*?

Gabriel covered his face with his wings. "You've every right to be ashamed of me, but how could you fling it in my face like that? Using that as a weapon means there's nothing sacred between us. When I thought all along there was everything."

Fling it in his face? When Gabriel had been the one flinging it in his face that Raphael hadn't been there for him? The rage flared inside, but Raphael pushed it down.

"Look." He struggled to steady himself enough to do damage control, sweeping his wingtips forward just enough to touch Gabriel's. "Please don't say that. I am not now and never have been ashamed of you."

Gabriel glared up for the first time, his eyes burning sharper than the stars. "Don't you dare lie to me."

Raphael backed off. "I'm not lying."

Gabriel flared his wings. "You *said* you were ashamed." He advanced, and Raphael backed away. "You told me your feelings hadn't changed. You told me there was never any doubt."

"When—?"

"Always!" This anger had blown up out of nowhere, and Raphael flailed for a reason, or even when he might have said these things. *Always?* When he couldn't remember saying it even once? Gabriel snapped, "We're bonded, remember? Why do you think I wouldn't feel how mortally embarrassed you are *every* time the subject comes up?"

Images pushed into Raphael's head: snow banks, snow forts, a tortured conversation driving into a Cherub's heart like icicles.

Raphael gasped. "I wasn't ashamed of *you*." He grabbed Gabriel by the arms. "I'd never be ashamed of you."

Gabriel looked unsteady. "Even though you'd do anything short of throwing me into Hell to get me to shut up about—"

"I let you down!" Raphael pushed him away. "The one time you really, honestly, truly needed me, I over-reacted and couldn't be there for you!" Gabriel looked shocked, but Raphael couldn't stop because it just kept coming. "You were burnt to the ground and rebuilt, and I wasn't there for you, and it was my own lousy fault! And then over and over you kept saying how everyone helped you, but it wasn't *everyone,* was it? It was *everyone but me*. And they all know it, and you know it, and you'll never let me forget it, and I can never make that up."

Gabriel only said, "I didn't hold you accountable for that."

"That's great." Raphael turned away. "So you never even expected anything better of me. That makes it more shameful."

Gabriel glowered at him. "Be rational for a minute. It's not a matter of expectations. I'd have lost contact with you regardless. I couldn't feel you from the moment God took the Vision away. He suspended all my bonds, not just yours. The only thing you lost was the ability to know about me."

Gabriel actually sounded like himself. Raphael pressed on. "I also lost the ability to tell Michael how to help you."

"So by extension you lost the chance to be sobbing right alongside Remiel while I responded to Satan's commands like a domesticated dog. I'm glad you didn't get to witness that. You'd be twice as ashamed of me then."

Raphael snapped, "I'm *not* ashamed of you."

Gabriel regarded him with no expression. "Do you really expect me to believe you carried that for six hundred years? And then didn't learn enough from it to apply the brakes this time?"

Raphael clenched his fists. "You have to believe me!"

Gabriel pulled back. No, clearly he didn't have to believe it. He was so hard to read, especially when he went into that Cherub mindset and weighed everything like a scientist gathering data.

Raphael groped for whatever he remembered of that snowball conversation. What had he said back then? "My feelings haven't changed. There was never any doubt: the whole time you were gone, I only wanted you back. You're my best friend, and I love spending time with you, and I'm proud to serve God at your side."

Gabriel closed his eyes. But the steel was yielding, and he wasn't withdrawing anymore. Raphael could feel Gabriel processing. Re-working new information in with the old; re-interpreting; challenging.

Raphael finally said, "You asked me, so let me ask you too: why would you stay around if you thought I felt that way?"

"Because I love you." Gabriel's light dimmed. "I'm sorry I let you think I blamed you. I was too ensnared in your opinion of me."

Raphael hovered in front of Gabriel so they were eye-to-eye. He rested his hands on Gabriel's shoulders.

Gabriel brought his wings around Raphael and put his hands into Raphael's hair. He prayed.

Raphael joined him. *Father, I don't know how to fix this. Please let me be trustworthy for him.*

God, Gabriel wove into Raphael's prayer, *he can't prove himself trustworthy unless I trust him first. Please give me the strength to trust him. Please help me get past this.*

Peace settled across both of them, and then Raphael felt the Holy Spirit talking directly to Gabriel. He couldn't pick out the specifics, but it felt like encouragement. It felt like reassurance and an invitation to faith.

With a deep breath, Gabriel reached into Raphael's heart and started drawing off fire.

Relief washed through Raphael like a tidal wave. Gabriel's thoughts and sensations flooded him, and Raphael reflexively reached for Gabriel's heart.

"I'll ask again." Raphael looked him in the eyes. "Please accept my gift."

Empowered and burning like a torch, Gabriel ventured again into the star field then paused, looked back over his shoulder at Raphael. Flushed, Gabriel returned to Raphael and took him by the hand to show him everything. Raphael followed, listening to Gabriel machine-gunning descriptions of the different kinds of singularities, of the ripples in space and the way things nestled within them. When they reached something Gabriel didn't understand, the Cherub overflowed his own mind and annexed Raphael's intelligence, and then they both were learning.

Gabriel's eyes glowed. Taking a deep breath, he half-closed his eyes and tilted up his chin ever so slightly as if swallowing, and started exuding rings.

Wide-eyed, Raphael let the first one ripple past, then scrambled to catch the last part of the second pulse, and by the third he'd opened wide and absorbed the rings into himself.

Because— He'd thought— He hadn't dared to hope— He'd figured it would never happen again, but here was Gabriel, casting rings for him, and—

Gabriel resonated now with a richness Raphael hadn't felt for six hundred years. For centuries, Gabriel must have been suppressing parts of himself to protect Raphael from having to be ashamed of him. The trees—had he hidden his trees only to protect Raphael? But now he was opening wide so Raphael could see all of him, and in response Raphael gave Gabriel complete access to his soul, to his deepest regrets about not having been there for him. Gabriel let him feel for the first time how pivotal, how important it had been that he come under God's discipline and learn, really learn, humility.

Gabriel looked him in the eyes, and Raphael felt Gabriel saying thank you, but in his heart he wasn't sure if the one saying it wasn't himself.

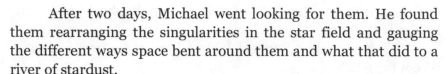

After two days, Michael went looking for them. He found them rearranging the singularities in the star field and gauging the different ways space bent around them and what that did to a river of stardust.

Sensing Michael, they turned simultaneously, the same motion, the same relaxed expression on their faces, and even the same features.

Michael gave a relieved sigh.

Gabriel flashed to him and touched wingtip to wingtip, then took Michael's hands in his own. There had been so many unspoken words, so many assumptions, so many little avoidances; Gabriel was projecting sadness and wonderment even as he put it into Michael's heart. There had been so many things they'd avoided talking about for so long, but they were covering it all, all the things they hadn't even realized they'd been avoiding, the way they'd both assumed the blame for the other's feelings, all the little hurts that had added up to one tremendous alienation and a breach of trust.

Michael squeezed Gabriel's hands, then looked up to meet Raphael's eyes, and he thanked God for an answered prayer.

Gabriel gave a little tug, and Michael let the Cherub bring him out into the star field to see, see what Raphael had given him and all the things they'd discovered together.

Gabriel and Raphael received the summons at the same time, and they flashed to Jesus where he stood with the eleven disciples and his mother on the top of a hill at Bethany.

Uriel took Gabriel's hand, and when Gabriel smiled, so did the Throne. Mary noticed them and looked relieved.

Jesus spoke to the eleven, words for each of the men, a kiss on the cheek. He hugged his mother and kissed her on both cheeks, then stepped back.

Mary was struggling to keep her face passive, but her mouth kept twisting. This was it. She knew it, and Gabriel moved nearer to her even though some pain even angels couldn't deflect.

Peter asked if now was the time to restore the Kingdom of Israel, and Jesus said no. "It's not for us to know the time. That's under the Father's authority. But I'm sending the Holy Spirit, and He'll fill you with power so you can go tell the story all through Jerusalem and Samaria and Judea and even to the ends of the world."

Then, before the disciples, he rose off the ground.

They watched him, the eleven men and Mary, and Raphael went with him, but Gabriel stayed at Mary's side to give strength to her heart. *That's the sword. Her soul's been pierced.*

Beside Gabriel, Uriel said, "Men of Galilee? Why are you looking up into the sky?"

The disciples all turned, and Mary turned toward Uriel too, meeting her guardian's eyes.

Uriel said, "Jesus has been taken up into Heaven, and he'll come back to you in the same way."

The disciples looked startled, but then Uriel vanished from their sight. Gabriel stayed close to Mary. *He won't leave you orphaned.*

Mary replied, *An orphan has no parents. But there's no word for a mother whose child is gone.*

It's hard being apart, even though you know he's waiting for you, Gabriel sent. *Pray and wait for the Spirit. He's the Consoler and sanctifier. I'm sorry you can't be together.*

The disciples returned to Jerusalem. God called Gabriel back to Jesus's side.

Gabriel reappeared in the remnants of Sheol, now cleared out of the air. Ophaniel reported immediately that by their calculations, they'd secured anywhere between 99.97% of the particles and 104%. "We can't get a more specific measurement," he added.

Jesus moved among the people again, but this time there was no tension, only joy. These were the ones who had lived well and lived generously, who had always tried to do what was right even when they didn't know what it might be. They'd followed the natural law, and then when offered the chance to hear the news, had heard it with joy and chosen to be with God. An extension, really, of the decisions they'd been making all their lives.

"Now," Jesus called, "come with me! Come and share your master's joy!"

He rose above them all, and the souls followed, human souls and angel souls. He extended his arms, and then they were no longer in the void where Sheol used to be but outside the front gates of Heaven. Zadkiel and Saraquael opened the gates, and Jesus led the stream of souls through.

Some angels began playing music while others sang, and they ushered in the human souls. There were reunions and embraces and congratulations. Raphael left Jesus's side and went to stand with Gabriel.

Jesus took a seat at a raised throne, and God the Father said, "This is my Son, your King."

The angels cheered. The humans did the same.

Jesus said, "And now — play!"

Raphael laughed out loud, and the party began.

The more curious human souls began exploring Heaven, and angels volunteered to show them around. Others remained, socializing or asking questions. Gabriel started fielding requests from people who wanted to learn everything, everything about the universe right now, and he found himself barraged with requests for tours of his library.

"I hope I can have a chance too," said a voice at his side, and he turned to find Tobias.

Raphael joined them. "Tobias," he said, "son of Tobit, you've met my friend, Gabriel. Thank you." He swallowed. "Thank you for looking out for him at a time when I couldn't."

Michael appeared at Gabriel's side. He had a new sword in its scabbard, embellished with a cross. "Jesus wants you to come to the front."

Jesus had a group of angels standing with him, waiting their turns. Nivalis knelt before him, he with his hands on her head. She kept her arms crossed over her chest while he blessed her, and then he released her and she stood. When she saw Gabriel and Raphael, she went to them.

Her uniform had changed to black and silver, and she wore a black armband. "I'm so sorry about Judas," Gabriel said again.

She looked sad, but solid. "I've asked permission... I'm not the only one who lost her charge. There's lots of us, and more will come in the future. So I've gotten permission to form a new team of angels. The grief squad. So we can help others through when the worst happens."

Raphael hugged her, and she melted against his shoulder. "It doesn't make it good," she whispered, and her voice broke. "But helping others makes it better."

Remiel was standing in front of Jesus now, receiving new earrings and a new sword, and finally a kiss on the cheek. When she stepped away, Jesus said, "Ah, Gabriel. You're next."

Gabriel stepped forward and bowed. Jesus said, "Did Uriel tell them that just as they saw me leave, I'd return the same way?"

"Uriel told them that."

Jesus said, "And when that happens, would you agree I'll need someone to announce my coming?"

Gabriel frowned. "I disagree. Surely you as the Divine Word don't *need* anyone to announce anything," and Jesus laughed out loud.

"You'd agree it's fitting, though," Jesus said, and Gabriel replied, "You already know I'd agree to that."

Jesus pressed a hand against Gabriel's chest, then pulled back to draw light from his heart. Before Gabriel's wide eyes, he opened his hands, and there appeared a silver device. Gabriel gasped as Jesus extended the instrument to him.

Gabriel raised it, sighted along the edges, and pushed on the three valves in the middle. "What are these?"

"That, my friend, is a trumpet." Jesus laughed. "A trumpet the world has never seen before."

"This isn't a ram's horn. This is metal. It..." Gabirel fingered the valves and probed through the coiled tubing with his mind. "These valves change the length of the tubing by opening and closing the different pathways. You can change the notes and the tone!"

Raphael said, "It's amazing!"

"And its yours," Jesus said. "When the time comes, I'm going to want you to make an announcement, and I want everyone to listen when you do. Until then, play it and enjoy."

Gabriel bowed.

Jesus turned to Raphael. "And you, my friend."

He hugged Raphael, and Raphael gripped him as tightly as he could, bringing his wings around Jesus and bowing his head. "Thank you for letting me be your guardian. That's the only gift I'd ever have asked for, and you already gave it to me."

Jesus chuckled. "Of all of them, you're the one who's most convicted, most determined to serve me. You never wavered, and you're wholly mine."

Raphael closed his eyes.

Jesus said, "I'm going to give you a gift anyhow." He opened his hands, and between them appeared a bowl filled with minuscule pearls. In the light of Heaven their creamy skin gleamed with pastel blues and pinks. "This is joy. I want you to keep these and hand them out to whomever you see fit."

Raphael picked up one of pearls, rolling it gently between the tip of his thumb and forefinger. "Anyone?"

He looked over at Gabriel, but Gabriel raised his trumpet. "Not me. I've already got my gift."

Jesus laughed. "Peter and the others are going to head into the world and tell everyone the good news of their salvation. It's not going to be easy for them, and some people are going to need a little extra help. The joy of the gospel is my gift to my people, and I want it to pass through your hands on its way."

Raphael accepted the bowl, and as soon as he held it, the bowl and all its pearls dissipated into his heart. "They're all there for you, waiting," Jesus said. "You've got enough fire inside to keep them warm and ready for my people when it's time for them to come to me."

That done, Jesus turned toward the assembly and raised his hands. Cups appeared, all filled with wine. He raised his glass and said, "A toast! Today we're enjoying our wine new in the Kingdom of God."

Acknowledgments

As always, I owe a debt of gratitude to my critique partners who give the most amazing and insightful feedback. Thank you so much Ivy Reisner, Wendy Dinsmore, Kaci Hill, Sarah Begg, and Normandie Fischer. I'm especially thankful for Amy Deardon's guidance as I continue to figure out the indie publishing process.

On the personal side of things, thank you also Madeline and Evan, for reasons you two know. Finally, special thanks to James for his patience while I'm worlds away.

I especially need to thank my readers. Your support and encouragement never stop amazing me, and I thank you for the gift of your time and the chance to share my world with you.

Thank you so much for reading *Sacred Cups*! Please consider leaving a review at Amazon or Goodreads (or both.) A review doesn't have to be more than a couple of sentences saying what you liked or didn't like, and authors will love you for it!

 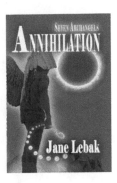

The Seven Archangels stories all stand alone, so you can read them in any order you want. If you'd like to see the start of the story, that's *Seven Archangels: An Arrow In Flight.*

Or you can find out what happens when Satan figures out how to annihilate an angel. In *Seven Archangels: Annihilation* he starts with Gabriel. Who's next?

Tabris is a guardian angel who killed the boy he vowed to protect. He expects to be thrown into Hell, but then God gives him a second chance – another assignment. Yet in protecting this other child, Tabris can't be sure he's not fighting the wrong enemy.

If you'd like to hear from me when new books appear, feel free to email me at JaneLebak@gmail.com. I've also got a Facebook page at http://www.facebook.com/JaneLebakAuthor.

Thanks again for reading my story, and I hope to hear from you!

CPSIA information can be obtained
at www.ICGtesting.com
Printed in the USA
FSHW022116031219
54740FS